ANCIENT BLOODLUST

The child and the cat made their way through the dark woods. The girl rained down ancient curses on the men who had disturbed their rest cycle. She and Pet had been awake too long now to again seek the sanctuary and safety of sleep.

The only control they had over their destiny was to survive. But for now they must eat, and eat well, in order to regain their strength. For the ordeal ahead of them would be severe. They knew armed men would be hunting them. They had been through it all before.

The cat's ears perked up. The pair stopped. They both heard sounds of panting. Moonlight glinted off a parked car. Young voices drifted through the spring air.

The cat and the girl slipped as silently as death's touch up to the parked car. Within seconds, the low voices turned into screams of terror. Blood splattered the windows and cushions of the car. Frantic thrashings rocked the vehicle. A cat's yowlings and a girl's grotesque smacking of lips filled the air.

Then silence once more filled the woods. A bloody child's face appeared in the rear window. A cat appeared by her side. They looked at one another—and smiled in satisfaction...

THRILLERS BY WILLIAM W. JOHNSTONE

THE DEVIL'S CAT   (2091, $3.95)
The town was alive with all kinds of cats. Black, white, fat, scrawny. They lived in the streets, in backyards, in the swamps of Becancour. Sam, Nydia, and Little Sam had never seen so many cats. The cats' eyes were glowing slits as they watched the newcomers. The town was ripe with evil. It seemed to waft in from the swamps with the hot, fetid breeze and breed in the minds of Becancour's citizens. Soon Sam, Nydia, and Little Sam would battle the forces of darkness. Standing alone against the ultimate predator—The Devil's Cat.

THE DEVIL'S HEART   (2110, $3.95)
Now it was summer again in Whitfield. The town was peaceful, quiet, and unprepared for the atrocities to come. Eternal life, everlasting youth, an orgy that would span time—that was what the Lord of Darkness was promising the coven members in return for their pledge of love. The few who had fought against his hideous powers before, believed it could never happen again. Then the hot wind began to blow—as black as evil as The Devil's Heart.

THE DEVIL'S TOUCH   (2111, $3.95)
Once the carnage begins, there's no time for anything but terror. Hollow-eyed, hungry corpses rise from unearthly tombs to gorge themselves on living flesh and spawn a new generation of restless Undead. The demons of Hell cavort with Satan's unholy disciples in blood-soaked rituals and fevered orgies. The Balons have faced the red, glowing eyes of the Master before, and they know what must be done. But there can be no salvation for those marked by The Devil's Touch.

CAT'S CRADLE

BY WILLIAM W. JOHNSTONE

ZEBRA BOOKS
KENSINGTON PUBLISHING CORP.

ZEBRA BOOKS

are published by

Kensington Publishing Corp.
475 Park Avenue South
New York, NY 10016

Third printing: December, 1989.

Printed in the United States of America

Dedicated to Sheriff R. R. "Mitch" Mitchell and Chief Deputy Sheriff B. B. Harmon and the staff and personnel of the Madison Parish, Louisiana Sheriff's Department.

Cruel, but composed and bland,
Dumb, inscrutable and grand,
So Tiberius might have sat,
Had Tiberius been a cat.

Arnold

THE CONCEPTION

It was an ancient rite. An evil supplication to the old gods. The woman was anything but a willing participant. She jerked and screamed and struggled, howling her fear and horror at what had been planned for her; planned by the unseen ones she really did not believe in.

Very soon she would be a believer.

Under dark night skies that had yet to see few examples of a dawning of civilized behavior, the woman was dragged toward the altar. The altar was draped in black, the cloth adorned with savage pictures of a cat. Hundreds of torches flickered dancing light, the leaping flames creating hundreds of shadows, turning the vastness of surrounding sand a deep purple black.

A very old cat sat alone on a large square stone and watched the woman being dragged toward the black-draped altar. The cat's yellow unblinking eyes stared without visible expression. It yawned its boredom. It wondered if this conception would be the one that would relieve it of this life. It hoped so. The last few had produced terrible offspring; and they had been destroyed. Horrible multi-headed creatures. Some half cat, half snake. Others too hideous to describe.

The old cat was tired. Tired of it all. It wanted its companion. But it knew its companion was dead. Dead now for several years. They had been together for hundreds of years, and loved one another as only sisters can.

Then the cat seemed to smile. It sensed this mating would be successful and acceptable.

The cat knew its life was almost over. It knew freshborn would soon take its place. The cat knew these things and welcomed them. It welcomed the end of its life and the beginning of new lives.

The old cat turned away from the scene. It was far too old to enjoy the sights and sounds of sexual matters. It could not even mentally recall the pleasures. The cat began its slow long walk down the stone stairs of the plateau.

The woman screamed as she was penetrated. Gruntings filled the hot desert night. The woman moaned as the hot winds blew. Then it was over.

The cat walked down the steps without looking back. Callused but gentle hands picked up the animal and placed it on a silken pillow.

The old cat closed its ancient eyes.

It died.

THE INCEPTION

The woman died giving birth, as it was planned. As it must be. Her body was thrown into the river and devoured by crocodiles.

She had delivered twins; as it was planned. They were perfect. Animal and human. Both female. The baby girl's eyes were dark, her hair black as midnight. A birthmark was visible on her left arm. It was the shape of a cat's paw. The baby kitten was black, with yellow eyes. The surrogate mother who nursed both the newborn, fearfully, painfully, was killed after two months. Her body was tossed into the river and eaten. All attending priests and priestesses were sealed into a tomb and left to die, forever silencing the secret they and they alone knew.

It was the time when the man called Jesus Christ walked the sands, spreading His message. Only a few years before that man would be nailed to a rough wooden cross to die.

And the girl who was called Anya, and the cat who was called Pet watched it all.

And thoroughly enjoyed the suffering.

Then they were entombed alive, and would remain thus until they were called. As all gods must be. It

9

would be hundreds of years before the archaeologists would come and disturb their resting place, unleashing the horror.

ENGLAND, 1865

" 'Tis a foul night out, Love," the man said, forcing the door closed against the howling winds that blew hard against the cottage on the North English coast.

"Aye, 'tis that," she said, without turning from or ceasing her stirring of the stew that bubbled in the blackened pot that hung over the fire. She knew it would bring on the ire of her husband, but she spoke her mind. "And them unseen ones is about on this night as well."

"Bah!" her husband said, giving her a stern look. "I'll na' hav' no more of that talk in this house, woman. The royal messengers hav' said that nonsense is to cease. All that talk of werewolves and man-like creatures that change shapes is causing unrest among the ignorant. Are ye ignorant, woman? Them things do na' exist. Now put the food on the table and sit down, 'fore I take a strap to ye."

The woman muttered darkly, but softly enough so her husband would not hear. She filled the bowls and sat down, paying only scant attention as her husband blessed the food, asked for help in paying the taxes, and prayed for guidance to overcome the babblings of an ignorant woman.

A timid knock on the door could just be heard over the raging of the storm.

The woman paled. "Don't answer it!" she begged her husband.

"Woman," the man said, exasperation in his voice, "are ye daft? Hav' ye lost all sense of compassion? 'Tis not a fit night for any living thing to be out."

"Any *living* thing," she said.

"Fool!" He walked to the door. He did not notice that his dogs had not barked. He opened the door, the winds and rain lashing him.

The woman sat on her table bench.

At first the man could see nothing. Then, as lightning flashed, he lowered his eyes and looked at the soaked shape of a young girl. She cradled a cat in her arms. The girl looked to be no more than nine or ten years old. She was very pale. And the cat looked more dead than alive.

The cat stared at the man through cold yellow eyes.

"Child?" the man said. "Are ye tryin' to catch the death out tonight?'

"If ye'll give me shelter in your shed for this night, sir," she said, "I'll sure clean the house come the dawnin'."

"I'd be a pinchpenny man to take wages from a child for a act of kindness, now wouldn't I, girl? Come in the house and sup with me and my old woman." He waved the small girl inside and once more fought the door closed.

The woman's fear had left her at the sight of the harmless looking girl and her cat. She smiled as the cat leaped from the girl's arms and made itself comfortable some distance from the roaring fire. It began licking itself dry, ignoring them all. Aloof and silent.

The woman gave the child a piece of dry cloth with which to dry herself, and an old rag of a dress to cover herself while her clothing was hung before the fire to dry. The child was given a bowl of stew and a hunk of bread.

"Do ye hav' a name, girl?" the man asked. "And what are ye doin' wanderin' about on such a cruel night as this?"

"My name is Anya," the girl said. Her dark eyes gave away nothing. Never changing. "And I'm traveling."

"Without neither parent?" the woman asked. "Are ye a runaway?"

"No, mum. I have no parents."

Suspicion sprang into the woman's eyes. "Would ye be a gypsy, then?"

The child suddenly smiled, the smile changing her entire face, making her appear much more innocent. "No, mum. I'm just alone." She cut her eyes to the cat. "Except for my cat, Pet."

The cat paused in its licking at the mention of its name. It looked up, looking at the girl, then resumed its grooming.

"Are ye travelin' far, then?" the man asked.

"London. 'Tis there I'm to be in the service of a grand gentlemen and his lady."

"Ahh. Well," the woman said. "You'll rest well this night and come the morrow we'll give ye food for travelin'."

"I thank you, mum."

Later, in the darkness of the quiet, sleeping cottage, on her pallet to the left of the fire, Anya regurgitated her undigested food. The food was not palatable to either female. They would both dine later.

13

As the rains and winds intensified, the cat and the girl rose from the pallet to pad silently to the bed where the man and woman lay, deep in sleep under the heavy covers.

Anya and Pet shared a secret thought. The girl nodded her head. Anya leaned forward, her mouth close to the man's throat as Pet leaped onto the bed.

"A terrible, terrible thing," the constable said, pushing back the crowds that had gathered around the cottage. "It's a sight none of you wish to see."

The storm had blown itself out, leaving in its wake a sky of murky gray. And death.

"It is true?" a man called from the crowd. "Have they both been drained of blood and eaten on?"

"I'm not at liberty to speak of that," the constable said. "And you'd best hold your tongue of such talk. I'd not be spreading rumors were I you."

A young man dressed in a dark suit and carrying a small leather bag came out of the death cottage and vomited on the ground. He wiped his mouth with a handkerchief and motioned for the constable to approach him.

"Sir?"

"Did the man and woman own a cat?" the young doctor asked.

"No, sir. Dogs, but no cats."

"Then where did the cat tracks come from?"

The constable shook his head. "I can't say, sir. And I don't know where the dogs have gone."

"I want what is left of the man and woman to be placed in coffins immediately. The coffins sealed. No one must be allowed to see them. Is that understood?"

"Aye, sir. As you wish."

On the edge of the huge crowd, a young girl with a cat in her arms watched the goings-on through dark expressionless eyes. The cat slept in her arms. Both girl and cat appeared bloated.

The girl's coloring had improved dramatically.

The girl turned and walked away.

BOSTON, 1890

Boston police were still baffled and no closer to solving the more than a dozen brutal and grotesque murders that had occurred the past month. Surely a madman was on the loose.

A fiend.

"I'll not have that filthy animal in this house," the matron of the orphanage told the dark haired, dark eyed little girl. "I didn't want you here to begin with. You're a trouble-maker, girl. The other children shun you. But I'm a good Christian woman, and I'll not turn you back out into the street. But you must get rid of that cat. Throw it out. Do you understand?"

"Yes, ma'am," the child said.

That night the orphanage burned to the ground. A dozen children and the matron died in the blaze. The police were able to determine that many of the bodies had been killed prior to the fire. And gnawed on.

Some said that they saw a young girl carrying a cat in her arms leaving the building just before the fire consumed the place. Others said they heard hideous screaming coming from the place before the fire started. But neither could be substantiated.

ST. LOUIS, 1915

The killings seemed to be tapering off. But for several weeks the city had been in the grip of a near-panic. While no one had yet to print the word, many citizens believed a vampire was on the loose.

"Where did she come from in the first place?" the director of the orphanage asked.

"She just appeared off the street," the head nurse said. "Three weeks ago. She was dressed in a garment that was out of style twenty-five years ago. She was very pale and sickly. And the cat appeared to be near death. Now both are robust. And inseparable. And we all have reason to believe she leaves the home at night. With the cat."

"And several of the children have become very ill." It was not put in question form.

"Extremely ill. And we don't know from what. One is so weak she can barely raise her head. And she's so *pale.*"

"Are you suggesting this new child has something to do with the sudden rash of illness here?"

The nurse hesitated. "I . . . don't know what I'm suggesting, sir. Only that all this illness started after the girl came here."

Neither of them noticed the cat sitting on the window ledge outside the office. Four stories up from the ground level. Had they seen the cat, they might have noticed its eyes had changed colors. They were no longer yellow. They were dark. Like the girl called Anya.

The cat appeared to be listening. Very intently. Its head was cocked to one side, the dark eyes staring and unblinking.

A knock came at the door.

"Come," the director said.

A large woman entered the office. She was dressed in whites. She had a worried look on her broad, pleasant face. "Mrs. Bradford?" she said, looking at the head nurse.

"Yes?"

"Young Missy has died."

Director and head nurse stood up. "Of what?" the man asked.

The nurse looked frightened, confused. "Sir, there doesn't appear to be any blood left in the poor child."

The cat disappeared from the ledge.

Neither the cat nor the girl named Anya were ever seen at the orphanage again.

NEW ORLEANS, 1940

The unexplained killings had tapered off, much to the relief of the NOPD, who had, to date, been unable to solve a single one. And they had been more than just killings. These were macabre. Grotesque. Blood-sucking and cannibalistic.

The big street cop stood trying to catch his breath. The little girl sure was fast on her feet. He looked down a dark alley; thought he caught a glimpse of something moving very slowly. There! Right next to that building.

What the hell was it? Holy Mother! It wasn't human, but it wasn't animal. It seemed to be a combination of both.

The cop stepped closer, blinked his eyes, shook his head. Stared.

The cop stepped closer and froze in fright and horror at the sight before his street-hardened eyes. He again blinked. What he was seeing was impossible.

But there it was.

It was a big cat. No! It was a little girl. No . . . Oh,

my god! It was . . . they were . . . *joined*.

The cop had caught the pair in their most vulnerable moment; that instant when cat reentered feline shape and girl was once more taking human form.

They both were covered with blood.

The cat and the girl looked up as the cop clicked on his flashlight, the harsh beam reflecting off bloody teeth that snarled at him.

The big cop screamed in terror and ran for the lighted street. He heard the sounds of feet and paws behind him. He heard the low growling and snarling and fear made him very swift.

The footsteps and paw paddings were getting closer.

The cop said a silent prayer and began really picking them up and putting them down.

"*Murphy!*" he screamed at his partner, standing across the street, chatting with a lady of the evening. "Murphy! Kill it. For God's sake—*kill it!*"

Murphy pulled his service revolver and looked wildly around him. The lady of the evening hauled her ass, looking for a john to sell it to.

"Kill what, Rufus?" he yelled. The street was empty.

Patrolman Rufus Gremillion chanced a glance over his shoulder. He stopped in the street and looked in all directions.

There was no one behind him. No creatures. No monsters. Nothing.

Rufus bent over, trying to ease the stitch in his side. He caught his breath. "No more booze for me, Murphy," he proclaimed. "That's it. From this moment on, I'm taking the pledge. No more booze. Ever."

"What did you see back there, Rufus?" Murphy asked. He had almost shit his pants when his partner

20

started hollering.

"A glimpse of hell, Murphy. A glimpse of hell."

And he never spoke of it again.

The killings stopped.

NEW YORK CITY, 1965

The girl and the cat were both getting fat and lazy, for food was plentiful in this city, and they were feasting each night. It was well, though. For soon they would have to enter their twenty-five year cycle of rejuvenation. And the time was getting close. And they still had not found a suitable place for their long rest.

It was none too soon. The residents of New York City were getting edgy, even more fearful than usual of traveling alone at night. Too many blood-drained and gnawed-on bodies were being found.

Tonight would be the final night of feasting in the city, and then the child and the cat would move on to find a suitable place to sleep.

The girl had noticed something else, too. As the years rolled by, it was not only customs and language and dress that changed—that was easy to cope with. But it was becoming more and more difficult for a young girl to travel the country alone. Almost impossible unless one moved at night, and even then, one had to be very careful.

No telling what problems the next life-cycle would bring.

BOOK ONE

1

Ruger County, Virginia. 1985.

"Dad?"

"Ummm?" Dan Garrett looked up from his paper at his son. The boy—no, that wasn't correct, the father amended—his son was a young man; junior at the university.

"What were you doing in 1965?"

"Walking the floor at the hospital, waiting for you to be born." He grinned and winked at his only son.

Carl Garrett laughed. "Come on, Dad! Get serious, will you?"

"All right. What, specifically, about '65, did you have in mind?"

"New York City."

"The Big Orange," his father said, his grin spreading.

"Apple, Dad," his daughter corrected. "It's known as the Big Apple."

"I knew it was some kind of fruit." Dan winked at his wife.

The daughter grimaced. "You're impossible."

Carl looked at his sister, Carrie. "If you're *quite* through? Thank you. I'm doing a paper on the great unsolved murders of the past one hundred years, Dad. There was some really neat murders in New York City back in '65."

"Really *neat* murders?" Dan questioned that.

"Were," Carrie said to her brother.

Carl cut his eyes. "Huh?"

"There *were* some really neat murders," Carrie said.

"*Was* is correct," her brother said, sticking to his statement.

Father stepped in. He wasn't sure himself and he was afraid he'd be asked. His wife, a teacher at the local high school, smiled at him. He knew she was hoping he'd be asked to settle it. "You're a trouble-maker," he said to his wife. Cutting his eyes back to his son, he asked, "What about those murders in the Big Grape?"

"Apple, Dad," Carrie said. "And it's *were*."

"Shaddup, Dink," Carl said, calling her by the nickname she detested.

With her hand held behind the magazine so her parents could not see what she was doing, Carrie flipped Carl the rigid digit.

He laughed at her. "Naughty, naughty."

Dan looked around the room at his family. "Did I miss something?"

Both kids laughed.

"What is going on!" Dan said, a tone to his voice that both brother and sister knew only too well. Cool it. Enough is enough.

"The murders in New York City," Carl brought it back. "You see, they were all drained of blood."

"Gross out!" Carrie said.

"Carl," his mother cautioned. "We just finished supper. If you don't mind?"

The boy grinned. It was just too good to miss. "No, I didn't mind at all. It was good."

Dan looked at his son. "Whoa, boy."

That was the time to back off, slow down, take it easy, WYM-time. Watch Your Mouth.

"Sorry, Mother," the boy took the vocal cue from his father.

"Fine, Carl."

"Anyhoo," the boy said, "back to the Vampire Murders."

This time, Dan folded his paper and laid it aside. "The what?"

"That is what the NYPD named them. The Vampire Murders. I'm serious about the bodies being drained of blood. And that's not all." He grinned, doing his best Vincent Price imitation.

"You look like Pat Boone," his sister shot him down.

"Drop the other boot, boy," Dan said.

"The bodies had been partially eaten, too."

"That's all," Evonne Garrett said, rising from her

27

chair and moving toward the front door. "Come on, Carrie. Let's go out on the porch. It's nice and peaceful out there."

"No way, Mother," the just-turned-seventeen year old said. "This is getting good in here."

"Yukk!" the mother said.

"What's the matter, Vonne?" Dan said with a laugh. He winked at her. "Every time a scary movie comes on the tube, you can't be pried away from it."

"That's different, Dan. That's a movie. This is real."

Dan chuckled as his wife left the room. He looked at his son. "Go on."

"Well, in 1965, Dad, what were you doing?"

"In '65, son, I was with the FBI. Five years later I got shot and put out to pasture. I came back home to Ruger County and joined the Sheriff's Department. Then I ran for sheriff. To my surprise, I won. The rest is history."

"And you never heard of the Vampire Murders?"

"Carl, I probably did at the time. I've just forgotten about them."

"Were you in Washington back in '65?"

"I was all over the United States between '65 and '69."

"Working on civil rights cases?"

"I didn't do much of that. I was with a . . . special Bureau team."

And the son and daughter knew the father would not tell them what it was. And they knew not to push it.

"Shot up and Presidential decorated," Carl said

28

with a smile, "and the man doesn't remember the murders of the century."

"Chalk it up to old age, boy."

"You said it, not me." Carl and Carrie laughed.

"Have you stopped discussing Jack the Ripper?" Vonne called from the porch.

"Yes, dear," Dan said. "You may come in now and clean up the gore."

From the front porch, came the rubbery sounds of the wet raspberry.

Ruger County, Virginia is located in the center of the state. Rolling hill country, rich with history and tradition. Lots of old homes. Ruger County is, for the most part, a quiet, peaceful county. The largest town is Valentine, which is the county seat. 3600 population. There are three incorporated towns in the county. Bradford, Ashby, and Callaway. The county population stays right about 10,000. Real violence is rare; that's not counting the occasional fights between husband and wife.

FBI agent, then deputy, and finally sheriff of Ruger County for the past ten years, Dan Garrett and his deputies keep a loose but steady hand on the pulse of Ruger County. They know who the trouble-makers are, and can usually intervene before anything of a deadly nature occurs.

Not always, but usually. And in the field of law enforcement, that's a pretty good average.

The town of Valentine holds the county's only hospital. Small, but extremely well-equipped and fully staffed with highly competent personnel. Old Doc Ramsey built the original facility back in the mid-'30's. His son, Doctor Quinn Ramsey, took over in '65, building a brand new hospital. Quinn is the county coroner. His wife, Alice, is the county's expert—one of many—on Virginia. More specifically, her own family tree. And, so the rumor goes, and goes, if one is ever foolish enough to be trapped at a gathering by Alice's rapid-fire interlocution, one is left with the disconcerting sensation of having one's eyes bug out, dry mouth, rapid pulse, and one's shoes seemingly welded to the floor.

One of their friends actually passed out while talking to Alice one day. On the phone.

"Goddamn woman could rot a fence post," a local farmer was once accused of saying.

He stoutly denies it.

But really, Ruger County is a very serene place to live and raise a family. A lot of proven but so-called old-fashioned ways are still clung to. And many people are wising up to the fact that many old ways were and are the best.

One movie house. That's in Valentine. One drive-in theater. That's in Bradford. A few honky-tonks. Damn few. Beer only. Buy your hard liquor at the state-owned stores. A lot of out-of-staters don't like that system; but it suits the residents of Ruger—most of them—and it's their county.

No radio or TV stations located in the county. Get lots of music and TV out of Richmond—seventy miles away, or from Charlottesville or Lynchburg. And if that's not good enough for you, stick a satellite dish in your back yard and prop your feet up.

There are a few small factories in the county. All but one of them located in and around Valentine. Couple of small lumber mills.

The whites outnumber the blacks, and for the most part, both sides get along well, with only a few agitators on both sides. Those people are, for the most part, ignored. Every now and then some minor racial trouble will flare up, usually in the form of nigger-baiting or honky-hating. If the sheriff's deputies get there in time, all concerned are going to the pokey. White and black.

Best thing to do is just try to get along.

About 9950 pretty good folks live in Ruger County. Fifty-five cronks. And one colossal bore.

Alice.

The tallest mountain in the county is Eden Mountain. 1200 plus feet. The government is mining something out of Eden. They're taking the mountain down from the top and won't tell anybody what they're taking out of there. Top secret hush-hush stuff and all that stuff. People in the county are used to it. Nobody ever went to the damned ol' mountain anyway. People have been known to get lost in there. Damn place is full of caves. Local drunk got lost in there 'bout fifteen years back. Lost for two days. Scared the hell out of him. Got religion in there, too. Went in a wine-head and came out a born-again Baptist. Hasn't touched a drop since then. Hair turned gray in spots. Claimed he saw a dark-haired little girl and a cat in there. They were sleeping and he couldn't wake either of them up.

31

They weren't dead; they were sleeping.
Of course, nobody believed ol' Eddie Brown.
Yet.

The rumbling and grumbling and grinding and
blasting and roaring of equipment woke the girl and
the cat. They were both disorganized and confused
and irritable. Their rest cycle had been disturbed far
too soon. And worse yet, if they could not find a new
resting place, they would not be able to return to
sleep. Unless . . . this was their final destination.
Perhaps.

Anya and Pet looked at one another in the darkness
of the cave. Light or dark meant nothing to either of
them. They saw the same whether it was day or night.
They would wait out the rumbling until it stopped,
then they would attempt to find another refuge. If it
wasn't already too late. And they both felt that might
well be the case. If so, they would have to endure a
human-like and child's play-pet existence for a time.
It had happened before; they knew how to deal with
it. But neither of them liked it. It increased the
chances of discovery. Unless this was the home of the
Old Ones. Perhaps.

No one had told them their reign on earth would be
easy. No one had told them anything. They knew only
they must survive. And search. Try to find the source.
The Force.

And now that they were awake, they were hungry.

Voices drifted to them. Lights flashed in the darkness. That made the child and the cat even more

32

irritable. How *dare* anyone interrupt them.

"Hold it, Jimmy. Whoa! We've hit another cave. Back off."

"'Bout quittin' time anyway. You wanna check it out now or wait 'til morning?"

"Let's do it now. Help me enlarge this hole and we'll get some light down here."

Anya and Pet were trapped. The miner was blocking their escape route. A roaring filled the cave as the hole was enlarged. Heavy boots hit the floor of the cave. They heard the clicking of the flashlight. It would not come on.

The miner flipped the switch several times and cussed. He shook the flashlight. "Get me another torch, Jimmy. This one won't work." He sniffed the close, stale air. "Jesus, what is that smell?"

It smelled like . . . like, unwashed human bodies. Stale flesh. And something else, too, but the miner couldn't pinpoint it. Then the man found the words he sought: Old blood. And evil. *Evil!* Why would he think that?

Heavy flashlight in hand, the engineer inspected the immediate cavern for serious breaks or instability. Everything looked good.

"You okay, Al?" Jimmy called.

"Yeah. But God, what a horrible smell down here."

"Gas?"

"No. It isn't gas. I don't know what it is."

He heard a very slight rustling sound coming from the right angle turn in the cave. He froze, listening intently. Silence greeted him.

Rats, he thought.

He shone the light into the darkness of the cave. The beam picked up nothing human or animal. He stepped toward the sharp bend in the cave. That terrible odor once more assailed his nostrils. He slowly made his way around the bend and lifted the light.

Sudden fear rooted the man to the spot.

The powerful light froze a young girl in place. She held a cat in her hands. The girl's dress was tattered and torn and filthy. And out of style. Years out of style. It was really no more than rags hanging from her slim body. The child couldn't have been more than nine or ten years old. And she was half-starved looking. The cat in her arms looked so thin Al couldn't tell if it was dead or alive.

Then the cat opened its eyes. The cold yellow reflected back into the light.

"Girl," Al found his voice. The one word echoed in the cave.

Both the girl and the cat screamed at the man. The inhuman-sounding yowling jarred the engineer. He took several steps backward.

"Goddamn, Al!" Jimmy yelled. "What in the name of God was that?"

"Get down here, Jimmy! Now!"

"On my way. Hang on."

The girl and the cat jumped at Al. The girl's eyes were black embers glowing in the harsh light. She knocked the light from Al's hand as long, dirty fingernails dug grooves in his face. The blood leaped from the deep slashes. The cat landed on Al's head, digging in, its front paws slashing at the man's face.

34

One clawed paw ripped an eye from a socket. Al's hard hat was knocked loose. In his pain and confusion and fear, Al stumbled backward, losing his footing in the darkness. He fell heavily, smashing his head on the rock wall.

Then purple darkness took him, swallowing him. He thought he heard laughter, very hollow-sounding, very evil. Demons filled his mind. They were horrible.

Then, in his mind, he saw the face of . . .

2

Dan Garrett stood up, stretching his lanky frame. Now on the shady side of middle age, the man could still wear the same size jeans he wore in college. He exercised several times a week, but could not do much jogging, since the bullet that knocked him out of the FBI had shattered a knee. After several operations, he limped only when tired. He ran fingers through salt and pepper hair—and rubbed the beard stubble on his face.

Getting old, he thought. Come in from work, open a beer, pick up the paper, sit down, and promptly fall asleep. Wonderful.

He tried the paper again. He was just getting into a story when the phone rang. He stilled the ringing.

"Dan?"

"Yes."

"Quinn Ramsey here. Did I catch you at supper?"

"Oh, no. We never eat until around seven."

"Good. Just don't eat and go to bed on a full stomach," the doctor added, almost as an after-

36

thought.

Dan laughed at his long-time friend. The men had gone all the way through school together. Grade school all the way through the university.

"Sorry, Dan. Sometimes I have difficulty keeping my work at the office."

"Believe me, Quinn, I do know the feeling. What's on your mind?"

"Well . . . Dan, can you come to the hospital? It's . . . the damndest thing. I'd just rather not say anything about it until you have a look."

"Sounds serious, Quinn."

"It is. Frightening is a better word."

"All right, Quinn. I'll be there in ten minutes."

Dan walked toward the front door, then paused, remembering he had forgotten his pistol.

He shook his head and laughed. Hell, it can't be that serious.

Dan walked out of the intensive care unit and removed his mask and gloves. His face was shiny with sweat and his eyes looked glassy from the unexpected. He lifted his eyes and looked at Doctor Ramsey.

"What in the name of God happened to that man, Quinn?"

"We don't really know what happened. And neither does the man who brought him in. They were both working inside Eden Mountain. Just about quitting time. Al—the man you just saw—dropped down into a newly found cave to check it out. Jimmy—that's the man who brought him in—stayed top-side. Jimmy heard howling, then screaming. Whoever, or *what*ever it was, was gone when Jimmy arrived to help his

37

friend. What we do know is this: the man has a severe concussion, one eye clawed out, and many deep lacerations on his face, head, arms, and chest."

Sheriff Dan Garrett, not known for being a profane man, startled the RN standing nearby when he blurted "But the man looks like a fucking *mummy*! He looks like he's five hundred years old."

"Steady, Dan. I know, I know. Believe me, my reaction was even more profane than yours. His . . . condition is precisely why you wore gloves, gown, and mask, and viewed him through glass. He's being kept in an absolutely controlled environment. You all right now, buddy?"

"Yes. Sorry for the outburst. Quinn, how old is that man?"

"His driver's license says he's thirty-two years old."

Dan felt the blood rush from his face. He was suddenly not all right. He took several deep breaths and cracked his knuckles—a habit he'd been trying to break. "When did the . . . ah, aging process begin?"

"Apparently the instant whatever it was attacked him and drew blood. I have Doctor Goodson in from the university. He's in the lab now. Doctor Goodson was . . . ah, shocked at the man's appearance. First time I ever saw that man change expression. He was one of my professors in med school."

Dan shook his head. He didn't know Doctor Goodson from a can of beans. "Who is Goodson?"

Doctor Ramsey looked pained. "I'll keep it in layman's terms."

"Please do."

"Doctor Goodson wrote the book—or books—on aging. If there is anything he doesn't know about it, it's because it has not been discovered."

Dan said, "The university does have one of the finest med schools in the nation."

"*The* finest," Quinn corrected.

Dan smiled. "You wouldn't be prejudiced, would you, Quinn?"

"Of course not," the doctor's reply was stiff.

Dan jerked his thumb toward the intensive care unit. "What did your expert have to say about that guy in there?"

Quinn Ramsey once again looked pained. "Doctor Goodson's exact words at first glance?"

"Yes."

"Holy shit!"

The child and the cat made their way through the dark woods. The girl rained down ancient curses on the men who had disturbed their rest cycle. She and Pet had been awake too long now to again seek the sanctuary and safety of sleep.

They were awake and that was the way it must remain. They had no other options. But where were the Old Ones?

The only control they had over their destiny was to survive. And now, to search. The Old Ones must be found.

But for now, they must eat, and eat well, in order to regain their strength. For the ordeal ahead of them would be severe. They knew armed men would be hunting them. They had been through it all before.

The cat's ears perked up. The pair stopped. The girl and the cat exchanged glances and thoughts. They both heard the sounds of panting. The cat leaped ahead, slipping through the woods, the girl following as silently as the cat's light step, the rags of her tattered dress flapping. Moonlight glinted off a parked car. The car was rocking on its springs. A young man's gruntings and a young woman's moaning drifted through the spring air.

The cat and the girl slipped as silently as death's touch up to the parked car, one taking the right, the other the left.

Within seconds, panting and moaning and grunting had changed to screams of terror and howls of pain. Blood splattered the windows and cushions of the car. Frantic thrashings rocked the vehicle. A cat's yowlings and a girl's grotesque smacking of lips filled the air. The rocking of the car ceased. The screaming bubbled off into nothing.

Silence once more filled the woods. A bloody child's face appeared in the rear window. A cat appeared by her side. Both were covered with blood. They looked at one another. They smiled in satisfaction.

Al the engineer died.

"Died of *what*?" Dan persisted in his questioning. "Of what?"

Goodson said, "Old age."

"But the man was only thirty-two years old!"

Doctor Goodson sat looking at the table top. Doctor Ramsey sat looking at Doctor Goodson. Dan stood over the medical men, looking at both of them, expecting, demanding answers.

Dan said, "Either you don't know, or you're not leveling with me. Which is it?"

Goodson looked up at the sheriff. "We don't know, Dan. I've never seen anything like it. And that is the truth." He looked at Quinn. "How many people know of this?"

"Of the rapid aging?"

"Yes."

"The emergency room personnel. One RN. Doctor Harrison. The intensive care personnel who were on duty. You, me, Sheriff Garrett."

Doctor Goodson sighed, feeling his age. "I've got to get some people in here from CDC. We're over our heads with this." He looked startled for a moment. "Where is the man who brought him in?"

"I sedated him and put him to bed," Quinn said.

"Did you notice any cuts or scratches on him? Think, Doctor."

". . . no. But . . . He wasn't wearing gloves. What are you thinking?" Then it hit Quinn. "Oh, God!"

"If that man had even the smallest cut and the blood from the engineer infected him . . . Damn!" He stood up. "Let's go see him."

But Jimmy was gone. No one on the floor had seen him leave.

Jimmy looked at his hand and felt like puking. The hand had shriveled and now had no feeling left in it. It was like a part of him had died.

It had.

He had gotten out of bed to go to the john. That's when he'd noticed his hand. He had panicked, not fully awake from the shot the doctor had given him. He had not known what to do. He had dressed in his dirty work clothes and walked out of the hospital. He hadn't seen a soul in doing so.

He knew he should go back to the hospital, get

41

some help. But goddamnit, they hadn't been able to help Al. God, he was scared. He had watched Al shrivel up and turn into some kind of mummy-looking creature right before his very eyes. Jesus God! He had seen it but had not believed his own eyes. What had happened to Al was impossible.

He raised his cold, shriveled, ugly hand. But it wasn't impossible. Christ, it was happening to *him*. And the aging had spread all the way up to his elbow. It looked like . . . it looked hideous.

He had to do something. He had to think. He was shaking all over.

Wild, unreasonable panic struck Jimmy. He couldn't think straight. But he had to do something, and do it damn quick.

What was that line in the Bible about plucking your eye out if it offends you?

Something like that.

All right, then. If it was God's will, then that's the way it would be.

Jimmy went stumbling and falling around the line of trucks and equipment at the mining site. He fumbled open the lock on the tool shed, clicked on the lights, and began throwing tools around. Finally he found what he was looking for.

A hatchet.

Taking a piece of rope, Jimmy tied it as tightly as he could around his arm, just above the elbow, cutting off the flow of blood. He propped his arm up on the fender of the truck.

He took a deep breath and gripped the wooden handle. He raised the hatchet. Moonlight reflected off the head of the small axe. He brought the axe down as hard as he could. The sounds of his screaming filled the quiet night. Half his arm bounced off the gravel.

Through his pain, Jimmy heard dark laughter echoing around him. Lightning licked across the sky. A heavy, sulfurous odor filled the air.

Then Jimmy saw the face of . . .

He began screaming in his unconsciousness.

3

Sheriff Dan Garrett gathered his force of deputies around him in the now deserted hospital cafeteria. The deputies listened in shock and horror and all with some degree of disbelief as Dan explained what had happened.

Then he showed them all the body of Al.

There were no more unbelievers among the deputies.

Dan described Jimmy and told his men, "Find him. When you find him, not if, *when*, don't try to take him alone. Call for help. I mean that. I don't want any hotdogs lone-wolfing it this night. And for God's sake, *don't* touch him. Repeating that: *Don't* touch him. Just call in his location and stand back, keeping an eye on him. Move out!"

When the deputies had gone, Dan sat in the room housing the hospital's radio equipment. He would monitor from there. He looked up as boot-heels echoed hollow in the hall. Sergeant Scott Langway of the Virginia Highway Patrol stepped into the room.

"Dan," the patrolman said. "I got here as soon as I could. Big pileup east of here, right on the county line. Nobody seriously hurt, but traffic was backed up for two miles. What's going on?"

"I'll let Doctor Ramsey brief you."

Doctor Ramsey brought the patrolman up-to-date, speaking quickly, but leaving nothing out. When he had finished, the highway cop stood very still for a full ten count. He looked at Dan, then at Quinn.

"Is either of you putting me on?" he asked.

"It's no joke, Scott," Dan said.

"I want to see this man."

"Come with me," Quinn said.

Dan had no desire to view the mummy-looking man again. He used that time to call his wife. Her days married to a field agent with the FBI had stayed with her. She asked no questions. Just said she'd put a plate of food in the fridge for him to have when he got home.

"Stay safe," she said, then hung up.

Dan sat down at a table and looked at the paper cup of cold coffee in front of him. He tried very hard not to think of the horrible possibilities of this . . . this *situation*. Tried, but failed.

And as every cop with any time behind a badge at all has thought at one time or another, Dan thought: Why me? Why here? Why on my beat? Why?

And as always, there was no satisfying answer.

Jimmy came awake to cold numbing fear and white hot pain. He looked at his mangled arm. Blood seeped past the tightly bound stump. The severed arm, from the elbow down, lay on the ground, a shriveled ugly thing. It made Jimmy want to puke just

45

looking at the thing. He couldn't believe he'd actually had the courage to do it.

But now what? And what in God's name had he dreamed?

He sat up. He was weak, but not as weak as he thought he'd be. His arm—what was left of it—hurt like hell; but it was bearable. He looked up as headlights swept the parking area of the mine site. The car crunched over gravel and slid to a halt.

"Freeze!" the voice shouted from behind the blazing headlights. "Don't move."

Jimmy raised his bloody stump. "It's okay, now," he called. "I cut it off."

"Jumpin' Jesus!" the deputy said. He fumbled for his mike, found it, dropped it out of shaky fingers, and picked it up again and called in. His voice broke. He hated it that his voice was so shaky. He couldn't help that. God, the nut case had whacked off his own arm. The young deputy felt like tossing his supper.

"Stay right there," Dan instructed his deputy. "I'm on my way."

In less than five minutes, a half dozen cars and one ambulance ground to a halt in the gravel of the parking lot. In one of the cars, behind the wheel, sat a still-badly shaken Sergeant Langway of the VHP. He had viewed the dead engineer. In a lot of ways, he wished he had not.

Masked, gloved men approached Jimmy, sitting on the gravel, his back to a pickup.

"Did I do the right thing, Doc?" Jimmy asked, his voice just audible. He was in shock, and losing ground.

The now flat-topped mountain loomed dark behind the men.

"I'm sure you did, son," Quinn said, his voice slightly muffled behind his mask. He looked at the dead, shriveled arm and hand on the gravel. "Get that," he told a medic. "And be careful."

Dan's radio began squawking metallically. Dan stilled the tinny sounds.

"All units to tach," the dispatcher said. "Ten-thirty-five from Ruger nine."

Dan switched his radio to tach and to hell with the constitutionality of it all. "Go, Nine."

"I just found Mary Louise Turner and Billy Mack Evans out near Whispering Creek, on the old Hogg Road. Both of them naked. They're in Mr. Evans' car. Both of them are dead. Tore up real bad. Blood everywhere and the bodies have been eaten on. You copy this, Sheriff?"

"Ten-four," Dan radioed. "I'm rolling now. Stay with it, Nine."

Sergeant Langway met the sheriff's eyes. "Going to be a long night, Dan."

"Yeah," Dan replied.

None of the cops, county or state, or any of the doctors, nurses, or medics, had ever seen anything like what had been done to the young couple. After the initial viewing, Doctor Goodson had ordered the cops away from the mangled, eaten bodies and blood-splattered car. The medical people, all sworn to silence by the state police, viewed the carnage under harsh light from portable spotlights set up by the state police.

Dan had given his tersely worded orders to his people; "Keep a tight lid on this. No press. *None at all!* Anybody leaks this, I'll have his or her ass, roasted and served up. Understood?"

They all understood, knowing full well that Sheriff

Garrett meant every word of it.

"Look," Doctor Goodson said to Quinn, pointing. "See where the flesh had begun to age around the bites?"

"Stopping the aging process at the moment of death," Quinn said.

"Yes. And the bites are both human and animal-like. We have, at least, a madman loose."

"Madwoman," Dan said, peering over the doctor's shoulders. He wore a mask and gloves. "Maybe."

Goodson looked around. "Why do you say that, Sheriff?"

"By the size of the human bites. A small mouth did that. And those are not animal-like tracks. They're paw prints from a cat."

Goodson looked again. "You're right," he conceded. "Very observant, Sheriff."

"Yeah," Dan said drily. "A madwoman with a killer house-cat."

"Did you know, my good fellow," Carl's roommate at the university said, "that in ancient Egypt, there once existed a secret religion who believed in cat people?"

Without looking up from his books, Carl said, "If you call me 'your good fellow' one more time, I'm going to jack your jaw, Mike."

"My word, you certainly are testy this evening."

"Busy, buddy, busy."

"You do recall the line about all work and no play, et cetera and so forth?"

"Mike, you're going to get your lazy ass tossed out of school if you don't start bearing down. And you'd better damn well start realizing that."

"As Ol' William once wrote: 'It maketh not a damn to me'."

Carl laughed at his friend. Built exactly like his father, Carl leaned back, away from the desk full of books, and stretched. Lean and lanky, the young man pushed back a lock of thick, unruly hair and rubbed his tired eyes.

The last paragraph on the many-times-photocopied page caught his eyes. He leaned closer and read: The rash of murders that to this day remain unsolved in St. Louis held more than one macabre note. In addition to the human teeth marks there were found other marks that at first were dismissed as rat bites. Experts later testified the bites were made by a cat. The same cat had gnawed on all the bodies, as had the same small person. The human bites are thought to be female.

He looked at Mike. "What was that you said about cat people?"

"Ahh! Got your attention, didn't I? O-ye-of-little-confidence-in-your-ol'-buddy's academic abilities."

"I have confidence in your abilities as a bull-shitter," Carl said. "Besides, I thought those people worshipped Ra?"

"No, you heathen. Ra was a sun god of Heliopolis. A hawk-headed man. This was a very small group of men and women. No more than a couple of thousand at the most. The high priests and priestesses were thought, so it is rumored, to have supernatural powers. For instance, the cat and the goddess could change shapes, one becoming the other. They both were worshipped. And they were said to live for an incredible length of time. Hundreds and hundreds of years."

Carl shook his head. "Mike, you have such a fantastic memory. A recall that is awesome. Yet your grades are terrible."

Mike grinned. "You wanna be president of my fan club, Carl?"

"Asshole," Carl muttered. "Tell me more about these cat people."

"Are you serious? I thought you were going to be a pig?"

"A police officer, Mike. Besides, pigs is beautiful."

"Oh, God!" Mike feigned great disgust. "Spare me. Why do you want to know about ancient religions? Pigs are not only beautiful, they're notoriously stupid."

"Would you like to come home with me this weekend and tell that to my dad?" Carl grinned.

Mike rolled his eyes. "Ah . . . *no*! Besides, your father is an educated pig. There is a great deal of difference between that and an ordinary pig."

Carl laughed. He couldn't get mad at Mike. He knew Mike was only putting the needle to him. His friend had absolutely no beef with the police. Mike was built like a big overstuffed teddy bear—a very wealthy teddy bear, and an enormously strong teddy bear. One of the feather-headed jocks at school had attempted to fight Mike once. Once. Mike had very nearly crushed the life out of the young man. Mike was six feet tall, and about three and half feet wide. He was even-tempered until provoked. When that happened—look out! He was also a genius, with only one love, and that one love was not the major forced on him by his parents. His father and mother had set up a very generous allowance, but Mike could not touch the principal until he was twenty-five, only the interest. And that was considerable.

"The cat people, Mike?" Carl persisted.

"Gods and goddesses, ol' buddy. High priests and all that type of stuff. I'll tell you a truth. There really isn't that much known about them. Like I said, a secret religion. The religion, cult, whatever, supposedly began when the Sahara was green."

"The Sahara Desert? It was *green*? What are you talking about?"

"Fertile. Like Virginia. I don't mean with oaks and hickory trees and stuff like that. But, well . . . *fertile*. Like in the ability to grow things. The Sahara began to die about seven to eight thousand years B.C. That is well documented by wall paintings in a sandstone plateau in the Tassili N'Ajjer. That is about the time the cat people were really getting down and doing their thing. When the desert began to die, they moved on . . . somewhere. No one knows for sure because it was all very hush-hush, and those not affiliated with the religion were scared to death of them."

"What did they eat?"

"I beg your pardon?"

"I mean, well, were they cannibalistic?"

"Oh, yes. Bloodthirsty. They were a savage, barbaric group of nutsos. It's written—somewhere, I forget where I read it—that only the high priest could impregnate the chosen woman. Thus insuring that she would deliver twins, a girl baby, and a cat. But they weren't successful all the time. Really hideous monsters and creatures could be birthed. And it's all tied in with the devil—or something very much like the devil. The bite of the girl or the cat could produce some strange effects on the human body. Changing it. Some say that when the girl and the cat were nine or ten years old, they were entombed alive. But they didn't die. They could come and go at will. Especially if they were called upon."

"That's wild, Mike. How come I never heard anything about this bunch?"

"Because it's unproven. Myth. Personally, I think

51

it's all a bunch of shit."

Carl looked at the report of the murders. "Yeah," he said. "I guess so."

The bodies—what was left of them—of Billy Mack and Mary Louise were body-bagged and taken to the hospital. Doctor Ramsey, with Doctor Goodson assisting, both of them gloved, gowned, and masked, began the autopsy. Gruesome things at best, this one was particularly difficult for Doctor Ramsey, for he had delivered both young people. Both men were shocked to discover the hearts were missing from both young persons. The entire stomach cavity had been eaten. The eyes, lips, and much of the tongue was gone. And from the size of the bites, the human bites, both doctors were certain the attacker was a very small person; no bigger than a child. But a very savage child. Surely insane. What other explanation could there be?

Quinn lifted his eyes, meeting the eyes of Goodson. "Lycanthropy, perhaps?"

"I thought of that," Goodson said. "But which definition of it?"

"Are you serious!" Quinn blurted the question.

"Quite."

Lycanthropy is a form of insanity in which a person imagines himself to be a wolf or other wild beast. The second definition is the assumption of the actual form of a wolf by a human being.

A werewolf.

"Assuming such things actually exist, which I doubt," Quinn said, "what about the second set of bites? A wolf and a cat teaming up?"

"I am merely attempting to exhaust all possibilities, Doctor," Goodson remarked. Something, some old memory was nagging at the man. He could not bring the memory into mental light. Perhaps it would come to him.

The doctors scrubbed and changed into street clothes. In the hall, Quinn met Dan Garrett and Sergeant Langway.

"Have you notified the parents yet?" Quinn asked the men. Goodson had returned to the lab.

Both lawmen appeared to be in a mild state of shock. It was not fear. Not the fear of physical harm to themselves. Both men had used their service revolvers more than once. Each had killed in the line of duty. They had both seen the mangled remains of traffic victims. They both had witnessed the horror of the worst kinds of child abuse, from incest to savage beatings that resulted in the death of the child. They both had seen the best and the worst of humankind.

But neither had ever seen anything like what had happened this night. And both feared it was going to get much worse before getting any better.

They were correct in thinking that.

Quinn cleared his throat. The lawmen looked up. Quinn repeated, "Have you notified the parents yet?"

Langway shook his head. Dan sighed, saying, "What do we tell them, Quinn? How can we tell them they can't view the bodies when the car was not involved in any type of traffic accident? Do we tell them the truth? And have you considered the ramifications of doing so? How about the press? How about the panic among the citizens if we level with the press? We'd have every nut from five states converging on us. You want that?"

"Not to mention every citizen in the county shooting at shadows," Langway said.

"Yes," Dan agreed. "I'm not going to lie to the press. But for the sake of those kids' parents, I am going to stretch the truth a bit. They were murdered;

that's a fact. They were badly mutilated; that's a fact. Quinn, I'm leaving it up to you to see that the funerals are closed casket services. You and Ed Hathaway at the funeral home have shared a few secrets, have you not?"

"Certainly." He looked at Langway. "When will your lab people be through here, Sergeant?"

"Couple of hours. They'll coordinate with you about releasing the bodies."

Dan said, "Scott, have your people finished going over the car?"

The trooper shook his head.

"Then impound it," Dan said. "And cover it carefully before moving it. I don't want anybody who isn't directly connected with this investigation to see that car. Hell, what am I saying? I don't have to tell *you* the drill." The trooper nodded his head.

Chief Deputy Chuck Klevan said, "We've got to buy ourselves some time. Some breathing room."

"For a fact," Langway agreed.

"How is the miner who whacked his arm?" Dan asked.

Quinn cringed at Dan's wording. "Serious but stable. He's in shock. Lost a lot of blood. But his action seems to have stopped the aging process."

"Let's hope so . . ." Langway murmured.

4

Anya and Pet found shelter in a deserted house near a patch of woods. They could go no further that night, for both were bloated from gorging themselves on the young people. Both knew they were in trouble; but both were confident they would survive. For they knew they were at the source of their searching. The Old Ones were here. They had made a mistake in seeking the Source in the cities. They had, for years, taken the easy way in their searching. And they had been wrong. But now everything was right. But they had to buy some time. A few more days. That was critical. Anya had been receiving messages. *Their search was over!* They were so close to freedom.

The girl and the cat looked at one another in the darkness that was light to them. Messages passed between them. Messages and memories they and they alone shared. Ancient messages and reminiscences. But one was not so old—not to them.

They had been asleep for hundreds of years. No one had called them to come forth. And now they knew why. They knew they were very nearly the last of their kind. There were others, but they were scattered and few in number. And none knew where the other was.

Then the British explorers came to the old lands, with their shovels and picks and brushes, digging in the sands. And they disturbed the resting place of Anya and Pet.

Those archaeologists had learned the terror of disturbing that which should have been left alone. That expedition had vanished from the face of the earth, with no trace left on the sands that were forever shifting, forever silent, except to those who knew the ancient tongues.

Anya and Pet had surfaced into a world that bore little resemblance to that in which they had been born and reared. Released from their underground entombment, with no one to guide them, they had made their way to the sea, stowing aboard a ship that had taken them to England. From England, they had traveled to America. America had been much less crowded. They felt they could survive here, for as long as they were meant to live.

And neither knew just how long that might be. Only that they must endure and survive until the voices called them home for their final rest. Neither Anya nor Pet could comprehend that what they were doing would be construed as evil. They were from another time, another place, and were doing only what they had been born to do.

Anya and Pet rested for several hours, then a light mist covered them, a living shroud while they shifted beings, changing shapes and forms, Pet becoming Anya, Anya becoming Pet. On silent feet, the cat padded out of the house into the woods, passing several homes after careful inspection. The cat finally came to a home with a bedroom window open. And no dogs. The human cat slipped the hook on the screen, slipped through, and silently prowled the quiet sleeping home, coming to a child's bedroom. There,

56

the cat found jeans and underwear and shirts and tennis shoes that would fit its counterpart. One by one, the cat carried the articles of clothing to the open screen and dropped them to the ground. Once more outside, the cat patiently carried the clothing into the woods, making several trips, hiding them carefully. Then the cat returned to the deserted house and slipped under the mist that had covered that which was but really wasn't. They once more became female human child and feline.

They rested.

"Who in the hell are you?" Dan questioned the young woman.

"Mille Smith," she replied.

"Shit!" Sergeant Langway muttered.

"*The* Mille Smith?" Quinn asked.

"The one and only," she said with a smile.

All present, with the exception of the youngest Virginia trooper, knew all about Mille Smith. And they knew that smile was as phony as a shark's smile. Mille was very pretty, very shapely. She was tanned, with short brown hair and dark eyes. She had won a Pulitzer at the tender age of twenty-two. She had garnered more literary accolades (some of them so far to the left she walked crookedly after receiving them), covering Somoza's fall in Nicaragua. She naturally had taken a hard line position against Somoza. She had roamed Central America, filing story after story, always subtly taking sides against her own country's policies.

Mille was a hard-nosed, not always fair, investigative reporter who had many more enemies than she did friends. She could be brash and vulgar and extremely obnoxious. She was also cunning and tough. Like many reporters, she was always highly critical of the police, believing them all stamped from the same mold, regardless of country.

Had she been of age, she surely would have been a revolutionary back in the '60's.

All the men present in the hospital corridor wondered if Mille had heard enough of the conversation to pique her curiosity.

"What can we do for you, Ms. Smith?" Doctor Ramsey asked.

"Tell me what's going on, for starters," the woman replied, meeting the man look for look.

"What gives you the idea anything is going on?" Sergeant Langway asked.

She laughed at the trooper, not knowing, or caring, that she had, at that instant, made another enemy. "I was traveling through this county," she said. "On my way to Richmond, before you ask, even though it's none of your business where I was going, when I saw all the flashing lights. I hung around, followed you all here when you came back to town. Now what's going on. I'm a member of the press, I have a right to know."

Sheriff Garrett said, "Well, for a normally quiet county, Ms. Smith, we've had a mining accident that killed one man and badly injured another. Then on top of that, we had two young people murdered tonight. In Ruger County, that's a lot of goings-on for one year, much less one night. That's the trouble."

"Really, Sheriff?"

"Really, Ms. Smith."

"Sheriff?"

"Yes, Ms. Smith?"

"I don't know whether you're lying, or just full of shit!"

Dan rose to his long, lean, lanky height and faced

the woman, towering over her five foot, four inches. "Ms. Smith, I don't know what you're really doing here, or even why you want to waste your time looking into the events of this night. But you, or no one else talks to me like that. Now I have no beef with the press. Print or electronic. Past or present. You may talk to Pat Leonard of the local paper. You may speak to the people at the *News Leader* or the *Times Dispatch* in Richmond. You may speak to any reporters from the TV or other newpapers that serve this area. When you do, you will find I cooperate fully with them. But don't you get hard-nosed with me."

"Is that a threat?" Mille yelled.

"This is a hospital, young lady," Quinn said. "Keep your voice down or I'll have you ejected."

Mille flushed and cut her eyes back to Dan, towering over her. God, she hated cops! Even hicktown cops.

"No, that's not a threat, Ms. Smith," Dan said. "But it is a warning. Now, if you are here legitimately seeking a story, that's fine. If I can release any information to you, I will. Openly and willingly. But if I feel any part of that information will jeopardize whatever case I might be working on, I will not release it." He looked up as Pat Leonard, owner and editor of the local weekly paper entered the corridor and joined the group. Pat's eyes widened as he caught sight of Mille and recognized her.

"Are you quite through preaching and lecturing me, Sheriff?" Mille asked.

"For this evening, yes."

"How wonderful," she said sarcastically.

"Is it true about Billy Mack and Mary Louise, Dan?" Pat asked.

"Yes. I'm afraid it is. But I haven't notified their parents, yet. So hold up until I give you a call, okay?"

59

"Sure, Dan," Pat said.

Mille looked at the man. "Since when do reporters take orders from cops?"

Pat looked at her, sighed, and shook his head.

"You're a real pussycat, aren't you?" Mille said. She swung her gaze from Pat to Dan. "How old were the kids?"

"Both sixteen, Ms. Smith. Born and reared here in Ruger County. We all knew them."

"Yeah, yeah, I know. Just one big happy family, right? How about the third victim?"

"He was a miner working on Eden Mountain. I can't give you his name because we have not yet been able to locate next of kin. Is there anything else, Ms. Smith?"

And with a reporter's intuition—much like, although Mille would never admit to *that*—a cop's sixth sense of trouble, she knew the sheriff was lying.

But why? she questioned. What in God's name would they have to hide here?

"No, Sheriff. Not a thing. I'll just be on my way."

"Good night, Ms. Smith."

Mille looked at Pat. "Come on, Tiger. You can buy me a hamburger."

She turned and walked away, Pat Leonard leaving with her.

Nice ass, the youngest trooper thought.

"Think she bought it, Dan?" Langway asked.

"I don't know. Maybe. But if I had to make a guess, I'd say no. Damn! The last thing we need at this moment is a lot of press people snooping around."

"I concur," Quinn said. "But we have yet another problem."

"The dead engineer," Dan said.

"Precisely. I suggest we keep him in cold storage until the CDC people get here."

60

"Yes," Doctor Goodson said, making his first appearance out of the hospital's small lab since the autopsy. "I know the people from CDC; old and good friends of mine. Gentlemen, we've got serious problems. And I mean, *serious* problems."

All eyes swung toward the doctor.

"I've been testing saliva from the wounds of all three victims," Goodson said. "There are two points I'd like to make. But before I do, let me say this: I have *never* seen anything like what I've been looking at for the past hour. Never. They could have come from the same person, or *thing*. But of course, we all know that is impossible."

Sergeant Langway looked confused. Hell! He was confused. "What are you saying, Doctor?"

"Point one: The saliva is neither human nor animal. It's . . . I don't know what it is. Two: Assuming that both a human and animal was involved, they . . . well, they're one and the same."

"That's impossible!" Quinn said.

"Goddamn!" the young trooper said softly.

"Yes," Goodson said thoughtfully. "I am fully aware of that, Quinn. That is why I checked and rechecked, time after time. The results came up the same. But while it is highly infectious, it is not airborne. So we can all relax a bit on that point. Gentlemen, the murders of the kids cannot be held back from the press for very long. Once the parents are notified, it'll be news. I wish us all good luck after that. Sergeant Langway will have to inform his superiors as to the events of this night. If we're lucky, maybe we'll have seventy-two hours before the press gets wind of this. They always do. The state police are through with the bodies of the young people. The man from the funeral home can pick them up. I'm told he can keep his mouth shut and the caskets will be sealed as soon as the young people are ready. That isn't exactly kosher, but it would be best for the parents not to know all the gory details of what happened to their children. I'm an old man; I've got to get some sleep. I suggest that you all do the same." He rubbed his chin. "This isn't over. This is national news stuff, boys. And it's going to hit the news."

"Should we inform the governor?" Langway asked.

Goodson shrugged. "That will be up to your superiors, but I'm sure he'll be kept up to date before this thing is all over."

The old doctor turned and walked away.

"Optimistic type, isn't he?" Langway said.

"I think that he knows more than he's telling us," Quinn said.

"Well," Dan said. "I've got to go tell the parents the bad news."

5

The remainder of that night in Ruger County was quiet, much to the relief of the lawmen and the doctors.

The death car was covered with tarps, tied down, and moved to the Virginia Highway Patrol's impoundment lot for that division.

Friday morning's dawn managed to push through the low-hanging clouds over Ruger County. Before Sheriff Dan Garrett had swung his long legs out of bed, the mist had changed to a very light, cold rain; very cold for this early in May.

Sitting on the side of the bed, Dan rubbed his face as the events of the previous evening came roaring back to the surface. Returning in dead, gnawed-on, shriveled, bloody Technicolor.

Dan pushed them from his mind, momentarily, and showered and shaved and dressed. He did not put on his uniform that day, choosing civvies instead. In the kitchen of the quiet house, with the light rain for company, Dan poured coffee, dropped bread into the toaster, and picked up the note his wife had left for him on the table.

We have a teacher's meeting after school. I'll be late. Carrie is spending the night at Linda's. Carl will be at Mike's for the weekend. You mumbled and jerked and tossed all night long. Whatever you're working on, I hope you wrap it up soon.

Love

"So do I, babe," Dan said. "So do I. But don't count on it."

Why do I think that? he questioned.

He shook it away and buttered his toast and drank his coffee. He pulled on his boots and slipped into a shoulder holster rig, dropping his .38 Chief's Special into leather. Locking up the house, he got in his car and drove to work.

He turned on the radio and his mood improved as the DJ played a song from Dan's high school days: Sam Cooke singing "You Send Me."

Dan was humming along with the golden oldie when his radio crackled.

"Ruger One," he spoke into the mike.

"See Doctor Ramsey at the hospital, Sheriff," dispatch said. "He just called for you."

He found Quinn and Doctor Goodson sitting with two men in the doctor's lounge. The men were introduced as Doctors Alderson and Doucette. Dan shook hands, poured coffee, and sat down.

"Give me the good news first, Quinn," he said.

The doctor shook his head. "There is no good news, Dan."

"Tell me. Okay. So give me the bad news."

"What happened to the engineers last evening is impossible," Quinn said.

Dan paused in the lifting of coffee cup to mouth. "I beg your pardon?"

"What happened to the engineers is, medically speaking, impossible," Doctor Doucette said. "We checked the dead man this morning; did some preliminary work in the hospital's lab. The man has been mummified. We found traces of myrrh, cassia, sodium carbonate, honey and various spices. That method of preserving went out with the Pyramids— more or less. It's impossible."

"Myrrh?" Dan said, placing his cup gently on the table. "Like in the Bible?"

"Yes," Alderson said.

"What is cassia?"

"A variety of cinnamon. Comes from the cassia-bark tree," Doucette said. "It's called senna. Most senna comes from Arabia. There is a species of wild senna that grows in the eastern part of North America."

Sergeant Langway stepped into the room. He had been standing just inside the door, listening. He was accompanied by a man wearing captain's bars. Captain Taylor. He was introduced all around and the troopers poured coffee and sat down.

"Then the man has been embalmed?" Captain Taylor asked.

"Not by anyone around here," Quinn said.

"How about the severed arm?" Dan asked.

"Same thing," Alderson said. "Mummified."

Dan whistled softly; a slow expulsion of breath.

"I took shavings from around the wounds of the

65

young people," Goodson said. "Same thing."

Captain Taylor said, "Sergeant Langway has brought me up to date on this. This falls in my division. I'm a cop, not a medical person. So I have been instructed to work with you people on all matters pertaining to medicine. What happened to the kids, however, is on the books as murder. And that's my bailiwick. I'd like to keep what I just heard quiet for as long as possible. But like it or not, it's all going to come out into the open. And when it does, all hell is going to break loose. We'd better discuss how we want to handle it."

Alderson waved his hand impatiently. "I'm not concerned with the police work. My—our—concern is seeing that this . . . well, person who is the carrier, is found and isolated. As quickly as possible. I am, however, concerned about the panic the news of this could bring. But the public has to be notified."

"I don't believe we can separate legal from medical," Goodson said. "It's all tied in. I've notified the university that I'm staying on here for a time. Right now, we had all better get busy."

"What do we release to the press?" Dan asked.

"As much of the truth as possible," Captain Taylor said. "Without creating a general panic. I think we can legally, and without jeopardizing the case, hold back . . . ah, certain aspects of the events. We can state that the young people were killed gruesomely— that's certainly a fact—and mutilated. We don't have to say they were . . ." He swallowed hard. ". . . eaten. The engineer was killed in a mining accident. Now that's a federal project out on Eden Mountain, so the Bureau has to be advised of this. You do that this morning, Sergeant."

"Yes, sir."

Dan said, "The guy who whacked off his arm . . . that's going to be touchy. I think he should be kept in isolation for a time. We don't need to go public with him—yet."

"I agree. But God help us all if that Mille Smith female gets wind of us holding back information."

"Mille Smith?" Captain Taylor said. "What's she got to do with this?"

He was brought up to date.

"Tell our people not to hassle her, Sergeant," Taylor said. "Don't give her any slack, but don't lean on her. That woman has lawsuits against half the cops in the world."

"And she doesn't like me," Dan said.

"Dan," Taylor said. "That woman doesn't even like herself."

The cat and the girl slipped silently and unseen to where the clothes were hidden. Anya dressed in the unfamiliar modern clothing and buried her old, tattered, and bloody garments. She sat on a log and looked at her companion, looking at her.

Both of them knew their searching was over. Now the waiting had begun. And that was dangerous. For they must remain in this area—undiscovered.

"You must call your kind," Anya said to Pet. "The time is very close."

The cat cocked its head and seemed to smile.

Mille Smith had driven as far as Richmond and checked into a motel. Something big was going on back in Ruger County, and she, by God, was going to find out what it was. Whenever cops start lying—something, Mille felt, they were all experts at—something smelly was behind all the lying.

67

Carl Garrett could not concentrate on his classes that day. Something Mike had said the night before had triggered something buried deep within the dark reaches of his brain. He couldn't pin it down. But it would come to him. He hoped.

Doctor Goodson sat alone in the doctor's lounge, sipping hot tea while he was deep in thought. He had not been entirely honest with his co-workers. He had seen something very similar to this rapid aging process. But it had been more than forty-five years back, before he got out of college. He had been with his father and mother, on one of his father's sabbaticals, in Egypt. He recalled his father's laughter at the guide's explanation of the illness of the native, and his consequent death. His father had dismissed the man's explanation as ignorant, superstitious mumbo-jumbo.

But now, the son was not so sure.

And Anya and the cat rested.

The weather front that had drifted in from the west seemed to be stalled over Ruger County. For the past three days, Friday, Saturday, and Sunday, the skies had been sullen and gray, misting occasionally, and the temperature had remained on the cool side. Then it warmed up. All knew the bottom was about to drop out.

Monday morning, the residents of the county awakened to a roaring series of thunderstorms that rattled windows and made driving very hazardous. It was a lousy day for a double funeral; but when is there ever a good day?

Billy Mack and Mary Louise were given to the wet earth. No one had been allowed to view the remains. Doctor Ramsey, a distant cousin to the Evans' family, had made the official I.D. And no civilian had yet been told the entire truth about the murders.

The kids had been killed and badly mutilated. Period. The car was impounded. The insurance investigator took one quick look at the interior, lost his breakfast, and declared the vehicle a total loss.

People knew, of course, the murderer, or murderers, were still on the loose. They armed themselves and double-checked doors and windows.

Then, as in any rural area, news of the strange mining accident began to drift throughout the county. Mining operations had ceased and the miners had left town. The operation was closed indefinitely.

And people began to wonder why—aloud.

Mille Smith was always ready to listen with a very attentive ear, nodding and ohhing and ahhing in just the right spots.

"Ma'am, I heard that engineer was drained of blood. Terrible thing to see. 'Course it's all rumor."

"Is that right?" Mille said.

"Yes, ma'am."

"They tell me "—always that elusive *they*—" hit a pocket of poison gas. Never going to reopen the mine. That's what I heard."

"Interesting," Mille said.

"It's the Lord's will," a lady told her. "And His will

be done."

"Right," Mille said drily, and moved on down the street.

"I don't think they know what the hell happened," another citizen said. "And I don't think they ever will."

Mille didn't talk with Eddie Brown, and only Eddie Brown felt he knew what had happened in that cave. But damned if he was gonna volunteer anything. He'd been the butt of enough jokes. Eddie felt this was the perfect time for him to go on his annual retreat. Be silent. Be prayerful. Meditate. And most important of all: Keep his mouth shut about what he'd seen—and he saw it, he was sure of that—in that cave. 'Cause he'd been stone, cold sober. He remembered thinking—at the time—what a disgusting feeling it was.

Anya and Pet had moved only at night, and then, very cautiously. They had eaten well again, on Sunday night, feasting on a drunk man who had been staggering along the gravel road near where the pair had been hiding. This time, Anya had taken the man's money and put it in her pocket. Pet had looked at her curiously, not understanding fully. They had never used the paper and coins before.

"I'll explain," Anya told her sister. "Later."

They had walked on, leaving the partially eaten man in the ditch.

They came to a cabin in the woods and approached it warily. It was empty. And it had the appearance of not having been lived in for some time. Months, at least. They would rest there.

Eddie Brown was glad to get away from the town. All that talk about the murders and the mountain was making him nervous. Even though the cabin was only a few miles outside of Valentine proper, it was isolated. Eddie looked forward to his stay.

Eddie hadn't held a steady job since coming home from the war back in '46. He had never seen combat, so he couldn't attribute his lack of ambition and taste for booze to shell shock. He just liked to loaf around, shoot the breeze with his cronies, and booze it. He had married a lady of some means, and that woman had fallen off a ladder and broken her neck during the fifth year of their marriage. She left everything to her darlin' Eddie. Eddie didn't have to work.

So, in his grief, he became the town drunk. Good excuse as any.

Then he witnessed that terrible sight while lost inside Eden Mountain. Well, not exactly *terrible*. But it did scare him. Scare him so he became a born-again Baptist. And it was a good thing he did become a born-again Baptist, for his time on this earth in his present form was rapidly running out.

Eddie got out of his car and walked up to the porch of the small cabin and set his suitcase on the porch, by the front door. He unlocked the door and stepped inside. He did not notice the rear window slightly ajar. A noise spun him around, looking in all directions.

He saw the girl and cat he'd seen in the cave. But the girl was dressed differently this time. Instead of a dirty dress, she wore jeans.

Eddie panicked as the girl and the cat both snarled at him, fouling the air with a stench he could not readily identify. Then it came to him. Old. The smell

71

was very old.

He screamed as the cat leaped on his face, its claws tearing long strips from his flesh. The girl leaped for Eddie, her small teeth tearing open his arm. The hot blood poured from the man as the girl and the cat attempted to ride him to the floor.

Eddie became strong with fear. He kicked and screamed, breaking loose. He ran across the small room and dove head-first out a window. He rolled to his feet and ran for the woods. He felt light-headed, but attributed that to his sudden burst of energy.

Eddie's suitcase was still sitting on the front porch. A small puddle of blood oozed out from under the front door, to gather at the base of the suitcase.

The rains intensified, the lightning licking and dancing around the heavens, the thunder rolling in heavy waves.

Anya and Pet followed Eddie into the woods. They soon gave up when they sensed the change in the man. They returned to the cabin and rested.

Tuesday dawned clear, and the conversation in the cafes and various other watering holes of Valentine was about the storm. It had been the most violent any of them could remember, with downed power lines, uprooted trees, and blown-off roofs of barns and a couple of houses. Luckily, no one had been injured.

The CDC men were still in town, as was Doctor Goodson, all working in the lab at the hospital, and all keeping a very low profile.

And the FBI had made their quiet entrance.

"What do you think, Dan?" Special Agent Dodge asked the sheriff over coffee in the sheriff's office. "Do you think our party, or parties, have left this area?"

"I don't know," Dan replied. "It's a terrible thing for a cop to wish on another cop, but I sure hope they have."

"I think they've pulled out," Captain Taylor said, refilling his coffee cup from the large urn, "I think they—whoever or whatever they might be—somehow managed to wriggle in that small cave opening and were hiding there. That poor guy just happened to be the one who discovered them. While they were running, they came upon the kids. Does that fit anyone else's thinking?"

Before anyone could reply, the radio crackled. "Ruger fourteen to base. Go to tach, please."

The cops gathered around the radio.

"I've got a DB just off the C & O tracks. On Willis Road. Same M.O. as the others. It's fresh."

"Stay with it," Dan radioed. "We're rolling." He looked at Captain Taylor.

The trooper said, "I'm glad I'm not betting my hunches today. I'd lose my damned drawers!"

6

The man was identified as Donald Drake. He was not from Ruger County; a transient from around the Richmond area. He had been drained of blood and partially eaten. Doctor Ramsey said the body was not more than twenty-four to thirty-six hours old.

The lawmen exchanged glances. The FBI agents looked at the mutilated remains, the savage gnawing bites, both human and animal, and shook their heads. One of the younger agents walked off into the bushes and vomited on the ground.

"That young man been with the Bureau long?" Dan asked innocently.

"Less than a year," the agent-in-charge said. "This was his first opportunity to earn the puke badge."

"He earned it the hard way," Captain Taylor said. He looked at Dan and sighed.

"I know," Dan said. "This complicates it. We've got to comb this countryside. And, I've got to level with the people. It's going to hit the fan when I do, but they have a right to know what is among them. I'd be derelict in my duty if I did anything else. But Jesus, it's going to a goddamned circus around here when the press is informed."

Before anyone could concur or disagree, Dan's radio came to life. "Ruger nine to Ruger one."

Dan picked up his mike. "Go, nine."

"Tach."

Frequencies reset, Ruger nine said, "I'm parked in front of Eddie Brown's cabin, Sheriff. Something is very wrong here."

"What, nine?"

"I . . . I don't know Sheriff. Eddie's car is in the drive, and it's cold. Been here for some time. The rains have washed out the tracks. But his suitcase is still sitting on the front porch. I just get the feeling it's been out there for a long time. You want me to check it out?"

Dan hesitated. He knew only too well how accurate a cop's hunches can be. "Negative on that. Stay put until backup arrives. Don't get out of your car." He glanced at his watch. "Backup ETA approximately ten minutes."

"Ten four, sir."

Captain Taylor was already moving, ordering by radio one of his men to Ruger nine's location.

Dan turned back to the dead man in the ditch. "Mark the body's location and shoot it. Rope this place off and go over it inch by inch. Chuck, call Pat Leonard at the paper and tell him to be at my office at noon for a briefing. Ask him if he will notify the other papers in this area."

"That damn nosy libber is still in town, Dan," Chuck reminded his boss.

"I know," Dan said, suddenly feeling tired. "Can't be helped. It's still a free country." He thought about that for a moment. "Even for left-wingers like her."

Anya and Pet had left the cabin through a back window when the deputy's car had driven up. They were a full two miles away when the highway patrolman pulled up. The deputy and the trooper approached the cabin very cautiously, pistols drawn. The deputy was the first to spot the drying blood gathered around the base of the suitcase. He pointed it out, saying, "Do we check the cabin or call in?"

The trooper hesitated. "We'd look stupid if the man had some sort of natural accident and is bleeding to death in there while we stand around out here shaking in our boots. Let's check it out."

The men stepped up to the porch, one going left, the other turning right. They looked in through the windows, seeing the blood on the floor, the overturned chairs, and the shattered rear window. No sign of Eddie Brown or anyone else.

Cautiously, they made their way around the small cabin, meeting at the rear of the building.

"Nothing," they both said.

They checked the ground. The heavy rains had washed away any tracks and also the blood from Eddie's wounds. Then they saw the broken small limbs and uprooted bushes left behind when Eddie ran into the woods.

The woods loomed dark and suddenly very unfriendly before the lawmen.

And neither wanted to enter those woods. It was more the use of common sense—not knowing what they might be up against—than fear.

"Let's call it in," the deputy said.

But before they could reach their cars, they heard the sounds of fast-approaching cars coming up the road toward the cabin.

Sheriff Garrett, Captain Taylor, and agent Dodge of the FBI.

76

"What'd you have?" Dan asked his deputy.

The deputy explained, briefly.

Dan nodded. "Let's go in."

Inside the cabin, Dan's eyes followed the drying trail of blood from the front door to the shattered window. He saw the paw prints clearly in the dried blood, along with the small print of tennis shoes. "Don't get any of that blood on you," he warned the others. "It might be, probably is, highly contagious."

"But not airborne?" Dodge asked.

"Not according to Doctor Goodson and the men from CDC."

Outside, Dan said, "Seal it off, Billy. Captain Taylor, can you get those troopers you talked about in here?"

"How many do you want?"

"I don't know. As many as it takes."

"Twenty-five to start with?"

"Sounds good to me."

"They'll be here within the hour." The Virginia Highway Patrol can place one hundred combat ready troopers anywhere in the state within one hour.

"I can probably get a few more Bureau people in here quickly," Dodge said.

"I would appreciate all the help I can get," Dan said.

"You got your speech all prepared for the press?" Taylor asked.

Dan shook his head. "I wish."

"I don't mean to take anything away from you, Dan," the Bureau man said. "But I've probably had more experience fielding questions from reporters. If you like, I'll handle it."

It was tempting for Dan. Just dump it in someone else's lap. God, it was tempting. "No," he said. "It's my county."

The news of the newly found body spread through the county with the speed of that much talked about wildfire. Dan had ordered his people not to talk to anyone about the dead, but he was making no effort to hide the fact that a killer, or killers, was loose and on the rampage in Ruger County.

Whether or not to tell the press about the possibilities that one or both of the madmen, or madwomen, were carriers of a deadly "virus," as Doctor Goodson called it, was solely in Dan's lap. He talked with all concerned about it.

"We don't even know what it is they're carrying," Chuck said. "Every time I try to think about it, I come up short. It's like a science fiction movie. How the hell would you explain it?"

Dan didn't know.

"I'd dump it in the CDC's lap," Sergeant Langway said.

Captain Taylor's smile was wan. "You'll be captain someday, Scott."

And he left it at that, leaving Scott to read whatever into his remark.

"If you tell the people that these . . . murderers can turn them into mummies," a deputy said, "they're not going to believe you unless you show them the body of the dead engineer and the arm of the other guy. Then we'll have a damn circus on our hands."

Dan looked at agent Dodge. "What do your people say about it?"

"Off the record and it didn't come from me?"

"Yes."

"Sit on it for a few days."

All present agreed they should do that. And all knew they were taking a terrible chance.

Reporters from Richmond, Charlottesville, Petersburg, and Lynchburg were gathered at the sheriff's office when Dan opened the news briefing. Among them Mille Smith.

"Looks like when bad luck strikes a place, it sometimes decides to hang around for a while." Dan told the men and women. "And we're having our share of bad luck. I have not prepared a statement; so I'll wing this as best I can."

Then it hit him, plunging him into numbing silence. Eddie Brown had reported seeing a small girl and a cat in a cave inside Eden Mountain back when he was lost, years ago. That was before Dan had joined the department. Was there a connection? God, surely not. There couldn't be. The girl would be in her twenties now.

Dan mentally filed that and got down to business. He kept his fingers crossed that no one would ask for an exhumation of the graves of Billy Mack and Mary Louise. Both mothers were in bad enough shape as it was. Seeing the bodies might well kill one of them.

"Here is what we know for sure," Dan began. "You all are aware of the deaths of the teenagers. No need to go into that. You've all carried the stories. We believe that the miner who was killed inside Eden Mountain was killed by the same party or parties. He was the first to be killed. He probably surprised them in the cave and was attacked. We're assuming it was two . . . people." He stumbled over that.

"Why are you assuming it was two people, Sheriff?" a reporter asked.

"Because the marks on the bodies seem to indicate more than one person was involved."

"We know the kids were brutally murdered, Sheriff.

79

But we don't know how. What kind of marks?"

Here it is. Dan kept his expression as bland as possible. "The bodies we found had been beaten and punctured with some sort of . . . multi-tined instrument." Not exactly a lie; just stretching the truth a bit. "And we found another body this morning bearing the same sort of marks."

"Another body, Sheriff?"

"Another body, a white male, not from this area, was found this morning. Murdered. Same M.O. We'll release his name when we locate and inform the next of kin. And," he sighed, "another resident of Ruger County is missing. All signs seem to indicate that this person also met with some sort of foul play. I will not release the name until we know for sure."

Mille stood up. A young veteran of countless press conferences and briefings, she could feel the hostility emanating from Sheriff Dan Garrett and the other cops in the room. All directed toward her, and her alone. It pissed her off even more. "How about the other man, Sheriff?"

"What other man, Ms. Smith?"

"The other miner."

"He had an accident in the parking lot just below the mountain. He lost the lower part of his arm. His left arm. He's in the hospital in very serious condition. Infection, shock, and loss of blood."

"He was not attacked by these so-called 'unknown parties?' " Mille asked, the sarcasm heavy in her tone.

"I can give you an unequivocal no to that question, Ms. Smith. He was not attacked by the party or parties we seek in connection with the other murders."

"I'd like for him to tell me that, Sheriff. When can we see this man?"

"You will have to speak with Doctor Quinn Ramsey

about that."

Mille stood her ground, refusing to yield the floor.

"Sheriff," Mille said, "I overheard you and some other officers and men talking in the hospital. You were all talking about being bitten. Being bitten by what, Sheriff? And what did Doctor Ramsey mean by, and I'm quoting the doctor directly here: 'His action seems to have stopped the aging process.' End quote. Whose action, Sheriff? Were you talking about the miner who had the so-called accident? What's *really* going on here, Sheriff?"

Dan didn't falter; his facial expression was neutral. Closed. "Exactly what I am trying to relate to you all, Ms. Smith. What you overheard while you were eavesdropping was police business, and if, or when, I feel it necessary to divulge that information, you will be among the first to know. Next question."

"I resent the implication that I was eavesdropping, Sheriff!"

"I don't particularly care what you resent, Ms. Smith. Right now, I've got more important matters on my mind than your ruffled feathers. When the citizens of this county, those men and women who live and work and pay the taxes here, tell me that I have to answer to you, that's when I'll resign. Now please sit down and have the good manners to allow your colleagues to ask some questions. Unlike you, Ms. Smith, they represent the people of this area, and are not seeking sensationalism."

Mille sat. But she was so angry she could scarcely contain her inner ragings. She knew she was flushed; she could feel the heat in her face.

Goddamn smart-assed, country-redneck-pig! she thought. You'll pay for this!

Her spleen silently vented, Mille forced a very sweet smile on her pretty face and demurely folded her

81

hands in her lap.

The other reporters looked first at Mille, then at Sheriff Garrett. Unlike Mille, they knew Dan Garrett's background: Graduated with honors from the university; Army intelligence for three years; decorated FBI agent, deputy, then sheriff of Ruger County. Well-liked and respected. And one hard-nosed son of a bitch when he had to be. Sheriff Dan Garrett would take no crap from anybody, anytime.

A reporter stood up. Dan nodded at him. "Are you gathering all the law officers we've seen here for a manhunt, Sheriff?"

"That is correct. My chief deputy is meeting with them now, and I'll be joining them as soon as this briefing is concluded."

Conclude it right now as far as I'm concerned, you jerk! Mille fumed.

"Sheriff, do you have any thoughts about the mental condition of the people you're after?"

"After seeing what was done to the bodies, my first thoughts were that the people who did that were extremely savage. They are the most brutal killings that I have ever seen. As to whether they are insane—" He shrugged. "—that will be up to a psychiatrist to determine."

You're lying, Sheriff, Mille fumed. You're lying, the state police are lying, the doctors are lying, and when the FBI opens their mouths, they're going to be lying, too. I'm sitting here right on top of one whale of a story, and I'm going to pry open this can of worms. And when I do, I'm going to wipe the floor with you, Garrett.

She thought: I've got to get in touch with Kenny Allen. I need somebody to do some legwork, and he's the best. I'll call him just as soon as this farce is over.

Kenny Allen was the same age as Mille. They had

gone through school together, from grade school through college. They shared many things in common; two things above all else: they both hated cops; any type of authority figure brought out the viciousness in them. And they both felt the press was the guardian of everything fine and decent and moral. It didn't make any difference who they hurt getting a story. Their method of news-gathering was this: everybody has some dirt in their past—let's find it. It doesn't make any difference who gets hurt in the process, or whether the dirt has anything to do with the story at hand. Anybody who gets in the way of the press gets kicked in the mouth.

Mille forced her attention back to Cowboy Dan Garrett and his lying mouth.

"Anyone have any further questions?" Dan asked.

Yeah, Mille thought. Where do you want the flowers sent? 'Cause when I get through with you, you won't be able to get a job anywhere . . .

7

Sheriff's deputies highway patrolmen, FBI personnel, and selected volunteers combed the countryside of Ruger County for days. They found two pot patches, a small cache of illegal automatic weapons, a still that hadn't been in operation for more than thirty years, two illegal aliens from El Salvador, one whore house, the rusted remains of a stolen car that had been missing for two years—and scared the living hell out of a deacon of a local church who was pumping away at the wife of another deacon.

And that was all the lawmen turned up.

No more bodies were found. No trace of Eddie Brown could be found. And no trace of the people responsible for the brutal deaths.

Nothing.

"Nothing," Dan told Vonne over supper. "I've got to believe they've left the county."

Friday evening, and Carl was home from school, his friend Mike with him.

"I don't mean to lighten what has happened," Carl said. "But there hasn't been this much activity in Ruger County since Mrs. Zigler ran off with that truck driver."

Dan laughed, and the laughter felt good, the tension gradually leaving the man. Vonne had fried chicken, made lots of mashed potatoes, a big bowl of gravy, biscuits from scratch, and fixed corn on the cob. Dan had pitched in, making his famous (more or less) deep-dish apple pie.

Mike was digging in. "Don't eat this way at my house," he said, wiping a bit of gravy from his chin. "Our cook wouldn't think of frying chicken. We'd have broiled chicken breasts a la poo doo, or something like that. I try to avoid eating at home whenever possible."

The Garretts knew it wasn't the food that kept Mike as far as decently possible from his parents' home. He did not get along with mother and father. Mike was as common as an old shoe. His parents, both of them, were relatively newly rich, and they, as the saying goes, liked to put on the dog. Mike's only passion in life—other than girls and food, not necessarily in that order—was archaeology, and he was brilliant on the subject. But his parents would not hear of Mike majoring in that. Hideous thing! Grubbing about in the dirt like a common laborer. That just wouldn't do for their son. What would the neighbors think?

The neighbors thought the Pearsons were obnoxious and obvious now. The neighbors would have applauded Mike's choice of vocation.

So Mike's parents insisted in Mike majoring in business and then going into the family business. Consequently, Mike's grades were just barely above passing. He said he was getting his own degree in his chosen field by reading everything on the subject he could get his hands on. When he came into his inheritance, then he would major in what he wanted to.

"No word about that poor Eddie Brown?" Vonne asked.

"Nothing," Dan said. "But if he's alive, it'll be a miracle."

"The manhunt over, Dad?" Carl asked.

"Pretty much so. Most of the troopers and extra FBI people have left."

"Eddie Brown," Vonne said. "What did I once hear about him?"

Dan knew. He kept his mouth shut.

"Oh, yes! Wasn't he the one who insisted he saw something strange when lost in Eden Mountain?" Vonne asked.

"I believe so," Dan said, conscious of young eyes on him.

"What did he see?" Carl asked.

Carrie wasn't paying any attention. All this stuff bored her.

"A young girl and a cat. Both asleep. He tried to wake them, but couldn't," Dan said. "I just recalled that," he added.

Nobody listening believed him.

The young men exchanged glances.

Dan caught the looks and said, "You two know something I might need to know?"

Carrie stood and asked to be excused. "After you help me clear the table and do the dishes," Vonne sat her back down.

No argument from Carrie. The kids did as they were told, when they were told to do it. Vonne and Dan had instilled their values in the young people, and stuck with that teaching regardless of what other parents did.

Dan and the boys helped clear the table and stack the dishes, then went outside to sit on the front porch. There, under Carl's prodding, Mike told Dan all he could recall about the strange religion and the stories about twins being born, sisters, a human female, and a female cat.

"And these stories have persisted all these thousands of years?" Dan asked.

"Yes, sir," Mike said. "There probably is some modicum of truth in them. By that I mean a group of people who did worship cats thousands of years ago. But like so many myths, they've been embellished considerably down through the years."

"And they were supposed to have supernatural powers?" Dan asked.

"Yes. And . . ." He paused.

"Something?" Dan asked.

"I'm trying to recall it, Mr. Garrett. Ah! Yes. The cat people were supposedly somehow aligned with the devil. Do you want me to see if I can find more about this group, sir?"

"Can you do it without jeopardizing your grades?"

Mike's laughter rang merrily in the night. "Mr. Garrett, my grades are the least of my worries. Ah!" he said, holding up one finger and narrowing his eyes conspiratorially. "Now I get it. You're thinking these crazies might have found out about the old religion and are practicing it here, right?"

That wasn't what Dan thought at all, only what he wanted Mike to believe, and the young man bought it. "That's it, Mike. Will you help me? On the QT, of course."

"Our lips are sealed, Sheriff," Mike said, punching Carl in the ribs. "Right, my good fellow?"

Carl sighed.

At a motel in Richmond, Mille met with Kenny Allen. Since the pullout of the troopers and the FBI

87

super-pigs, press interest in the mysterious happenings in Ruger County had waned. But Mille was still feeling the sting of Sheriff Dan Garrett's irreverence toward what she considered the untouchable press corps. The fact that most of the other reporters present that day of her rebuff had found it all rather amusing had not entered her mind.

The First Amendment, done in beautiful calligraphy, hung in her bedroom in her apartment in Washington. Mille took that amendment very seriously, and read into it much more than the founding fathers had intended. Very seriously. Religiously. Fanatically. If Mille had been a praying person, she would have built an alter, with the First as the centerpiece.

She glared at Kenny, not believing what he had just told her. "Are you telling me you can't find *any* dirt on Dan Garrett?"

Kenny shook his head. He looked like a large frog. A very ugly frog. He would have looked a great deal better had he done something with his hair, long, fine, and stringy. Kenny was not the type long hair enhances. He looked like an ugly hairy frog. Without warts. And a frog had more scruples.

"The man is Mister Clean," Kenny repeated. "His service record is spotless."

"Army super-spook," Mille spat the words. She didn't like military types either. Uniform lovers. Just as bad as pigs. Maybe worse. An army type had beat up her older brother once. After her brother had spat on the sergeant.

"He had to have screwed up in college," Mille persisted.

"Well, he didn't. I tell you the man is clean."

"No wild frat parties? No chasing women? No hard drinking? Come *on* Kenny!"

"Garrett didn't belong to any frat house. He didn't

88

have time. He worked his way through the university. He has maintained a three-beer limit ever since he was old enough to drink. I don't believe the man has ever been drunk. He's a top-notch lawman, Mille. You're wasting your time and your money."

"It's my time and my money, Kenny," she reminded him.

Kenny shrugged. She could well afford it. No sweat there.

"Don't tell me that hotdog hick sheriff has never had a fling with another woman?"

"Solid family man, Mille."

"Bull!"

Kenny shook his head. "I tell you, Mille, I've checked him from head to toe. Nothing."

"All right. Maybe. He never had a prisoner abused in his jail?"

"Yes. One."

"Ah-*hah*!"

"He fired the deputy who beat the prisoner and then brought charges against the man."

"Damn!" Mille looked disgusted.

"I'd give it up, Mille."

"No way. All right. Let's go after his family. How about his kids?"

"Clean. Neither one uses any type of drugs and very little alcohol. The oldest son is a junior at the university. The daughter is in high school. They're clean."

"I suppose the son is going to be a cop like his father?"

"That is correct."

"What's the daughter going to do?"

"That, I couldn't say."

"How about Garrett's wife? She married a pig, there can't be much to her."

89

"Clean, Mille. Solid and respected."

"Too good to be true. Kenny, you know as well as I do, *everybody* has dirt."

Kenny drained his beer and popped open another, taking a toke on a joint. He offered the joint to Mille. She hit on it and passed it back.

"What's the matter, Mille?"

She waved him silent and sat for a time, staring at the motel wall and its tacky paintings. Her mind was busy, hard at work. Had Mille been a bit more moral, had her attitude not been misdirected by the older brother (who had been a dope-head, a pusher, a thief, a violent demonstrator back in the '60's, and who finally met his end from a policeman's gun), Mille could have been and probably would have been a much more respected world-class reporter, for she was brilliant, with a fine mind. The fact that her brother had pulled a knife on the cop didn't matter; the fact that the cop had done his best to talk the young man into dropping the knife didn't matter; the fact that her brother had a rap sheet in a dozen cities didn't matter; the fact that her brother had jumped bond, broke probation and skipped didn't matter. He was her brother, and he could do no wrong. What had happened to her brother was not her brother's fault. Oh, no. It was society's fault. It was the fault of the cops. The system. But not the fault of her brother.

"All right," Mille finally broke the silence. "A multi-tined instrument. That's what the stupid sheriff said. But the rumors are the people were scratched as well. My brother was going to Columbia in '65. I remember him telling me about a rash of murders in the city. And something else, too. What was it?" She smiled. "Got it! the bodies were scratched and drained of blood. And partially eaten. By both human and animal. And in one case, at least, the flesh

90

around the wound had . . . decayed? No. *Aged!*"

Mille sat straight up in her chair. She said, quoting Doctor Ramsey, "His action seems to have stopped the aging process. Do you suppose, just maybe, the same thing that happened in New York City is, or has happened in Ruger County?"

"Mille, I don't believe in spooks and hants and all that stuff."

"Well, I do, Kenny. At least I believe in the unexplained." She wrote him a check. She could afford it. Her parents had sued the city after the cop shot and killed her darling, precious, wonderful brother—and won. Since Mille adored her sibling they had given the money to her.

"You get to New York City. You find out everything and anything you can about those murders. Then get back here fast."

Kenny was gone within the hour.

Kenny had majored in journalism, but soon discovered he was not very good at it. He completed his major, however, earning his extra money by working part-time for a local private detective.

Kenny had found his true talent. Snooping. Spying. Meddling. Prying. Making a pest of himself until his prey would say anything just to get rid of the ugly, freaky looking little guy.

Mille stretched out on the bed and smoked another joint. She smiled a grim smile of satisfaction.

"Now, Sheriff," she muttered. "Now, I'm going to nail your ass—but *good*!

The creature stumbled through the thinning woods. It was almost to the edge of Valentine's city limits. It lifted its head and surveyed the situation through slanted yellow eyes. Its head ached. The head had every right to ache. The brain was full of pus and corruption, eating away at the mass of once intelligent matter. The face had changed as well as the eyes. The skin was now wrinkled and dark. From the neck down, a thick pelt of long dark hair had grown. The shirt it had worn had grown very uncomfortable, so the creature had ripped it off, tossing it aside. The trousers were torn and ragged, flapping with every step, exposing the hairy legs.

Thick drool leaked past the creature's lips, dripping down on its hairy chest. It shook its aching head and snarled. The stinking drool flew from its lips.

The creature stumbled across the deserted highway and slipped unnoticed into a wooded area near a field, which lay behind a residential area near the outskirts of Valentine. Something clicked and bounced metallically as the creature lurched across the blacktop. A small pin that had been attached to the thing's belt fell onto the road. It was a pin denoting ten years of faithful service and attendance to a local church.

Congratulations, Eddie Brown.

Welcome back.

8

Monday morning.

The ringing of the phone jarred Dan out of the first really good night's sleep he'd had in two weeks. He fumbled for the phone and succeeded in knocking it off the night stand onto the floor.

Muttering low curses, while Vonne smothered her giggles beside him, Dan found the receiver and stuck it to his ear—upside down. He reversed it and grumbled his hello.

"How terribly enthusiastic," Vonne said.

"Sheriff? This is Andy downtown."

"Yeah, Andy. What's up?"

"Ah, Sheriff. We kinda got ourselves into a sort of a bind here. One of the chief's neighbors, Mizzus Milford, she called chief about an hour ago and said for him to get right over to her back yard, 'cause there was some sort of big creature out there. The chief went over to take a look-see."

Dan waited. He could not understand the edgy feeling that had suddenly gripped him. "All right,

Andy. So?"

"He never came back, Sheriff. His phone don't answer, and don't nobody answer the phone over to Mizzus Milford's house."

Unexpected sweat popped out on Dan's forehead. Something ugly and slimy and ancient touched his inner belly. It uncoiled and roamed around before once more settling down.

It isn't over, Dan thought. Goddamnit, it isn't over! It's *back*!

"You there, Sheriff?"

"Yeah, Andy. Getting into my pants now. I'll call my office and we'll be right over to check it out. You want to meet us there?"

"There ain't nobody here but me, Sheriff," the old man replied.

And you're too old to be wearing a badge and you're scared and only doing this to supplement your not-enough-to-live on income, Dan thought. And I don't blame you for being frightened.

Dan had argued for ten years for the town of Valentine to contract out the sheriff's department; let them handle both city and county. Dan's personnel were all much better trained and much better equipped. A growing number of communities were choosing to go that route and it was working out well.

But Valentine resisted. Maybe someday, Dan always said.

"Sheriff?"

"Yeah, Andy. Pulling on my boots. You stay put. I'll take care of it."

"Thanks, Sheriff. It's probably nothing, right?"

Don't bet on it. "Sure, Andy. Check with you later."

He felt Vonne's eyes on him in the darkness of the

94

bedroom. He turned to look at her. "Trouble, Dan?'"

"I think so." He reached for the phone, then pulled his hand back. He'd call dispatch from his car.

Rolling, he radioed in and asked who was working this section of the county, telling dispatch to have them meet him at the Milford house.

He drove through the dark quiet streets. He could not explain nor fully shake away the eerie feeling that had somehow attached itself to him, clinging to his flesh like a huge, invisible leech. Once, he stopped and pulled down his pump sawed-off shotgun, making sure the tube was filled. Buckshot. Three inch magnums.

He drove on.

For a rural area, with not a large county population, Dan had argued and fought and bullied and finally succeeded in building his deputy force into a respectable number. He had ten, fully trained and fully equipped full-time deputies. Eleven, counting Chuck Klevan, the chief deputy sheriff of the county. Dan's personnel were all graduates from the university's criminal law and law enforcement training programs, and three had been through the FBI's training school. Dan made certain his people were the best he could find—for the money paid—and that all stayed abreast of the ever-changing laws and procedures.

Deputy Susan Dodd was working this end of the county this night, Ruger County's only female deputy sheriff. But Susan was a very good deputy, asking for and receiving no more slack than any of the other deputies received—which from Dan Garrett, was damn little. Susan had spent three years in the Army, working as an MP. While she was not a large woman, there was no backup in her, and she would use her baton very quickly, as some of the rowdier residents of

95

Ruger County had painfully discovered when they attempted to hassle and intimidate her. That, plus the fact she was belted in both judo and karate, made her a dangerous person with which to attempt any type of hostility.

Susan was waiting at the Milford house. She got out of her patrol car and met Dan on the sidewalk.

The dark sleeping homes stood sightless and quiet on both sides of the residential street. Behind the chief's house, and Mrs. Milford's home, lay a large field.

"I haven't checked it out, Sheriff. I was waiting for you. But just listen for a moment. Can you feel it?"

Dan stood very still, all senses tuned. He knew what his deputy meant. That intangible feeling that any good street cop soon develops. *Nobody was alive inside the Milford home.*

"I sense it, Susan. Pray we're both wrong."

"I already did, Sheriff."

Dan climbed the steps and tried the doorbell first, leaning on the button for two full fifteen second rings. He waited. Nothing. The house remained dark and silent.

"You check out the chief's house, Susan. He's a widower," Dan reminded her.

Dan stood on the large porch while Susan checked out the house next door. She checked it thoroughly. She was back at the Milford house in a few minutes.

"Nobody inside that house, Sheriff," she reported. "The chief's bed is rumpled and his sidearm is gone from its holster. His car is parked in the garage. The engine is cold."

"All right. I've tried the doorknob. It's locked. Get your shotgun from your car."

Riot gun in her hands, Susan rejoined Dan in front

96

of the Milford home.

"Take the left side of the house," Dan told her. "I'll work the right. Give me a whistle when you reach the end of the house. Let's not blow holes in each other."

Susan nodded.

They split up, working their way cautiously down the side of the house, the beams from heavy duty flashlights spotting the way, working left and right.

Susan whistled.

"What'd you have?" Dan called.

"Blood, Sheriff. A lot of it."

Dan quickly joined her and knelt down, careful not to disturb the scene before him. They both saw the torn and bloody bits of a nightgown. And saw and smelled the stinking drool. Dan shifted his flashlight, the beam picking up strands of long dark hair caught on the branches of the shrubbery.

Susan sniffed the air, her nose wrinkled at the foulness. "What is that smell?"

"I don't know, it's coming from that stuff," he said, pointing to the drool. "Don't touch it." He looked up as lights clicked on in the neighboring house. "Sheriff's Department!" Dan yelled. "Leave your lights on but don't come outside."

"Yes, sir!" a man called.

Dan looked again at the white, ropy looking drool. He shook his head. "Stuff's making me sick. Susan, check the Milford house. Use the phone to call dispatch. Get Chuck over here."

"Do I call City, too?"

"Not yet."

Then Dan was alone, squatting by the pools of blood, the drool, and the mangled bits of nightgown. He knew what those other pale and crimson bits were on the ground, too. Torn pieces of human flesh.

He felt eyes on him; the sensation turning his sweat cold. He slowly swung around, standing up, his eyes searching the gloom and the dark pockets of shadows. He automatically checked to see if his shotgun was off safety. Cop's reflex action. The bushes at the rear of the house rattled drily. A groan drifted to him.

"Nick?" Dan called. "Nick Hardy!"

Another pain-filled groan. It was human-sounding, but just barely.

Dan could not see the long dark shape slowly slithering its way toward him, staying close to the hedgerow by the side of the house.

Dan heard no more groaning. He did hear a faint hissing sound. He looked around him. Nothing. The back door opened and Susan stepped out.

"Andy had already called Chuck. They're rolling. I thought I heard a groan out here."

"You did. So did I. And something else too."

"What?"

"I don't know. Turn on the outside lights."

The back yard was filled with light. But the light only served to darken and deepen the pockets of shadows around the bushes and hedges of the huge old back yard.

A scream of pure anguish came from the rear of the yard.

"Shit!" Susan said, nervousness in her voice.

"Oh, Jesus God!" the hidden and mysterious . . . voice called. "Help me!"

"Nick!" Dan shouted, unable to pinpoint the location of the voice. It was weak and hollow-sounding.

"Sheriff!" Susan called. "Look!"

Dan whirled around, looking in the direction Susan was pointing.

98

His stomach rolled a time or two and then his cop's mind willed it to settle down.

A mangled and partially eaten human leg lay next to the hedgerow. The multi-colored house slipper was still on the foot.

Susan and Dan both heard the faint sounds of hissing.

The sounds did nothing to sooth already stretched and jangled nerves.

An inhuman howl ripped the night just as headlights flashed, swinging into the driveway of the Milford house.

Car doors clinked shut. "Dan?" Chuck called. "It's Chuck and Billy."

"Shotguns, both of you!" Dan called. "Be careful. I don't know what we're up against."

That howling again.

"What in the hell is that?" Billy called.

"I don't know. But something has eaten Mrs. Milford, and maybe the chief, too," Dan called.

"Jesus!" Chuck said.

The hissing came again, much closer.

"Look out!" Susan called. Her shotgun roared in the night. Dan whirled around and caught a glimpse of the most hideous thing he had ever seen, outside of a horror movie. It was . . . Christ! he couldn't begin to describe it.

It was a man. He thought. Naked from the waist up. And covered with long hair.

Dan lifted his shotgun and pulled the trigger, knowing when he did he had missed. The man—for want of a better word—howled and hissed as he disappeared.

"Chuck, Billy!" Dan called. "Cover the north side."

"What the hell are we lookin' for?" Chuck called.

Dan hesitated. "It's man-sized. Naked from the waist up. Covered with long hair. Dark wrinkled face."

Billy looked at Chuck. "Is he *serious*?"

Dan heard that. "Move!" he roared, shoving another shell into his shotgun. He wanted it fully loaded. He would have liked to have had a flame thrower. Maybe a bazooka. A platoon of Green Berets would be nice, too.

Dan ran to the rear of the Milford yard. He almost lost what was left of his supper.

Nick Hardy's intestines lay on the ground and hanging in the bushes in bloody gray ropy strands. Dan's eyes found the chief. The flesh from one arm was chewed off; the flesh from one leg chewed off, from ankle to knee. The whiteness of bone shone in the dim light. A great gaping hole was all that was left of the man's stomach. Blood was splattered all over the dewy grass.

"Dan?" Nick whispered, his hand feebly reaching for the man. Life was nearly gone.

"I'm here, Chief. Hang on."

"Don't con me, young fellow." Nick whispered. "I'm done and you know it. It was something out of hell, Dan. Its eyes were yellow and slanted. Like a cat. Dark and wrinkled, like a mummy. Body all covered with hair. It ate old lady Milford and then turned on me."

"Ate her!"

But Nick would never speak again. Not in this world. His eyes rolled back in his head and he stiffened in Dan's arms, then relaxed, free of the pain and the woes of this life.

Dan thought: Eyes yellow and slanted like a cat?

100

Face like a mummy?

What in God's name was it?

A crashing noise came from beyond the northern-most house. Garbage cans turning over.

A hissing, howling sound reached Dan, the sound heavy and ominous. His skin prickled with chill bumps. Nothing human made that sound. The inhuman sound was followed by a rustling, scratching, scraping noise. Dan listened. It was coming from the weed-filled empty field that bordered the block on the edge of town.

"It's heading for the field!" Dan yelled. "Fire into the field. Open fire!"

Gunfire ripped the night as shotguns and pistols poured lead into the vacant field. But Dan knew the odds of them hitting anything other than air was slim.

"Chuck!" Dan yelled. "Get on the horn. Call Sergeant Langway. Get as many troopers in here as possible. Go!" He caught his breath, then yelled, "Stay out of that field. Nobody goes into that field. Susan! Get every deputy out here, on that dirt road behind the field. Cars pointed toward the field, headlights on high. Move!"

But Dan knew as swiftly as that . . . *thing* could move, it would be long gone before his people were in position.

He went in search of what might be left of Mrs. Milford. He found very little left.

Red dawn found the town of Valentine swarming with heavily armed police. And a lot of confused and frightened citizens.

And reporters.

"I don't give a good godddamn what you like or

101

dislike!" Dan told the superintendent of schools and the principal of the high school. "I said the schools are closed until I say reopen them. Is that clear?"

"I don't take orders from you!" Mickey Reynolds, the principal of the high school said.

"The hell you don't!" Dan informed him.

Mickey grabbed Dan's arm as the sheriff turned to leave and spun him around.

Mickey felt cold sweat pop out on his body as he looked into the flat, emotionless eyes of the sheriff. Dan said, his voice very low, "You have five seconds to get your goddamned hands off me or I'll lock you up so far back in the jail somebody will have to pump sunlight to you."

Mickey removed his hand. Quickly. "You can't keep me from going to my office."

"Be my guest, Mr Reynolds," Dan said. He walked away.

"Monster!" Mickey snorted, but not loud enough for Dan to hear. "Monsters, indeed. How ridiculous!" He walked to his car and drove away, toward the school.

The superintendent of public schools knew there was bad blood between Dan and Mickey. Had been ever since high school. But Dan Garrett was right in this matter. The safety of the children came first.

The creature, AKA Eddie Brown, was so bloated it knew it must find some sort of shelter to sleep and digest its heavy meal.

It was not confused, disoriented, or frightened. It knew, without knowing how it knew, where it was and how to get about. It headed for a cluster of buildings. Back when it was . . . well, back in some

102

other . . . *life*, it supposed, the rotted brain unable to form the thoughts, it used to hide in the darkness of the buildings. But which one. Then it came to the creature.

It slipped in through an unlocked basement window and settled down among the boxes and crates and other dusty and long-forgotten materials. It snuggled up against several old wine bottles. The bottles were familiar to the creature. Somehow.

It rested in the basement of the Valentine High School.

9

"It's all wide open now, Dan," Captain Taylor said. "The lid's blown off the pot."

"And the press is gathering," Chuck said glumly. "But I ain't seen that goddamn libber yet," he added. Women's lib turned Chuck off. Completely. He saw pictures of the famous, or infamous, march in New York City years back. When he saw some of the women waving their bras, he almost swallowed his bridgework.

"You will," Taylor said. He looked at Dan. "She's out to get you, Dan."

"I know it," Dan admitted. "And she'll probably succeed in doing it, too."

Odd thing for him to say, Taylor thought. He had just arrived from Division and had not yet seen the mangled and half eaten bodies. He was not buying Dan's story about the creature.

"A monster, Dan?" Taylor asked.

"Yes," Dan stuck to it. "I saw it and so did Susan. We both fired at it. I don't know what it was. I know

104

only that I have never seen anything like it. Not in my worst nightmares. But is it connected with the initial murders?"

Captain Taylor shook his head. He ventured nothing.

Sergeant Langway walked up. "Captain. We got a lot of good footprints. The thing was barefooted. From the depths of the depressions, it weighs about two hundred pounds. It scraped itself on several bushes, for we found lots of long dark hair. They do not appear to be human."

"Yeah," Dan said. "It was covered with long hair. Had slanty yellow eyes. Like a cat."

Taylor looked as though he would have liked to toss a net over Dan Garrett. "The light was very bad in there, Dan."

"Not that bad. I know what I saw."

"And we found some . . . deposits," Langway said. "The medics from the hospital have them for analysis."

"Deposits?" Taylor said. "Excrement?"

"No, sir. More like drool."

"It was about six feet tall," Dan said. "The trousers were ragged, with a leather belt."

"Six feet tall, two hundred pounds," Taylor said. "Covered with long hair. Ragged pants and a leather belt. Cat's eyes." He shook his head. "Computer's gonna blow a fuse when we put this in it."

Dan's eyes were on the hills around the town. He thought: a scratch from whatever it was they had been, or were, chasing, could change a human being into a mummy. But could it make other changes in the human system? Maybe. And maybe he was really reaching on this. Whatever. It was worth a shot. Dan pointed with his finger.

"Eddie Brown's cabin is right up there. You can almost see it from here. Our people followed the trail we assumed Eddie made when running from those who attacked him. You with me, Captain?"

"Yeah, so far. But I don't know what it is you're driving at."

"Bear with me, Captain. It's wild."

"Any wilder than a six foot tall, two hundred pound hairy human being with cat's eyes who eats people?"

"Yes."

"Oh, that's dandy. Please proceed." The captain's tone was very dry. Like a desert.

"First I want to find out where that creature crossed the highway," Dan said.

"*If* it crossed the highway," Taylor qualified that.

"It crossed the highway," Langway said.

Taylor cut his eyes. He wondered if it was time for his sergeant to take a vacation. A nice long rest. "And just how did you arrive at that conclusion, Sergeant?"

"Well, sir, the footprints were very erratic. So unless it staggered and stumbled right down the center of town, it had to have crossed the road."

"Uh-huh," Taylor said. That's what Langway needed all right. A rest. "Very well, Sergeant. I'll accept your . . . hypothesis. For the moment. Go on, Dan."

"When we find where the . . . thing crossed the road, I want the road closed until we can search the blacktop on both sides. Carefully."

"What are we looking for, Dan?" Taylor asked. Other than a padded room and rubber dollies for both of you. And no sharp instruments either.

"I don't know," Dan said, hedging that. He knew, but he also knew the captain thought him a basket case. So he'd play it close to the vest for now. For if he

106

told Taylor what was really on his mind, the man might very well go whooping and hollering and running up the road, screaming for a net. "I'll know it when I see it."

"Sheriff Garrett!" A reporter called from the crowd. "When do we get some kind of official statement from you, sir?"

Dan looked at Captain Taylor. "Will you handle the closing of the road?"

"All right, Dan. I'll . . ." He started to say: Humor you. "I'll handle it." He glanced at Langway. Come to think of it, the sergeant's eyes *did* look a little weird. "Close it off, Scott. Find out where your . . . monster crossed, and start combing the area."

"Yes, sir."

Dan, with Taylor by his side, walked to the knot of reporters. He looked for Mille Smith. Ms. She was not there. Yet.

Dan waved the crowd silent. He was conscious, and self-conscious of the several mini-cams pointed at him. He cleared his throat and said, "The chief of police of Valentine, Nick Hardy, and a neighbor, Mrs. Gladys Milford, were murdered last night. Chief Hardy had gone to investigate a prowler call from Mrs. Milford. This area, as you are all well aware of, is now cordoned off by Virginia State Troopers, Ruger Country deputies, and several platoons of the local National Guard. We don't know how many people were involved in the recent killings; or whether they have any connection with the earlier murders, which are still under investigation. Just as soon as we know more, we'll let you know. Thank you."

Ignoring the shouted questions, Dan and Captain Taylor turned and walked away. Agent Dodge of the FBI fell in step with the men. He had just arrived at the confusion.

"You're learning, Dan," Dodge said. "Keep it brief and then walk away—quickly."

"Here in Ruger, I just haven't had much practice with the press," Dan admitted.

"You forgot your Bureau training so soon?" Dodge kidded him.

"Working undercover as I did for those years, I really didn't have much chance to put it into practice."

"That's right," Dodge said. "I forgot. You were with that . . . team, weren't you? Tell me about the murders. The latest ones."

Dan brought the man up to date. Then, with a grim smile, he said to Captain Taylor, "You haven't seen the bodies, yet, have you, Captain?"

"Eh? No. No, I haven't."

"Why don't you and Dodge see the bodies and then I'll meet you at the search site?" Dan suggested.

"Good idea," the FBI man said. "See you there, Dan. Oh, by the way. What are you boys looking for up at the road?"

With a straight face, Taylor said, "A two hundred pound, six foot tall, hairy creature with cat's eyes that eats people."

The FBI agent was still sputtering and stuttering as Dan got in his car.

"You asshole!" Captain Taylor said, when he joined Dan at the search point. "You might have warned me. I've known Nick for twenty years."

"I thought it best to shock you with the truth. Remember that old line about seeing is believing?"

Taylor took several deep breaths. He slowly nodded his head. "All right, Dan. Sorry I lost my temper.

108

Sorry I made fun of you and Langway. Accepted?"

"Sure. We're all in this together. Let's go to work."

"Found something over here, Sheriff," a deputy called.

Dan looked at the small pin. It had been run over a couple of times, but the wording was still readable. He really didn't want to look on the back for initials. He was afraid his theory might turn into fact.

"What is it, Dan?" Taylor asked.

"A church pin. A ten year pin."

"That mean anything to you?" Dodge asked.

"Only if there are initials on the back," Dan said slowly.

Chuck took the pin from Dan's hand and turned it over. "E.B.," he said. He lifted his eyes, meeting Dan's eyes. "You thinkin' what I'm thinkin,' Dan?"

"Yeah," Dan said, almost reluctantly. The pin really didn't prove anything; but it did drive another nail in support of his theory.

"E.B.?" Taylor said, taking the pin and looking at it. "What? . . ." He cut it short and looked at Dan. "E.B. Eddie Brown. Now you just slow down, Dan. Whoa! Now I can only take so much of this before it begins to boggle the mind. You don't think . . . You can't mean . . . You're not implying? . . . Oh, *hell*, no! No way, Dan!"

Dan shifted his eyes, looking at the FBI man. There was something . . . *curious* in the Bureau man's eyes. Something Dan couldn't pinpoint. What was he doing back here? These murders didn't fall under federal jurisdiction. And Dodge had not returned alone. He had brought a half dozen other men with him. Suddenly Dan just didn't trust Dodge. And for no good reason he could firm up in his mind.

"Are you holding back from me, Dan?" Captain

Taylor persisted.

"In a way, Captain," Dan admitted. "You see, I spoke with the medical people over at the hospital this morning. I guess while you and Dodge were over there seeing what was left of Hardy and Milford, Goodson didn't show either of you the severed arm from the engineer, did he?"

Dan stole a quick glance at Dodge. The man's eyes were hooded.

"Well, no," Taylor said. "At least not to me. But we separated for a few minutes." He indicated Dodge. "He went with Doctor Ramsey. What about the arm?"

"It's growing," Dan said.

"What?" Taylor seemed stunned. "Bullshit, Dan. Dead, severed arms don't *grow*! Do they?" he asked in a near, whisper.

"The engineer's arm is growing. It went from a dead, lifeless object, to a living thing. It's alive."

Taylor rubbed his face. He swallowed hard. To hell with Dan and Scott—*he* needed a rest. "What is the arm growing, Dan?"

Dodge's face was emotionless. He knew all about the arm.

Dan said, "The doctors tell me they don't know. It keeps growing . . . well, matter, I guess you'd call it, and then rejecting it. Goodson said it appears to be seeking some specific form that it is, as yet, unable to produce. And something else: Jimmy's blood type is O positive. The doctors haven't, as yet, been able to type the new blood from the severed arm. It's not even the same color."

"What the hell color is it?" Taylor asked.

"It has a greenish tint to the red."

"But the arm is *human*!" Taylor said.

110

"Not any more," Dan said. "Goodson says he doesn't know what it is."

Captain Taylor looked at Dodge. The FBI man had nothing to say. He turned back to Dan. "Why do I get the feeling you have yet another shoe to drop?"

"Chuck just brought the word to me about the dead engineer, Al."

"What about him? I thought he was a mummy."

"He is. He's also gone."

10

Mickey Reynolds unlocked the door to his office
and stepped in. He leaned against the door jamb for a
moment. He didn't like it when the kids weren't here.
Place was just too quiet. Unnaturally so. The building
seemed dead without the kids. Mickey liked kids.
Always had. And he was a good administrator, tried
hard to be a Christian and a law-abiding man.

He just didn't like Dan Garrett.

Never had.

They were the same age; went to school together,
first grade all the way through the university. Different majors. It was just that Mickey had been in love
with Evonne since the first grade. And then that
damn Dan Garrett comes along and shoots him out of
the saddle.

He sat down in his chair, behind his desk. He
smiled, and then laughed, leaning back in his chair.
No, he thought, that just isn't true. He never was *in*
the saddle. And, he sighed, Dan was right in closing
the schools. Don't blame the sheriff for something
that isn't his fault. Love or life.

Mickey closed his eyes and indulged in a few moments of reminiscing, recalling the old days. Class of '57. God! where has the time gone?

He opened his eyes and swiveled in his chair, looking around at the shelf behind him for his old yearbooks. He had forgotten what they all looked like back in high school. So long ago. Then he remembered that when his office had been renovated, four or five years back, the workmen had moved all the albums and took them down to the basement. Mickey wondered if anyone had cleaned up all those wine bottles he'd seen down there? Probably not. Nobody ever went into the basement.

"Well," Mickey said aloud, getting out of his chair. "Nothing else to do today. Might as well lose myself in nostalgia."

He walked out of his office and toward the stairs that led to the basement. He removed a ring of keys from his pocket.

"And ladies," Alice Ramsey said to the monthly gathering of the local chapter of the Daughters of the Confederacy. She was winding the meeting up, or down, depending entirely on one's point of view. "Remember, next month Mrs. Grace Grillingham from the Sixty-nine Club of Richmond will be here. Right here in this home. And I know none of you want to miss *that*!" She gushed the last. Alice was one hell of a good gusher.

The ladies applauded.

The Richmond 69 Club is, supposedly, comprised of descendants from the original first 69 families to settle in Virginia.

Naturally, Alice belonged.

113

Dan, one evening while he and Vonne were visiting at Quinn's home, looked at the hundreds of applications from people wishing to join the 69 Club. He told Quinn, "I don't see how the men ever got the time to put a crop in. With all these descendants, they must have been screwing morning, noon, and night."

Alice had overheard the remark. She didn't speak to Dan for a year.

Emily Harrison, wife of Doctor Harrison, was a marginal member of the Daughters of the Confederacy. It was a little dubious as to just exactly which side her great grandpappy fought on. He was found hanging by his neck from a tree limb on the side of the road. The top half of the body was dressed in Union blue, the bottom half wearing the Rebel gray. But the DOC gave Emily the benefit of the doubt and let her in anyway. Doctor's wife, you know?

Emily pulled Alice off to one side after the meeting. "Have you any idea what is going on at the hospital?"

"No." Alice looked blank for a few seconds. "Is there something I need to know about?" Alice was just a little bit of an airhead, too.

Emily sighed. "The *murders*, Alice!"

"Oh. Oh! Well, Sheriff Garrett will take care of that gruesomeness. He is a good sheriff, even if he is a bit disrespectful toward that which is most important."

"Huh?" Emily said.

"Never mind, dear. You weren't here."

Thank God for small favors, Emily thought.

Alice babbled on. "Ladies should not concern themselves with such matters as murder and all that. It just isn't proper."

Emily looked at the woman strangely and nodded her head. Emily had been an emergency room RN before she married Bill Harrison. If there was *any-*

114

thing she hadn't seen, she didn't know what in the flippin' flap it was.

"Come, dear," Alice gushed again. "Let's have a glass of tea and talk about next month's meeting. We have so much to plan."

Emily looked around her. Everyone else had left. Oh, damn! she thought. I'm *stuck*.

A thumping came from the back porch. Sort of a slow thump-thump-thumping.

"Now what in the world is that?" Alice said.

"One way to find out," Emily said.

"Oh?"

"Go look."

"Oh. But I've dismissed the help. Oh, well. You know where the glasses are. You pour the tea and I'll go see what all the commotion is about."

The thumping was growing louder.

Alice walked out of the room, toward the back door. Walking is perhaps the wrong descriptive: gliding would be more like it. Like on a protected pillow of air. It fit her well.

Emily found the glasses, filled them with ice, and poured the tea. Pre-sweetened. Yukk! She hated sweetened tea. Stuff was so sweet she could feel her teeth turning into sugar cubes.

She heard some sort of . . . she didn't know what it was. Sort of a strangled sound. She turned around. Alice was standing in the archway. Her face was chalk-white and she was shaking all over.

"Alice! What's wrong?"

"Uh-uh-uh!" Alice said, pointing toward the back porch. "Gibjubuhdo."

"What?"

"Mum . . . mum . . . mummy!"

Shock, Emily thought. The woman's in shock. She

ran to the woman and gave her a good pop across the face. She grabbed her by the shoulders and shook her.

"Damnit, Alice. Talk to me!"

Alice cut her eyes to the back. Emily looked and froze to the floor.

Emily's first thought was: somebody's playing a joke on us. She was used to that. ER people will do anything to relieve the tension.

Emily quickly realized the scene before them was no accident. It was just too hideous. It would have taken a professional Hollywood makeup artist hours to do this. And the smell was sickening.

And she knew that smell. Decaying flesh. Rot. Maggots working overtime, eating through putrefied flesh.

The mummy-looking—and that's exactly what Alice had been trying to say—*thing*, wrinkled and stinking, took a hesitant step forward, unsure of its surroundings. It opened its mouth and screamed at the women. The air was suddenly fouled.

Emily moved. She jerked Alice forward and practically slung her into the hall. "Move!" Emily shouted.

The mummy-man screamed again and lumbered forward, knocking the table to one side.

The women ran into the den. Emily slammed the door and locked it. She grabbed one end of a heavy sofa.

"Grab the other end!" she told Alice.

"Heavens, darlin,' " Alice found her voice. No surprise to Emily. "We can't move that big ol' thing by ourselves."

"Lady," Emily said, her eyes narrowing dangerously. "Move it!"

Her sharp words were like a slap in the face to Alice. The woman grabbed her appointed end of the sofa and together they moved it against the door. They piled a large chair on top of the sofa. Emily pointed to the phone on the small desk.

"Call the cops. Move."

Emily looked around the den as the inhuman sounds from the godawful looking thing grew louder in the hall. It was beating on the wall, sending small pictures and prints to the floor. She saw Quinn's gun cabinet and ran to it. Locked. She picked up a poker from the fireplace stand and smashed the glass, jerking out a twelve gauge shotgun. She checked it. Unloaded.

"Oh no!" she groaned.

She found a broken box of shells and filled the tube. She was just conscious of Alice's frantic phone conversation.

"Tell 'em to get the hell over here!" Emily shouted.

"Get the hell over here!" Alice repeated automatically, startling the local city dispatcher. Mrs. Ramsey just didn't talk like that. Alice hung up the phone.

"What did they say?" Emily asked, clicking the shotgun off safety.

"They said, 'yes, ma'am'. You know how to shoot that thing, Emily?"

"Yeah. I know how. I used to rabbit hunt with my brothers down in Alabama."

The den door began splintering. A horrible grunting, panting, savage sound filled the hallway. Emily lifted the shutgun.

"If that big ugly thing comes through that door, I'm gonna fill his ass full of lead."

"Emily?" Alice said.

"Yeah, Alice."

"I'm glad it's you here instead of some of those other helpless biddies."

117

Emily smiled. "Alice, you're a fraud."

The woman returned the smile. "Of course, I am. But isn't it such fun? And don't you tell anybody or I'll tell everybody your great grandfather was a Yankee sympathizer."

Emily laughed. "Hell, Alice—he *was*."

The den door smashed open, the force of the blows knocking the chair off the sofa. The mummy-looking creature jumped into the den.

Mickey rummaged around the poorly-lighted basement, inspecting box after box. No luck. A noise spun him around, his heart hammering from sudden fear.

"Who's there!" he called into the darkness.

But the darkness remained silent.

"Come out here!" Mickey called.

A hissing greeted his words. The hissing was unlike anything Mickey had ever heard.

Then he got mad.

"All right, kids. Now come on out here. You don't have anywhere to run. Now come on out and face me."

Then the thought came to him: What if it isn't kids? What if it's those crazy people who killed last night? Oh, God!

The hissing grew louder, an angry sound to it.

Mickey looked around him, his eyes finding a length of 2x4 on a crate. He picked it up. He sniffed the closed air as a very foul odor drifted to him. He backed up, the 2x4 in his hand.

Not kids, he thought. Definitely not kids. But what in the hell is it?

The hissing changed to a yowling type of sound. Much like what big cat might do. A panther? No, no,

118

that's silly. No panthers in this area for years.

And what was that terrible smell? It smelled like . . . then it came to him. Rotting flesh.

Mickey gripped the 2x4 and stepped forward. Whatever it was, one good bash on the head should do it.

Mickey was suddenly jerked to the floor, slamming down hard, knocking the wind from him. White hot pain filled his left leg. Screaming from pain and fear, Mickey kicked out with his other leg. Then he saw what had him. Horror overrode the pain.

Nothing real looked like that! He screamed in terror.

He smashed the 2x4 onto the thing's head, feeling the sharp teeth clamp down harder on his mangled leg before releasing him. The creature jumped back, howling in pain, retreating into the darkness. Mickey crawled toward the stairs. The thrashing and screaming of the beast filled the basement as Mickey panted up the stairs and out into the hall. He slammed the door and locked it.

He crawled and then ran/limped a hundred feet down the deserted hallway until the pain in his badly bitten leg caused him to stumble and drop to the coolness of the corridor floor. He crawled to the nurse's office and found the first aid kit, ripping it open. He poured iodine on the gnawed flesh of the leg. He leaned back against a wall and rested, taking some assurance in the burning healing powers of the iodine.

Phone! he thought, as pain misted his mind. Got to get to a phone and call the police. Guess Dan was right. Monsters did attack Mrs. Milford and the chief. He was unaware of how curiously uncaring he was becoming. Almost as if some new being was

119

taking control of his mind and body.

That was correct.

"I'll just rest for a minute before I do that," Mickey said. Rest. Got to have some rest.

He closed his eyes as a very odd sensation filled him. He slipped into a coma-like sleep as strange dreams—more like visions—filled his mind. His blood was battling, and losing, against ancient invaders, from a time long before the human body was even begun to be understood. His visions were ancient dreams, taking place high above the sands. They were horrible dreams, filled with human sacrifices and orgies. And a small child and a cat.

Mickey let the dreams take him deeper and deeper.

The shotgun boomed and the butt plate slammed against Emily's shoulder, the crashing report loud in the room. The shot hit the creature in the shoulder and arm, bringing a scream of pain from the hideous thing. Green slime splattered against the wall. Emily fired again. This time the shot struck the mummy-man in the side. More green slime slopped as the shot tore open the wrinkled, foul-smelling flesh.

The creature howled and lumbered awkwardly down the hall, back toward the rear of the house.

Emily was only then conscious of sirens winding down. "Mrs. Ramsey!" a man's voice called. "Mrs. Ramsey, where are you?"

"In here!" Alice called. "In the den. Watch out. That . . . monster just ran out the back door."

It did indeed.

The young city patrolman ran around the side of the house just in time to run headlong into the arms of the wounded, painfilled creature. The maddened once

120

human object put both its hands into the cop's mouth; one hand pulled down, the other hand pulled up. It tore the young man's head apart, leaving only the lower jaw and tendons attached to the neck. Blood gushed several feet into the air. Holding the severed head in its hands, the creature ran into the back yard and disappeared behind another house.

Alice ran out onto the back porch, saw the glistening lower teeth and jaw of the cop, who was flopping in near-death on the ground—and promptly lost her brunch. She was leaning against a porch railing about ready to go into screaming hysterics when Emily ran on to the back porch. She took one look at the still-jerking young cop, mentally fought her stomach's urge to rebel, and ran for the phone, jerking Alice inside with her, slamming and locking the back door.

Emily snatched up the kitchen phone and dialed the sheriff's office.

"This is Emily Harrison. I'm at Doctor Quinn Ramsey's home. Some sort of creature just attacked us. It just killed a city policeman; tore the man's head off. *Please* send someone over here right away. I'm armed with a shotgun and I know how to use it, so sing out when you get here. Now *hurry!*"

"Yes, ma'am!"

Dan heard the trouble call and was the first to arrive at the Ramsey home. He left his car at a run, shotgun in hand. Captain Taylor and Langway pulled in about ten seconds after Dan.

"Alice!" Dan called. "Emily! Where are you. Answer me."

The front door slowly opened. Dan was conscious of people standing in windows of surrounding homes. Pale, frightened faces looking out. Alice and Emily stepped out onto the porch. Dan lowered his shotgun.

121

Both of the women looked to be badly shaken, but otherwise unhurt. Emily pointed to the rear of the house.

"You ladies all right? Dan asked.

"Yes," Emily said. "That . . . *thing* ran around that way, Sheriff. The young cop is around back. He's dead, or very nearly so."

"Stay in the house," Dan told them. "Close the door and lock it."

The women stepped back inside. The door closed.

A deputy squalled up, tires sliding on the surface of the street. Dan called, "Contact the hospital. Tell Docter Ramsey and Harrison their wives are both okay. Advise them as to what's happening. Move!"

"I don't *know* what's going on, Sheriff," the deputy said. "I just got back in late last night from pickin' up a prisoner in Seattle."

Dan shook his head. "Sorry," he said. "Radio the hospital. Tell them the escaped mummy is out here."

"The escaped *what*?" the deputy looked dumbfounded.

Dan ignored that. "Tell Doctor Ramsey and Harrison to get a team together and get over here. They'll know what you mean."

"Yes, sir!" The deputy muttered something else too low for Dan to hear.

Dan had a pretty good idea what it was.

And he didn't blame the young man.

Susan pulled up. "Rope this area off!" Dan yelled to her.

Dan, Taylor, and Langway made their way cautiously around the side of the house. They pulled up short at the blood-splattered back yard.

All three stood in disbelief for a full thirty seconds, shocked silent at the gory sight before them. Then a

122

foul odor assailed their nostrils.

"Whew!' Langway said. "What is that smell?"

Dan saw the long, trailing smear of stinking green slime. "And what is that stuff?"

A camera clicked behind them. All turned to look at Mille Smith. She smiled at the men, mockingly, tauntingly.

"Yes, Sheriff," she said. "What is that crap? I'd be so interested in hearing your explanation."

11

Mickey looked at his watch. But he couldn't quite make out the numbers on the dial. They kept changing before his eyes, the modern numbers fading into a system Mickey's mind could not comprehend. Yet.

He thought perhaps he'd been out for at least half an hour. But he didn't really care.

Mickey struggled to recall what he was doing on the floor in the nurse's office. Then he remembered. He checked his leg. The leg, from the knee down, was blackened and withered.

A heady feeling of indifference that Mickey had never experienced in his life overcame him. His mind was reeling, attempting to understand the strange language that filled his brain. He know who he was, but also knew that he was that person only in part. He was also another person.

But he didn't know who.

"Why, hell," he said aloud, his voice much deeper and hollow-sounding than ever before. Then he laughed for a moment, and crawled to his hands and knees. He stood up. His bad leg supported his weight. Strangely, he experienced no pain from the horrible bites. He did not find that odd. He tried to remember what he was doing here, why the school was so deserted?

He could not.

Mickey had no memory of the creature in the basement. No memory of the events that forced the closing of the schools. He was not sure of his own name. The names of his kids. His wife.

His wife. Oh, yeah. Her face came into his fevered mind. God, he hated her. And those whiny kids. Why did he ever mate with that woman?

Mate? Yeah. Mate.

"Oh, yeah," he said, as he stumbled along the hall toward his sanctuary.

His sanctuary?

" 'Cause that damn Dan Garrett stole the other female from me." What was her name? "Evonne. Lovely Evonne. Vonne."

Feeling confused, Mickey paused on his way to his refuge as the sounds of someone hammering on the front doors reverberated down the empty halls.

He lurched and stumbled toward the front door. At a corner, he paused, gathering his strength. For some reason, he knew he must not let anyone see him limping. He didn't know why he should do that. He just knew he must.

He peeked around the corner. His eyes were savage as his mind fought to stay in the present time frame. There she was. Pretty, petite, dainty little Denise. Standing by the locked doors all by herself. Mickey licked his lips as ancient, past-life memories flooded his mind. Denise, daughter of the richest man in the county. Pouty brat drove a Cadillac to school. Thought she was better than everybody else. All her daddy had to do was drop a word here and there and little Denise got whatever she wanted. For God help the person who didn't see things her way. Daddy

125

would fix it.

Mickey still smarted under the tongue-lashing he had received from Paul Moore. In public. And there was nothing Mickey could do except stand there and take it.

Mickey smiled. He walked to the front door and unlocked it, swinging it open. "Yes, Miss Moore?"

"I have to get something, Mister Reynolds." She breezed past him with a toss of her head.

No 'How do you do, sir.' No 'Please' or 'Thank you' or 'I'm sorry to disturb you, sir.' Just walk right in like she owned the goddamn place.

Mickey's eyes clouded over. He felt as though he was being propelled backward in time. Bloody scenes of torture and deprivation filled his mind as infected blood coursed through his veins. He could see himself standing by an altar with a curved knife in his hand. He brought the knife down into a naked body lashed to a rectangular flat-topped stone. The stone had likenesses of cats carved into it.

Mickey smiled. He laughed aloud. Power filled him. Raw, wild, ancient power. He looked at the blue jean clad rear end of Denise.

"Hey, whore!" he called.

She stopped as if hit between the shoulder blades. She turned and looked at the man. "I *beg* your pardon?"

Mickey started toward her.

"You're violating a restricted area, Ms. Smith," Dan told the woman. "How did you get past my deputy and don't tell me you didn't see the crime scene tape."

"That crime scene crap is unconstitutional, Sheriff," Mille retorted. "It's a free country, regardless of what you and the rest of your SS buddies would like to make it."

"That 'crime scene crap,' Ms. Smith is not unconstitutional. Ms. Smith, don't you realize your life is in danger here?" Other deputies pulled up. Dan told them to cordon off the neighborhood. He turned to leave just as Mille snapped two more shots.

Susan ran up and stopped short at the sight of Mille. "How in the hell did you get past me?"

"Easy, you sow. That is what they call female pigs, isn't it?"

Dan said, "Susan, take Ms. Smith's camera and expose the film. Find out the cost of a fresh roll and reimburse the . . . lady. Do that after you escort Ms. Smith to the civilian side of the ropes."

Susan reached for the camera and Mille jerked away.

"I'll sue you, I swear!"

Susan drew her baton.

"I've been hit by bigger pigs than you," Mille said.

"Probably," Susan said. "But I'll bet you haven't been hit any harder."

Mille looked into the openly hostile eyes of Susan. With a sigh of resignation, she snapped open her camera and exposed the film.

"Take the film," Dan ordered. "And please escort Ms. Smith out of this area."

Mille gone, Taylor said, "That's iffy, Dan. Real iffy. She just might have a case against you."

"Mille is the very least of my worries at this point," Dan said.

A shout of panic and shock filled the air, followed by a shotgun blast.

"Hold your fire," Dan shouted, as the men ran around the side of the house. "Sheriff's department!"

"Hold my fire, hell!" a man yelled. "You get that

thing outta my back yard."

The lawmen slid to a halt at the citizen's back porch. He held a double-barrel shotgun in his hands. Fear in his eyes.

"What was it?" Dan asked.

"Jesus Christ, Sheriff. I don't know. I never seen anything like it. It looked like . . . don't laugh. It looked like a mummy! He ran into my old workshop over there. He's still in there," the man added grimly. "Some kind of green stinking stuff is leaking out of him. It. Whatever."

"Did you hit it?" Taylor asked.

"Yes, sir. But this is light bird shot. I didn't do it much damage. Hell, I didn't even slow it up."

"Is there a back door to that shed?" Dan asked.

"No, sir. Not even a window in the back. Window on each side and that one you see right there in front. That's all."

"All right. Thanks for your help. Go back inside and stay low."

"Yes, sir, Sheriff. I'm *gone*."

The citizen back inside the house, Taylor said, "How in the hell do you order a . . . mummy to come out with his, its, hands up?"

Chuck and Herman joined the tight knot of lawmen, both of them armed with riot guns.

"You got some trouble out front of the house, Dan," Chuck said.

Dan looked at him. "Man, I got some trouble back *here*!"

Chuck shook his head. "That Smith female took a swing at Susan. Susan knocked her down. I mean, knocked her flat on her butt."

"With her baton?"

"No. With her fist. Those two women just don't appear to be real fond of one another."

128

Suddenly a savage roaring came from inside the small shed. Taylor and Langway lifted their pistols. The others lifted their twelve gauge shotguns. The door of the shed shattered, pieces of wood flying about the back yard. A terrible odor drifted to the men. The mummy, aka Al the engineer, stepped out into the sunlight. Green slime leaked from its wounds. It held out its arms and roared at the men. Then it charged, holding the young cop's bloody head in one hand.

"Fire!" Dan shouted.

Anya and Pet had taken refuge in some sort of two story garage/storage building near a large brick home about three miles outside of Valentine. The place was filled with boxes and crates. The pair had eaten again, and eaten well. They would need no further nourishment for days. They were bloated with human flesh and blood. They had covered their tracks well, being careful not to disturb the dust and cobwebs of the second floor of the building. They knew from past experience that dogs could not track them, for they could change their scent, confusing the animals. Anya had changed clothes and dropped them in a hole in the ground, miles from their present location.

Anya and pet carefully picked their way over the boxes and crates until they reached the end of the huge building. There, feeling safe, they rested. And waited for the rebirth.

Mickey panted and grunted as he violated the girl. He had used his fists to hammer Denise into submission. He had plans for her when the rape was concluded. Bloody plans. Mickey's head was filled with all sorts of confusing ancient visions and instructions in a language he was now able to understand.

His leg was beginning to rot, but he paid no attention to the smell.

.357 magnums and 12 gauge shotguns roared, the lead tearing great holes in the creature. They fired again and again, but the creature kept on coming, howling and staggering across the yard, leaking stinking slime from its many wounds. Captain Taylor took careful aim and shot the creature directly between the eyes, slamming the head back. The mummy-man fell to the earth and died. Again.

Green slime poured from the wounds, the stench of the thick, hideous-smelling fluid almost making the men sick to their stomachs.

"I am not believing this," Taylor said, reloading swiftly. "I am going to wake up and find it's all a bad dream. Everytime I fix a peanut butter, pickle, mayonnaise, and onion sandwich, on rye, I get nightmares."

"Yukk!" Langway said.

"Double yukk!" Chuck said.

Captain Taylor looked hurt.

Doctors Ramsey and Harrison stepped through the gunsmoke, gloved and masked medics with them. Dan looked at the medics. He did not recognize any of them. He put out an arm, halting them.

"I want pictures first," Dan said. "Do it, Chuck."

Chuck nodded and ran to his car.

"It's beautiful," Quinn whispered. "It's just awe-inspiring."

The lawmen wondered, at the time, what in the hell the doctor was talking about. But before they could ask, Chuck was back with his camera. Quinn held up a hand in a warning gesture.

"Better let one of the medics do it, Dan. For safety's sake."

Dan nodded and the medics moved up to the body, taking pictures as Dan called out what angle he wanted.

Another medic whom Dan did not recognize moved up to Quinn's side and whispered to the man. Quinn smiled behind his mask. Dan could see the man's eyes change.

"Are you sure?" Dan heard Quinn said.

"Yes, sir. The arm has begun growing and has showed no sign of rejection for more than an hour."

Dan pretended to be giving all his attention to the medics with the camera. He heard Quinn say, "The new growth. What is it?"

"It appears to be similar to a fetus, sir."

12

Dan waited for Quinn to tell him about the severed arm's so-called ability to reproduce life. Quinn said nothing about it. The stinking carcass of what had once been a living human being was covered and loaded into an ambulance. Dan did not think to check his camera when the unfamiliar medic returned it to him.

But for now, there was nothing the lawmen could do about the news. Ruger County was, within the hour, filling with more reporters. The major TV networks were represented, with everybody jockeying for position.

Thoroughly irritated, not fully knowing what was going on, Dan finally passed the buck, dropping it into the laps of the medical people.

"I'm a cop," Dan told the reporters. "My job is law enforcement, not medicine or science. You want answers to those questions, talk to the doctors."

"Don't screw it up," Dan told Quinn. "We're sitting

132

right on top of a general panic right now."

Dan thought the doctor's smile was a bit strange, touched with a mysterious quality.

But what the hell would he be covering up? And more importantly, *why*?

But the doctors, none of them, had any intention of screwing anything up. The medical people had plans of their own, and they did not include Dan. The doctors put on their best cool professional faces and met the press head on.

And lied.

Dan had one of Captain Taylor's plain clothes troopers tape record the press conference for him. He turned it off halfway through. He was disgusted. The doctors, all of them, especially Quinn, were lying. According to them, Al had contracted some strange illness while working in South America. Something closely akin to Hansen's Disease. No, they couldn't explain it. It was hideous though. Produced some sort of mummy-looking effect upon the skin. Terrible thing. Certainly was. No, Mrs. Ramsey and Mrs. Harrison were being treated for shock. Better leave them alone. They've had a terrible time of it.

"Yeah, sure," Dan said. He clicked the recorder off.

He went home late that afternoon. He could not recall ever being so tired, so drained, so mentally exhausted.

What pissed Dan off more than anything was the wild tale Quinn told about Al being the one who attacked Chief Hardy and Mrs. Milford. And that goddamn Dodge backed him up on it.

Dan took a long hot shower, tossing his stinking clothes in the hamper, and fixed a sandwich and a glass of milk. He fell asleep in his chair before he got halfway through eating the sandwich. Evonne spread a light blanket over him, and went on to bed, letting her husband sleep. He finally came to bed about ten o'clock.

At midnight, the phone rang. Dan jarred awake and answered it.

"Sheriff? Chuck. Sorry to wake you. I know you were asleep. So was I. We got more problems. Denise Moore is missing and so is Mickey Reynolds. And something funny is going on."

"Funny like ha-ha? I sure could use a good laugh."

"No. Funny like in weird. Odd. A half dozen big tractor trailer rigs have pulled in. Real secret like. Bowie reported it to me. Power crews been working out at that old truck terminal north of town, and that's where the rigs are tucking themselves in. They're painted like they might be military rigs. But they look like some sort of mobile labs to me, Dan. You know what I mean; you've seen them. I went out there. They got armed guards around the place and won't let me in."

Dan's temper flared, hitting the boiling point, then bubbling over. "Well, goddamnit, they'll let me in. Is Captain Taylor and Dodge still in town?"

"Oh, yeah, Dan. Dodge is part of it."

It began to jell in Dan's mind. "Federal, huh? Okay. It's beginning to clear up for me. How about Captain Taylor?"

"Out at the motel. So is Langway."

"How about the reporters?"

"Most of them gone. They seemed satisfied with the press conference."

"Yeah. I just bet Quinn and Dodge put on quite a show. Get Taylor and Langway. Meet me here at the house as soon as possible."

"Rolling." Chuck hung up.

Dan felt eyes on him. Vonne lay wide awake,

looking at him. "What is it, Dan?"

"I really don't know, Vonne. But whatever it is, I get the feeling it stinks."

"You're leaving in the middle of the night?"

"Yes. Go on back to sleep. I don't know how late I'll be."

Taylor and Langway rode together out to the old terminal. Chuck rode with Dan. "Bring me up to date on Mickey and Denise," Dan said.

"Mr. Moore called the office about seven o'clock. His daughter hadn't come home."

"Why in the hell did he wait until seven o'clock at night to report it? I'm not snapping at you, Chuck. Sorry."

"It's okay. I feel the same way about it. I don't spy on my kids, but I have a pretty good idea where they are most of the time. Rich folks just don't do things like ordinary people. I never have understood them. I don't know. About ten minutes after Moore called, Mrs. Reynolds called. Her husband was missing. Herman and Bowie checked it out. No one at the high school. No vehicles, nothing. Place is all locked up and dark. Mickey is a grown man and Denise is eighteen. Adults. You know there isn't much we can do this soon. Moore is yelling about how he'll have our jobs and all that crap. You know the drill."

"Moore can't do jack-shit. All right. All we can do is follow procedure. Chuck, I just remembered something about that terminal."

"Yeah. And I know what it is. When that company filed for bankruptcy, there was a bunch of federal things involved. Something about payroll taxes and income taxes and SBA loans. The government seized it all. It's federal property, now. 'Bout two hundred

135

and fifty acres of land, plus the buildings."

"Damnit!" Dan said, hitting the steering wheel with the palm of his hand. He pulled over at a crossroads.

"I know the feeling," Chuck said. "Sometimes I wish I'd gone into farming instead of police work. Too late, now. Been a cop since I got out of the Army. Hell, I was cop in there, too."

Taylor and Langway pulled in behind Dan's car. The men got out, shadowy figures moving about in the dust and the glare of the headlights.

Dan explained the situation

Taylor sighed in frustration. "You thinking like I'm thinking, Dan? This is a coverup?"

"That's exactly what I'm thinking."

"But what the hell are they covering up?" Langway asked.

"I don't know," Dan said. "Exactly."

Taylor said, "Well, if the Feds are involved and they don't want to let us on that property, they damn sure don't have to. But by God, I sure would like to know what's going on."

A low slung sports car drove slowly by. All the men knew who it was.

Mille Smith.

She blinked her lights and honked the horn, driving on past.

"Doesn't that female ever sleep?" Taylor asked.

"Do vampires need sleep?" Chuck asked.

The men laughed at that and stood for a moment, until Mille's lights had faded, driving on past the turnoff to the terminal. The cops continued on, turning off the main highway on another road, staying with that for just over a mile to the old terminal. They came to a halt at the closed and locked gates. Signs had been added to the gates.

FEDERAL PROPERTY—POSITIVELY NO ADMIT-
TANCE—ALL TRESPASSERS WILL BE PROSECUTED.

Another sign, a larger one, read: WARNING—
ARMED GUARDS AND TRAINED ATTACK DOGS PA-
TROL THIS AREA. DO NOT ENTER.

"Bastards move quickly when they want to, don't
they?" Langway asked.

"Yeah," Dan said. "You got both noun and adverb
right." He reached up and rattled the chained gates.

"Back off," a low voice warned, coming out of the
darkness.

"This is Ruger County Sheriff Dan Garrett! Goddamn you, don't tell me what to do in this county. Get
your ass out here so I can see you."

"Easy, Dan." They all recognized the voice of agent
Dodge. "This is all the way out of your hands. Don't
push it."

"Get out here where I can see you, Dodge. You've
got some explaining to do."

Dodge appeared out of the purple night, another
man with him. The second man shoved a small
leather ID case through the gates.

Dan opened the case and Chuck put his flashlight
on the two-fold. The man's picture was there, sealed
in plastic, and beside the official seal of the United
States Government read: FEDERAL OFFICE OF SPE-
CIAL STUDIES.

Dan said, "I never heard of the Office of Special
Studies."

The man smiled. "Would you like to see one that
reads Treasury Department:? Or how about Justice
or I.C.C. or Secret Service? Just ask, Sheriff. I can
produce it."

"I just bet you can, too," Dan said, sarcasm heavy in his voice.

"How about CIA?" Captain Taylor asked. "Wouldn't that be closer to the truth?"

"Now, now, Captain Taylor," the man said. Taylor was not surprised to learn the man knew his name. The man chuckled. "You know the Agency is not allowed to operate within the continental limits of the United States."

Taylor's returning chuckle held little humor.

"Go on back home, boys," Dodge said. "It's completely out of your hands. Besides, I understand in addition to all your other troubles, you've got some new disappearances to contend with."

"My, word gets around quickly," Dan said. "What's going on in there, Dodge?"

"You just do not have a need to know, Sheriff. And if you repeat that, you just might find yourself in a whole lot of trouble."

"Now, please leave," the OSS man said.

"Is this America or Russia?" Chuck asked.

But agent Dodge and the man from the Office of Special Studies had melted back into the night.

"Now what?" Chuck asked.

"Will you call the governor, Captain?" Dan asked. "Maybe he can shed some light on this."

"At first light," the trooper said grimly. "I do not like this one damn little bit."

The cops spun around as men appeared behind them, boots crunching on the pea gravel of the driveway. The men were dressed in military field clothes, but wore no insignia of any kind. They carried M-16s.

"You gentlemen are advised to leave this area, now," one of the men spoke. His voice was very flat-sounding. "We are closing the road leading from the

138

highway to this facility."

"And if we don't choose to do so?" Dan asked.

"Oh, you will leave, Sheriff. One way or the other. The choice is yours."

"I'll tell you one goddamn thing, buddy," Captain Taylor said, his voice low and menacing. "You people might have the authority to keep me out of *there*"—he pointed toward the dark outline of the terminal—"but when you put your asses on the highway system in this state, they belong to *me*. And you can read into that any goddamn thing you like."

"Are you quite through, Captain?" the nameless man asked.

"For the moment," Taylor replied.

"Fine. Then *you* hear *me* out. This is a matter of the highest national security. If you wish to engage in a muscle-flexing contest . . . well, I don't have to tell you who is going to win. Oh, it's quite true you might harass us a bit on the highways—for a very short time. But you do not control the skies."

Captain Taylor bowed up, sticking his chin out. "And just what in the hell do you mean by that?"

"That means they'll airlift in everything they need," Dan said.

"Those helicopters I heard about five this . . . yesterday afternoon," Chuck said.

"You're very quick, Sheriff," the man said. "I'll keep that in mind. Now, if you will all leave? . . ."

"We're leaving," Dan said, before Captain Taylor exploded all over the place, which would do no one any good. Dan didn't believe the government men would actually shoot any of them, but why take chances?

Off government property, the men stopped just before reaching the highway.

"What in the hell is going on back there?" Captain

139

Taylor questioned.

"Some sort of medical experiment, for sure," Dan said. "But damnit, why be so hush-hush about it?"

No one could say.

"We'll call dispatch," Dan said. "See if they have anything new on the missing people. If not, I suggest we call it a day—or night—and try to get some sleep. Let's meet at my office in the morning and see what else has developed."

In the bus garage of the high school, the white Cadillac of Denise Moore was parked in between two buses that were in the process of being repaired. The naked body of Denise was spread-eagled and tied on the hood. She was alive; but just barely. Blood leaked down both fenders and across the grille. It had gathered in pools on the concrete floor. The ropes that held Denise's ankles were stained red, tied to the bumper. The windows of the Caddy were lowered, the ropes that bound her wrists tied to the steering column. The girl had been repeatedly raped and then tortured. Strange shapes had been cut into her flesh; cuttings that depicted cats and stars and strange monuments. It had taken Mickey hours to do all that he had been instructed to do. Silently instructed in a strange language he now knew was his own. The metamorphosis of Mickey was almost complete. He had aged, his skin darkening and wrinkling. Drool leaked from his mouth. His eyes were maddened.

Mickey had hidden his car after hiding the Cadillac. He could not now use his car, for he had forgotten how to drive it. Finished with Denise, Mickey inspected his work. He was pleased. He staggered down the dark streets of town toward his home. Now Mickey was ready to surprise his wife. He had re-

140

ceived his instructions.

That which had been Eddie Brown had staggered from the basement of the school and into a patch of woods just north of the school. From there, it had made its way to a marshy area not far from a small creek. Eddie stayed as far from the water as possible. The smell of the water infuriated him. He beat his fists on the ground, suppressing howls of fury. He ran from the smell of water, hiding in a thicket. There, it rested. As it rested, the stinking drool leaking past his lips fouled the thick pelt of new-grown hair on his chest.

Dan climbed wearily into bed beside his wife. Forcing his mind to slow down, stop racing and reeling with all the new developments, he willed himself to sleep.

Captain Taylor was in his motel room just outside of the town of Valentine. A motel room with a phone; which had almost taken an act of congress to procure. A widower, Captain Taylor spent as much time on the road as possible. He did not like to stay at his own home. His house was lonely since his wife died.

Taylor decided not to wait until dawn to call the governor. He called him right then.

It did not come as any surprise to learn the governor had suddenly decided to take a vacation. In St. Croix.

He would be gone for a couple of weeks. At least.

"Bastard!" Taylor said of his boss.

Doctor Quinn Ramsey lay sleeping soundly in his bed. Occasionally, a small smile would play at the corners of his mouth. His dreams were pleasant as he dreamed of great medical accolades being heaped on him for his discoveries. What a medical find this tragedy had turned out to be. A nightmare had turned into a gold mine. He was going to be famous. He just knew it. He'd be written up in all the journals. Maybe *People* magazine would interview him.

Just think of that.

Mille Smith lay in her bed in the motel in Richmond. She was wide awake; didn't matter, she had enough speed to keep her going for a week, if it came to that.

This one was going to be the big one for Mille. The biggest of the big. This story would put her right up there at the top of the list. It contained everything a good muckraker needed: police cover-up, gory murders, mystery, withholding of evidence—now a young woman and an older man are missing; probably shacked up someplace, with the old dude fulfilling his fantasies. And now the government—had to be the government, Mille couldn't think of anything else—had stepped in, doing something strange and secret at that old terminal. It hadn't taken Mille long to find out the government owned the property. Public record.

But what were they doing out there?

And was it connected with the murders?

Had to be.

And what in the hell was that creature she'd got a glimpse of yesterday? She'd never seen anything like it. It had to be some sort of nut case all dressed up in

142

a Halloween costume. Forget about those lies at the press conference. All that junk about some mysterious disease contracted down in South America. The doctors were covering up because the local hotdog sheriff shot an unarmed mental patient. And she didn't believe that story about the doctors' wives being attacked either.

And what in the hell was Kenny doing up there in New York City? She hadn't heard from him. But she knew if there was anything to be found, Kenny would find it.

She finally closed her eyes and slept.

Ruger County lay quiet under the night skies. A picture postcard setting.

Except for the Mickey Reynolds' house. Which was a mess.

13

Tuesday.

Surprisingly, Dan felt well-rested when he awakened. He showered, shaved, dressed, and had breakfast with Vonne. Since schools were still closed in the county, Carrie had elected to sleep late. Dan brought his wife up-to-date—telling her as much as he could.

"What does it all mean, Dan?"

He shook his head. "I don't know. But I can't help but believe Quinn is involved in this up to his butt. He's the coroner. Chuck told me last night—this morning—the body of the engineer we killed is gone from the morgue. And Jimmy had been moved out sometime between dark and when Chuck called me."

"Where would they—whoever they might be—take the body and Jimmy?"

"Probably out to that new . . . whatever it is out at the old terminal. It's big, Vonne. It had to be to get the power company boys out there in the middle of the night running all those lines."

She looked at her husband, looked at the new lines in his face. Was there more gray in his hair? She thought so. "One good thing came out of this, though."

"Oh?"

"You're off the hook. Just play the old military game, Dan. Remember it from our days in the service?"

He smiled. "CYA. Cover Your Ass. You're right, Vonne. And that is exactly what I'm going to do. I can play that game with the best of them."

Someone knocked on the door.

Dan answered it. Agent Dodge of the FBI—and Dan was beginning to wonder if the man really was FBI—stood on the porch.

"One side of me says you're not very welcome here, Dodge. But the sheriff side of me is very curious. So come on in and have a cup of coffee."

"Thanks." Dodge stepped inside. "All I ask is that you hear my side of the story."

"That's fair. Fine. I've told my wife all I could about the case."

"Suits me. I'm married too, buddy." That slick smile came too easily to Dodge's lips.

The man reminded Dan of a lot of new, young, fast-up-coming politicians. Always on.

And Dan didn't trust any of those who smiled all the time.

Dodge passed on Vonne's offer of breakfast, settling for a cup of coffee.

Dodge said, "Dan, none of this was my idea." Dan didn't believe that either. "Nor anyone's at the Bureau. You know we don't operate this way." That much was true; but Dan was convinced now, more than ever, that Dodge was no Bureau man. "This was literally taken right out of my hands."

"That big, huh?"

"Real big, buddy. Goes nearly all the way to the top. It's very big."

Dan nodded his head. He poured a second cup of coffee. "Yeah, I can see that, Dodge. Tell me, what is the Office of Special Studies?"

"If you're thinking it's the Agency, forget it, it isn't." Dan never thought it was. The Company would never be that high-handed, showing arms, in public—not around something as press-drawing as multiple murders. "The Agency," Dodge continued, "has really cleaned up their act stateside. The OSS—no relation to the old OSS—is a relative newcomer; but one with enormous power. Sugar Cube knows of their existence, but there is nothing The Man can do about them. I'll level with you, Dan. I don't know much about them." Liar! "It's both civilian and military and government. They work out of an obscure office in Maryland. Their ties go deep into the Pentagon. They've got a lot of clout. And something else: I was told to cooperate with them. Right down the line."

"Let me finish it, Dodge. Big money behind it from the various conservative fundamental religious groups around the country. Right?"

Dodge fiddled with his coffee cup. "Well, off the record, yes."

"All right, Dodge. Let me ask something else: What do I do?"

"Stand clear and pass the buck. The latter is off the record. Dan, keep your own skirts clean. And don't push this thing."

"That is something to be considered. I'll think about it. Those tractor trailer rigs at the terminal. Those are portable labs?"

146

"Yes."

"Extensive ones?"

"The very best that can be put together. They've got a hospital out there, Dan."

"I see. All right. So it's big and it is—putting aside all the B.S.—government?"

Dodge said nothing.

"The . . . creature was shot yesterday; it's out there? And Jimmy, too?"

"Yes."

"Quinn Ramsey is involved in this?"

"Oh, yes. Doctor Harrison too. And the new CDC people; might as well list them all for you."

"But they aren't really CDC people, are they? And never mind the crap, Dodge. I know they aren't. They never were."

Dodge's smile was filled with grudging admiration. "How'd you put that together, Dan?"

"I had one of my deputies follow them. None of them ever flew back to Atlanta. Always to Washington."

"Cute, Dan. But I wish you hadn't done that. I really do."

Dan shrugged his total indifference as to what Dodge did or did not want.

"All right, Dan," the government man said. "You want the whole nine yards?" Dan nodded. "Then here it is. They're from the military's chemical and biological warfare center. That tell you anything?"

"Oh, yes. The continuing search for the ultimate weapon to use against our enemies."

"You got it, buddy."

"Doctor Goodson?"

"He was, to use his word, 'appalled.' He pulled out and went back to the university. Then he changed his

147

mind and returned. Said he might be able to do more good staying around, looking over the shoulders of these people."

"Good for Doctor Goodson." I have an ally in camp. He kept that thought silent. "The highway patrol?"

"I . . . understand they have been instructed not to make waves." Short and to the point.

Big, Dan thought. Real big. Bigger than a county sheriff alone can cope with. But how big? "By whom?"

Dodge lifted his shoulders.

Lying son of a bitch! "And you're here to tell me to do the same." It was not put in question form.

Dodge sighed; put a hound dog expression on his face. He was a really terrible actor. "Yeah. I'm afraid that's so, buddy."

Dan fought to keep his temper in check. He gave it his best effort. "Well, *buddy*, you'd better make sure no reporters get close to me. 'Cause I'm damn sure going to lift the lid off this stinking, slimy, wriggling, cover-up can of worms."

Dodge flushed, his eyes hardening in expression. He pointed his finger at Dan.

"You want that finger broken or just badly bent?" Dan asked.

Dodge tucked his finger back into his fist and lowered his hand. "No need to get hostile, buddy. I'm here only to help."

Dan laughed at him.

"Believe me, Dan. I can produce more muscle than you can—if that's the way you choose to play it."

"I'm sure you can. But I intend to play legal, Dodge. You are familiar with that word, are you not?"

"There is no can of worms, Dan."

"You can't be serious!"

"Like a crutch, buddy."

"You want to explain that?"

"There is no mummy-man. No severed arm. It's been destroyed. There is no one named Jimmy. He was released and went on a long recuperative vacation. Doctor's orders."

"Oh, come on, Dodge! That's shit and you know it."

"Prove it, buddy."

"Man, I've got pictures!"

"You have no pictures. Not of anything pertaining to this subject."

"I've got pictures of the kids. Al and Jimmy. Donald Drake. And . . ." He cut it off as Dodge smiled at him. Suckered! he thought. I've been stiffed. Taken like a rookie. "Why do I get the impression I'll never see any of those pictures again? And why do I get the feeling those medics of Ramsey's never took any pictures of the dead engineer?"

"You're learning, buddy. All gone. Accidents do happen when dealing with cameras, you know?"

"I see." Dan was conscious of his wife's pale face; her eyes staring at him. "Well, there is still the matter of Mille Smith. She *saw* the mummy-man."

"We're working on that."

Dan picked up on the 'we're' part of it. He kept his expression closed. "Dodge, there are a couple of points I'd like to make."

"I'm listening, buddy."

"One: you have no right to expose the people of this county to more danger. Two: the murderers who brought all this about."

"The people are in no danger, buddy. We're not

149

savages. Jesus Christ! That terminal is cordoned off with armed guards. You know that. And we—all of us—will be working very closely with you and your people in capturing the people responsible for the murders."

"Suppose I don't choose to accept your offer of *help*?"

"You don't have a choice in the matter, buddy."

"Are you threatening me, Dodge?"

"Not *you*, directly." He cut his eyes to Evonne.

Dan got it. "You lying—"

"Anything else, buddy?"

"Yeah."

"Name it."

"Get your goddamned ass out of my house— *buddy*!"

Dan laid it out for Captain Taylor, Sergeant Langway, Chuck Klevan, and the rest of the people. He did that after ordering a thorough search of the sheriff's department for the pictures of the murder victims.

The prints were gone.

"How in the hell did they get in here to do that?" a deputy questioned.

"Easily," Dan told them. "Can any of you dispatch people remember taking a phone call that seemed a little strange? Maybe one that lasted for an unusually long time?"

"Yes, sir," one of the night dispatch people said. "The same day that mummy thing was killed. That night, I mean. Some nut called in. Kept me on the line for about fifteen minutes. Wildest crap I ever heard." The dispatcher paused, a rueful smile on his lips. "Sure. And while I was busy trying to make some sense out of the call, giving it all my attention, somebody just walks right in the office and helps themselves. Right, Sheriff?"

"That's it. When I was with the Bureau, I worked similar ops, but never on a police station."

The deputies were angry, and it showed on their faces. Fellow officers—regardless of agency, they were still brother cops—had stiffed them. Battle lines had been drawn; the enemy identified.

"Get back to work," Dan ordered.

The deputies on duty returned to the roads. The off-duty dispatchers left to go home. Four Virginia Highway Patrolmen entered the room. They were dressed in civilian clothes. Dan knew them all, but not well.

Captain Taylor said, "In a very roundabout way, with nothing firm being said, I was ordered to work very closely with this new bunch out at the terminal. Give them my fullest cooperation. I told my C.O. that if he wasn't my C.O., I would tell him where to shove his orders. He said he understood my feelings."

"Did they pull the national security bit with you?" Chuck asked. "They sure did with me. Sounded like a broken record."

"They tried," Taylor said. "I told that damned Dodge to get the hell out of my motel room before I jammed his phony I.D. up his butt. Sideways. I don't believe that man is Bureau."

"He may be Bureau," Dan said. "But if so, he's working both sides of the street. I would imagine all agencies have been infiltrated by these OSS people. They've got to be big and very powerful. And very secret. And I think they've been around a lot longer than Dodge is telling us. And I'm thinking this bunch

151

is the same bunch we ran up against out west back in the sixties. Some of you may recall the flap about mutilated cattle. Those responsible were using cattle to try to perfect some sort of weapon to use against the Russians. Germ warfare. Between 1965 and 1970 some five thousand head of cattle were found, mutilated. It's still going on, but on a much smaller scale."

"Yeah," Langway said. "Wasn't there a movie about that?"

"Yes," Dan said. "It's based on fact. I worked on the case for two years."

"With what degree of success?" Taylor said.

"Very little," Dan admitted. "We ran up against a stone wall every way we turned. Big coverup."

"Nice folks," Chuck said.

"Don't underestimate them. They're highly trained and will kill you before you can blink. I lost a good friend out there. And there's something else too. I don't think Dodge likes what he's doing. That's just a hunch of mine."

"Are you saying they would turn on us?" Langway asked. "Violently?"

"If it's the same bunch, yes."

"And you think it is?" Chuck asked.

"Yes. Patriotic to the point of fanaticism. They're very dangerous."

Taylor said, "Well, they sure got to someone high up in this state. Very high. And I don't know how. Probably with old dirt. But," he smiled, "they couldn't touch anybody with the state police. They tried, though. My C.O. was really angry. And that's putting it mildly. But he takes orders like the rest of us." Taylor laughed. "However, it was said to me that if I elected to take some leave time, Scott Langway and three or four other troopers and I, we could. And

152

if we wanted to spend that vacation time here in Ruger County, why that was up to us. I told the man I sure could use some vacation time. So did Langway. And Troopers Lewis, Collins, Hawkes, and Forbes."

Dan nodded. "How long do you have . . . off?"

"Just as long as it takes, Dan," Taylor replied. "And that's firm."

Dan looked at the four troopers who were now on "vacation." "You men realize you could very well be putting your jobs on the line, don't you?"

"I took a medical leave of absence, Sheriff," Trooper Lewis said. "Old Vietnam injury."

"Even though it's going to come as a surprise to her," Collins said. "My wife's havin' a baby."

"I got a lot of time accrued," Hawkes said. "I can spend it any way I like."

Forbes said, "My daddy's sick. I gotta help him put in a crop."

"You guys are the worst bunch of liars I ever heard," Chuck said.

The troopers grinned. They were all under thirty, in top physical condition, all of them rarin' to go.

Taylor said, "These boys, Dan, represent a part of this division's Special Weapons and Tactical Team. Coincidence, I'm sure," he added with a straight face.

"Of course," Dan said, with an equally straight face. "And you all are now on official vacation?"

"That is correct," Taylor said.

A deputy stuck his head into Dan's office. "Sheriff? Just got a call from a neighbor of Mickey Reynolds. She said there was some kind of big ruckus over there last night. Lights stayed on all night long. She says she hasn't heard a peep from that house this morning, and all the shades are pulled. She says that's real odd."

"All right," Dan said. "Chuck, introduce the, ah, visiting vacation boys around, will you? I'll go take a look at the Reynolds' house."

"I'll tag along if you don't mind," Taylor said.

"Glad to have you."

The duty dispatcher stuck her head into the office. "Another body's been found, Sheriff."

Dan was torn between investigating the DB call and going to Mickey's house. The latter prevailed. Something nagged at him; something in the back of his mind said that the Reynolds' house was important. Check it out.

Taylor rode with Dan, both of them dressed in civilian clothes. Both of them carrying pistols in shoulder holsters. They parked in front of the Reynolds' house and sat for a moment, looking at the home. All the drapes and shades were pulled tightly closed. The house seemed to emit an empty force.

"I don't like the feeling I'm getting," Taylor said.

"Yeah. I feel the same way. Come on. Let's check it out."

Dan rang the doorbell and then banged on the front door. Nothing. He tried the doorknob. It turned in his hand. He cracked the door. Something howled and screamed and flew at the men.

It was a cat. The cat leaped into the front yard, went to the bathroom, then sat on the lawn, looking at the men.

"That thing took five years off my life," Taylor gasped.

"At least," Dan said. He called, "Mickey? Betty? Anyone home?"

Silence greeted his words. Stillness, and something

154

else: the sharp odor of sweat . . . and a foul odor that was somehow familiar to Dan.

"Smells like a locker room in there," Taylor said. "One that hasn't been cleaned for about a month."

"Yeah." Dan pushed open the door, allowing morning sunlight to flood the small foyer. Then it came to Dan. What he was smelling was the same thing he'd smelled in the back yard of the Milford house.

The house looked as though it had been trashed.

"Good Lord!" Taylor said, peering over Dan's shoulders at the mess.

"Let's check the back," Dan said.

"I'm with you."

The back screen door was hanging open, one hinge broken. The kitchen door was shattered. A toaster lay on the porch floor, amid sparkling shards of broken glass. The toaster was bent and broken.

"Domestic quarrel?" Taylor ventured. "You know these people, I don't."

"I doubt it. Mickey was not a violent man. Of course, I realize that doesn't mean a damn thing. People do snap."

"Just a suggestion. We don't get to work many family fights out on the highways. Just a lot of broken up bodies, caused by ignorant, arrogant, uncaring drunks." Taylor was still very much a highway cop, with a highway cop's contempt for those who drink and drive.

The men stepped onto the back porch, Dan leading the way. The kitchen was as littered and torn-up as the living room.

The many drawings and paintings on the walls pulled the men into silent staring. Finally, Taylor summed it up.

"They're . . . *hideous!*"

155

"Yes," Dan said. But he was looking at something else. He pointed it out. "Cats. Cats of all sizes and shapes. And very crude drawings of human sacrifices." He stepped closer and touched one of the red drawings. He sighed with relief. "Red crayon. At thought I first they were done in blood."

Taylor stepped closer, inspecting the wall. "And a small child. The cat seems to be following the child in this drawing."

"And the child is carrying the cat in this one. What do you make of it?"

"I just don't know."

"That makes three of us," the voice came from the back porch.

"Yes, Anya said, but he was looking at something else. He pointed toward "Chee Only of all flesh and species. A no mode distance of human consciousness. He helped closer and see—a none of the observance extracted with ——— had extracted Anya. Clothes was none Cer the chandra. Taking mind toward ——— see a chefl there Similarly when the raining across the the city.

14

The only visitor to the second floor of the storage garage had been a stray cat. Silent messages had passed between Anya and Pet and the cat. The cat had left. Anya and Pet knew they were as safe as they had been in days, for no one had been in or near the large brick home since their arrival. They could sense the home was unoccupied. At least for the time being. They elected to remain in the garage.

They knew they were safe, momentarily. They also knew they were trapped. But they had to stay; the rebirth was near.

It was not safe to travel the countryside. Too many men were hunting them. They had spent several days attempting to leave this area, testing what they both suspected. Each time they tried to leave, silent voices called them back. Then they were sure. Silent stirrings were all about them. Old voices, long mute, were silently echoing about this area. And the Master was close. Waiting, watching. Anya and Pet could feel the Old Ones struggling to rebirth.

The time was drawing near. Pet had done her duty, calling on her kind for help. They waited, gathering in groups.

Anya and Pet waited, listening to the silent voices. More and more had been added. Dark laughter joined the voices. Moans of those long-dead echoed around the area, unheard except to those who worshipped another god. The Dark One. Master of Filth. Lord of Evil. The Prince of Darkness.

He was here!

Anya and Pet laughed and laughed.

"Like a bad penny, Dodge," Dan said. "You keep popping up where least expected."

Dodge looked around him at the torn and ruined kitchen; the many drawings on the walls. "You were going to tell me about this, weren't you, Sheriff?"

"Well," Taylor said drily, "even though we're not professionals like you, Dodge, we were sorta going to muddle through. I mean, give it our best shot and all that. Country cops that we are."

Dodge smiled. "You don't like me very much, do you, Captain?"

Taylor's eyes told him the silent answer.

"I'm just like you, Captain. I'm taking orders and doing a job. I thought you were on vacation?"

"Oh, I am. You want to try to force me to take it elsewhere, Dodge?"

"Not at all." Dodge reached into his jacket pocket and produced a sheet of paper. "These are orders from your governor, gentlemen. Anything that happens in Ruger County, from this day forward, as far as the ongoing investigation is concerned, and I think you both know what investigation I'm speaking of, must be coordinated through my department. And that's me, boys. You want to read this?"

Taylor almost tore it out of the man's hands. He scanned the paper. "It's legit," he said.

Dodge spread his hands. "Would I lie?" he asked innocently.

"I think you'd do anything," Dan said. He read the orders and handed the paper back to Dodge. "And I don't believe you're Bureau."

"I started out with them. I was a good agent. I'm still associated with them . . . in a roundabout way. And that's all either of you need to know."

"Dodge," Taylor finally had it with the man. "You're a real jerk."

"I'm sorry you feel that way, Captain. I . . . uh . . . really am."

"Sure."

Dodge shrugged it off. "Well, back to business. What about all this?" He waved his hand.

"We don't know," Dan said. "We were about to make a search of the house when you started shooting off your mouth. May we continue our investigation?"

"Certainly. Don't let me interfere."

"What do you have on our governor, Dodge?" Taylor asked.

"Maybe he's just being a good citizen, cooperating with us?"

"Sure!"

Dodge shrugged. "I don't know, boys. That's the truth. I really don't. Boys, don't crowd these people. They play rough. Believe it."

"You sound as though you might be having some second thoughts about this bunch," Dan said.

Again, the man shrugged it off.

The trio roamed the house, carefully inspecting each room. There were paintings and drawings on every wall, but no sign of life. Or death. Just that almost sickening odor. They could find no traces of blood, even though all knew there had been a terrible struggle in the house. Between somebody.

159

"What do you think, Sheriff?" Dodge asked.

"I don't know." Sometimes, Dan thought, Dodge could be almost likeable. Almost. "But it might make things easier between us if you'd level with me about what is going on out at the terminal."

Dodge leaned against a wall and looked at Dan and Captain Taylor. He smiled, then said, "I went in the Navy at seventeen. A year later I was in Navy Intelligence. They found I had an aptitude for that sort of work. I took some college courses and when I got out, I finished up at NYCC. I've been a cop all my life. Just like you, Dan, and you, Captain Taylor. A cop. Not a medical person. You want me to level with you? Okay. I don't know what is going on out there. But it scares me. I think they're screwing around with blood samples and chromosomes and chromospheres and God only knows what else. I told you it scares me, and it does. They have that arm out there that's growing a new body. Yeah! A new *body*. And that mummy-thing you guys shot! You think it's dead? Forget it. It's alive and well."

The men listened with a mixture of horror and fascination.

"It scares me that it could get out of control. Like that time out west with the cattle. I was working the north range, Dan, while you boys were on the southern range. I saw it all. Like you, I *know* what went on out there. And this is the same bunch, boys. Older, wiser, and one hell of a lot rougher. I was against setting up the labs here in the county. I'm on record as being opposed to it. And I don't care whether you believe that or not. Yes, I do care. I'm sick of this business. I just want to go back to being a cop. But I know too much. Too goddamn much. And just exactly what I predicted would happen, is happening. Right here in Ruger. But they wanted the materials and labs

160

close. So I was over-ridden. That's it, boys. Turn me in and you won't see me again. But I wouldn't blame you if you did. They are doing experiments out there. That's all I know. And I'll even take a PSE or polyograph on that."

Both Dan and Taylor believed the man. Dan said, although he was not all that sure he wanted to hear the answer, "And what is happening that you predicted?"

Dodge waved his hand. "It's spreading. The infection. The aging thing. The disease. Hell, I don't know what it is. But the OSS doctors don't care about that. Dan, what I'm telling you now can't leave this room. You talk and you're dead. And you, too." He looked at Taylor. "But before you're dead, you'll be laughed out of the state. Because these guys are so good, so proficient, they can have the area wiped clean and be gone in twenty-five minutes. I've seen them do it with a hell of a lot more gear than they have out there now. And all you'll have for proof is your thumb stuck up your rear."

"That . . . incident that took place up in Missouri a couple years ago," Taylor said. "Something about a chemical spill. That was no chemical spill, was it?"

"Well," Dodge grimaced. "Yes and no. It wasn't supposed to have happened. But it did. You see now how good they are at covering up?"

"Tell me about these OSS doctors," Dan said.

"When I kicked up a fuss about the people in this county, the doctors said they weren't concerned about them. That this was as good a county as any to contain if an accident did happen. I tell you, boys, this thing spooks me. I think we're dealing with . . . don't laugh . . . something, well, that we just don't understand. Like a . . . higher power maybe."

"You mean, like *god*!" Taylor blurted.

"No," Dodge said, a definite edge to his voice. "I mean, like the devil."

"Dodge! . . ." Taylor said, irritation in his voice.

"No, I'm serious. That mummy is speaking in some kind of strange language. One of the doctors working out there, whose hobby is ancient languages, says he never heard of this language. But he has managed to pick out three or four key words. The mummy is calling for the Dark One. The Master. I don't have to tell either of you what the Dark One is, do I?"

Taylor felt a chill move slowly across his back. Turning his head, he looked again at the drawings on the wall. He stepped closer and looked hard at one. It was . . . indescribable in its revulsion. It was not a man, not an animal. It was a *thing*.

He crossed himself. "I swear that was not there a few minutes ago," he said.

"I believe it," Dodge said.

The ringing of the phone startled them all. Dan picked it up and listened for a few seconds. He replaced the phone in the cradle and looked at Dodge.

Dodge was looking at the drawing Taylor had pointed out. It was changing before their eyes. "Our Father, who art in Heaven," Dodge said. The words trailed off in his dry mouth.

Taylor and Dan stared at the drawing, horror filling them. The red crayon drawing was leaking, running in wet lines down the wall. With trembling fingers, Dodge took a napkin from the kitchen table and touched it to the liquid, staining the paper.

"It's blood," he whispered. "Blood."

He backed away from the wall. He wrapped the napkin in a piece of foil picked up from the floor and put it in his pocket.

"I'd like to see the report from the lab on that,"

Taylor said.

Dodge looked at the trooper. "I'm not so sure I do." He shook himself, touched the pocket where he'd put the foil. He took several deep breaths and looked at the wall. The hideousness was no longer there. Just a long wet sticky trail of blood. "See what I mean," he whispered.

"When did you first start thinking this had something to do with the devil?" Taylor asked.

"When it first occurred. Don't ask me why or how—I don't know. But I believe it." He looked at Dan. "What was that phone call?"

"A couple of my people just found the Moore girl. At the high school garage. She's alive, but just barely. She's been tortured and strange markings cut into her flesh. Cats and kids and strange symbols. The ball's in your court, Dodge. Where do we take her?"

Dodge looked tormented. He sighed. "This is going to make me sound awfully hard-hearted . . ."

"We don't have a choice," Captain Taylor said. "So let me say it. If she's been infected, and we take her out of the county, we endanger more lives. But if we call your people, Dodge, the girl gets used as a human guinea pig. That about wraps it all up?"

"Yes," Dodge said. "That's it."

Both men looked at Dan.

Dan looked at the sticky smear on the wall, the pool of blood that had gathered on the floor. He was placed squarely on the horns of that much-talked about dilemma. He cursed. He handed the phone to Dodge. "Call your people. Tell them to go to the school and get her. I don't have the right to endanger others."

Dodge's eyes were sad as he took the phone. "I'm sorry, Dan. I really am. I want you both to please believe me."

"We believe you," Taylor said. "And we're sorry,

too."

Dodge said, "Look, if you guys think I'm hard, wait 'til you meet some of the boys who do this sort of work all the time."

When Dan and Taylor arrived at the high school, a tractor-trailer rig was backed up to the bus garage. Dan knew what would be inside the trailer. Denise's car. He looked in. He was right. When he stepped into the garage area, half a dozen coverall-clad men and women were just finishing up. They did not speak to him, and that did not hurt Dan's feelings a bit.

In the time it had taken Dan and Captain Taylor to finish up at the Reynolds' house and drive to the high school, all apparent traces of what had happened to Denise had been erased. Dan knew a careful investigation would show all kinds of blood and tissue embedded in the concrete floor and walls, but to the untrained eye, the place was clean.

And the cover-up continued, and Dan kept getting in deeper and deeper. With no apparent way out.

The man who had been with Dodge on the other side of the gates the night before was leaning up against a bus, smoking a cigarette.

Dan walked up to him. The man lifted his eyes. Cold, unreadable. "What do I call you?" Dan asked.

"Lou will do, Sheriff."

"Do I get to see the girl?"

"Oh, sure, Sheriff. You're into this cover-up all the way now. No point in holding back from you. You blow the whistle on us, you gotta blow it on yourself as well."

"I'm under orders to work with you, Lou."

Lou smiled knowingly. "But we're holding the paper containing that order, Sheriff."

Dan grunted. They had him boxed. No way to go but forward. "Cute," he said.

Lou removed a dozen Polaroids from his coverall pocket and handed them to Dan. He studied Dan's face closely as Dan inspected the pictures.

Dan and Taylor were silent as they viewed the prints. It was difficult for Dan to believe the girl had endured the savage torture. In some of the prints, Denise's naked body had been washed clean, allowing the cuttings to be more clearly shot.

"What did you wash her with?" Taylor asked.

"Hosed her down," Lou said.

Dan looked at the man, amazed at the insensitivity.

Lou shrugged. "She's gonna die anyway. No big deal."

Taylor said, "And the girl is still alive? After all of this?"

"Yeah. Barely. She probably won't make it. She's lost a lot of blood. The cuts themselves aren't that deep. But maybe the doctors can learn something from her. Who knows?"

"And if she does make it?" Dan asked.

Lou's smile did not waver. "We have people who can . . . ah . . . fix it so she won't remember anything. Like a fading bad dream. Miracles of modern medicine and all that."

"And if she dies?" Taylor asked.

"Her body will never be found. If by some chance it is, it's just another Jane Doe."

Neither Dan nor Taylor could believe the coldness of the man called Lou.

"What happens to her car?" Dan asked.

Lou's grin spread. "You really wanna get into it deep, don't you, Sheriff?"

Dan felt sick at his stomach. "Forget I asked."

"Aw, come on, boys," Lou said. "This is nothing. I

165

worked in East Germany for two years. You should see some of the stuff that goes on over there. Hell, boys. The little lady is just one person out of two hundred and thirty five million. That won't even make a blip on a stat chart. Hey! Where's a good place to eat in this burg? I'm hungry."

15

Dan and Taylor both noticed that on the back of the worker's coveralls was the lettering: HPB TRUCKING. As they drove out to the site of the DB call, they saw several more of the workers, all dressed alike. They were shopping at a supermarket, picking up a paper, having lunch at a local cafe, making themselves a part of the community. Friendly, courteous, fitting right in. They would cause less suspicion that way.

"I wonder how often this scenario is played throughout the nation?" Taylor asked.

"More than the average citizen realizes," Dan said. "I personally know of one government agency—which shall remain nameless, and it isn't the CIA—that is into many, many businesses. They use them as fronts. And they all make money, too. That way, they don't have to go to congress for additional funding when a project comes up they want a hand in."

"Are you kidding me?"

"Dead serious."

"Why doesn't someone blow the whistle on them?"

"People do try, from time to time. But it would take ten teams of accountants, working around the clock, ten years to even scratch the surface. By that time, the businesses would be gone. Besides, they're run by civilians who don't realize who their real bosses are. And it's like the man said, 'everybody has dirt.' Once it's found, that person is in the pocket of whatever agency finds it."

Taylor shook his head. "I suppose, in the long run, it's necessary."

"Most of the time. At least that's what I keep telling myself. I have to sleep like everyone else."

"Yeah."

Dan ordered the blanket removed from the cold dead body. This one was the worst yet. The body had been savagely gnawed on; pale white flesh from the blood sucked from it.

And Dodge was there. The men looked at each other. Dodge said, "You know this man, Sheriff?"

"No. From the looks of him, he's a transient. Hitchhiker, probably. Did you go through his pack, Chuck?"

"Yes. Dirty clothes. A paperback book about some sort of transcendental meditation. And three joints."

Taylor grunted. "A dead *dumb* hitcher. The smart ones stopped carrying grass on them a long time ago."

Dan looked at Dodge, glad to be taking his eyes off the mangled flesh of the man. "I guess you want what's left of him?"

"I guess so."

"I want a pass giving me gate authorization at the terminal any time of the day or night."

"I'll see if I can arrange it. No promises, Dan."

"I understand."

"HPB Trucking a real outfit?" Taylor asked.

"Oh, yes. Has a lot of government contracts. HPB

pulls a lot of SSTs."

"A lot of what?" Deputy Herman Forrest asked.

"Safe Secure Transports," Taylor told him. "Nuclear stuff."

They stood and watched as the body was bagged and loaded into the station wagon. The back windows of the wagon were slightly darkened. The sign on the doors read HPB TRUCKING.

As if reading Dan's mind, Dodge said, "It's better this way. Reduces suspicion. The regular hospital personnel handle the routine calls, using hospital equipment."

"Didn't they get suspicious; angry about being displaced?" Taylor asked.

"Not after being given a talk about national security and five thousand bucks apiece," Dodge straightened that out.

"HPB must make a good profit," Dan said drily.

"Oh, it does. The, ah, regular personnel are fully unionized and have good benefits."

"Isn't that just dandy?" Taylor said.

Two long trailers had been placed end to end, making one long fully equipped and staffed lab. Two other trailers were placed along side, one on each side, side doors facing and interlocking. One of the side trailers was the mobile hospital; the other the morgue, autopsy room, and small cold storage for stiffs. In case of a power failure, a huge portable generator would kick in ten seconds after any failure, maintaining a constant temperature inside the trailers.

Another long trailer sat, for the time being, idle. But it could be fully operational in minutes, if needed. It would be needed. Much sooner than anyone could possibly realize.

169

Denise lay on one of the two operating tables. Vital blood flowed through a needle in one arm; an antibiotic was going IV into her other arm. She was naked, her tortured youthfulness under the gaze of the doctors.

"What a mess," one doctor said, working on the left side of the girl.

Goodson was observing. "She's young and strong and healthy," he said. "She's got a fighting chance."

"Sixty-forty," another doctor said. "That jerk Lou gave us yet another problem we didn't need by hosing her down."

"Yeah," another gloved and gowned and masked doctor said. "Pneumonia. I've told him a dozen times at least to take it easy."

"This poor child needs to be in a hospital," Doctor Goodson said.

Bennett, the chief of the OSS medical team, said, "Look around you, Doctor. You're looking at ten million dollars worth of equipment. This is a completely sterile environment. This is a battle hospital. There is nothing a permanent hospital could do that we aren't doing here, at this moment, for this particular case. We're scientists, yes; but we're doctors, too. If she can be saved, she will be. If you don't like what we're doing here, you are free to leave. You know to keep your mouth shut, and why. Careful with that stitch, Robert. One more. There. Good. No scarring. Nice work."

"Your concern for the girl is touching," Goodson said.

The doctor's eyes showed humor above his mask. "Isn't our work professional enough for you, Doctor?"

Goodson grunted. He had to admit the men were as good as he'd ever seen. Better than most. But damned if he was going to tell them so.

Goodson remained silent, listening to the OR chatter.

"BP?"

"Stabilizing. Looks good."

"Pulse is strong and steady."

"By God! I think she might make it."

"I certainly would like to talk with her. It's important we know something about the person who attacked her."

"Tomorrow, perhaps," Bennett said. "I want to study the pictures of those drawings carved in her skin. They are the strangest I've ever seen."

Suddenly, Goodson grew weak-kneed as a white hot flash of recollection and old memories flooded the man's mind. He had known they would; that had been one reason he'd stayed. The words from that old Egyptian came roaring into the light of full recall.

Goodson's father had asked about what he had heard was the Forbidden Ones. Some sort of religion. He had asked that question of several hundred Egyptians. It had become an in-house joke around the Bedouin camps. Finally one old man had acknowledged that he had heard of such a thing. He had been the first to even admit that much.

"You are speaking of the Cat People," the old man had said. "No one wishes to speak aloud of them. For no one outside of their group ever sees them and lives."

"Obviously," the elder Goodson had said, "you are the exception."

"I was lucky, and it was a lifetime ago."

"Who are they?"

The old man had looked fearfully around him. "They are of and for the Dark One."

"The Dark One?"

"You call him the devil."

The old man had said he was dying, and knew it. It no longer mattered whether or not he kept his silence. The Cat People could do nothing to him. He had made his peace. Dying was something he did not fear. It was living that was to be feared.

The old man had then begun speaking in a rush of words, almost a babbling. He had spoken of human sacrifices, of human and animal being born of woman. Twins, a girl and a cat who would live and reign for hundreds, perhaps thousands of years. The pair possessed strange powers and feasted on human flesh and blood. And their bite was highly infectious. The bite could produce rapid aging. It could infect and cause a mummy-like condition. It could change human life into a form of animal. The girl and the cat had powers over other felines. And the girl and the cat were carriers. If it stops there, he had added.

"Carriers?" the elder Goodson had questioned.

"That which causes dogs to go mad."

Goodson's father had not pursued the "if it stops there," part of the old man's statement.

Goodson stepped away from the operating table and walked into another compartment of the trailer. There, he removed his mask.

Not a religious man, Goodson rejected the concept of the devil. Let God, if He existed, combat the devil. The medical profession had something else to worry about in Ruger County.

Goodson sat alone for several minutes, deep in thought. With a sigh, he put his mask back on and reentered the OR. He could not keep this to himself. No matter how he detested what these OSS people were doing.

Bennett looked up, meeting Goodson's eyes.

"There is something you all had best be aware of,"

Goodson said.

"Oh, Doctor Goodson? Would you please enlighten us?"

"There was evidence of human bites on the girl, right?"

"That is correct. Savage bites on both inner thighs and on the stomach."

"That's what I was afraid of. We have yet another problem on our hands, gentlemen."

The OSS doctors looked at him in silence, waiting.

"We might be looking at a rabies epidemic here in the county."

16

Doctor Goodson stepped out of the trailer he was using as a home away from home. He looked up into the clear blue Virginia skies. He sighed. An old man's sigh, from a man who had seen the best and the worst of what humankind had to offer. He had been correct in his assumption that Denise was a victim of a rabid bite. As far as it went, that is.

It was rabies, all right. At least a form of it. But unlike any type he had ever seen. There was no doubt the girl was infected. And there was nothing the medical profession could do about it.

It was spreading faster than a brush fire in dry country. Denise's nervous system was showing signs of rapid deterioration.

Goodson looked toward the north. He muttered, "You idealistic young fool!"

The reason for that strange statement, and Doctor Goodson's overriding reason for staying with the OSS people, with the project—his term for it—was because of his nephew; his brother's son. Benjamin Goodson

174

had opted for Canada rather than be drafted during the Vietnam War. Before he left, however, he had been a radical, taking part in bombings and other violence. He had been in Canada for years, living under a different name.

Of course the OSS knew about Benjamin Goodson. Of course the OSS had told Goodson if he didn't keep his mouth shut about what was going on in Ruger County, his nephew would be hauled back to the U S of A, one way or the other, and prosecuted on half a dozen charges. And that meant prison. Of course Goodson did not want that to happen.

Dirt. Pressure. Rattling skeletons in the family closet. Everybody has a lever. The trick is in finding the handle and pulling it.

Doctor Bennett walked out of the mobile hospital and to Goodson's side.

"The girl will be dead in twelve to eighteen hours," he said.

"Mercifully so."

"That is one way of looking at it."

"How do you manage to sleep at night, Bennett?"

Bennett laughed. "Quite well, thank you. Goodson, everybody has a job to do. Some more distasteful than others. To some people. Ours involves national security. You have to look at it this way: if a few people are sacrificed to save millions . . ."

"Oh, shut up, Bennett!" Goodson said, considerable heat in his voice. "I don't want to hear that horseshit. Goddamn you, Bennett. We're talking about innocent people. This is not a war!"

Bennett chuckled, derision thick in his ugly humor. "Not a war, Doctor? You're wrong. It most certainly is a war. Don't you think we have counterparts in Russia? Of course we do. And they have more of them and are working much harder than we. If they got wind of this project, don't you think for an instant they wouldn't kill all of us to get it. And then isolate it, hone it, and use it against this country.

"Innocent people, Doctor? Really! How can a man of your experience and knowledge be so naive? Eddie Brown was a drunk. He hasn't worked, contributed, to anything in his entire life. Milford and Hardy were in their twilight years. Mickey Reynolds was a petty, pompous official. The young cop was a nobody; besides, cops are paid to take risks. The girl in there?" He jerked his thumb toward the hospital trailer. "Is—or was—a spoiled, arrogant brat. Innocent? Don't make me laugh, Doctor."

Goodson glanced at him. Talk about pompous and arrogant and petty, he thought. "You believe in the devil, Bennett?"

"Eh? Don't be absurd. Why are you asking me such a stupid question as that at a time like this?"

Goodson remained silent.

"All right," Bennett said. "Do *you* believe in Satan, Goodson?"

"I don't know. I didn't until about an hour ago. Now I'm not so sure."

Bennett laughed. "Well, Doctor, before you go to sleep tonight, be sure to look under your bed. Check carefully for ghosties and ghoulies and things that go bump in the night."

He walked away, chuckling.

Goodson recalled the old Egyptian. "I think I shall," he muttered.

"Just got a call from the same woman who called this morning," Dan was informed. "The neighbor of Mickey and Betty Reynolds? She said Mrs. Reynolds and the kids are back home now."

Dan looked at Taylor. Both men stood up. "She say anything about Mickey?"

"No, sir."

Dan and Taylor rolled up to the curb and stopped. They got out of the car and walked slowly up the sidewalk to the Reynolds' small front porch. Dan knocked on the door. Betty Reynolds opened it.

"Betty? Is everything all right here?"

The woman's eyes seemed too big for her face. Her face was very pale. Circles under her eyes. She wore a long sleeve shirt, so neither man could tell if her arms were bruised.

"Is everything all right, Betty?" Dan repeated.

The woman blinked. Focused her eyes on Dan. "Why . . . of course, Sheriff." She spoke in the flattest sounding voice either man had ever heard. Eerie sounding. Taylor resisted an impulse to look around him for . . . He mentally shook that thought away. He was just too damned old to be believing in ghosts and haunts and such.

"Ah . . . sure, Betty. Of course," Dan said. "Is, ah, Mickey home?"

"Mickey? Mickey? Oh! Why, no, Sheriff. He's at the school."

"At . . . the . . . school?" Dan said, very slowly. He blinked his eyes. Shook his head. Looked at Taylor. Silent cop talk. You take it!

"Mrs. Reynolds," Taylor said. "I'm Captain Taylor, Virginia State Police. You called the sheriff's office last night and reported your husband missing. Sheriff Garrett and I came over here this morning to talk to you. You were not at home. Your house had been ransacked. We thought there might have been a fight; some sort of trouble. We . . ."

Betty Reynolds opened the door wide. The men looked in. The home was immaculate. Neat as that

177

pin. Nothing out of place. She waved them inside.

Both men stood, too stunned to speak. Neither could quite believe their eyes.

Betty said, "You both must be mistaken. There's been no trouble here. My husband came in just after I called the sheriff's office. I'm so sorry I forgot to call you." She paused. She seemed to have trouble making her lower jaw stay in place. Her words were slurry. A bit of spittle oozed past her lips. "I've been shopping in Farmville all morning. Just got back about a half hour ago."

Dan sighed. He didn't know what to say. She was lying, sure, but? . . . Taylor said, "Do you, ah, mind if we look around?"

"Not at all, Captain."

The entire home was neat. No paintings or drawings on the walls. No broken glass or litter. The toaster was back on the counter.

With a huge dent in its side.

The back screen door had been repaired. But there was no glass in the once shattered kitchen window.

The men excused themselves and left.

When the front door closed, Betty picked up the phone and called the high school. She seemed to understand the gruntings from the other end of the line. More spittle oozed from her mouth. She grunted into the phone.

Had the men returned to the house and looked in, they would have seen Betty Reynolds and her kids, ages fourteen through eighteen, standing in the living room, holding hands and humming. Their cat sat on the TV, swaying back and forth to the humming.

The house was a mess, littered and trashy, the paintings and drawings very much in evidence on the walls.

When the front door closed behind the cops, the

toaster fell off the counter.

In the car, rolling toward the high school, Dan said, "She's lying."

"Hell, yes, she is. But why?"

"There is no way she could have straightened up that mess and removed all those drawings from the walls."

"But she did, Dan! They're gone."

"Were they really gone, Tay?"

"Old son, don't start with that. I'm goosy enough as is."

"All right, let's look at it like this: did we really see those drawings? Could it have been some sort of illusion? Or was what we just left some sort of illusion?"

Taylor shook his head. "What's next, Dan? Calling a priest to perform an exorcism?"

Dan forced a smile. "We might have to. I don't know of any Baptist preachers who would agree to it."

A devout Catholic, Taylor had a good laugh at just the mental picture of that.

"That was blood running down the the wall this morning," Taylor said. "Blood out of crayon."

"Yeah. I know."

Both men were then silent as they drove to the high school. Pulling into the lot, Dan said, "I don't see Mickey's car."

They parked and sat for a moment, staring at the empty building, neither of them liking the vibes they were receiving.

Dan picked up his mike and called in, giving his location. "Send backup and roll silent, please."

"Ten four, Ruger One. Rolling."

Taylor said, "One of these days, someone's going to come up with a code for a cop's hunch, huh?"

"I sure heard that."

179

The men got out and walked toward the high school. They tried the two double-doors in the front. Locked. Dan banged on the doors. Nothing. He looked through the glass of the doors. He could see only muted murkiness.

"I *don't* like the feeling I'm getting," Taylor said.

"Nor I. Let's wait for the backup."

The deputy's car rolled up, tires crunching on the gravel. Dan waved Bowie to a halt. "See if the back doors are unlocked. Call us if one of them is open. Look in, but don't go inside."

Bowie nodded and pulled around back.

"Your staff is young, Dan," Taylor observed.

"Yes. Most of them under thirty. I've been rebuilding since I took office. They're all good cops, though. Not a hotdog in the bunch."

"Ever have one of those?"

"Two of them in ten years. I fired both of them."

"I heard that."

Bowie got out of his car and walked up to one of the school's back doors. Locked. He tried the next one. The doorknob turned in his hand. He opened it wider and looked inside. He looked to the right. Nothing. The gym was empty and silent. He looked to his left.

And looked into the face of hell.

Finished with his finals, Mike sat in his car on campus and finished reading the last few pages of the old, dog-eared book. It was one of the few copies left in print on ancient religions. He'd had the book for several years, but had forgotten it. When he recalled it, he'd had to spend several hours in the attic of his parents' home searching for it.

The book had been published in the mid-1800's, in England. It had never been reissued because none of the stories in the book could be substantiated. Most religious experts and historians had scoffed at the book, ridiculing the writer, sending him into oblivion.

But shortly after the book was published, the author had been murdered. His body gnawed on, drained of blood. Cat tracks had been found in the blood around the half-eaten body.

"Shit!" Mike said, settling back in the seat and rereading the last story in the book. A chapter about a group called the Cat People. As he read, a cold, eerie feeling crept over him. Despite himself, he could not help but look up and glance around him.

"A child and a cat," he read aloud. "The girl and the cat are capable of changing forms, one into the other. They must survive on human flesh and blood. The bite is highly infectious, and can produce strange effects on humans, from rapid aging to a rabies-like condition. In times of great stress, the child, always named Anya, after a woman who supposedly mated with Satan, forming the religion, is thought to have the ability to call on Satan or one of his minions. The religion supposedly originated in Egypt but is rumored to be worldwide.

"Shiitt!" Mike said.

"What are you mumbling about?" Carl asked.

Mike jumped up, banging his head on the interior roof of the car. "Oww! Damn, you scared me."

Carl laughed at him.

"You all through with your finals?" Mike asked.

"Finished. What's wrong, Mike?"

"You mind some company at your house?"

"You know I don't. Mom and Dad are always glad to see you. Even if you do destroy Mom's food budget," he needled his friend.

Mike ignored the jab. He leaned over and opened the door on the passenger side. "Get in. I think I've

181

found what your dad is looking for."

"Do I have time to pack?"

"No."

Bowie recoiled in shock and horror and screamed as the dark-skinned, wrinkled-looking creature leaped at him, riding him down to the gym floor. He threw up his arm, shielding his face. Raw pain ripped through him as the thing's teeth tore great hunks of meat from the young deputy's right arm. Blood slicked the gym floor. With his good arm, his left one, Bowie managed to get his club out of the ring. He hammered at the head of the creature. Dark stinking blood leaped from the cuts on the man-like creature. What had once been Mickey howled in pain and rolled away from the deputy, strange gruntings coming from his mouth. Bowie rolled the other way, his left hand fumbling for his .357. Mickey staggered and lurched across the gym floor, slipping and sliding in his haste. Bowie fired, the pistol awkward in his left hand. He missed, the lead tearing up a section of the gym floor, the lead whining off. Mickey ducked beneath the bleachers.

Dan and Taylor were moving before the sounds of Bowie's screaming had echoed away. Together, the men kicked open the front doors of the school, running inside.

"The gym is in the back," Dan said. "That way." He pointed. "Bowie! Bowie! Sing out!"

"In the gym, Sheriff!" came the shout. "But Jesus God, be careful."

Taylor took one look at the bloody deputy and ran out the back to the deputy's car, radioing in for help and an ambulance. He jerked Bowie's shotgun out of the clamps on the front of the cage and ran back inside.

"Where'd he go, son?" Taylor asked.

"Under the bleachers, Captain."

"Hang on, boy. Help's on the way." Taylor quickly inspected Bowie's arm. Great hunks of meat were gone from the forearm. He could see the whiteness of bone. A pressure bandage would do no good. Using Bowie's belt, Taylor fixed a tourniquet, stopping the gushing of blood.

"That's against policy, Captain," Bowie joked. "Don't you know I'm liable to get me a slick lawyer and sue you for doing that?"

"I'll take my chances," Taylor said. "I'll say the devil made me do it."

Mickey had climbed up into the top of the bleachers, pushed open a crawlspace entrance, and was now making his way through the darkness, on his hands and knees, moving over the classrooms, toward the far end of the school.

"Was it Mickey Reynolds, son?" Taylor asked.

"I swear to you, Captain, I don't know what in the hell it was. It was a monster." The deputy's words ended with a low moan of pain. His arm was turning black, the skin wrinkling.

"Taylor?" Dan called.

"Yo!"

"Get on the horn. Tell the backups to surround the school."

"Right."

"Just like cowboys and Indians," Bowie said.

Mickey was scurrying like a rat through the darkness. He reached the far end of the building and kicked his way through the ceiling tile, dropping down into the science room. He opened a window and climbed out, running to the garage area. There, he caught his breath and raced for the creek that ran behind the school. He forced himself to wade through

183

the water, heading downstream, loathing every second the water touched his flesh. He angled toward the other side and carefully picked his way up the bank, staying in heavy brush, hiding his footprints. He disappeared into the back of a store in a small shopping center and crawled behind some boxes and crates.

There, he rested.

It was Chuck who first spotted the open window on the side of the school. He wheeled his car in close and jumped out, looking in through the window, spotting the hole in the ceiling. He yelled for Dan.

"He's out and runnin,' Dan," Chuck said. "Was it Mickey?"

Dan looked at the hole in the ceiling. "Damn! We don't know, Chuck. Bowie's going into shock. He's in bad shape. Arm all mangled."

"Bitten?"

"Yes."

"Oh, no!"

"Yeah. Goddamnit, Chuck, I've had it. Screw the OSS and Dodge and everybody concerned with this crap. This is getting too big and too ugly and too dangerous. No more coverups."

"No, Sheriff. We don't go public."

Dan and Chuck spun around. The man called Lou stood smiling at them. "We must not unduly alarm the citizens, gentlemen," he said.

"I'd like to see you stop me," Dan said. "Goddamn you, Lou—or whatever your name is—this crap has gone far enough."

"It's only just beginning, Sheriff," Lou said.

At that moment, none of the people involved could realize just how true the man's words were.

"That's your butt!" Dan popped.

Lou's smile never wavered. "That's an interesting

choice of words, Sheriff. We thought you might have a change of heart, being the public-spirited gentleman that you are." He reached into his pocket and pulled out a small gold chain with a tiny gold heart attached. "Recognize this, Sheriff?"

Dan lifted his eyes from the chain and heart. His eyes were filled with black hate and rage. "I'll kill you, Lou."

Lou laughed at him.

Chuck put out his hand, restraining Dan, as his eyes picked up the forms of half a dozen men moving closer. Lou's people.

"Easy, Dan. We're outgunned."

Dan stood and cursed the OSS man.

The gold chain and tiny heart belonged to Dan's daughter, Carrie.

"All we have to do is wait," Anya said. The cat looked at her, understanding. "The mortals have made things much easier for us. They have unknowingly released the Old Ones."

The cat stretched, arching its back. It seemed to smile. The cat padded to a window in the storage garage and looked out. Several dozen cats had gathered around the building. They lay resting and sleeping on the ground, dozing in the warmth of the sun.

"More are gathering?" Anya asked.

Pet looked at her, passing a silent message.

"Very good," Anya said. "When it is time, those who have interfered will learn the power of the cat. Right, Pet?"

Again, the cat seemed to smile. Turning back to the window, Pet yowled. The cats spread out, encircling the building. Some of them moved to the woods' edge, almost as if they were standing guard.

185

They were.

There were cats of all types and sizes and breeds. House cats to alley cats. Strays and pampered pets. But these would never again serve—as far as a cat ever serves—any human master. They had found another master.

Anya's eyes held a glow she had not experienced in hundreds of years. Her lips curved in a smile, a smile that was the very essence of wickedness. "I believe our being awakened was not simply a matter of fate, Pet. We were called. The human was an unwitting messenger. We were right in assuming the Old Ones were all about us."

Pet cocked her head. Her yellow eyes glowed.

Anya laughed. It was not the laugh of a young girl. The laughter held the pent-up evil of two thousand years.

17

"Relax, Sheriff," Lou said, his smile never leaving his lips. "Your little girl is just fine and dandy. She's at home, I believe. One of my people went into her bedroom last night and got this little bauble. I just wanted to show you how easy it would be—if it came to that. It doesn't have to; it's all up to you."

"Lou . . ." Dan sputtered, his rage just barely contained.

"Lamotta, Sheriff. Lou Lamotta."

"Sure, Lou. I'm sure that's your real name."

Lou shrugged. "It'll do, Sheriff. I've used it before."

Dan sized the man up. They were about the same age, but Lou was a mass of muscle. A big, solid, dark-complexioned man. Dark eyes that gave away nothing. Dan didn't think he could take the man with his hands. But he could goddamn sure shoot him.

Something flickered in Lou's eyes. "I wouldn't try it, Sheriff. It would be a stupid move."

"But a very delicious thought, Lamotta."

"You don't have the guts to do it, Sheriff. There's too much law and order in you."

"Don't put too much weight on that thought, Lamotta."

Lou nodded. His smile was gone. He, too, was sizing up the man in front of him. Lou reached the conclusion that Dan Garrett was harder than he at first thought.

"The thing in the school house?" Lou asked. "Was it Mickey Reynolds?"

"We don't know," Dan said. "The deputy's not sure what it was. It probably was Mickey." Damned if he was going to tell the man about the Reynolds' house. He was going to drag his feet whenever possible.

"Well, we have more problems, Sheriff. So I'll have your deputy taken out to our facilities. I say problems; if we can isolate and control it, we'll have the ultimate weapon."

"You idiot!" Dan flared. "You'll kill everyone in this county in search of a weapon that you thought might give you the upper hand over the Russians, wouldn't you, Lou?"

"Yes." He stepped closer. "Now you hear me out, Sheriff. You and your boys find this Reynolds character. And when you do, call us. You don't tell the people of this hick town a thing. Nothing. You know the drill, Sheriff. You keep your mouth shut. Tight! I've already talked with your deputies—most of them. I can nail two or three for income tax evasion. Don't make any difference whether it was deliberate, or not. Three of them are in some kind of military reserve or guard. I can have them jerked back in active so fast they won't know what hit them. And then it gets unpleasant for them. You want me to continue or do you get the message?"

Dan met the man's stony gaze. "I get the message," he said.

"Fine. I knew you were a reasonable man, Sheriff. But just let me add this one little thing. Don't screw up and talk to the press. 'Cause if you do, I'll take your daughter *and* your wife and pass them around to the boys." He grinned. "And the girls. I might even video tape it and play it back for you. And your son, Carl? He could very easily get picked up on a coke charge. Now do you copy all that?"

"Yeah." Dan popped back at him. "I sure do."

"Fine." Lou laughed aloud. "You're a real wimp, Sheriff. Now run along and do your little country hick sheriff bit."

Lou and his people stepped into the school and were soon out of earshot. Taylor walked up, joining Dan and the chief deputy.

"I heard it all, Dan," the trooper said. "I thought stuff like this only happened in the movies?"

"Strangely," Dan replied, "so did I."

"You think he means it?"

Before Dan could answer, Chuck said, "I do. I think he's just crazy enough to act sane. I think he'd do anything he felt had to be done. And I also think he'd enjoy doing it. He probably tortured little puppy dogs when he was a kid."

"And pulled the wings off little birds," Taylor added.

"Yeah."

Another deputy panted up. "We lost him, Sheriff. He went into the creek. We can't find out where he came out."

"Call Mr. Mathews. Get the dogs."

189

"Yes, sir. It'll be a couple hours before he can get here, though. Get everything lined out."

"All right. Get hold of him."

One of the older deputies, Jake, met Dan's eyes. "My oldest daughter is workin' up in Washington, Sheriff. You know. That damn Lou showed me a file on her. Told me if I don't cooperate, things could go hard for her. How in the hell can they move so quickly?"

"They're very powerful, Jake. He just threatened me, too. Threatened to rape my wife and daughter and frame my son."

"You goin' to stand still for it?"

"For the time being, Jake."

"Goddamnit, Sheriff! Is this America or Russia?"

Dan just shook his head. He really didn't know how to answer the man's question. He knew only this: he was going to get out from under the totalitarian rule of Lou and his OSS people. If he could, without risking the lives of his family.

Dan looked at Chuck. "He get to you, too, Chuck?"

"In a manner of speaking," the man said tersely.

And Dan knew that Lou had made a very vindictive and mean enemy in Chuck. Mountain born and reared, the wiry chief deputy grew up with the stories of blood feuds and shots in the night. Lou had made a very bad mistake in threatening Chuck.

Standing across the street from the high school, Pat Leonard watched all the police activity. A state trooper had just told him they thought they had the man responsible for all the murders cornered. But something nagged at Leonard; the trooper seemed evasive. He got the impression the man was trying to

190

tell him something. But what?

Pat was a small town newspaper owner and editor, but one with a lot of big city experience. Savvy. He had started out as a cub working the night beat in Richmond. From there he'd gone to Washington. Then spent ten years in New York City before returning home to take over the local paper after his dad died. Nobody had to tell Pat that things weren't as they seemed in Valentine. Too many local deputies with worried expressions. Too many strangers in town. And nobody in their right mind would reopen that old terminal. Too many debts against it; too far off the beaten path.

Pat didn't know what was really going on here in his little town and county. But he damn sure intended to find out.

He got into his car and drove out to the terminal. But he didn't make it that far. He was forced to stop at a new fence just off the highway. The road leading to the old truck terminal was effectively blocked. Too far off for pictures. He got out of his car and walked up to the gates.

"Can I help you, sir?" a guard asked.

Pat turned to look at the man. Where in the hell had he come from? And why would the man be wearing a pistol and one of those handy-talkies? What was so important about an old truck terminal?

"Just curious," Pat said. "The signs say this is government property."

"That's right."

"Housing a civilian trucking firm? HPB?"

"Also correct, as far as it goes. HPB is under contract to the government. The truckers who'll be pulling out of here work exclusively for Uncle."

191

"Hauling what?"

The man smiled. "I'm afraid that's classified, sir."

"Oh. Hush hush and all that, huh?"

"Just classified, sir."

"I see. Well, thanks for the information."

"You're certainly welcome, sir."

When Pat returned to his office, Lou was waiting for him.

"How's your deputy?" Taylor asked.

"Goodson says he's stable," Dan said. "But the man spoke in double talk. Like he was trying to tell me something. Trying to get me to read between the lines."

"Could you?"

"No. I couldn't make any sense out of it. And on top of that, the Reynolds family is gone. Mother and kids. I sent one of my men over there to pull them in for questioning and they're gone."

"Getting stranger and stranger," Taylor said. "Dan . . . what I'm about to ask . . . do you have any contacts left in Washington?"

"Like . . ."

"The CIA?"

Dan smiled. "Funny you should ask that, Tay. Yeah, I do. I'd like you to have one of your, ah, vacationing troopers get the gear and electronically sweep this office for bugs. I'd like that done just before I call. Can you arrange that?"

"Easy. I'll have it done first thing in the morning. Forbes is the wire expert."

"Fine. I'll call him after that's over." Dan looked up as Carl and Mike walked into the office. He

192

introduced them to Captain Taylor and waved the boys to a seat.

"What'd you characters do now, bust out of college?"

"Naw, Dad," Carl grinned.

"So what's up?"

"Strange things still happening here in Ruger, Mr. Garrett?" Mike asked.

"You could say that."

"Sheriff Garrett, do you believe in the devil?"

"Yes. I believe in heaven and hell, Mike."

"Captain Taylor?"

"Yes, son. I do."

Mike laid the worn old book on Dan's desk. "The last chapter in that book tells of a strange religion— stranger than the others detailed in there. Cats and kids and Satan." Mike related everything he had read about the Cat People. Then he leaned back in his chair and said, "The girl and the cat have to rest in twenty-five year cycles. If they're disturbed, well, all hell—literally—can break loose. Mike told me about the paper he did on the New York City murders. That was twenty years ago. Is there a connection?"

"Maybe," Dan said. He and Taylor exchanged glances. The trooper said, "It's a place to start, Dan. I'm about ready to believe anything."

"Has any of that stuff been verified?" Dan asked, pointing to the book.

"No, sir. But shortly after it was published, the author was killed. The body was partially eaten and the blood sucked from it. Small footprints and cat tracks were found in the blood."

Taylor sighed. "Maybe there is a connection."

"You boys through with finals?"

193

"Yes, sir," they both said.

"Carl, you and Mike go on home. Stay there. Keep an eye on your mother and sister. Don't let them out of your sight. Both of you are good shots. I know, I taught you. Carl, you get those M-one carbines out and load up the thirty round clips. Keep them handy."

"Dad? . . ."

"I'll explain when I get home. Thank you both for this information. Now take off and stay at the house."

The boys gone, Taylor looked at the old book on Dan's desk. For some reason he could not explain, he did not want to touch that book. "I don't want to believe it, Dan."

"Neither do I."

Dan stilled the ringing of the phone. He listened for a moment, then hung up after a terse, "Thanks."

"Denise Moore died a few minutes ago. That was one of the so-called doctors out at the terminal. He didn't tell me what she died of."

"You a praying man, Dan?"

"Not in a long time. You think prayer is the answer to this?"

"Damn sure wouldn't hurt."

Dan's intercom buzzed. "Dogs are ready, Sheriff."

"Okay."

"You going to autopsy?" Goodson asked.

"Not yet. I want to keep an eye on the deputy." He jerked a thumb toward the body of Denise. "She'll keep for a few hours."

The man left, closing the door to the cold room of the portable morgue. The body of Denise lay on a narrow table, the sheet covering her from the waist down. A peculiar humming filled the small room. Several of the jars and bottles began vibrating. Surgical gauze began unwinding and dropping to the floor. The sheet lifted from Denise's body and slowly slipped to the floor. Those areas on her body where the doctors had stitched suddenly opened, blood oozing out.

Denise opened her eyes.

BOOK TWO

Darkness, and worms, and shrouds, and sepulchers.
                                                    Keats

1

"I don't like to be threatened," Pat said, not backing up an inch from Lou.

"Why, I'm not threatening you," Lou replied, a look of innocence on his tanned face. "I haven't said a threatening word, have I?"

Pat's laugh was not pleasant-sounding. "Implying. Inferring."

"No, no, Mr. Leonard. Not at all. I'm just appealing to your sense of patriotism, that's all."

"Sure, sure. Come on! That's pure crap and you know it."

Lou smiled and pushed the desk phone closer to Pat. "Call your wife, Mr. Leonard. Every husband should be concerned about his spouse, don't you think?"

Pat's eyes narrowed. "What are you trying to say, you bastard?"

Personal insults rolled off Lou with the man taking no offense. He's been doing this type of work for years. Very little bothered him. Besides, Lou was crazy. Functionally insane. "Nothing, Pat. Nothing at all. Just call your darling little Sissy."

"How do you know my wife's name?"

"I know lots of things, Pat. I even know what size bra she wears." He laughed and stared at the newspaper editor.

"I guess," Pat said, "that somehow, you've gotten to Dan and his people. Maybe the state police, too. But you won't intimidate me. I'm calling the FBI and then I'm calling AP and alert them to this story."

Lou shrugged his shoulders. "Well, Mr. Leonard, I certainly won't try to physically stop you."

Pat caught the "physical" part of it. He picked up the phone.

Lou said, "Your wife still takes her shots every day, doesn't she, Pat?"

Pat paused, his finger poised over the dial. He lifted his eyes. "My wife is diabetic, yes."

"I'm curious, Pat. What would happen to her if she were to go, oh, say, four or five days without her shots? Would that cause her any difficulty?"

"You lousy—! You wouldn't do that?"

"Mr. Leonard," Lou's voice was low and soothing. "I have not said I was going to do *anything*. My, my, but you do have quite an active imagination, don't you? I merely asked a question, that's all."

Pat placed the phone back in the cradle. He sighed and nodded his head. "Very well. Okay, Mr? . . . "

"Lamotta. Lou Lamotta. Okay—what?"

Pat glared at the man. "What is it that you want from me, Mr. Lamotta?"

Lou's face brightened. He grinned hugely. "I just *knew* you were a true blue American, Pat. I knew that when I read that you're a veteran. I'm a veteran, too. We'll have to get together sometime and talk about the service. All right, Pat. Let's lay out the ground rules."

"Where in the goddamn hell have you been?" Mille

barked.

"Doin' what you sent me to New York to do!" Kenny said. "Jesus, Mille! I'm not Superman, you know?"

"What'd you find, Kenny?"

"Let me sit down and take a load off, Mille. Damn. I been on a flat out dead run ever since I pulled out of here."

Beer in hand, his ragged tennis shoes off, one big toe sticking through a hole in a very dirty sock, Kenny grinned. Like that famous cat.

Mille smiled back at him. "You got it, didn't you?"

Kenny pointed a finger at her and said, "Bingo, Mille-baby. We got the big one."

Dan thought the day would never end. Paul Moore had burst into his office, demanding and threatening and finally breaking down, sitting in a chair and crying like a baby, his face in his hands.

Dan never thought he'd ever feel sorry for Paul Moore—rich, arrogant, pompous, and almost always totally obnoxious. But for a moment, he did feel sorry for the man.

Then Moore had shattered the momentary emotion by lifting his head and roaring, "I'll have your job! I pay your salary, you know? You and all the rest of these losers you have wearing badges. Now where is my daughter?"

Dan had shown him the way out of his office.

Mathews' dogs had been less than useful. They could turn up nothing. They had acted confused and frightened. Unable to track. And for some reason, they were very leery of cats. And one deputy had commented that he could not remember ever seeing so many cats.

The long day finally ended, much to the relief of the day shift of deputies. Taylor said he was going back to the motel, take a long, hot shower, have a quiet supper, and go to bed. "Boss must be gettin' old," Trooper Collins said to Trooper Lewis.

Luckily, Taylor had not heard the comment.

Driving home, Dan noticed but did not pay any particular attention to the large numbers of cats wandering the countryside. No one really paid much attention to the growing number of felines. Yet.

Vonne met Dan on the front porch of their home. She was angry, and made that very clear at once. "I've been trying to reach you by phone all afternoon, Dan. I want some answers and by *God*, I want them now. What the hell's the idea of sending those boys home with orders to arm themselves and guard *me*?"

Dan raised his hands in surrender. "Can I please get inside and have a beer? Please? I'm going to level with you all. But, Jesus, Vonne, give me a break, will you?"

The boys had taken Dan very seriously. Both his military carbines were loaded up and leaning against a wall in the den. Both Carl and Mike had pistols close by them.

Dan removed his hat and tossed it on the rack. "Carl, get me a beer, will you? And get one for yourself and Mike, too. I know you boys drink, so you might as well drink in front of me."

"And fix me a bourbon and water," Vonne said.

Dan looked at his wife, surprise in his eyes. "Is it New Years' Eve?"

"What do I get to drink?" Carrie asked.

"Iced tea," her mother settled that quickly.

"I'm not a child," Carrie said.

And that prompted Dan to change his mind about excluding Carrie from the conversation. He had

202

thought about doing that; but Lou had mentioned his daughter, so she certainly had a right to know.

He sat them all down in the den, fully aware that his house might well be bugged, and took it from the top, leaving nothing out. When he had finished, he popped open another beer and leaned back in his chair. He looked at his family—they all thought of Mike as family. "That's it, gang. All of it."

Dan looked first at Carrie. The girl was uncertain whether to smile or look serious. She wasn't at all sure if her dad was putting her on, or not.

"It's all true, Carrie," Dan said. "Don't doubt it for an instant. From now on, you don't leave this house without my permission, or unless you're accompanied by your mother, your brother, or Mike. Is that clear?"

"Yes, sir. What about Linda? She's going to come over tomorrow and spend a few days with me. Her parents are going out of town."

"I'll talk to her." He looked at his wife. "From now on, lady, you go armed. At all times. You're as good a shot as any woman in this county. With the exception of Susan Dodd, perhaps. You put that .380 in your purse loaded full. And you bear in mind the lawman's motto: I'd rather be judged by twelve than carried by six. All right?"

She laughed at him. "You're *serious*! Come on, Dan. It's stopped being funny."

"Funny!" Dan roared, losing his temper. "God-*damnit*, Vonne. Do you think this is some sort of a stupid *joke*?"

Carrie's eyes widened. Daddy just didn't talk to Mother like that.

"Don't you yell at me like that!" Vonne flared.

"My word!" Mike said.

Carl wisely kept his mouth shut.

Dan gripped the arms of his easy chair. He took several deep breaths, calming himself. "Listen to me—all of you. You are all in danger. From all directions. Lou Lamotta is a psycho. A fanatic. I can't stress that enough. He would do anything—*anything*—to keep the lid on this . . . this matter. I don't want to turn you all into a bunch of paranoids, but you've got to exercise caution from now on. Mickey Reynolds is loose and running; he's changed into some sort of . . . of monster. That's the only word I can use to describe him. And only two . . . beings know what else is out there," he waved his hand, "prowling the countryside."

"Two beings, Dan?" Vonne questioned, her voice small as the full impact of what her husband was saying struck home.

"Two beings, Daddy?" Carrie echoed. "Who are they?"

Dan's eyes briefly touched each person in the room. "God and Satan."

Wednesday.

Dan awakened early, before dawn, and as quietly as possible, showered and shaved and dressed. He unlocked the door to his steel gun cabinet and took out a half dozen ingram M-10's and a box of extra clips for each mini-submachine gun. The clips held thirty .45 caliber rounds. He turned around at a slight noise behind him.

"Getting that serious, Dad?" Carl asked, eyeballing the armament.

"Yes, I think so, son. Help me carry this stuff out to the car, will you?"

Outside, the sun just breaking over the rolling

204

Virginia hills, father and son stood by Dan's prowl car and chatted.

"This OSS bunch kind of has you in a bind, don't they?"

"Yes," Dan said. "But I've got an idea how to loosen the knots."

Carl didn't push. His dad would tell him in time.

Dan looked around him. "I always wanted a place in the country. But now I wish I'd bought closer to town. We're damn near isolated out here."

"We'll take care of things out here, Dad," the son assured him. "There is no backup at all like Mike. You remember what happened when he was fifteen, don't you?"

Dan nodded. A gang of thugs and street slime had broken into the Pearson mansion outside the city. They had terrorized Mike's mother and grandmother. The fifteen year old Mike had slipped into the mansion through a back door, got a shotgun, and loaded it up with three inch magnums. He killed two of the punks, spreading them all over the den, badly wounding two more.

He then had taken the empty shotgun and beat in the head of the fifth punk. The punk with the fractured skull had found a bleeding heart lawyer and sued the Pearson family for damages. And won.

"He made believers of that bunch, didn't he, boy?" The fact that the street crud had collected damages still left a sour taste in Dan's mouth.

"He sure did, Dad. We'll handle things here at home. Put that worry out of your mind."

"If it gets down to it, son, don't hesitate. Don't play like it's the movies. Just pull the trigger and blow the jerk away. Aim between the neck and the waist and pull the trigger. You're a cop's kid, boy, and you're going to be a good cop. But you're not a cop yet, so you don't have any of the cop's restrictions." He squeezed his son's shoulder. "I'm depending on you, Carl. And I know you'll do what you have to do. Head's up, now, boy."

"Yes, sir."

Forbes was at the office when Dan arrived. He had been working for several hours. He had checked all outside terminals. He had taken apart all the office phones and declared them secure. He had then electronically swept the offices. They were clean.

"Of course," he reminded Dan, "someone might have a long range mike pointed at this office. If that's the case, there is very little you can do about it."

"You're such a comfort to me, Forbes," Dan had said with a grin.

"I know, sir," the young trooper said, returning Dan's grin. "Ain't life hell?"

Captain Taylor and Chuck arrived at the office together. Dan passed out the M-10's, keeping one for himself. Taylor declined the little spitter, saying he'd stay with his model 1100 Remington. It was his personal shotgun, and with the extender tube, carried nine three inch magnums. Dan checked with the night watch; nothing new to report. Taylor, Chuck, and Dan sat in Dan's office, drinking coffee and chatting until nine o'clock. Dan placed the call to his friend at CIA.

After going through several people, Dan finally got his friend on the line. "Gordon? Dan Garrett here."

"Dan? Good Lord! A voice from the past. You still wearing your cowboy boots and tin star?"

"Nope."

"No?"

"Gold star."

"Oh, excuse me! Hey, old buddy! What's going on with you?"

"Is your phone clear, Gordon?"

A short pause. "It is now. I gather this is not a purely social call, right?"

"I wish it were. I won't stall around, Gordon. What do you know about the Office of Special Studies?"

The pause was a bit longer. "Tell me you don't have that bunch in your area?"

" 'Fraid I can't do that, Gordon. I'm up to my neck with them."

"I hate to hear that, Buddy. I really do. Okay. The OSS. Well, they're legit. More civilian but with a lot of government mixed in. Powerful, powerful, old friend. A lot of senators and representatives back what they do—in a quiet sort of way. If you know what I mean, and you do. Let me make this as uncomplicated as possible. You remember The Team? Well, after that Utah mess up, the name was changed to Code Blue. Then to the OSS. You with me?"

"I'm with you."

"That's about it, buddy. They keep a very, very low profile. They're into a lot of legit businesses, and they make profits out of them to keep going. That plus a lot of, ah, well-meaning but badly misinformed Red haters kicking in big bucks. Lou Lamotta still with them?"

"Yeah."

"He's crazy, Dan. A real honest to God psycho. But he's so good at what he does, they'll put up with his kinkiness in exchange for his expertise. The man is a human computer. His recall ability is truly astounding. What are they doing down there, Dan?"

"You got a seat belt on your chair, Gordon?"

"For years, pal."

Dan spoke for several minutes, taking it from the top, leaving nothing out. When he had brought his CIA friend up to date, Gordon was silent for a full ten count.

Then the man started laughing. "Come on, Dan. You really had me going for a couple of minutes. Mack put you up to this didn't he? It's my birthday. This is the wildest birthday present I've ever had. Come on, 'fess up, Dan."

"I'm telling you the truth, Gordon."

The pause grew longer. When Gordon again spoke, his voice was no more than a whisper, with Dan straining to hear. "The truth? You're not putting me on? Mack really didn't put you up to this?"

"I haven't seen Mack in years, Gordon. I don't even know where he is. Gordon, I need some help on this. I can't fight the OSS with what I have. They've gotten to some people in very high places in this state. I need help bad."

"Jesus Christ, Dan! I thought . . . I mean . . . Dan, what can I do? If just ten percent of what you told me is true, man, we're talking heavy, heavy stuff. If just a word of the OSS being there leaks out, you're going to have Russian agents crawling all over your little county. They'll be coming in there as fishermen, tourists, truck drivers, backpackers—you name it."

"It's all true, Gordon. Every word of it. Who can you trust in the Agency?"

"Oh, those days are over, Dan. Wait a sec. Just hold what you got. Personally, I'd like to put that lousy OSS all the way out of business. Everybody thinks we're behind it. Gives us a bad name. Can you stay put for fifteen minutes?"

"I'll be right here." He gave the man his office number.

"All right. I'll call you back. You're sure your office

208

and phone is clear?"

"I just had an expert from the Virginia State Police sweep it."

"I'll call you back in fifteen minutes. Twenty tops."

"I'll be here." Dan hung up and looked at Taylor. "We might have some help on the way."

"Man, I hope so."

Chuck grimaced and said, "Oh, no! There's that damn libber again. I thought we were through with her."

Dan looked up. Mille Smith was standing outside his office, looking at him through the glass. The young man by her side was the freakiest looking individual Dan had seen since the hippie heyday.

2

Doctor Reed thought Bennett had placed the body of Denise in cold storage. Bennett thought Doctor Roberts had stowed away the body. Goodson thought Doctor Avery had slid her into the cold box. All of them were far too busy trying to save the life of Deputy Bowie to give the dead girl a second thought.

Bowie was showing signs of going the same route as the mummy-man. Goodson was quietly but frantically studying sample after sample of skin tissue, trying to find some way, some drug, some*thing*, to reverse the aging process. Nothing was working. Nothing. He threw down his pen in disgust and rubbed his tired eyes. Nothing made any sense. Mickey had attacked both the girl and the deputy. One contracted a rabies-like condition, the other showed no signs of rabies, but instead had begun aging like the engineer, who was attacked by . . . what? Or whom?

That was the key, of course. Very unprofessionally, Goodson muttered, "We're wasting our time until we find the initial attackers. They're the carriers. They've got to be found."

He left the lab and walked into the small intensive care unit. The OSS doctors were standing around Bowie's bed, none of them knowing what to do or try next. "I'm going to take some more samples from the girl," Goodson told Bennett. "So far I'm drawing a blank."

Bennett pulled out the first drawer of cold storage. Nothing. He tried the other three. Same thing. Empty except for the bag containing some remains of Nick Hardy. Goodson walked over to the fourth trailer, which had been pressed into service after Al the engineer refused to die—astounding them all— and looked in on Al. The poor mummy-like man was in leather restraints, secured to his bed. Al rolled his eyes and looked at Goodson. He began speaking in a strange tongue. Almost a pleading tone in his voice.

"If I knew how to put you out of your misery," Goodson said. "I would."

The mummy's brain, heart, and other vital organs had suffered horrible damage from the slugs and buckshot from the police. Then it had begun repairing itself. The doctors could but stand and look in disbelief. The creature had sustained what should have been a dozen fatal hits. But it simply would not die.

Goodson walked to the bed and looked at what had once been productive human life. "What are you?" he asked. "What in God's name has happened to you?"

The mummy-man began speaking to Goodson. The doctor recognized the words as Arabic, but it had to be ancient Arabic.

And Goodson knew from reading the profile on Al that the man had never studied languages or been outside the continental United States.

Everything about the man was impossible. It flew in the face of science.

Could another being be inside the man? Something . . . something from the nether world?

Goodson shook those thoughts away. He didn't know what to believe or think or . . .

Goodson looked at the guard when leaving and said, "What would you do if the creature broke loose, son?"

"I really don't know, sir," the guard replied honestly.

"I see." Goodson looked at the man's sidearm. "Well, Diogenes would not have been totally disappointed had he come here."

The guard blinked. "Sir?"

Goodson shook his head. "Nothing, son. Just the babblings of an old man." He walked away and conducted a thorough search of all the trailers. Irritated, he walked back to the main unit.

"What have you done with the girl?" he asked Bennett.

"The Moore girl?"

"Yes."

"She's in the cold room."

"No, she is not," Goodson said.

Bennett looked at Roberts. "Didn't you put her in the vault?"

"No. I thought you did."

"Are you sure she's missing?" Bennett asked Goodson.

"Goddamnit, man! I'm not in the habit of confusing the living with the dead. Of course, I'm certain."

Fear touched Bennett's eyes, disappearing as swiftly as it came. "Well, she couldn't have *walked* out of here."

Goodson met his eyes. "I wouldn't bet on it," he

said.

"Game time is all over, Sheriff," Mille said with a smirk. "I'm going to lift the lid off your slimy little coverup and blow you out of the water."

"Oh, Ms. Smith? That's interesting. Where did you get the idea we were covering up anything?"

"Don't insult my intelligence and I won't insult yours, Sheriff."

"All right, Ms. Smith. You seem to have the floor. So proceed."

Mille looked at her notepad. "In 1965, Sheriff, in New York City, there was a rash of murders. Same M.O. as what's been occurring in Ruger County. In 1940, the same thing occurred in New Orleans. Same M.O. In 1915, it happened in St. Louis. Same M.O. It was 1890 in Boston. Same M.O. In 1865, in England. Same M.O. Are you going to sit there and tell me that you and the rest of the cops were not aware of that?"

Dan did a little work on his adding machine. "Twenty five year difference in all those dates, Ms. Smith. Twenty year difference in '65 and '85. How do you account for that?" Dan recalled Mike's words. Was it possible? Had the rest cycle been disturbed? Was the religion real after all? What were they dealing with here in Ruger?

"I don't know," Mille said. "But there are too many similarities to be coincidence."

"You may be right, Ms. Smith," Dan surprised her by saying. "But, no, I was not aware of all those murders." Dan was doing some fast thinking and stalling. Gordon was due to call back at any moment. And as much as he disliked Ms. Mille Smith, he would not have consider handing her over to Lou

213

Lamotta.

Maybe there was another way? Dan had run her. He knew from the computer printouts about her brother. He knew the young woman was mentally warped when it came to her thinking about police officers. Dan was anything but a fool. He knew there were a lot of rogue cops in the U.S. And he had never adopted the attitude that so many cops form: that everyone is guilty and must be proved innocent. He did not practice nor tolerate a double-standard of justice. No person was above the law. The wealthy of Ruger County had not supported Dan's bid for sheriff. Never had. They knew the man would come down as hard on them as he did on anyone else. And did just that.

No, the average man and woman had put Dan in office, and were keeping him in office. And that was the overriding reason this coverup rankled Dan so.

He lifted his eyes and looked at Mille. "I'll make a deal with you, Ms. Smith."

She recoiled as if hit with a stun gun. "I'd sooner make a deal with the devil!"

Dan smiled without mirth. "That . . . might be closer to the truth than you realize, Ms. Smith."

"What?"

"I want you to sit on this story, Ms. Smith. In return, and I'll put it in writing, I will give you first shot when it's time to break the news."

She shook her head. "I don't believe you, Sheriff. You're lying."

"No, Ms. Smith. I'm trying to level with you. I've got ten thousand men, women, and kids in this county to worry about. Ten thousand reasons to make a deal with you."

Mille cocked her head, staring at the man, trying to visually find a chink in his armor. "You'll give me

214

exclusive interviews, and that is including yourself?"

"Yes."

"How long do I sit on it?"

"That, I can't say for sure. But I don't think it's going to be a very long wait."

Mille stared at Dan for a long half minute. Finally she said, "I want you to level with me, Sheriff." Something about this hick cop struck a responsive chord deep within her. The man sounded so sincere. Big ol' basset hound eyes. Crap! Mille would never admit it aloud, but she had run up on one or two pretty decent cops in her life. Well, maybe three or four. "You tell me the whole story. The truth—all of it. In return . . . sort of a guarantee, I guess you could call it . . . insurance . . . you can write up an arrest warrant against Kenny and me. We'll sign it. You can say . . ." She sighed. She reached into her purse and tossed a small bottle on Dan's desk. "That's full of coke. Give him yours, Kenny."

Kenny looked like he was about to shit. But he did as Mille instructed, tossing a similar container onto Dan's desk.

Dan smiled and shook his head. He looked at the bottles of white powder. A lot of lines in those bottles, he thought. Why do they do it? he asked himself the age-old question that straight cops have asked for years. Young and successful and they want to ruin their lives. He shrugged it off and pushed the bottles back to the young woman and man. He stuck out his hand.

"We've got to have some trust in this, Ms. Smith. You'll understand why I say that after you learn everything that's going down. But right now, I would like for you to go with Captain Taylor." Seeing the sudden suspicion on her face Dan quickly said, "It's not what you think. I'm expecting a phone call from a

215

friend. In government. Federal government. He may agree to help us on this matter. If he does, he'll be putting his job, his career, up for grabs, and possibly be facing a prison sentence just for helping us. Not to mention putting his life on the line."

The suspicion faded from her face. She said, "Has to be someone in the CIA. Super spook."

Very quick, Dan noted. She's smart as hell. Without changing expression, he said, "Captain Taylor will lay it all out for you. Then when I'm free, you can ask me any questions you like. Deal?"

She shook his hand. "Deal, Sheriff."

Chuck looked very dubious about the whole thing.

Kenny looked at the chief deputy and inwardly shuddered in disbelief. The deputy looked . . . *freaky!*

Denise stood naked in the woods outside the terminal compound fence. She looked down at the yellow cat which sat at her feet. The cat rose and walked away. Denise followed. The sharp briars that grabbed her bare feet and calves did not bother her. She was long past feeling any pain. Birds flew away at her approach. Squirrels and other woods animals remained motionless in their hiding places until she passed. She never blinked her eyes. They stared straight ahead. Her eyes were a curious shade of yellow.

Denise walked through the woods until a very faint bubbling sound reached her. She turned toward the source, following the putrid smell that wafted from the ground.

A small pool of liquid had appeared in the ground. She knelt down beside it and drank deeply from the hand-sized bubbling pool, the cat beside her, lapping at the foul-smelling liquid.

When they had drunk their fill, Denise and the cat rested for a time by the pool.

Eddie Brown had cautiously made his way into town during the night. He now lay in the dusty darkness of a church basement. A cat sat on a boxful of old worn church hymnals. The pair waited.

For the call.

Mickey Reynolds had moved from the shopping center back to the school. Some primitive sense of survival had told him the school would be the safest place. The hunters would not likely look for him there. Not again. He made his way to the basement of the school, crawling behind some boxes and crates. He looked up through the darkness. A cat sat on a box, looking back at him.

They waited.

Alice Ramsey and Emily Harrison sat in Alice's lovely home, drinking coffee.

"Do you have any idea what in the world is going on?" Alice asked.

"Only that it has something to do with the reopening of that old truck terminal outside of town."

"Something, well, very strange is going on. Quinn actually snapped at me this morning when I asked him about his . . . abnormal behavior of late. He's never, ever, done that before."

"You have any binoculars, Alice?"

"Why . . . yes. Quinn does. Of course. What? . . ." Her face brightened. "Oh, yes, I see. Do you?"

"Yes."

Alice looked at her watch. "We'll have to change into outdoorsy clothing. I'll meet you back here in an hour, all right?"

"I'll be here."

"Here's what I can do, Dan," Gordon said. "I've been authorized to take a short leave. Short, depending on how long it takes to wrap this up. Give me an hour to pack some things, and I'll be on the road heading for your location. I'll be bringing a female operative with me. June Pletcher. I have to stress this, Dan: we have no official power. None. You know the rules. Lamotta doesn't know either of us. We're coming in as IRS field agents." He laughed. "If Lamotta does check us out, he'll find that it holds up. We've worked that angle before stateside."

Dan smiled. He knew that a certain section of the CIA paid about as much attention to the law forbidding their work inside the borders of the U.S. as a hog does to table manners. "Shame on you, Gordon."

"I know, buddy. I pray for guidance every night before bedtime. See you mid-afternoon." He hung up.

Dan felt a slight sense of relief. Gordon would be coming in under specific orders. If there was a possible way to end the power-play by the OSS, Gordon would find it and do it. And if it had to be concluded with gunplay, that was fine with Gordon.

Dan motioned for Taylor, Mille, and Kenny to come inside his office. When they were seated, Dan looked at the young woman.

"You've been briefed?"

"Yes."

"Now you see why we're sitting on this thing,

218

Mille?"

Mille sighed. She looked at Taylor, then lifted her eyes as Chuck entered the room. "Is this on the level, Sheriff? I just can't believe you people are serious. I mean, I can't believe any of this."

Dan shrugged his shoulders. "Believe this, Mille: I wish it was all a bad dream. Unfortunately, I can't show you the pictures we took of the victims. The OSS stole them out of this office."

Mille's smile was as thin as weak ice. "You mean the brotherhood of the badge was violated?"

Taylor grunted. "Lamotta is no cop, girl. I don't know what exactly what he is."

Dan said, "Let me stress this, Mille: don't get crossways with Lamotta." He looked at Kenny. "Either of you. The man is a psycho. He's vicious." He told them about Lou's threats. "See what I mean?"

"I've been trying to tell people that stuff like this goes on," Mille said. "Nobody wants to believe me."

"It doesn't go on very often, Mille," Dan said. "And we're all trying to end the abuse of power. I may have found a way. I'll know in a couple of days."

"Sheriff, go public with it," she urged. "It's simple."

"I can't do that, Mille. Not yet."

She opened her mouth to protest and Kenny said, "Shut up, Mille. It fits. It's beginning to jell. I'm thinking about that deal we stumbled into about five years ago. We were just out of college—you remember?" She nodded. "What was the name we uncovered? Yeah. Code Blue, I think. Something like that."

She looked at Dan. He said, "Same bunch, Mille. Different name."

"Monsters, Sheriff?" she questioned.

"That's the only word I can think of for what we've all seen."

Mille stood up. "We're going to prowl some, Sheriff. If we discover anything—anything at all—we'll call you. That's a promise."

"I would appreciate it, Ms. Smith."

"Mille," she said with a smile.

"Mille," Dan said with a smile. And a very uneasy alliance was formed.

Chuck, looking at Kenny, still looked very dubious about the entire matter.

Kenny, looking at Chuck, wondered how anyone could look so . . . *straight*?

The teenagers strolled through the woods not far from the truck terminal. A tiny creek lay to their left. Two boys, two girls. The boys were seniors in high school, the girls juniors. None of them believed any of the stories being whispered around town. All that barf about monsters. Everybody knew that cops were stupid; they probably made up all that garbage 'cause they were so dumb they couldn't catch the real killers. All the kids were having a big laugh about it.

The four kids shared a very vulgar vocalizing about what Denise and Reynolds might be doing, together, at that very moment.

Who would have thought it? Been lots of jokes about that, too.

"Reckon how long she's been giving it to him?" one wondered aloud.

They all laughed.

The young people had not noticed the flitting shadows that seemed to be trailing them as they ambled along. The small quick shadows were all around them. In front, in back, on both sides.

And more were gathering, gradually tightening the loose circle around the strolling quartet.

The kids were having a good time, enjoying their unexpected break from school. Their parents didn't believe there were any monsters about the county. So, heck, let the kids wander a bit. Nothing's going to happen.

Uh-huh.

Had the kids been a bit more observant, they might have noticed the flitting shapes following them, pacing them, gathering numbers. But that would have only heightened their fear, lengthening the fear period. There was no escape for the teenagers.

No one really knows the cat population in America. Some conservative guesses put it in the millions.

"I heard we're not even going to have finals this year," one of the girls said. "Really!"

"Boy, that'd be great."

"No, I'm serious. They're just going to average out our grades and that'll be that."

"Failed again," a boy said glumly.

Young laughter in the woods and rolling hills. Very soon it would be stilled. Forever.

They walked further away from the fence line. One of the boys thought he heard a faint bubbling sound, accompanied by a very foul odor. The wind changed. The bubbling sound and putrid odor faded.

"That's not what I heard," he said. "I heard when the killers—the *monsters*!—are caught, back to school we go."

"Great," a girl said, "there goes my summer job."

"Aw, maybe not. Depends on when they catch the guys who done it."

"I thought it was monsters?"

More young laughter.

The older of the boys stopped, holding up his hand

221

for the others to stop.

"What's wrong?"

He shook his head. "I don't know. Weird. Listen. I don't hear nothing."

"Hear what? There isn't anything to hear."

"That's what I mean. There's nothing. A few minutes ago, all the birds were singing. Now it's just . . . it's just dead quiet."

"So what?" a girl demanded. "Just means we scared them off, is all. Right?" She looked around her as something caught her eye. Something was moving through the trees. Then the movement stopped. "Something is kinda weird around here," she said.

"Year," the boy said. "That's what I mean." He looked around him. He saw the cats, sitting patiently, motionlessly, watching them. Fear touched the boy, lightly at first; why be afraid of a cat? Ten cats. Jesus Christ, he thought, his eyes shifting rapidly. There must be three or four hundred cats. Never seen so many cats. What are they doing? What do they want?

The cats began swishing their tails, looking at each other, as if seeking some silent signal.

To do what? the boy thought.

"Good Lord!" a girl said, pointing. "Look at all the cats."

The kids stood in silence, looking at the silent cats, looking at them.

"Aww," the second girl said. "That's Nanny." She pointed. "That's my neighbor's cat." She knelt down. "Come here, Nanny," she called. "Come on, Nanny. Here, kitty, kitty, kitty."

The big house cat slowly and majestically rose to all four paws. It blinked at the sound of the voice. It stretched, arching its back. It padded softly to the girl, never taking its eyes from her face.

The cat's tongue flicked in and out.

"You see!" the girl said. "You guys are all chicken. Come on, Nanny."

The cat drew closer.

"Hi, Nanny!"

Nanny leaped, snarling and spitting and howling. Its sharp teeth bit all the way through the girl's lower lip. Blood spurted. The other cats began moving, hissing and howling and running toward the kids. Nanny's claws were flashing. One paw, claws extended, caught the girl in the eye, ripping the eyeball from the socket. The girl screamed and rolled on the ground.

The scent of fear and blood filled the warm air. The cats, hundreds of them, moved as one being, the blood-scent arousing them, flinging them back in time, back to when they were pets of no human, masters of all their territory, feared hunters.

The cats leaped on the teenagers, claws and teeth ripping and tearing. Some covered the head, quick claws tearing great, long strips of meat from the face.

The first girl to be attacked, now with both eyes torn from her face, rolled and screamed in agony on the ground. One of the boys ran to help her. Fifty cats rode him to the ground, their teeth and claws ripping and shredding the warm human flesh. While some tore at the meat, others lapped at the salty blood springing forth.

One of the young men was in the last trembling throes of death, his legs jerking as life left him, the cats tearing at his throat.

One girl, shock releasing her from her frozen fear, tried to run from the savage attack. Too frightened to scream her horror at the bloody and unexpected assault, she wheeled and ran. But the cats soon brought her down, kicking and wailing, the girl finally finding her voice. The short chase only heightened the cats' delight and appetite. What fun is prey without a chase? Boring. This was fun. This was the way it used to be, that thought was in the felines' minds. This is the way it will continue to be. For it had been promised them.

The screaming stopped. Young life was over. The cats slopped through the gore and blood, licking their chops, stretching, then bending their heads to dine again. Like a chicken-killing dog; a coyote who brings down a family pet; a bear who savored his first taste of human flesh, these cats would never again be content with food from a sack or can. They had now tasted the warm flavor of fresh human meat and blood.

They were once more hunters. They were once more feared and respected. The way had been shown to them.

And all over the country, the packs were forming.

3

"We might have a small problem, Sheriff," Lou's voice came down the line, into Dan's ear.

"Now what?" Dan asked, waving for Taylor to pick up the extension. The trooper did, very carefully. He nodded at Dan.

"The Moore girl is gone."

"*Gone?* Would you mind explaining that, Lou?"

"Yeah. Gone. Like in she ain't here."

Sheriff and trooper exchanged looks. "Well, what the hell did you people do with her?"

"Well, Sheriff, we didn't do anything with her. We, ah, kind of think—" He sighed. "—that she might have walked out of here."

Taylor sat down heavily at that news. His eyes expressed his shock.

Dan said, "Lou, Denise is *dead*!"

"No, she ain't, Sheriff. She's just like the mummy-man, alive."

Captain Taylor crossed himself.

"Lamotta? . . ."

Lou's voice hardened. "Don't start with your civic speech, Sheriff. Now more than ever we have to keep a lid on this thing. You and your boys find her, Sheriff.

My people are spread too thin as it is. You find her, Sheriff. Just do it. And keep your mouth shut about it."

He hung up.

"Spread too thin," Dan said. Before he could give that any further mental working, he glanced at Taylor. The man's face was pale. Not from fear, Dan knew, but from shock. He didn't think the captain was afraid of anything.

Taylor said, "Dan, how do you kill something that is . . . that is already dead?"

Dan shook his head. "Dead people don't come back to life through any . . . scientific means."

Taylor looked puzzled for a moment. "What are you saying, Dan?"

"You remember when we talked about seeing a priest?"

"Yes."

"Maybe it's time for us to include the religious community in this."

"This is the ickiest place I have ever seen," Alice complained. Cockleburrs had gathered on her jeans legs, a branch had just popped back and swatted her across the face, she had chiggers working at her ankles, and she could swear she was covered with fleas.

Alice just was not the outdoorsy type.

She had packed enough gear to go on an extended safari. In a rucksack, she carried half a dozen sandwiches—with the crust trimmed, of course—a bottle of water, suntan lotion, insect repellent, a book describing poisonous plants and poisonous snakes indigenous to Virginia, a small portable radio, an address book, her binoculars, a small first-aid kit, a flash-

226

light, extra batteries, pad and pencil, extra socks, and various other articles she felt might be useful when wandering about the wilderness. Including a roll of toilet paper. Scented, of course.

As it would turn out, Alice had planned well, even though the women were a few miles outside of Valentine and about fifteen hundred feet off the main highway.

Emily carried only a .22 caliber automatic pistol in a holster, and two extra clips for the weapon.

"Do you really know how to shoot that thing?" Alice asked.

"You bet your butt I do," Emily replied.

Alice suppressed a giggle. It was such fun being naughty.

The women walked deeper into the timber. They would occasionally catch a glimpse of the chain link fence surrounding the terminal grounds. They could see, in many places, where the old fence had been repaired. Warning signs gleamed brightly on the fence every hundred yards or so. They followed the timberline for a few moments, losing sight of the fence.

Alice stopped, looking around her. "Oh, Lord!" she wailed. "We're *lost*!"

"Oh, hell, Alice," Emily said, pointing. "The power lines are right there. They were to our right coming in here. Just keep that in mind."

"Emily, you are so . . . so *woodsy*."

Emily didn't quite know how to take that. "Alice, weren't you ever in the Girl Scouts?"

Alice looked horrified. "Heavens, no!"

"Stupid question," Emily muttered. "Figures."

"I was in the dance." Pronounced daunce.

"That's good, Alice. Great."

"What activities did you engage in as a child, Emily?"

227

Emily hid a grin. "Well, down on the farm we used to get a kick out of watching the bulls do it to the cows."

Alice was silent for an unusually long time.

"We had rabbits, too," Emily said.

"That's . . . nice."

Then, a long forgotten but somehow familiar odor drifted to Emily. She held up a hand. "Hold up, Alice. You smell that?"

Alice sniffed daintily. She held a hanky to her nose. "Yukk! What is that?"

"Blood, Alice. Lots of blood." Emily had worked too many accidents not to know that smell. "Come on."

Alice pulled back. "Where are we going, dear?"

"To see what is causing that smell."

"You go, dear. I'll just rest here for a moment."

"There are bears in these woods."

Alice could move very swiftly when she set her mind to it. "I'm ready whenever you are, Emily." She looked around her for grizzlies.

"I thought that might move you. Turn *loose* of me, Alice."

The women made their way slowly through the brush, the odor becoming stronger. Death, Emily thought. Human death. The human body emits an odor all its own at violent death.

Something felt squishy under Emily's tennis shoe. She looked down.

She was standing on a length of human intestine.

She lifted her eyes and saw the carnage that lay before them. Half eaten bodies, the stomach cavity all chewed out, the faces gone, exposing the whiteness of skull. Yards of intestines. Hearts and lungs and livers lay all around them. And the ground was slick with blood.

Emily heard a thump behind her. She didn't have to look; she knew what it was. She looked anyway. Alice had hit the ground.

With the toe of her tennis shoe, Emily prodded Alice's buttocks. They tightened. An unconscious person's buttocks will remain loose.

"Come on, Alice. You can get up. I know you're only faking it."

Alice opened her eyes. "My mother always told me that in cases of great stress, a lady should promptly faint."

"Your mother was full of prunes. Get up."

Alice groaned, closing her eyes.

"Whoever did this might still be around."

Once again, Alice exhibited an almost Olympian ability to recover from great adversity. On her feet, she stared at the carnage. Turning her head, she upchucked. Emily didn't blame her a bit. Alice pointed at the remains of one girl. "I know . . . I think . . . that one is . . . was . . . Carla Andrews."

But Emily was paying little attention. There was nothing that could be done for the kids. Except bodybagging. She had detected some slight movement in the woods around them. She pulled her pistol from leather and jacked a round into the chamber, locking the full cock.

Alice watched her. "What's wrong? I mean, other than the obvious." She swallowed hard.

"Back toward the fence, Alice. Move slowly. Don't panic and run. *Don't run.*"

Alice then noticed the movement. The movement became solid shapes. Cats. What looked like hundreds of cats.

"Cats?" Alice questioned softly.

"Yeah, Alice. Cats."

"But? . . ."

229

"Move, Alice. Keep your eyes straight ahead." The cats were circling the women. A multi-colored moving, living mass, slowly tightening the circle. Emily had never liked cats; didn't trust them. Never had. Cats were cruel and she knew it. "Don't look back, Alice."

Alice, of course, promptly stopped and turned around. "Oh! Yes, I see. Look at all the kitties. Aren't they precious?"

"No, they're not. Move, Alice."

"But Emily. Why? . . . Where did all the cats come from?"

"Hell, Alice. I don't know. Maybe they're having a convention. Keep moving. Change directions right now. Turn right."

"But you *told* me to walk toward the fence, Emily!"

"We can't go that way now. The cats are blocking our way."

"Oh, for heavens sake, Emily. They are not."

"Alice, don't argue with me!" Emily had seen the cats tightening the loose circle. The women's only chance was to head into the woods.

Alice immediately began flapping her arms at the cats. "Shoo, kitty! Shoo, now!" She looked at Emily. "Emily, why aren't they moving?"

The cats sat on the ground and stared at the women, motionless, unblinking. Cruel-looking.

"Alice, you wanna knock it off? Goddamnit, don't get them upset."

"What is the matter with you, Emily? My word, they're just cats!"

"Yeah, sure. Alice, look at the light-colored one. No, don't stop walking. Just look at it. What do you see?"

She looked. Blinked. Her face paled. "Why . . .

230

I . . ." She almost fainted—remembered. "They're covered with blood. All of them are covered with blood. Do you think that the cats? . . ."

"Keep walking. Yeah, Alice. I think the cats attacked the . . . those people."

"But why? Why would they do such a thing? Emily, do you think this might have something to do with the strange behavior of Quinn and Bill?"

"That's what I'm thinking, Emily. Among other things, that is."

The cats began steadily pacing the women as they walked, always staying about a hundred feet from them. But following them, their eyes unblinking and savage-looking. There were cats of all descriptions, from pedigree to alley cat. Big cats, little cats, large cats. They followed the women silently.

When the cats had failed to attack, Alice said, "Emily, this is ridiculous. There is no reason for house cats to attack people. Right?"

"Right, Alice. Keep walking."

"Then why would they turn on people?"

"Keep walking. Don't stop. Alice, I don't feel like riddles. I don't know why. But they did. And they look like they're still hungry."

Alice moved a bit faster.

"Slow down, Alice. Angle a little bit more this way. Alice? Look around. See which way I'm pointing. That way. You see that old house over there? Let's head for it."

"Oh, Emily! That isn't a house."

"Well, what the hell do you call it?"

"That's a run down shack. And it's all falling in."

"Alice, I don't care—we have no choice. I can't shoot four or five hundred cats. Now, move!"

The women began walking faster, angling off. The cats sensed the urgency in the women's steps, and the changing direction. They picked up speed, pulling closer to the women. The women began running, a fright scent drifting to the pursuing felines. The scent enraged them, filling them with a primitive emotion that lies just beneath the surface of any cat or hunter-dog: the german shepherd, the husky, the chow, the doberman.

"They're getting closer, Emily!"

"Yeah, I know," Emily panted. "Just keep going, Alice.

The cats began yowling and snarling as they ran, closing the distance rapidly. One leaped on the rotting old porch just a step behind the women. Emily whirled around and shot the cat through the body, killing it.

The gunshot was familiar to the animals. En masse, they stopped for a moment. That was all the time the women needed. They rushed into the old shack, both of them looking wildly around them for a place, any place, to hide.

"There aren't any windows in this old shack!" Alice yelled, just a step away from hysteria.

"Hang on, Alice!" Emily yelled. "We'll make it."

She shoved the woman into a closet, stepping in behind her and slamming the door.

Cats filled the small shack. They crawled on the roof, covering it with small bodies. They yowled and howled and screeched their rage at their escaping prey. They flung themselves against the closed closet door, claws ripping at the old wood. One stuck its paw under the door, between the door and the floor, the paw searching for flesh. Alice lifted her foot and stomped the paw with the sole of her tennis shoe. The cat screamed in pain.

The din in and around and on top of the old shack was tremendous.

The women sank to the dusty, rat-droppings-littered floor, scared and exhausted.

"Emily?"

"Yes, Alice?"

"What are we going to do?"

"I don't know. We'll think of something."

Carrie shook her head, stopping her friend's repeated questions. "I *can't* tell you any more than that, Linda. Daddy will explain it all when he gets home. He said he would. Okay?"

"It's got something to do with all that monster talk around town, doesn't it?"

Carrie nodded.

"Wow! This is exciting." She leaned closer to her friend. "And just think—having two college men to protect us, too."

Carrie looked at her brother and at Mike. "College *men*? If you say so, Linda."

"I think Mike's cute."

Carrie sighed. Mike was like a brother to her. And brothers are okay, but not *cute*. At least not until Carrie had a couple more years on her. If she lived that long. If anyone in the Garrett household lived through the next few days. And nights.

"Come on, Carrie," Linda urged. "At least tell me a little more about what's going on."

But Carrie knew better than to disobey her dad. She shook her head and remained mum on the subject. "Wait until Dad gets home. I told you."

"All right. Big secrets. Oh! I meant to ask you. Is your cat still around here?"

Mike and Carl listened to the girl's chatter more attentively with that question.

"Huh? Oh . . . sure. I mean, I guess. She's around

233

someplace. She's a weird cat. Doesn't like to come inside. She's out around the shed, I suppose. No, wait a sec. Come to think of it, I haven't seen her in a couple of days. Why do you ask?"

"Well, it's probably nothing, but all the cats in our neighborhood have disappeared. Including our Nanny. They just . . . well, went away. Isn't that weird?"

"Yeah. Now that you mention it, it is. Real strange."

"I guess Nanny will come back home."

"Oh, sure. She'll come back when she's hungry. Speaking of that, let's fix a sandwich and go in my room. I got the new Rick Springfield album."

The cats were forgotten. "All *right*!" Linda said.

The girls gone, the boys waited until the stereo was blaring.

Carl looked at Mike. "You heard that about the cats, right?"

"Yeah, I heard. You thinking what I'm thinking?"

"Since I'm not all omniscient, I haven't the vaguest idea. But the odds are good that I am. I wonder if it's just a fluke, or countywide?"

"You think we should call your father?"

Carl thought for a moment. "Yeah, I do."

His mother stepped into the room, a puzzled look on her face. "Boys? Would you both please come look here?"

The boys rose and followed her into the kitchen. "Is it lunchtime already?" Mike joked, patting his stomach.

"You're a bottomless pit," Carl said.

"If nominated I will not accept. If elected I will not serve. But show me some food, and I'll always eat."

"You might not want to eat after seeing this," Vonne told them. "Either of you."

"What's up, Ma?" Carl said, grinning at her.

She pointed toward the kitchen window. "Look out there and tell me what you make of that."

Both young men stepped to the window over the sink. They looked out.

Both lost their grins.

"Holy cow!" Mike said. He blinked, rubbed his eyes, and looked again.

The same sight greeted him.

"Damn!" Carl whispered.

The side yard and as far in the back yard as the boys could see was filled with cats. Several hundred cats. They were on the lawn furniture, on Mike's car, perched on tree limbs, and sitting on the roof of the shed.

They were all looking at the house.

Motionless.

Unblinking.

Silently staring through cold eyes.

4

"I think you really stepped in it this time, Mille," Kenny said. "I tell you this, I could have died when you tossed your stash on that cop's desk."

She smiled, recalling the look on Kenny's face as she did so. "He's fair," she defended her action. "I think we've found us a real gem. An honest cop."

Kenny wasn't so sure. "Maybe. But that damn chief deputy looks freaky."

Mille could not contain her laughter as she glanced over at Kenny.

"What's wrong with you?" he asked.

"Nothing. Nothing at all, Kenny. All right. Let's assume the sheriff is leveling with us. Where do we start? And don't tell me the beginning."

"Let's drive the back roads, Mille. Together. Personally, I think that monster tale is just that—nonsense. At least I hope it is. But if it isn't? . . ." He trailed that off into silence and sat looking out the window.

"Two heads are better than one," she finished it for him.

"Something like that, Mille."

She picked up on the flatness of his tone and again glanced at him. "Something is sure eating at you, Kenny. Want to talk about it?"

"I'm struggling with myself, Mille. Inwardly. Major decision-making time, I guess. Something that's going to affect my whole life." He looked at his reflection in the glass.

"Jesus, Kenny. Are you going to get married? Is that it?"

"No, no. A much bigger step than that, I'm afraid."

Then it came to her. "Oh, my God, Kenny! You're not thinking about joining the *Army* are you?"

"No. Bigger than that. Mille, if I asked you something, would you give me a totally honest answer. I mean, level with me."

"You know I would."

"Mille—" He sighed. "What do you think about me getting a haircut?"

Suddenly, there appeared to be a shortage of dogs in the county. There were as many dogs as before, they were just not as visible as before. As some animals will show signs of concern and agitation before a violent storm, the dogs in Ruger County sensed some sort of danger all around them. And they became very wary. It was not anything tangible; just something that touched a nerve within the animals. And the animals had enough sense to pay attention to it. The dogs made themselves as inconspicuous as possible. When they did venture away from home, they traveled in small packs. Once bitter enemies became close allies.

Territory meant nothing now. The dogs sensed survival was the paramount issue.

But few human residents of the county noticed the change in the animals. A few would, but it would be too late for those humans who worked outside, and usually alone.

Or for those who enjoyed the night.

"Cats?" Dan questioned the telephone call. "Like in house cats, boy?"

"House cats, Dad," Carl said. "I've never seen anything like it in my life; so many of them gathered together. And there hasn't been a fight among them. None of them. That's why I think something is very wrong. They're just . . . watching the house. Staring at it."

"Stay inside," Dan told his son. "Pull all the windows down and lock them. Close the doors." A queasy sensation was creeping into his stomach. A very uneasy emotion. Loose ends were beginning to draw together. But Dan didn't like the knots that were forming.

Dan was conscious of Taylor watching him closely.

"Dad? You there, Dad?"

"What? Oh, yes. Yes, I'm here son. Lock it down, Carl. I'm on my way home." He hung up.

"Now what?" Taylor asked.

Dan told him.

"Cats?" the man questioned. "Like in kitty cats?"

"I'm afraid so. Like in kitty cats. Come on. Get your shotgun."

Dan stopped at dispatch on the way out. "Anybody calling in about bunches of cats gathering?"

Dan was conscious of Deputy Ken Pollard looking strangely at him.

Dispatch looked up. "Sir?" she asked.

"Cats?" Dan repeated. "Large bunches of cats gathering?"

"No, sir. But it's very odd."

"What is?"

"My mother called this morning from Ashby. All upset. Her old cat is gone and so are her neighbors' cats. On all sides of her. All up and down the street. Gone. And my cat is missing, too. Come to think of if, I . . ." She paused, brow wrinkling in recall. "I saw a large group of cats coming to work this morning. Maybe . . . oh, fifty or sixty of them. Maybe more. Quite a bunch of them."

"These cats," Captain Taylor asked, "what were they doing?"

Dispatch looked at him. "Nothing, sir. They were just sitting in a vacant field. Wait . . . come to think of it, they were all sitting in a straight line, staring out at, well, I don't know what they were staring at. But they were, well, like . . . soldiers."

Dan noticed Ken listening very intently. Then Dan remembered driving home the afternoon before. All those cats he'd seen wandering about.

Dan said, "I want you to go to tach and alert all units to be on the lookout for large groups of cats. Never mind any dogs." He paused. Hell, he couldn't remember even *seeing* any dogs the past twenty-four hours.

"I haven't even seen any dogs lately," Taylor said.

"Come to think of it," Chuck said. "My hounds are sure acting funny."

"Funny how?" Dan asked.

"Nervous like. Maybe, well, scared, might be the word I'm lookin' for. But scared of what?"

"Large groups of cats, maybe," Dan said. He turned back to dispatch. "Have the units log the cats' location and approximate number. I'm enroute to my house now. Captain Taylor will be with me. Get on that please."

"Yes, sir."

On their way out, Dan noticed Pollard on the telephone. He thought nothing of it.

Rolling toward his house, Dan said to Captain Taylor, "What is that line from Alice in Wonderland?"

"Eh? Oh, yeah. What was it? Yeah. Curiouser and curiouser. Sure fits this situation, doesn't it. Oh, God, Dan. Look over there to your right."

Dan looked and once more that sick sensation filled his stomach.

A large group of cats, perhaps fifty or sixty, filled the branches of a huge old tree. They sat perched like miniature leopards; a real life diminution of a wildlife special. All the scene lacked was a veldt and baobab tree.

"I have never seen house cats behave like that," Taylor said.

"Yeah," was all Dan could say.

The scene unnerved both men. They were silent the rest of the way to the Garrett house.

Dan pulled into his drive and stopped midway. Both men sat and stared.

The yard was filled with cats. Several hundred of them, at least. They sat and stared at the men, staring at them.

Dan's radio shattered the silence. "Base to Ruger One."

"This is One. Go."

"Doctors Ramsey and Harrison just called in. Both their wives are missing. And Mrs. Armstrong, Miller, Bradbury, and Como have all called in, hysterical. Their kids are missing. They were in the Armstrong

240

car, but said they were going walking out near the old truck terminal."

"Oh, no!" Taylor gasped.

"All right," Dan spoke into his mike. "Send someone out to the terminal, check the woods around there. I want a pair. No one lone-wolfs it. Understood?"

"Ten-four, Sheriff."

Dan hooked the mike just as a large yellow tomcat jumped up on the hood of the car. It sat, looking through the windshield. The cat put a paw against the glass, the claws extended. It dragged the paw down the glass slowly, producing a noise much like fingernails on a blackboard.

Both Dan and Captain Taylor cringed.

The cat actually seemed to be grinning at the men. Almost as if it knew it was taunting them.

Dan turned on the wipers. The cat studied the moving blades for a few seconds, then reached up and slapped the blades. Dan honked the horn. The noise did not bother the cat. Dan was intent on watching the cat and did not notice what the other cats were doing.

"Dan?" Taylor brought him out of his study. "The cats are moving, circling us."

Dan looked around him. The cats were moving, slowly circling the car. Their eyes did not . . . Dan struggled for a word . . . did not appear *normal*. He had never, or could not ever recall, seeing eyes so savage-looking on a house cat.

Dan said, "I feel like I'm having a bad dream. Pretty soon, I'm going to wake up."

"I hope I'm in that dream and we're going to wake up fast," Taylor said.

Dan looked up, spotting the faces of his family looking out the front windows of the house. He

241

motioned for them to stay inside. Vonne nodded.

The men had rolled up the windows on the car after pulling in and spotting the cats. They sat and watched the cats circle them. Dan's eyes widened as he detected a pattern in the circling.

"Look at that!" he said to Taylor. "The group closest to us is moving clockwise. The next group is going counter-clockwise. The next group clockwise, and so on. Cats just don't *do* things like that."

"It's almost as if they . . . are being controlled," Taylor said. "But by whom? Or what?"

"Look out!" Dan yelled, even though they were protected by the heavy glass.

The cats hurled themselves against the car, throwing their bodies against the metal and glass, howling and snarling and spitting, their sharp little teeth exposed.

Their claws scratched at the paint as the cats completely covered the vehicle.

"Hang on!" Dan said. He dropped the car into gear and floorboarded it, holding the wheel in a hard left turn. He cut tight doughnuts in his drive and the front yard, knocking cats spinning and squalling and howling, the tires squashing a dozen of them.

No room to maneuver his shotgun, Taylor rolled down the window and emptied his .357 at the cats, quickly reloading and firing again.

The cats began retreating into the meadow and woods around the home, but not before Carl and Mike ran out onto the porch, shotguns in their hands. They blasted the air with shot, sending bloody bits of cats hurtling through the yard. Vonne stood on the porch beside the boys, a .22 semi-automatic rifle in her hands. She emptied the tube, each small slug impacting with a cat.

Carrie and Linda stood in the living room of the

Garrett house, their hands over their ears.

When the gunfire had died away, and the echoes were bouncing off the rolling hills, at least seventy-five cats lay dead or dying in the yard around the house.

"Don't let any of the wounded cats get close enough to bite you," Dan warned.

He pulled his car as close to the house as he could get it. "Carl, you and Mike get that roll of chicken wire out of the shed. Get some cutters. We'll stand guard. For God's sake, be careful. We'll nail it over the window screens. Move, boys."

Dan grabbed up his mike. "Ruger One to base."

"Base."

"Go to tach. All units."

Six rolling units reported they were on tach and standing by.

Dan looked at Taylor. "This report is going to make me look like a fool."

Taylor's eyes swept the bloody yard. "Not after they see this."

"I have just been attacked by a large band of . . . house cats," he radioed in, a grimace on his face.

In a rolling unit, heading for the woods and pastures around the old truck terminal, Herman looked at Frank. "What did he say?"

Chuck grabbed up his mike. "Sheriff? Would you ten-nine on that last transmission?" He couldn't quite believe he'd heard what he thought he heard.

Dan keyed his mike. "I said, Captain Taylor and I were attacked by a large group of cats. Believe me, I feel foolish just saying it. But it's far from being a joke. It may well be just an isolated incident, but somehow I doubt it. Be wary of large groups of cats."

All units acknowledged the order. All units feeling a bit foolish as they did so.

"Now what?" Taylor asked.

"We put the wire over the windows and then I talk to Linda. I have to level with the girl. And then? . . ."

Taylor waited.

"I just don't know what to do."

"Join the club," the trooper admitted.

Not far from the truck terminal, by the tiny pool where the soul-less Denise and the cat waited, the cup-sized pool began bubbling, enlarging, as the tiny crack in the earth became larger. Putrid, noxious fumes drifted from the thick, colored liquid. Denise and the cat sat up at the slight noise. They looked first at each other, then at the pool. Something was trying to push its way out of the gurgling foulness. A grotesque, misshapen object that only slightly resembled fingers fought to clear the surface of the tiny pool. But the hole in the earth was not quite large enough.

Yet.

Denise, no longer of this earth, but unable to leave its physical confines, naked, torn, her flesh chalk-white, and the cat, sat by the pool and waited. They both knew, sensed, somehow, the wait was becoming shorter. Perhaps another day. Two days at the most, and that which had slept dormant under the crust of the earth for hundreds of years would struggle out of the pool. Then the promises of the Dark One, Master of the Night, would spring to being.

They waited.

On a table in a corner of one of the small labs in a trailer at the old truck terminal, the severed arm lay forgotten. Much more important matters confronted the doctors. But the arm no longer resembled that which it was. It had been steadily growing since the moment the axe separated it from the young man's body, producing new life forms. The worm-like objects would form, grow, and then break off from the arm. They dropped to the floor of the forgotten room, wriggling like maggots working on rotting flesh. A small pile had gathered. Every few minutes, another worm-like bit of new life would be added to the growing pile. They slithered and rolled and hunched their way under cabinets, tables, under the cases and filing cabinets.

They waited, and grew.

The concrete floor of the high school basement cracked. Not a large crack, no more than a sixteenth of an inch wide. Faint wisps of smoke floated out of the crack. In a moment, a thick colored liquid oozed out of the crack, gradually spreading out, covering perhaps a foot on either side of the crack. The thick liquid pulsed with a newly-freed life. It swelled and seemed to gasp for breath. Then the liquid settled down and was still for a moment. Then the pulsing began anew. The thickness protruding from out of the tiny crack became larger, better defined. The odor became a stench, a foulness from a long-forgotten grave. A once dead, rotting fetidness. A sigh drifted from the crack in the floor. The sigh expelled decaying breath.

The creature called Mickey Reynolds sat on the floor and looked at the growing pool of colored liquid. The cat watched just as intently. Neither feline nor once-human took their eyes from the growing pool of fresh, living, evil rot.

They watched, and waited.

What had once been Eddie Brown felt a growing wetness on the floor beneath where he lay, resting. His animal mind had heard a slight cracking sound a few moments before, but he had paid it no attention. It had not seemed to represent any danger. Now he sat up, peering through the gloom.

The floor had cracked, a thick ooze spreading out from the separating concrete. A foulness filled the basement as the thickness gathered, dark red in color. Groaning whispered hoarsely, faintly, from the crack in the dusty floor.

A thin, finger-like object pushed out of the crack, wet and slimy from the stinking fluid. It pushed out again and again, seeking freedom, but not yet able to attain the release.

Eddie and his new friend, the cat, waited and watched.

Betty Reynolds and her kids squatted in the ruins of what had once been a service station/motel by the side of the highway. It had not been used as such for years. The concrete floor of the old station had cracked, a thick, smelly, red-colored liquid oozed from the crack, spreading its thickness over a small portion of the dirty floor. A wrinkled object, vaguely resembling an ape-like finger, protruded from the crack. It worked in and out, up and down, attempting to enlarge the crack in the cement. Betty and her children squatted in their own filth. They watched and waited.

And on the second floor of the combination garage

and storage building, Anya began laughing softly. A laugh of the darkest evil, containing the ultimate of depravity.

Pet had instructed the gathering of cats around the building and the nearby house to stay close, but to conceal themselves, to be cautious, to be especially wary of any human invaders. For it was not yet time to make their move. Almost time. But not quite.

Pet looked around at its companion's dark, ugly laughter. Anya's eyes were gleaming in the gloom of the storage area; gleaming so brightly as to illuminate the pockets of dust and cobwebs. The girl's facial features were changing, becoming an old mask that reflected ten thousand years of lust and torture and evil. Her face kept changing, from that of a young girl, to an old, snaggletoothed hag. The girl's hands were curled into claws, opening and closing in time with her wild laughter.

Slowly, her face became once more that of a child, with the exception of her eyes. They glowed with evil.

Both the girl and the cat could sense, could smell the Old Ones attempting to push their way out of the earth's crust, slowly making their way through the tons of rock that covered them, rock placed over them by the Master of all that is good and kind and loving and caring.

Anya spat on the floor at just the thought of Him.

Pet padded to a corner and howled her contempt.

The moment was near—very near. Both knew it. A bit more patience was all that was needed. What a stroke of unexpected luck it had been for that engineer to have discovered their hiding place and roused them from their sleep cycle.

Anya's depraved laughter tapered off to an evil chuckling. Her hands were once more those of a young girl. Her eyes were once more dark and unread-

247

able. And the formerly unseen minions of the Dark One, those which lay under the earth's surface all over the world, were, in this locality, struggling to be free, hearing and heeding the call of the Master.

The moment was very near.

5

"All rolling units report," Dan radioed.

All units reported the same thing: no large bands of cats had been sighted. But the dogs they did spot were behaving strangely. Sort of cowed and very wary.

Dan had ordered one car to swing by the tree where he and Taylor had spotted the cats in the branches. The tree was void of felines.

"Then they've been warned off," Mike said, standing behind the men.

Taylor turned around, not sure he'd heard correctly. "Warned off? By whom?"

Before Mike could reply, a station wagon pulled into the drive. HPB Trucking on its doors. Lou Lamotta behind the wheel.

Dan reached into his car and took out his M-10, jacking a round into the chamber. He checked the fire selector, moving it a full one hundred and eighty degrees from semi to full auto. He clicked the safety from safe to fire.

Lou's eyes widened. He closed the wagon door carefully. "Hey, Sheriff. Whoa, now. I'm on your side, remember?"

"You're on nobody's side but your own, Lou You

wrap yourself in the flag like some sort of goddamn shroud. So let's not kid each other. Now what in the hell are you doing on my property?"

Lou smiled his damnable smile. "I intercepted your transmissions, ol' buddy."

Dan started to call the man a liar, then closed his mouth as an idea popped into his head. Somebody at the office was pipelining to Lou. Had to be. Dan had looked at the OSS's radio equipment. They were not equipped with de-scramblers. So the man had someone feeding him information.

Lou said, "I wanted to see these killer kitty cats. I've got some lab boys on the way to gather up the carcasses." He looked at the lethal little .45 caliber spitter in Dan's hands. His smile widened. "You'd really like to use that on me, wouldn't you, Sheriff?"

"I wouldn't like to, Lou. But I would." Dan's words came out low and cold and very menacing. "I place more emphasis on human life than you do. Even your life."

Lou got a kick out of that. He slowly nodded his head.

"Maybe I came on a little hard, Dan. With you. I read you wrong. So I'm backing off what I said. Forget I said it, if you can. You just don't understand the importance of my work, that's all."

"I understand the importance, Lou. Not the way you go about it. Don't forget, I worked out west when you people were butchering farmers' and ranchers' cattle—without compensating the owners for their loss."

"I don't forget anything, Sheriff."

Dan believed that. The man was brilliantly insane.

Dan had noticed his wife leaving the porch and entering the house. She returned, banging the screen door, a carbine in her hands, a thirty round clip stuck in the weapon's belly.

Lou looked at her, the weapon, and sighed.

Vonne said, "So you're the man who is going to rape me and my daughter, right?"

Lou sighed again, deeper.

"Would you like to try that now?" Vonne asked.

"No, ma'am," Lou said. "But I will most certainly remember that you threatened me."

Vonne lifted the muzzle of the carbine, aiming squarely at Lou's crotch.

Lou sucked in his gut and turned sideways. He'd rather be hip-shot than shot in the balls. "Jesus, Mrs. Garrett! Can't you people take a little joke?"

"As both a woman and mother of a daughter, Mr. Lamotta, I don't consider rape a joking matter." Lou had lost his smile. He forced it back to his lips.

"I guess not, Mrs. Garrett." He cut his eyes at the approach of two vans. "I guess I made a mistake by coming on high-handed with you people. But I can't undo what has been said and done." He looked at Carl and Mike. He guessed accurately that these were not the average give-it-hell and have-a-good-time college boys. He knew all about Mike's shooting of the punks, and he sensed, again accurately, that Carl had his father's no-backup in him. Both young men had shotguns in their hands and pistols belted at their waist. Captain Taylor had shifted positions. The man now held one of the meanest-looking shotguns Lou had ever seen. It had been Pachmayred and Parkerized, and the extension tube for the magazine ended just short of the muzzle. "Remington model 1100 mag?"

"Uh-huh," Taylor said.

"Nice weapon,"

"Just dandy.'

This guy has mean eyes, Lou thought. "You ever

251

shot a man with one of those?"

"Uh-huh."

"Messy, wasn't it?"

"But damned effective. I shot him from about fifteen inches. Blew his whole backbone out. Along with a lot of his guts. And other things."

Lou swallowed. "Uh . . . *yeah!* Well. I'll just be helping the boys and girls load up the kitty cats."

"You do that," Langway said, stepping out from the corner of the house. He held an M-16 in his hands. "I came the back way," he said to Taylor.

"Welcome to the party," his CO said.

Lou walked off, stepping carefully. He muttered, "Whole bunch is trigger-happy."

The lab crew quickly and very efficiently bagged the dead cats. They used very thick, heavy gloves that were, Dan suspected, steel wire enforced against bites. Many of the cats were only wounded. Those were hit with a knock-out drug of some kind and placed to one side.

Taylor watched for a few moments, then said, "You get the impression they've done this many, many times before?"

"Yes," Dan said, conscious of his family listening. "I do. With cattle in Colorado and sheep up in Utah. I've seen it."

"What were they doing with the livestock, Mister Garrett?" Mike asked. "Or rather, *why* were they doing it?"

"I was never able to find out. I was told it had to do with nerve gas. But I'll never be convinced that was the only reason."

The boys cut the chicken wire and nailed it over windows, folding a double layer over the bottom windows for extra strength.

"I feel like a jerk not being able to tell the people to

252

do the same," Taylor said.

"Much more of this and I will tell them," Dan said. "And Lou Lamotta can drop dead."

The young people grinned at that.

When the clean-up was concluded, and the OSS people leaving, Lou stuck his head out the wagon window and called in a fake southern accent, "Ya'll be careful now, you hear?"

"I detest that man," Vonne said, her arms around the shoulders of Carrie and Linda. "He makes my flesh crawl."

"I don't understand any of this," Linda said, fear in her eyes.

"Vonne will talk to you, Linda," Dan said. He looked at his wife. She nodded.

"What is interesting to me," Mike said, "is that that government man didn't even ask why or how the cats got here. He did not seem concerned or interested in the fact that . . . well, higher powers might well be involved in all of this."

"Higher powers?" Vonne asked from the porch.

"God and Satan," Mike replied.

"You think God and Satan are involved, son?" Taylor asked.

"Yes, I do," Mike replied without hesitation. "From everything I know about what is happening here, it's supernatural. And that takes it right out of mortal hands. I'm not terribly religious, but I think calling in a priest wouldn't hurt."

"Right in the middle of Baptist country," Dan said, unable to hide his smile.

"Dan!" Vonne scolded him. But she too saw the humor in her husband's remark.

"I just don't believe we—any of us—really know what we're facing here."

Like any good cop, Taylor wasn't afraid to explore

any angle, no matter how foolish it might sound at the outset. "All right, Mike. When do you think we might know what is going on?"

"Whenever God or Satan feels it's time."

"You think God is going to help us in this, Mike?" Dan asked.

"Not in any . . . obvious way, I should imagine. He stopped doing that a long time ago. But it sure wouldn't hurt to ask Him."

"I have been," Taylor said simply.

Dan leaned against the car and looked around him. A slow, rueful smile creased his face. "Lamotta may well be the most arrogant and obnoxious man in the world, but he's sure sharp."

"How do you mean, Sheriff," Langway asked.

"Even if we did alert the public as to what took place out here, they wouldn't believe us. We stood right here and let Lamotta remove all the physical evidence of the attack. We have absolutely no proof it ever took place."

Taylor looked around him, exasperated at himself for allowing that to take place right under his nose. "Well, I'll just be goddamned!" he said. He looked heavenward. "Excuse me."

Alice and Emily huddled in the cramped closet. They were scared, tired, sore, and hot. Emily had banged her watch on something and the damn thing had quit working. Alice had not worn a watch, so the women had no idea what time it was. To them, it seemed they had been in the closet for hours.

"Emily?" Alice whispered.

"Yes, Alice?"

"I have to tinkle."

"So do I. Hold it."

"I'll try. Emily?"

"Yes, Alice?"

"For some reason, I get the impression there aren't as many cats out there as before. Do you?"

"Yeah. I get the same feeling. You want to be the one to stick your head out this door?"

"I don't believe so, Emily."

Both women had heard the almost silent padding of the cats as many of them left the crumbling shack. The women had no idea where they went or why they had left. Or how many had left. Or how far they had gone. If they had indeed left.

Finally, Emily made up her mind—reluctantly. "I'm going to crack this door just a tiny bit, Alice. If nothing else, we'll know where we stand."

"Or squat," Alice said, with an attempt at humor.

Emily grinned at that. Alice was turning out to be an all-right person. Most of Emily's earlier feelings about the woman had vanished. She found herself liking Alice—the real Alice—once she had discovered the person beneath the snobbish facade.

Emily looked at Alice in the near darkness of the closet. "You ready?"

"Give it hell, Emily."

Emily chuckled and cracked the door.

Herman and Frank found Emily Ramsey's car. It was parked by the side of the road about a half mile from the truck terminal. They checked it out and discovered no signs of foul play.

"Let's drive up the road a piece before calling this in," Frank suggested. "Might find the kids' car."

"You're driving."

Just around the curve, they found a car registered to Clyde Armstrong. They radioed both finds in.

"Stay right where you are," Dan said. "I'll be joining you shortly. ETA five minutes." Dan looked at his family. "Get in the house and stay put. Don't come outside for any reason. And that is not a request."

Vonne smiled at him. "You're still a sexist pig, old man."

"Of course," Dan returned the smile.

The girls laughed.

Vonne waved at him. "Get outta here! And be careful."

Rolling toward the cars of the missing women and teenagers, Taylor said, "I wonder if Lamotta really heard that call?"

"I doubt it. I think he's got a pipeline in my office. But I don't know who it is. Anyway, we'll know if he's monitoring our tach frequency when we get to the site."

"I wish I knew how all this was going to end."

Dan glanced at him. "Do you, Tay? Really?"

Captain Taylor crossed himself and remained silent.

The old shack was empty. Except for stinking piles of cat crap that littered the floor. Emily cautiously opened the door a tad wider and looked out, her pistol in her right hand. Emily pushed the door open wider still. Nothing came leaping and snarling and howling at them. The only sound was the seemingly loud beating of the women's hearts.

Emily straightened up, her knee joints cracking as she did so. She carefully and thoroughly inspected the room. No cats. Still standing in the closet door, she looked out through the glassless windows. No cats could be seen. But as the wind changed, it brought with it a very foul odor. The stench, somehow familiar to Emily, wrinkled her nose as it assaulted her nostrils.

"Phew, Emily," Alice said. "What is that smell?"

"I don't know. But it's somehow familiar to me. I . . ." Then it came to her. Old blood and rotting flesh. She didn't mention that to Alice. But she wondered where the odor was coming from, and the source of it.

Emily stepped out into the dirty, cobwebby room. She inspected the other two rooms of the shack. No cats.

Alice turned as a movement caught her peripheral vision, right side. She stared in disbelief. Her heart hammered. "Alice?" she whispered. "Look toward your right, out that window," she pointed. "And tell me what you see."

Alice looked. Sucked in her breath. She stared in horror. "That's . . . oh, my God! That's the Moore girl." Her voice was just audible.

"Yeah, that's what I thought, too." Emily blinked. The figure would not go away.

"I'm going to close my eyes," Alice said. "And when I open, them, that . . . *thing* is going to be gone. I just know it."

She closed her eyes. Opened them. Denise stood not far from the shack.

Both women stood in shock, staring out into the clearing.

A word drifted to the women. But neither could make it out.

"Did you say something, Emily?"

"No. I thought it was you. It was you, wasn't it, Alice?"

"I didn't say anything!"

"Calm down. We're hallucinating, that's all. Let's

257

close our eyes and take several deep breaths."

That done, the women opened their eyes. Denise was closer to the shack.

"NoNoNoNoNoNo!" Alice said. "This is not possible."

The naked, torn, ghostly pale body of Denise gleamed brightly in the sun. She stood in the clearing, looking at the shack, a cat sitting on the ground beside her. She slowly lifted one arm and motioned at the shack. She spoke, the words very clear now.

"Come. Come. Come with me."

Alice hit the floor.

6

"No signs of foul play?" Dan asked.

"No, sir," Herman said. "Nothing to indicate that at all."

"All right. Both of you take your handy-talkies. Check them out. Get your shotguns. Stuff your pockets full of extra shells. I don't know what in the hell we're going up against here."

"Hell might be an apt choice of words," Taylor said.

Chuck pulled up, Susan in the car behind them. They were followed by the other "vacationing" Virginia state troopers. The troopers, including Langway, were all dressed in civvies.

Dan looked around him. Curious, he thought. No birds singing. No sign of any birds. The pastures and woods were still. Ominously so.

Taylor's eyes touched Dan's. "I just flat don't like it," the trooper said.

"I don't either."

"It's your ballpark, Dan," Taylor said. "We're just visiting. You call the shots."

"We'll sweep this area," he said, waving his hand. "No more than fifty to seventy-five yards apart. Weapons at combat ready. No heroics, people. Like I said, we don't know what we're up against. Creatures, monsters, cats—you name it."

"And The Blob!" Trooper Hawkes said.

Taylor gave the young patrolman a look guaranteed to freeze snowballs in the desert.

"A small attempt at humor, Captain," Hawkes said.

"Rodney Dangerfield doesn't have a thing to worry about," Taylor responded.

Hawkes looked hurt.

The wind freshened a bit, bringing with it a foul stench.

"Yukk!" Susan said. "What is that?"

"I came up on a pile of thawed bodies one time in Korea," Taylor said. "Frozen stiff during the winter, thawed out in the spring. Smelled something like that."

"Korea, huh?" Hawkes said, his face containing nothing but pure innocence. "I thought you fought in the First World War?"

Taylor stepped toward him. Hawkes trotted away, calling over his shoulder. "I'll take the far side. Waaaay over there!"

Taylor had to smile. He could remember being young and full of spunk.

"Move out," Dan said. "Slow and easy."

This time, Alice wasn't faking it. She was out cold.

Emily took what was left of the water and bathed the woman's face, all the while trying to keep one eye on the pale form of Denise. When she looked up from the reclining Alice, Denise and the cat had disappeared.

She got Alice awake and sitting up. She wiped the damp cloth over the woman's face. "Can you get up, Alice? We've got to get out of here."

Alice got her eyes in focus. "Denise Moore is *dead!* That could not have been her. Damnit, Emily, it couldn't have been."

"But it was." Emily helped the woman to her feet. "We both saw her. We both couldn't have imagined that. Come on."

Together, Emily leading the way, the women stepped out of the house onto the rotting porch of the shack. Both of them looked warily around for cats.

"That odor has changed," Alice observed.

"You're smelling yourself. You landed in cat shit."

"Gross! I don't see any of the little bastards. Do you?"

"No. But I'm wondering if they see us."

"I wish you hadn't said that."

"Let's go, Alice. Stay close to me."

"Don't you worry about that."

Chuck was the first to spot the women, slipping through the thin scrub timber. He called to them. Waved at them. They practically knocked him down getting to him.

Dan and the others stood for a full two minutes, listening to Alice babble about the attack, being pursued by thousands of cats, the mangled bodies of the teenagers, their taking refuge in a smelly old shack, and finally, the sighting of Denise.

They couldn't make sense out of anything she said.

261

Emily said, "Alice, please, slow down for a minute, will you?"

"Mrs. Ramsey," Chuck said, showing his understanding of Virginia's female aristocracy . . . so-called. "Perhaps you'd like to sit in my car and rest for a few moments? I'll take down your report when you feel like it."

She looked at the chief deputy like Elaine of Astolat must have looked at Launcelot. "Oh, thank you!" She was gushing again. "Mr? . . ."

"Klevan, ma'am." Chuck blushed. "Chief Deputy Klevan." He held out his arm and she took it. He led her off toward the parked cars.

"What a pair," Hawkes said.

"Alice is really a good person," Emily said. "She's just pretentious a lot of the time."

"What happened, Emily?" Dan asked.

Emily told her story with all the succinctness and perception of a good O.R. nurse. When she finished, the cops stood and stared at her.

Taylor cleared his throat. "You really saw the Moore girl, Mrs. Harrison? *Alive?*"

"No, sir. I don't believe she was alive. Not as we know the word."

For once, Hawkes didn't have anything cute to say. He looked a little pale.

"You mind explaining that?" Taylor said.

"Some kook had really done a number on the girl. She had been literally sewn back together. It looked like strange designs had been cut into her body. Nobody could survive that. And I've seen people who had bled to death. She looked just like that. Her flesh was pale white; almost tinted a light blue. She was naked. She called to us, but at first it was in a

262

language I couldn't understand. When she came closer, I could see the stitching in her flesh. When she again spoke, motioning to us, it was in English. She had a cat with her. They disappeared into a little patch of woods."

Hawkes was definitely pale. He looked nervously around him.

Taylor shook his head and sighed.

"And the bodies of the kids?" Dan asked.

"Let me get my bearings." Emily looked around her, spotting the high tension wires, looking for landmarks. "Right over there," she said, pointing.

"Thank you, Mrs. Harrison," Dan said. "Frank, escort Mrs. Harrison back to the cars and stay with her, please."

"Sheriff?" Emily said.

"Yes, ma'am?"

"Two things, please. First, I want to know what is going on in this county. Secondly, you'd better radio in for some body bags. There isn't much left of those kids."

"Mrs. Harrison," Dan said. "I think it's time for everyone in this county to be informed as to what is going on."

"I don't," the familiar voice came from behind the line of cops.

Mille and Kenny had left the car parked by the side of a gravel road and now stood at the edge of the lovely, peaceful-appearing meadow, the open field bordered on three sides by trees.

"What are we looking for, Mille?" Kenny did not like the great outdoors.

"I don't know. Nothing, in particular. I just need to walk around out in the fresh air. Clear my head and sort out some things."

"We're gonna have to be careful on this one, Mille," Kenny warned. "I think the sheriff meant it when he told us about that Lamotta creep."

"Monsters, Kenny?" she said, looking at him. "Creatures? Mummy-men? Killer house cats. A two thousand year old little girl and her cat? Think about it. Is the sheriff having a big laugh at our expense?"

"I thought about that first, Mille. I thought you were the one with no doubts."

"That doesn't answer the question. But, yeah. I'm having some doubts. Lots of them."

A pickup truck drove by, stopped, and backed up. A man's friendly face looked out at the pair. "Haven't you young folks heard about the monsters?" he asked with a grin. "It ain't safe to be out and about with them creatures roamin'."

"We haven't heard that one, mister," Mille said, straight-faced lying. "But I gather you don't think there's much truth in the stories?"

The man laughed, a good, strong, jolly type of laugh. "Young lady, I quit believin' in spooks a long time ago." He waved at them. "Ya'll take care now, you hear? And don't scare my cattle in that field."

"We won't," Kenny assured them.

He drove on down the gravel road and turned off on a dirt road, leading away from the pair. A mile down that road, he stopped, staring but not believing his eyes.

"Nice fellow," Kenny said. "He didn't even look twice at my hair."

"Are you getting self-conscious about your hair,

Kenny?"

"I guess so. Sort of."

They started walking.

"Well, the sheriff's story seems to be circulating, and obviously, not many people are buying it. I can sure see why."

For once in his young life, Kenny stood squarely beside the law. "I don't know, Mille. I believe the man. I don't think the guy knows *how* to lie."

They walked across the small pasture, full of early summer flowers and an occasional pile of cow dung. It was the cow droppings that masked that other odor wafting through the air.

And the warm, whispering winds also covered the sounds of footsteps slipping closer to the reporter and the investigator. Mille turned around in the pasture, some sense of warning alerting her. She looked around. She could see nothing out of the ordinary.

"What's wrong, Mille?"

"Nothing, I guess. I just felt like someone was watching us. I guess I'm getting spooky. It was my imagination, that's all."

"Sure. That's . . . Ooww!" Kenny spun around, his face contorted from pain.

A dart stuck out of his right buttock.

"Jesus, Mille. I've been darted."

"That's a tranquilizer dart, Kenny. Someone is . . ." A sharp pain in Mille's hip cut off her words. She jerked and looked down. A dart stuck out of her hip. "Goddamnit!" she said. "What's going on?"

Within seconds, both Mille and Kenny slumped to the ground, no longer able to control leg movement. They jerked spasmodically, thrashing on the cool ground. Finally, they lay still.

They could hear voices, but could not make out who was talking. A fine mist seemed to cover their open eyes, fogging vision, dulling the mind.

"Pull the van around on that dirt road close to the tree line," a voice said. "Over there. We'll carry them from here. Hurry! Take them to the terminal. They can cool their heels in lock-up. That'll get them out of our business. Move it."

Kenny and Mille slipped into unconsciousness.

Dan slowly led the way in the direction Emily had pointed out. The cops were spread out, weapons at the ready. They moved slowly and carefully through the meadows and thin timber and brush. Lou Lamotta walked by Dan's side. He carried an M-16.

"You're just determined to blow the lid off this thing, aren't you, Sheriff?" Lou asked.

"Lamotta . . ." Dan started to argue with the man, then realized it was futile. Lou Lamotta was a right-wing fanatic. Country came first, no matter if he had to kill off the entire U.S. population to save it. Dan knew then, that moment, with a veteran's cop's insight, that Lamotta was truly insane.

"Wouldn't you sacrifice one county to save the whole country, Sheriff?" Lamotta pressed.

"I don't want to argue about it, Lamotta," Dan said wearily. "You won't change. But I'll tell you this: you're nuts!"

Lamotta laughed. "Oh, I am, Sheriff. I don't deny it. I'm mad as a hatter. Certifiably insane. But I know how to deal with it. That's the only reason I'm not in some lockdown."

Taylor looked at the man and muttered an obscenity under his breath.

The smell reached them, stronger. A thick, almost tangible odor of death. Fifty steps more and they stood on the fringe of the slaughter-site. The cops stood looking on in shock and disgust; Lou lifted his handy-talkie and called in to his base. He gave their location and told his people to get moving.

Then, to the shock of the others, Lou began laughing.

He waved the cops back and squatted down, chuckling as he inspected the blood and gore and young death. "Cats," he said. "A bunch of goddamn house cats did this. Great God! If we could learn how to control their actions, just think what a weapon this nation could have. Right, Sheriff?"

Dan knew the OSS agent was putting the needle to him. He looked at Lou and shook his head in disgust.

Lou laughed at him.

Taylor spat on the ground and walked away from Lou, again muttering obscenities under his breath.

Langway seriously contemplated shooting the maniac. He glared at Lou, gripping his shotgun so hard his knuckles turned white from strain.

"Steady, Sarge," Hawkes said softly. "You're our leader, remember?"

"Old blood and rotting human meat," Lou said, talking to himself. "That's what the Harrison broad said she smelled. But this just smells like excrement. So where did she smell it? And does it have anything to do with the cats' behavior?" He looked up at Dan.

"I have no idea. But do I have your permission to continue my investigation, O Great OSS Man?"

Lou laughed and rose to his feet just as a man walked up to the site. Dodge.

"Where the hell have you been?" Lou snapped at him.

Dodge pointed a finger at him. "Cool it, Lamotta! I don't take all my orders from you—remember? I've been out of town."

"Doing what?" Lou demanded.

"None of your business."

"There will be a report written about your attitude, Dodge."

"Good. Dandy. You do that, Lamotta."

"My investigation, Lamotta?" Dan repeated.

"Yeah, yeah, Sheriff," Lou said impatiently, waving his hand. "Run along and play detective. And take that jerk," he looked at Dodge, "with you. Just stay the hell out of my peoples' way and remember to keep your mouth shut after you leave here." His eyes hardened and his smile changed to more of a snarl. "I've tried to be friends, Sheriff; tried to apologize for coming on so hard. You and your family tossed it back in my face. You got an attitude problem, buddy-boy. But I think I've found a way to circle around that and keep your mouth shut. You're so super civic-minded; concerned with the public's welfare and all that." He glanced at his watch. "So I guess it's time to get hard. I've had some of my people—I pulled a few more in—grab Ms. Smith and that freaky little hippie punk with her. They'll be my, ah, guests for the duration, buddy-boy. Now you get cute with me again, hotshot, and Ms. Smith and that fruit-pie get hurt—*bad*—and then, buddy-boy, I start on some local people. You copy all that, Sheriff?"

Dan stepped out of character and said, "You're a sorry excuse for a human, Lamotta!"

Lamotta laughed in Dan's face. "Yeah, I know.

268 -

Now, Sheriff, you run along and play cops and robbers. Stay out of my business."

Inwardly fuming, Dan said, "How about the parents of the dead kids?"

"Tell them their kids took off. We'll take care of the car. That's the story. You stick with it."

Dan and the others hung around until the OSS lab team made their appearance, arriving in a few minutes, exiting the back gate to avoid any curious eyes. Dan and his people, Dodge with him, walked away from the body-bagging being carried out by the OSS people. They stepped into the scrub timber, looking for the source of that odor Emily had spoken of.

But one of the new OSS people pulled in had already found it, and he was about to regret—briefly—his discovery.

7

The agent knelt down by the pool of red, foul-smelling liquid that bubbled out of the ground. The stench was so foul, even the blood and guts-hardened OSS man could scarcely keep his breakfast down.

He couldn't figure out what the liquid might be.

Looking around, he found a stick and stuck it down into the pool, about six inches deep. He was careful not to get any of the liquid on his hands. This stuff smelled terrible.

The stick was jerked out of his hands.

The agent fell backward, startled, landing on his butt. "What the hell?"

The hole from which the liquid bubbled, now more than a foot wide, bubbled and seemed to sigh.

The agent looked at the pool. "It's talkin' to me!"

The agent found another stick, a heavier one, and getting a good grip on the stick, jammed it down into the liquid and worked it around, in and out, with short, savage, jabbing motions. The stick struck something solid . . . sort of. He'd jammed a stick into a jellyfish once—it was kinda like that. Squishy/solid.

The agent jammed the stick deeper. The sighing from the hole changed timbre, becoming more of a groan, then changing into a low murmuring of anger.

"What *is* this?" the man said aloud. He tried to pull the stick out. He could not. He would pull the stick out only a few inches, then something would haul the stick back into the thick, crimson, foul-smelling liquid, almost jerking the man off his feet.

The agent got mad.

"Why, you—" he yelled, his face getting red from anger and exertion. He pulled on the stick, gaining a few more inches. "Gotcha, you creep!"

He was again almost jerked off his feet as the stick plunged deeper into the liquid-filled hole in the earth. He lost the stick and stood, watching the stick disappear, being pulled into the foulness. It was, he thought, almost as if someone, or something, with superhuman strength was hiding down there.

"That's ridiculous," he muttered.

"I'll fix you," he said, reaching into his pocket for a clasp knife. He found a pole this time, sharpening one end of it. Returning to the hole, he jammed the sharpened end into the hole with all his strength.

A furious howl of pain and rage erupted from the liquid. The agent stepped back, for the first time, fear touching his features.

The protruding end of the pole, almost five feet of it, waved and trembled. The agent stepped back to the hole and once more grabbed the pole. He jammed it again and again into the hole.

"Take that, and that!" he shouted, sweat running from his face.

He laughed.

Something from down under the liquid laughed.

"Naw," the man said. "That's impossible."

He did not notice the webbed, slightly humanlike hand slowly inching its slick and slimy way out of the liquid. The adjoined fingers were dark and wrinkled,

271

the end of the fingers curved claws. The hand clamped around the man's ankle.

The agent screamed as the hot wet fingers closed around his ankle and jerked, flinging him to the ground. He struggled to free himself. He could not. The hand was too powerful. He squalled his panic.

He dug his fingers into the earth as he felt himself being pulled backward, toward the stinking hole. "No!" he screamed. "God! Help me! Please!"

Laughter bubbled out of the liquid.

The foot, then the ankle, finally the leg, up to the knee, was slowly immersed into the thick red liquid. A chewing, smacking sound rose out of the bubbling matter.

The OSS agent began shrieking in agony.

The grotesque hand once more appeared out of the liquid, followed by a thick, scaly, hairy wrist and forearm. The clawed fingers inched upward, to the agent's thigh. They dug in, through the trousers and into flesh. Blood squirted out of the punched fleshy holes.

The man's screaming echoed through the scrub timber, the larger trees, the brush, and the pastures. His was a howling of anguish.

The clawed fingers dug deeper and deeper into the flesh, pulling, ripping long strips of bloody meat from the man's thigh. The pale, bloody pieces and hunks disappeared into the hole. More chewing and chomping sounds emanated from beneath the bubbling matter. They were followed by a lip-smacking sound of satisfaction.

The agent's struggling became weaker as shock and loss of blood took its toll. He was slowly, from beneath the ground, twisted and repositioned above ground, then steadily pulled down into the hole, his hip bones cracking as his body was forcibly dragged through the too-small opening. His upper torso was now all that was visible above the ground.

More chewing sounds sprang from the bubbling ground.

The agent, through his hideous pain of being devoured alive, found a root growing above ground and hooked his arms over and under the root.

The spawn of the devil beneath the bubbling surface of the earth pulled on the agent. But the man had died, in death, his arms locking him above the surface, around the thick tree root.

"God!" Taylor yelled. "Where was that howling coming from?"

"I can't tell!" Langway yelled. "I couldn't get a fix. That way, I think." He pointed.

"Jesus Christ!" they all heard Trooper Forbes yell. "Holy Mother of God!"

Then the sounds of Forbes' screaming reached them all, chilling them.

The cops began running toward the now-defined sound.

It took them several minutes to reach the scene.

They all, to a person, froze momentarily at the sight.

Forbes was covered with cats, only his boots visible as the snarling, clawing, spitting, biting felines rode him to the ground. As he fell to the ground, unconscious, some of the cats were knocked from him. The cops could see the irreparable damage.

Forbes' face was gone, his eyes gone, his lips gone, his ears torn off.

Captain Taylor crossed himself, lifted his shotgun, and put Virginia Highway Patrolman Forbes out of this world. Taylor emptied the Remington, knocking bloody pieces of cats spinning and hurtling through the soft early summer air.

273

The remaining cats seemed to melt into the landscape.

The cops looked at the bloody rags that once was Trooper Forbes. All knew Taylor had done the only thing that could have been done.

"If you hadn't, I was going to," Langway told the captain.

But the captain wasn't listening. His eyes were locked on the OSS agent.

They all looked through horror-filled eyes. They heard the nerve-jarring and mind-numbing sounds of the breaking of bones. They watched as the agent's torso was slowly pulled into the too-small bubbling hole in the ground. The man disappeared, the foul-smelling liquid covering his head.

The man's arms were all that remained above ground, pulled out of their sockets. They gripped the root in death.

"Jesus Christ!" Lou said, panting up to the site. He could do nothing but stand and stare in horror at all that remained of his agent.

The cops walked slowly up to the hole in the Virginia earth. The sounds of chewing and the cracking of bones grew louder, then faded away.

"It ate him," Hawkes said.

"Whatever *it* is," Dan said.

The liquid bubbled. "Uhhrupt!" the hole belched.

The agent's shoes and belt were puked up, to land on the surface.

The cops stood in silence, staring at the bubbling hole.

One of the OSS lab people came running up, nearly out of breath.

"You . . ." Lou had trouble speaking. He cleared his throat, finding his voice. "You get a sample of that liquid. But Jesus God, be careful doing it."

"Where's the rest of Randall?" the lab man asked.

"Whatever's down in that hole ate him."

The lab man looked at Lamotta, then at the hole. He put his kit on the ground. "Forget it, man!" he said. He turned and walked off.

Lou didn't say a thing. Just watched him go for a moment. Then he lifted his M-16 and shot the man in the back, knocking him sprawling, dead on the ground. Lou looked at the cops. "That ought to prove to you pansies I mean what I say." He looked at one of his men. "Get another lab boy out here and get a sample. Move."

"You don't have to do that," the female voice came from behind the men.

Emily stood beside a deputy, looking at the scene.

"I can tell you the composition of that liquid," Emily said. "In all probability," she added.

"And that is? . . ." Dan asked.

"Stale, putrid blood."

"Oh, gross!" Susan said.

The hole belched again. The agent's car keys were spat from the bubbling matter, to fall with a small thud on the earth's surface.

8

The farmer, what was left of him, lay a dozen yards from his pickup truck. His bones gleamed white under God's sun. He had been eaten down to the bone. Not one scrap of flesh remained on him. Nearby, a hole bubbled and spewed its noxious stench. Beside the hole, a small creature sat. It was hideously grotesque, slick and slimy from its passage through the life-sustaining liquid. The creature had arms and legs and a head. It was vaguely human-appearing. Its hide was all scales and hair. The head was huge, the mouth wide, with long misshapen teeth. The toes were webbed, as were the hands, clawed hands and feet.

The Old One belched, a foulness springing from its mouth. It scratched itself and stretched. It was still tremendously hungry. It rose to its feet, the legs still shaky. The arms hung down almost to its feet. It took a few steps, walking back and forth. It was neither male nor female. It was all things—all things evil.

It walked away from the permanent bubbling womb.

Dan and Taylor were shown, by Doctor Goodson, the engineer. Neither man could disguise his shock at the . . . *thing's* appearance. Both were glad to be out of the mummy-like man's sight. It was unnerving.

Goodson had then shown them Deputy Bowie; or more specifically, what Bowie was becoming.

The men stepped back outside, into the sunlight. Grateful for that light.

"Did you leave guards at the hole?" Goodson asked.

"Lamotta did," Dan replied. "A safe distance away."

"That goddamn Lamotta fed the body of the man he shot into the hole," Taylor said. "Said he wanted to see if whatever was down there was still hungry. It was."

Goodson was silently stunned at the OSS man's callousness.

"What does he have on you, Doctor?" Dan asked.

Goodson told him, speaking quietly. He ended with a question. "How do we break out of this . . . hold he has on us?"

"I'm working on that," Dan told him, and would say no more on the subject. "How about the sample taken from the hole?"

"Just what Mrs. Harrison said it was. Very old blood. But the cells . . . well, I've never seen anything like it. Never. I . . . can't describe them to a layperson. I don't mean to belittle your intelligence, but I'd be talking over your heads. It's even above *my* head."

"Try to simplify it," Taylor urged. "Good God,

man! Give us *something* tangible."

"Gentlemen, I can't tell you because I don't know myself. The cells are not human. They are not animal. They . . . I don't know what they are. And neither will anyone else . . . on this earth."

None of the men wanted to pursue that last remark. But they all silently agreed with the doctor.

"The cats taken from my yard?" Dan asked.

"We don't know yet," Goodson said. "But they're not rabid. That's about the only bright spot in this . . . mess."

"How are they controlled to attack? And why?" Langway asked.

"I don't know," Goodson said calmly, while inside he trembled with fear. "But I'll say this, and I never thought the words would leave my mouth." He met the eyes of the men. "You'd better get some religious people in on this." He took a note pad from his pocket and wrote a number on it. "The man's name is Father Michael Denier. He lives in Richmond. He is still a priest, but not active in any church. He's . . . he was forced into an early retirement about five years ago. If there is an expert in this world on the devil, Denier is it." He gave Dan the number and walked away.

The men looked at one another without speaking. Dan put the paper into his pocket. Finally, Taylor said, "Are you going to call him?"

"Yes," Dan said.

The cops had carefully looked around the terminal, wanting to see if they could spot where Mille and Kenny were being held. They could not. The terminal had several large buildings and half a dozen smaller ones. The pair might be held in any one of them. Or, the thought had crossed their minds, they could be a hundred miles away.

Lou had watched the eyes and faces of the cops, an

amused look on his own face. He knew what they were doing. He had already shoved the memory of the dead trooper far into that back of his mind. He'd lost people before. Two more didn't bother him. He just wanted whatever might be lying beneath the bubbling brew. And not for revenge. Lou's mind was working hard; he felt he had found the ultimate weapon. Now the problem was in harnessing it; controlling it for study and experimentation.

If the U.S.A. could harness it, and Lou felt they could, America could put the commies on the run; wipe out the Red bastards. Once and for all. Just turn the cats and that other . . . thing loose in Russia and let it go to work. Maybe the lab boys could take whatever it is in all that smelly goo and make a whole bunch of them. Turn it loose on the Reds. Let it eat them all up. Men, women, and kids.

Lou laughed aloud, watching the wimpy cops leave the area. He imagined himself at the White House, the president giving him the Medal of Freedom. Hot damn! Wouldn't that be a kick?

"The Bureau is not at all happy with the OSS, Dan," Dodge told the sheriff. "They've ordered a team into this county. They're supposedly in here now, working very quietly."

"I don't recall seeing any strangers lately," Dan said.

Dodge shrugged. "That's just what I was told, Sheriff."

"Oh, it's fine with me. But I think we're going to have to go a little higher than the FBI before this is all over."

"To the president?"

"Higher than that." Dan pointed heavenward.

279

"You're really serious?"

"Yeah."

By the time Dan had notified all the parents of the dead kids, lying again, telling them their kids had probably run away from home, it was mid-afternoon. The phone on his desk rang. His private number.

"First motel on the right coming from the north," the voice said. "Rooms twenty-eight and thirty. Backside. How do we play this thing, Dan?"

"Carefully," he told Gordon. "Lamotta's got eyes and ears all over the place."

"More than you know, buddy. Lamotta's playing the national security bit for all it'll stand on this one. But his high-handed tactics are wearing some folks' patience mighty thin. Some high-up folks in Foggy Bottom are getting edgy with the OSS. They think it might be time for them to pull in their horns. And the Bureau has a team working in the county. Construction or surveyors or something like that. The OSS really blew it this time, and I think this may well be the end of Lamotta. The OSS will always be around. But after all this coverup, their role will be sharply reduced."

"Reading between the lines, ol' buddy, I'm getting the impression we have to let this play all the way out."

"That's it."

"Wonderful. Well, we have to talk in depth, but damned if I know where or how."

"I'm IRS, Dan. As soon as Lou checks me out and finds my I.D. holds up, he'll back off. Not even the OSS wants to screw around with the IRS. I always check in with the local police and sheriff's department whenever I use the IRS bit. Courtesy call. I'll see you in about fifteen or twenty minutes."

"I'll sure be here."

Dan felt his office had been penetrated. He couldn't prove it, but he felt certain Lou had gotten to one of his people. But which one? He didn't know. Intimidation from the OSS was how, he felt sure. And he was equally certain it had not been a subtle approach. One of his peoples' kids had been threatened, their mother or father or wife or husband. But which deputy?

His intercom buzzed. "Pat Leonard to see you, Sheriff."

"Send him in." Dan leaned back in his chair and rubbed his temples with his fingertips.

Seated, Pat looked at Dan. Dan waited. Pat cleared his throat and said, "Some jerk named Lou Lamotta came to see me, Dan."

"That doesn't surprise me a bit, Pat. He's been seeing a number of people."

"What's going on in this town, Dan?"

Dan sighed. "Pat . . . tell me what Lou had to say to you."

"All right. Nothing firm was said by him. Goddamn master of double-talk, I guess. Not a damn thing that would stand up in a court of law. But I never felt so threatened. Yes, I have, by God! Down in South America, about ten years ago, while I was working out of New York. The state security police grabbed me and questioned me for several hours; accused me of working for the CIA. I . . ."

Dan smiled. Held up his hand. "You play along with me, Pat. I just got an idea. You're about to be investigated by the IRS." He chuckled and glanced at the clock on his desk.

Pat sat straight up in his chair. "I'm about to be what?" he blurted.

Dan laughed. "Just play along, Pat. I promise you I'll level with you in due time. Just hang in there with me for a time. For right now, just sit still and look very worried."

"That won't be too hard, Dan, I am worried!"

Fixing a smile on his face, Dan walked out of his office and over to the coffee urn. Pouring himself a cup of coffee, he said, to several deputies and a couple of Taylor's troopers, "Pat must think the sheriff's office has a lot of power. He's being investigated by the IRS and wants me to do something about it."

The cops grinned at that. All of them thankful it wasn't them being checked by the IRS.

Dan glanced at his watch, playing it close. "Damn fool told the IRS field agent to meet him in my office. Be here any time, now. I really wish he'd left me out of his personal business."

"Yeah, Sheriff," Deputy Ken Pollard said. "The IRS is liable to be on your case next."

"I heard that." Dan lifted his eyes as a man and woman entered the building. He recognized the man as Gordon Miller. Gordon was dressed in a rumpled suit and carried a briefcase. Dan knew the eyeglasses were for window-dressing only. The woman with him was short and stocky, her hair worn short. She wore slacks and carried a battered briefcase.

"That's got to be the IRS people, Sheriff," Ken said with a nervous laugh. Not at all like him. "They stand out like a sore thumb."

Exactly what Gordon wanted them to do, Dan thought. He knew full well most IRS agents didn't stand out any more than anybody else.

"You boys get to work," Dan told his people. "And be careful."

Dan suddenly remembered that Ken's younger brother was bed-ridden, paralyzed from the neck down after a swimming accident years back. The family was not well-off, and would not have been able to manage if it were not for government assistance. And lots of it. Ken would be Dan's first choice as Lou's pipeline.

Then he remembered Ken on the phone after they discussed the cat situation, standing around the dispatcher. It began to fit together.

Dan walked to the counter. Gordon fumbled around, spilling half the briefcase's contents on the floor as he searched for his I.D. He found his I.D. and showed it to Dan.

"I don't like to be a part of this, Mister Miller," Dan said. "Mister Leonard is in my office, now. He's very upset about your visit."

Gordon picked up on it immediately. "Well, now, this is highly irregular, Sheriff Garrett. But I assure you, you are not under any type of IRS audit. It's Mister Leonard we wish to speak with."

Dan knew Pat's lawyer was out of town, on vacation. He said, "Mister Leonard's attorney is out of town. Pat wanted me to witness this first meeting. I don't know why. I'm not even sure it's legal. And I hope it's the only meeting."

Gordon pushed up his glasses. "Highly irregular. But if that is what Mister Leonard wishes. All right," he said with a shrug.

"Right this way," Dan said, stepping aside to allow the pair past the counter. He cut his eyes. Ken Pollard was standing just outside the office front door, watching the proceedings.

"Now, Quinn!" Alice said, pointing her finger at her husband. "I want to know what in the blazes is going on, you . . . you . . . *idiot*!"

Quinn sat on the couch, open-mouthed in shock. His wife had never spoken to him like that before. Not in all their years of marriage. The doctor sputtered and stammered a couple of times.

Doctor Harrison looked awfully uncomfortable. He would not meet his wife's steady gaze.

"Goddamnit, Quinn!" Alice shouted at him. "Now you'd better tell me the truth this time. And I mean all of it."

"And that goes in triplicate for you, Bill," Emily said.

The doctors looked at each other.

"We can't," Bill said lamely.

"We were sworn to secrecy," Quinn added. "It's a top-secret government matter."

"Lies!" Alice blared at him.

"Husband of mine," Emily said, her eyes fixed on Bill. "It's choice-making time for you. Me, or your secret. Think about it, buddy. 'Cause if those cats that chased us this morning; those cats that killed those kids, is your top secret government matter, you don't have both oars in the water."

"Ditto on that from me," Alice said.

The doctors sighed. Bill said, "We got suckered, Quinn."

"Yeah," Quinn said. "First of all, ladies, let me say we made a mistake in going along with Lou Lamotta on this. And I'm going to apologize to this town, if they'll give me a chance to do so. I'll start by apologizing to the both of you, right now."

Alice sat down beside Emily to hear the man out.

"Veiled threats," Gordon said, after Pat had told his story. "Lamotta hasn't changed any." He clicked off the tiny cassette recorder. He looked at Dan.

Dan was getting some strange vibes from his old friend. Something was just not right about the man; something was not ringing true. Maybe he was wrong, he thought. He hoped he was.

Gordon said, "And you think one of your people is pipelining out of this office to Lou?"

Might as well play it out to the end, Dan thought. He wished those nagging doubts would go away. "Yeah, that's right. Ken Pollard." He told them about Ken's brother.

June laughed and said, "Lou can't do anything about that fellow's government assistance. He's simply running one of his famous bluffs and the guy bought it. Lou and the OSS are powerful, but not that powerful; not nearly as powerful as they would like people to believe. We know their power is waning. A lot of people would like to see the OSS put out of business."

"That's dandy," Dan said. "So would I. But right now, Lou is not my main concern. It's all these . . . well, unexplained—but very real—supernatural occurrences that have me worried."

Gordon and June looked at each other.

Did a signal pass between them? Dan thought. He felt it did.

Gordon looked back at Dan and said, "You've *really* seen all this, Dan?"

"I've seen it. Just as I described it to you."

Gordon smiled. Funny time for a man to be smiling, Dan thought.

Pat looked both sick and doubtful at Dan's story. "And you went along with it," he said accusingly. He shook his head. "Sorry, Dan. I shouldn't have said that. But I wonder how many more people this Lamotta has coerced?"

"That isn't important," Gordon said. He waved

that aside. "The hard fact is, buddy," he said to Dan. "You can't *prove* any of it."

"That's right," Dan said. Again, Gordon smiled. "And I'd come off looking like the world's biggest fool if I attempted to blow the story."

"That is correct, Sheriff," June said. She had a small smile on her lips.

What the hell is with these two? Dan thought.

"But the citizens of this county are in danger!" Pat protested. "Not only the people of Ruger, but the whole state. We can't just sit here and do nothing. That is," he qualified that, "providing I believe all this . . . monster stuff."

"Believe it, Pat," Dan said. "Eddie Brown and Mickey Reynolds and Jimmy and Al and Denise and Bowie are no longer a part of the human race. I'm numb. I should be running around shrieking; but it's so horrible, I suppose my mind has blocked out part of it. I saw the cats kill Trooper Forbes. I saw Lou's agent being devoured by that . . . that *thing* in the hole. I saw Lou feed the body of the man he shot into that hole; heard the body being eaten. I saw the cats attack. I saw what plain ordinary house cats did to those kids." He touched the pocket where he had put the piece of paper Goodson had given him.

Gordon's eyes followed the gesture. "What are you thinking, Dan?"

"About calling in some help."

"Who?" Pat asked.

Dan decided to hedge his bets. "A priest from up in Washington."

June laughed. And Dan didn't like the sound of the laughter. "Mumbo-jumbo," she said. "Superstitious hogwash."

"I agree," Pat said. "Dan, you're not Catholic. You can't believe in all that exorcism business."

286

"Washington, eh?" Gordon asked.

"That's right."

"Called him yet?"

"Not yet."

"Well, wait awhile on that, Dan. You probably won't need him."

"Whatever you say, Gordon."

Dan didn't know whom to trust.

9

"I got an idea, Kenny," Mille said.

The young man forced a smile. "I am certainly in a position to be open to suggestion."

They were being held in a small room at the back of the main terminal building. A very dirty room. One window, set up high, near the high ceiling. It was barred. The door was wooden, with a sheet metal covering front and back. The room had a tiny bathroom with only a ragged curtain for a door.

"I wonder what they did with our luggage?" Mille asked.

"Is that your idea?"

"No. I just was wondering. They must not be planning on keeping us for very long."

"They're going to kill us, Mille," Kenny said. "Wise up and think about it. They're not going to face kidnapping charges. And they know if we're released, we'd sure file charges against them. They're totally ruthless. We've had it."

"All the more reason for us to be planning a way out of this place, right?"

"I'm still listening."

"The lock on that door is weak. I've seen you pick better locks. Can you pick that one?"

"I've already thought of that. Sure, I could pick it. So what? They've got guards outside."

"One guard, Kenny. And along three o'clock in the morning, I'll give you odds he'll be sleeping."

"The others outside the building won't be sleeping."

"Do we have a choice, Kenny?"

"No. So let's hear your plan."

The severed arm was now covered with maggot-like worms. They were growing faster and faster, and breeding with each other as soon as they plopped to the floor. There was no place left for them to hide in the room. They covered the floor, squirming and hunching and wriggling about. Ankle deep. And still more were dropping from the infected arm, falling onto the others. The worms were a mottled white/gray, as thick as a big man's thumb. With very sharp little teeth.

And they were very hungry.

They had devoured their weaker brothers and sisters; eaten all the carpet; the insulation off the wiring; the plastic and leather and cloth of anything they could find in the room. But they could not escape from the room.

They began squeaking in anger.

Outside the trailer, the afternoon was waning, the sun now dipping into the western horizon. A guard stopped, not sure of what he thought he'd just heard. He took another step, then stopped and turned around. There was that sound again. A squeaking sort of sound. A lot of things squeaking. But what the hell was it?

He stepped closer to the trailer. Coming from in there, he thought. And there wasn't supposed to be anything in there. Not that he knew of. Just that severed arm was all, and that sure as hell wasn't squeaking.

He unlocked the door and stepped inside. The squeaking was much louder. And . . . the sounds of something moving, he thought, sensed. Yeah, there it was. Definitely not supposed to be anything moving in this trailer. He closed the door, the door locking automatically, and began investigating all the rooms. He'd find out what it was.

By the bubbling pool that had claimed one life and the carcass of the man Lou had shot, an OSS guard squatted and stared at the foul-smelling liquid. He was a safe and respectable distance away. At least fifteen feet. No way he'd get any closer to that mess.

Whispering came softly from beneath the bubbling liquid.

The man cut his eyes. *Whispering?*

The whispering became a bit louder. The agent moved a few feet closer.

"Help me," the words came from the pool of red-colored liquid. "Please help me, Wally."

Wally's eyes widened in shock. That was Randall's voice. But Randall was dead!

"No," the voice said, louder. "No, I'm not. Wally, please help me." The voice was stronger. "Please. I don't have any arms, Wally."

Wally knew that for a flat-out fact. He'd seen the arms body-bagged. He inched closer to the pleading voice of Randall.

The voice whispered again. But this time the words were too low for Wally to understand. He moved closer.

"Randall? Randall? Is that really you down there?"

"Yes."

Wally inched closer. "Really?" Something was wrong with Wally's mind. He couldn't think straight. Kind of like he'd had one drink too many.

"Help me, Wally. Please get me out."

"Get you *out*?" Wally said. "But, you're *dead*!" He looked around him. Felt like a fool.

"No. Bad hurt. Please, Wally. Help me. Get me out of this awful place."

The words got to Wally. He laid down his M-16. "Okay, Randall." He moved to the lip of the hole. "What can I do?"

He stopped abruptly as his head suddenly cleared. He looked around him. "This must be a trick. There is no way for Randall to be alive."

"Yes, it is," Randall's voice came out of the bubbling pool, a chuckling sound close behind the words. A dark, clawed hand reached out and clamped around Wally's ankle.

Wally began screaming.

In the high school basement, Mickey Reynolds looked at the ever-widening crack in the concrete floor. The red-colored fluid now covered the entire basement floor where he squatted with his companion, the cat.

Gazing down into the crack, Mickey could see eyes staring back at him.

Mickey grunted. The eyes blinked in understanding. He grunted again.

The creature beneath the floor spoke to him. "It is almost time. Only a few more hours."

Mickey knew that voice.

He should.
It was his.

"What a despicable place for my rebirth," the voice rose out of the bubbling foulness.

Eddie Brown nodded his animal head. He didn't know what the creature meant; his mind could no longer comprehend human thoughts.

"A church," the voice spoke from the stinking blood.

Eddie grunted.

The old blood covered the basement floor. The crack had widened to about ten inches across. What had once been Eddie Brown could see eyes looking at him from out of the liquid.

"Only a few more hours," the familiar voice spoke. "Just after noon tomorrow."

Eddie nodded. That voice calmed him. He knew that voice. Trusted it.

It was his own.

In the old service station/motel, the Old One was now able to get its head out of the wet, slimy crack in the floor. It looked at Betty and her kids.

"Can I help?" she asked.

"No," the voice sprang from the wide, ugly mouth. "I must do it myself. Soon it will be over. By noon of tomorrow."

She knew that voice, oddly feminine-sounding. But she couldn't quite place it.

It was her voice.

Anya and Pet sat by a dusty window and watched a

man and a woman park their truck and get out. They went into the house, returning in a moment to carry in their suitcases. A small dog ran around the yard, barking. The man told the little dog to shut up.

"They must not know of our presence until all the Old Ones have rebirthed," Anya said. "Warn our friends not to attack."

The cat blinked and trotted off.

"I say we pull all our people in and plan an attack for tonight," Dan said. "We can't wait any longer. The public must be warned of what's facing them. We tell the people to stay inside. We could coordinate the attack on the terminal with a charge of dynamite down that goddamned hole."

"You haven't been listening, Dan," Gordon said. It had reached the point where Dan thought the man's voice sounded oily. "I told you, we have to see this matter through. Those orders come from the top."

Dan didn't believe that and said as much—bluntly.

Gordon shrugged it off. "Dan, would you like to see this county grow?"

Dan blinked and stared at the man, not understanding what that had to do with their present situation. "What kind moronic question is that?"

"Would you?" Gordon said.

"As a lawman, I wouldn't. Not without more personnel. As a citizen, of course I'd like to see it grow. What are you driving at, Gordon?"

"A large industrial complex built right outside this town. Employing up to a thousand people."

"Drop the other shoe, Gordon," Dan said, disgust in his voice. He knew what the other shoe would contain. Another pack of lies.

"You might not like it, Dan."

"I'm sure I won't."

"You see this thing through, without spilling it to the national press, or to the residents of this county, and I place in the proper hands a signed, legal document attesting to the fact that a certain high-tech industry will begin construction on a large plant immediately. Others to follow."

"I have neither the authority nor the inclination to agree to that," Dan said. "The lives of the people in this county are incalculable, Gordon. You're as bad as Lamotta. I won't agree to that offer."

"I will," Pat said, executing a greedy flip-flop. More people meant more businesses; more bussinesses meant more advertisers; more advertisers meant more money. For him. "I'm chairman of the Ruger County Industrial Inducement Committee. Let me see that document."

"Come on, Pat!" Dan said.

June produced the document and handed it to the editor. Pat quickly scanned it. "This is legal and binding," he said, looking up.

"We know it," Gordon said.

"If the lives of the people of this county are physically threatened, you back off and the document still remains valid?" Pat asked.

"Of course," Gordon said smoothly. "We don't want to see anyone hurt."

Dan looked up at the ceiling, shaking his head at how easily the man could lie.

Pat said, "I want a codicil included that the companies will train locals for employment."

"That can be worked out," Gordon assured him. "Just write it in and I'll date it and initial it. We want to cooperate with the residents of this county."

"In return for? . . ." Pat asked.

"Your cooperation in our finding out about the

aging process and what is really under the ground here."

"That's fair," Pat said. He scribbled on the paper, conscious of Dan's eyes on him as he did so.

"You don't know what you're doing," Dan flared.

"I know what I'm doing," Pat said. "If you had any business sense you would too."

"May I use your phone, Dan?" Gordon asked.

"You can stick it in your ear if you want to," Dan told him.

Gordon laughed and dialed a number. He said, "Seal it off." He hung up. He looked at Dan, then at Pat. "All taken care of." He smiled.

"Gordon," Dan said. "You're as bad as Lamotta, you know that?"

"But in a much more subtle way, ol' buddy. Relax, Dan. Everything will be all right."

Dan's laugh was sour-sounding. "How do you think that lousy piece of paper is going to keep my mouth shut?"

Gordon smiled again. "Because, ol' buddy, we are going to handle this thing so smoothly and quietly we won't stir up a ripple. Right now, a state of emergency is being declared in Ruger County. And we don't need your permission to do that. We're moving against Lamotta and his people in," he glanced at his watch, "twenty-six hours. In ten minutes, a news flash will be on the air, telling people that an SST rig containing nuclear warheads has overturned in this county. It's a very dangerous situation. My people are on the way. The bridge on highway fifteen is closed, as are the bridges on twenty and fifty-six. Traffic on sixty heading west is being diverted down to Farmville and over. Sixty east is being blocked and diverted south on twenty-six down to four-sixty. Any traffic on fifteen north is being advised to turn back, or detoured east

295

or west on six-thirty-six. Your county will be shut down tight in six hours, Dan. In twenty-eight hours, everything will be returned to normal and no resident of Ruger will have been hurt, or even know what has taken place here. So relax, ol' buddy. It's all out of your hands."

"You're a real pal, aren't you, Gordon?"

"It's for the good of the nation, Dan."

"Yeah. Sure. Get out of my office." He looked at Pat. Jerked his thumb at the editor. "And take that loser with you."

"I'll remember this with editorials come election time, Dan," Pat said, his face flushing with anger.

"You do that."

His office clear of Gordon, June, and Pat (Dan thought it smelled better), he waved Taylor, Dodge, and Chuck in and laid it out for them. The men sat in silence for a moment, digesting it all.

Dodge said, "There are government agencies that can come in and take over in cases of dangerous SST wrecks. Including military units. But I think they've been duped, being used by Gordon and his people. I guess your buddy wasn't such a buddy after all. I wanted to tell you, but I didn't think you'd believe me."

"I want to pursue that, Dodge. 'Cause I don't know which side you're on."

"Later," Taylor said. "Right now, Dan, the question is: what do we do?"

"Play our only remaining hole card," Dan said, reaching for the phone on his desk. He pulled his hand back. "Chuck, go get Ken and tell him his brother's government assistance is safe. I thought that was iffy from the beginning."

Chuck nodded and left the office.

Dan dialed the number. It was answered on the

third ring. "Father Michael Denier? Yes. Good. My name is Garrett. Sheriff Dan Garrett of Ruger County. Oh? You what, Father?"

Dan listened and then lifted his eyes, looking at the men seated in front of his desk. "Father Denier says he's been waiting for my call."

Taylor crossed himself.

Dodge looked stunned.

Dan cleared his throat and spoke briefly with the priest. "I see, Father. Well, I guess that's good. I don't understand it, but . . ."

Dan listened intently. "How do you *know* these things, Father?"

Dan exchanged a few more words with the priest and then hung up.

"He says he'll be here in an hour. And no, he didn't need directions to my house. He said he knows the way. You heard me ask him if there was anything we could do until he arrived?"

The men nodded.

"He said try prayer."

10

Wally was putting up a much stronger defense than Randall. Wary from the outset, the man had intense fear working on his side. He managed to twist, grab his M-16, and flop over onto his back. He pulled the trigger. The three round burst caught the creature in the neck and face, all that was visible sticking out of the ground. Through fearful eyes, Wally watched the slugs impact, twisting and tearing their way through the dark, wrinkled flesh. One of the slugs hit the thing in its mouth, knocking out long teeth.

The hideous being laughed at Wally. It was Randall's voice springing from out of that wide, fanged mouth. The head and face slick and slimy from the hole. Wally fired again and again, the slugs knocking chunks of meat from the creature. The stinking chunks fell to the earth around the hole. They lay quivering, working their way into the earth. Living still.

Wally felt himself being pulled deeper into the hole. Almost unbearable agony ripped through the man as his leg was twisted, breaking, the bone popping, punching out of his flesh. He blacked out momentarily. When he regained consciousness, he was up to his waist, inside the hole. The heat of the liquid was worse than the pain in his leg.

Summoning what was left of his strength, Wally twisted and hammered at the ugly creature with his rifle. Pounding on the thing's slimy head seemed to have more effect than shooting it. Wally felt the creature's hand relax its grip on his one good ankle. He jammed the muzzle of the M-16 into one of the thing's eyes and pulled the trigger. The horrible being howled and screamed, releasing Wally's ankle. Its eye exploded in a gush of fluid. The creature shook its head and roared.

Wally found his way out of the hole and crawled and scurried like a big crippled bug over the ground. Scooting along, dragging his mangled leg, Wally made his way away from the hole. He looked back, over his shoulder. The creature was struggling to be free of the hole; but could not quite make it out. It sank back into the bubbling stench.

Wally found his walkie-talkie and managed to call in. Then he passed out, the darkness swallowing him.

"Have you switched sides permanently?" Dan asked Dodge. And can I believe whatever answer you give me? he thought.

Dodge, Taylor, and Dan stood outside the Sheriff's Department office building. The sun was boiling red,

299

slowly sinking over Ruger County. It was almost the color of blood, tinting the landscape an eerie hue.

Dodge nodded. "I never was on the side of the OSS. I've been working undercover for seven years with those people. Every time I'd think I had enough to go to court, the witnesses would turn rabbit on me. I'm sorry, Dan. But I couldn't let on to you." He looked at Taylor. "Either of you. Now it doesn't make any difference; Lamotta began suspecting I wasn't who I claimed to be several months ago. They've been edging me out slowly. And your pal Gordon Miller— that isn't his real name, by the way—is working both sides of the street, too. Maybe both sides *and* the middle. We think he's taking Red money."

"Holy smokes!" Taylor said. "And Miller knows all about the OSS?"

Dodge laughed bitterly. "Know about them? He's been part of them for years. So is the woman with him. We think she's a Red mole."

Who to trust? Dan thought. Trust? The question is: what can I *do*?

"We're all meeting the priest at your house, right, Dan?" Taylor asked.

"Yeah. We'd better get going."

"I'm going to shower and change first," the trooper said. "I got a feeling in my guts it may be a while before we get another chance."

"I'll sure go along with that."

"One more thing," Dodge said. "Governor Williams is working with the Bureau on this matter. He didn't cut bait. He just didn't have any choice in the matter. None of us knew it was going to turn out this way. I mean, come on, think about it. Monsters? Creatures? Satan? But the governor is fully prepared

300

to shoulder the blame. He's really a good man caught up in a hard bind. I guess, like us."

"Why all the goddamned cover-ups?" Taylor demanded. "Why not just come out and level with us all from the outset?"

Dodge sighed. "Because, gentlemen, sometimes government agencies work at cross-purposes with each other. It's usually unintentional—as in this case—but it happens. We told the governor to do one thing, another agency, without knowing we were even in on it, told him to do another. The governor said to hell with it all and went on vacation."

"In other words," Taylor said. "You blew it."

"Well, yes."

"Dandy," the trooper said, disgust in his tone. "Where do you super-cops get the idea that you can handle a state's internal problems any better than that state's troopers?"

Dodge had no reply to give, literally or figuratively. He knew the captain was right.

"I'm sorry about Forbes," Dodge said.

"Yeah," Taylor said, turning to leave. He called over his shoulder. "I'll have that chiseled on his tombstone."

Dodge took no offense. He understood the trooper's anger.

"He's a good, solid man, Dodge," Dan said.

"Oh, I know that. He has every reason to be angry. I don't blame him a bit."

"That document Gordon had Pat sign?" Dan asked.

Dodge laughed, his short bark void of humor. "Not worth the paper it's printed on. The company named is non-existent. The CIA has no authority to make

301

any such agreements."

"I thought as much. Come on. Follow me to my house."

The only thing left of the guard was the change in his pockets, his gun and ammunition, his keys, his watch and belt buckle. Everything else had been eaten.

They had attacked the guard's ankles, quickly eating their way up his calves, eating the muscles, bringing the man down, unable to use his legs. More vicious than piranha, the worms wriggled and crawled and squirmed their way over the floor of the trailer; they covered the white bones of the guard.

But the worms were still unable to leave the trailer. They were still trapped, and still growing, producing more and more of their kind. Little spawns of the Dark One. Even Satan has a sense of humor.

They began seeking escape from the confines of the trailer.

The doctors and their wives sat in silence in Alice's lovely home. They looked at each other, none trusting their voices to speak. They had just heard the news bulletin on the TV.

"I don't understand it," Emily said. "What does it mean? Is it real?"

"I doubt it," Quinn said. "I think if it were real, we would have been notified. We're the only Trauma Center in the county."

"They? . . ." Alice looked at her husband. "What does it all mean?"

Bill answered her question. "I think it means we're cut off. No one can get into the county, and no one can get out."

"Trapped," Emily said.

"I'm afraid so."

BOOK THREE

As long as I count the votes, what are you going to do about it?

Tweed

1

The man stood in the twilight, that time between light and dark, day and night. But he was no more fearful of the night than of light. He carried a small leather bag, much like a doctor's bag, in his right hand. Although he was just past middle age, his hair was snow-white, his face lined from years of studying and combating his enemy—Satan. And Satan was here. He could feel the presence of the Dark One. There was no doubt in his mind. And Satan was not alone. The Old Ones were struggling to be free.

The priest had been awaiting a call from this county for several weeks. Not looking forward to it, but knowing it was coming. The evil had intensified, slowly growing, the corruption building and bubbling under the earth's surface.

And the priest knew it was no fault of the county's ten thousand or so residents. The young goddess and her companion had been disturbed by an unlucky slap of fate. Or perhaps Satan had directed their footsteps to this county. The priest would probably never know.

Father Michael Denier had known he would be called. And he knew he was facing his own death by answering that call.

He stood in the front yard, looking at the Garrett house in the now-swiftly fading light.

"Mother," Carrie said, looking out a window. "There is a man standing out in the front yard. He's all dressed in black."

"The priest," Dan said. He walked out onto the porch and stood, looking at the man, looking at him. "Father Denier?"

"Yes. But please drop the Father. Call me Michael."

"I wouldn't be comfortable doing that," Dan said.

"As you wish."

"Please come in, Father."

"In a moment. First I want to bless this house and grounds."

Dan didn't know if he was allowed to watch this or not. Denier smiled. "I'm just a man, Sheriff Garrett. And all things pertaining to God can, or should be, viewed."

"How did you develop the power to read minds?"

"Most people have some sort of psychic ability. I merely developed mine."

"I see." The phone rang. Leaving the priest to his holy work, Dan walked back inside.

Vonne held out the phone to him. "It's for you. That damnable Lou Lamotta."

"What do you want, Lamotta?"

"That thing in the hole got another one of my people, Garrett. But this one got away from it. He's pretty badly chewed up. Leg's shattered. And that hole is getting bigger. Pretty damn soon, whatever in the hell it is down there, is coming out. I put more guards out there and threw up a cyclone fence—makeshift. It's not going to hold it in, though."

"Why tell me about it, Lamotta. Didn't you tell me

to stay out of your business?"

"Because you're just as big a jerk as you think I am, Garrett. You're just too dumb to see it. Do you think I'm a fool, Garrett?"

"I told you before, Lamotta. I think you're insane. Why are you asking me these things?"

"Come on, Sheriff. Don't act cute with me. Are you saying you didn't have anything to do with the rigged accident that's closing down this county?"

"That's right. I didn't even know anything about it until it was already in motion. My plan was to storm the terminal and blow the hole where that . . . *thing* is hiding. And hopefully, I'd get to shoot you in the process."

Lou chuckled, then sighed. "Company's in on this then. Probably that phony IRS agent that met with you this afternoon, right?"

"That's right, Lou." Why not, Dan thought. I sure don't owe Gordon a damn thing.

"I figured as much. I ran into a stone wall checking him out. And that broad with him is as phony as he is. You know, Sheriff," Lou drawled. "We just might become allies before this is all over."

"Lamotta, I can't think of anything any more disgusting."

Lou laughed at that. "Hang in there, Garrett. One thing about you, buddy-boy—you're predictable."

The connection was broken.

Dan replaced the phone in the cradle and turned, feeling eyes on him. Father Denier was standing in the open doorway.

"Where to start, Father?"

Denier spread his hands and shrugged.

Taylor, Dodge, Chuck, Mike, and Dan's family sat in the den, waiting, listening. Carrie and Linda sat on the floor, both of them looking scared.

Dan took a deep breath. "This is going to sound awfully stupid, Father."

"The Old Ones are working their way out of the earth," the priest said.

"You know about them?" Dan asked.

"Oh, yes." Denier stepped into the room, placing his bag on a table. "Satan planned well. He has minions all over the world. God condemned them to the bowels of the earth and covered them, buried them under tons of rock. Thousands of years ago. Religions then formed in an attempt to call out the Old Ones. Only one succeeded. They were known as the Cat People."

Mike stared at the priest. "Then . . . that chapter in the book I read is true?"

"What chapter in what book, son?" the priest asked. There was a strange smile on his face.

Mike picked up the old book. "This book, Father." He opened the book and turned to the chapter.

But no such chapter existed.

Mike practically tore the book apart in his frantic searching for the lost chapter.

"Stop it!" Father Denier spoke sharply.

Mike looked at the man, his face confused and scared.

"It isn't in there," the priest said.

"But it *was*!" the young man said.

"I know," the priest said gently. "But it's gone now. I've been through all this before, son."

Mike shook his head as if to clear it. "How . . . Why? . . ."

Denier shrugged. "To lure you here, perhaps. It worked. Obviously. Perhaps Satan has plans for you. I don't know. Perhaps the Dark One was merely playing games. He does that—often. Taking one drink too many when a person knows they have had enough.

310

Floorboarding your car's gas pedal, knowing you're breaking the law and endangering others. Lying when the truth would serve you better. Deliberately hurting someone you love. The list is practically endless. Satan is playing. Listen to me; let me say this and please believe me. Your lives will depend on a strong belief in God. Satan can do anything he wishes to do. Anything he wishes to do on the face of this earth. He can take possession of your mind and body. He can be a snake or a humble human being. He can be or control the winds, the lightning, the thunder, the rains, the entire storm. He can be a dog, a cat, any animal he chooses. He could well be sitting in this room at this very moment."

Chuck cut his eyes at Dodge. The chief deputy didn't know much about the Catholic religion; he always tried to steer clear of priests and nuns.

Denier said, "Only one force can stop the devil. God." He smiled. "Sometimes He sends Michael. God's warrior enjoys a good fight. But, as is usually the case, humans beat back Satan. With God's help."

"Through some human emissary," Vonne said.

"Usually," the priest agreed.

"In this case . . . you?" you asked.

Denier shrugged. "Perhaps. I've battled the Dark One before. Many times. We're old enemies. We despise each other."

"Have you ever seen the devil?" Carrie asked.

"No, child. No one looks at the face of Satan and lives to tell of it. I have seen . . . some of his forms; his helpers." Again, he smiled. "How old do you think I am, child?"

"Truthfully?"

"Yes."

"Oh . . . seventy years old."

"I'm fifty." He noticed the shock on the faces of

those in the room. "I've been at war with Satan all of my adult life."

Vonne said, "Dan tells me you are not an active priest."

Denier chuckled. "Well, I wouldn't put it quite that way. I don't have a church. I was, well, asked to . . ." He seemed amused at the mental recalling. "I was gaining too much attention and too much criticism as the man to see if one felt a loved one might be possessed by Satan. And if the time was short, I sometimes bypassed church protocol for the rite of exorcism. That wasn't the only reason I was shelved, so to speak. It's a very long story, and we don't have the time to waste on ancient history." Denier looked at each person in the room. Chuck squirmed a little bit when the man looked at him. He felt a hell of a lot more comfortable with an oldtime hell, fire, and brimstone spoutin' preacher.

"Tell me everything that has happened," Denier said. "Don't leave anything out. The smallest item might be the key."

Dan, embarrassed, apologized for his lack of manners. He introduced everyone in the room. Vonne sent the girls to get the coffee and cake she had baked that afternoon.

Dan took the lead, telling his story, struggling to recall every small detail. Vonne added a few more details about the cats that attacked; their curious movement of clockwise and counter-clockwise. Dodge told of the blood on the Reynolds' kitchen wall. Taylor told of the attack on Forbes and how he shot his own man.

"You did what you thought was right," Denier told the trooper. "Don't punish yourself by dwelling on it."

Denier had listened intently as the people told their stories. He drained his coffee cup and leaned back in

312

his chair. "The cats were, although I am quite certain they themselves did not realize it, dancing the witches' dance. If you could have been able to determine the sex of the cats, you would have noticed the females forming one circle, the males forming another, and so on."

"Witches!" Chuck said. "You mean, like in ghosts and things like that?"

"Yes," Denier said.

"Lordy!" Chuck said. He'd have to remember to get some garlic and hang over his front door. He was remembering his grandmother, from the mountains of West Virginia, telling him that would ward off evil spirits.

Chuck almost jumped out of his boots when Father Denier said, "Garlic won't help."

"It won't *hurt*!" Chuck said.

Denier chuckled, sobered, then shocked them all by saying, "There is nothing I can do."

2

The guard had brought them their supper. A loaf of bread, a jar of mustard, and some assorted cold cuts. He looked in on them and said, "Nighty, nite, kids. Sleep tight and don't let the bedbugs bite."

"Hell with you," Mille said.

He laughed and said. "Lights out at nine. Be good and you might get breakfast."

"You mean we won't have to look at your ugly face again tonight?" Mille asked.

" 'Fraid not," he replied with a sardonic grin and closed the door.

As soon as he left they went to work on the old cane-bottomed chair they had found in a pile of junk in the corner. When they finished, they both had clubs, about three feet long. They sat down, fixed sandwiches, and waited for the deep night.

The farmer and his wife sat watching television. As far as the man was concerned, the program was about as interesting as watching cows chew cud. His attention kept wandering off. He wished they'd put something good back on TV. Gunsmoke or Rawhide or Wagon Train.

He stirred in his chair.

"Don't say it," his wife said, never taking her eyes from the screen. She knew what he was about to say. She'd heard it many times.

"I don't see how you can sit and watch this junk," he said.

She shook her head and smiled. She knew what would be next.

"I think I'm gonna get me one them dishes and stick it out in the front yard."

"Over my dead body. All you want to do is watch naked girls."

"All I want to do," he said, "is watch a good cowboy gunfight every now and then. I wouldn't know what to do with a young girl if one come dancin' across the living room."

She laughed at him, leaned over, and kissed his cheek. This was a game they played often. Not much else to do with the kids and grandbabies long gone and living way off in the cities. Work a little garden, sit out on the porch and rock, and watch some TV at night. And play the game, arguing about the quality of programming.

This would be the last night for them to play the game.

The man looked at the rerun on TV and wished that stupid boat would sink. Didn't old people ever take cruises? Was the entire world made up of young people? It sure seemed that way.

Their old hound dog began barking. The barking suddenly tapered off into a choking, painful bubbling. Husband and wife looked at each other.

"Turn it off," he said, pointing at the TV.

She rose and clicked off the TV while he went to the closet and got his shotgun. He broke it down and loaded up both barrels. "Stay in the house." He put a handful of extra shells in his pocket.

The old man stepped out onto the back porch. He could see what was left of his old dog in the moonlight. Bits and pieces of Buck. Blood all over the place, glistening darkly, wetly, under the moon's light. The man felt sick to his stomach. Old Buck was, or had been, more than a dog; he was, or had been, a member of the family.

The man cussed, low and long.

"What is it?" his wife called.

"I don't know. It's bad, though. Something's killed old Buck."

"What?"

"If I knew, woman, I'd tell you. Don't come out here. Get that four-ten of yours and load 'er up. Do what I tell you, now."

The man's nose wrinkled in disgust as something foul drifted to him, floating heavily on the light night breeze. He had never smelled anything like it.

Yes, he had. Death! It smelled like death.

Then something else struck his mind. Pete didn't drive back that afternoon. He'd seen Pete drive down the dirt road, like he did everyday, 'cept Sunday, to check on them cattle of his. But today he never came back. And Pete would have had to come back on the dirt road. Only one way in, and one way out.

But he didn't come back.

And he knew he hadn't missed him. 'Cause it was a regular thing between the two men. Pete would laugh and honk and wave. Walter would return the wave from his rocking chair on the porch.

So where the hell was Pete?

An alien night sound spun him around, his damned old bad knee almost giving way on him. It was rough getting old. What the blazes was that . . . *thing* moving over there by the corner of the house?

Walter stepped closer, gripping the shotgun tightly, lifting the double-barrel.

"Phew, Walter!" his wife said. "What in the world is that awful smell?"

"I don't know." That thing he'd seen was gone. "You load up that four-ten?"

No. There it was. But what the hell is it?

"Yes. And I feel like a fool holding this thing."

"Better to feel like a fool for a few minutes than be forever dead, mother." There that thing was again. God! it was *horrible* looking.

"It's probably a bear. Mable told me there was some sightings last week."

"No bear, mother. Not this time."

"But? . . ."

"Hush up." His eyes had not left the thing by the corner of the house. It began to move, slowly. Kind of shuffling movement. But what in the good God almighty was it? He strained his eyes, peering into the ivory-tinted gloom. The damn thing looked . . . well, *slick*.

Slick?

He stepped closer. The thing growled at him. But it was not a growl like any growl he had ever heard before. It was—he didn't know what it sounded like.

"What's all that growling?"

"Goddamnit, mother, I don't know!"

"You watch your mouth, old man."

The thing came closer, shuffling as it came. Then it stepped into the light from God's moon.

"Jesus Christ!" the old man shouted, the shotgun in his hands forgotten. Fear numbed his mind. Froze his feet to the ground.

"Walter! What's wrong?"

"Lock all the doors, mother! And call the law!"

The man remembered the shotgun in his hands. The weapon felt strange. He looked down. The shotgun was melting in his hands, the metal white hot, the barrels drooping, the wood blazing with fire. His hands were blistered from the heat. When he released the weapon, the heat was so intense it took pieces of flesh from his hands. He screamed in pain.

The creature's eyes glowed in the night. The old man felt himself being pushed backward by some invisible force. His feet sailed out from under him and he fell heavily to the ground, landing on his bad knee. He felt the old bones give way and break. He yelled in pain.

"Walter!"

"Stay inside," he called weakly. "Call the law, mother. Don't come out here. For God's sake, don't come outside."

The woman ran to the phone and dialed the sheriff's office. She quickly told the dispatcher what she knew and told them to please hurry. She slammed the phone down, picked up her shotgun, and ran toward the back porch.

She looked out, saw her husband writhing on the ground. She jerked open the back door and ran onto the porch. The Old One turned at the disturbance. Its hideous face crinkled in what was, for the Old One, a smile.

The woman pointed her shotgun at the creature. The Old One laughed. Its eyes glowed. The woman screamed as her shotgun was torn from her hands, breaking several of her fingers as it was wrenched away. The shotgun sailed from the porch to the man on the ground. The butt of the weapon smashed

Walter's head, again and again, caving in the man's skull. The sounds of his skull cracking filled the once peaceful night. He screamed once, then fell into darkness. The retired farmer's blood and brains stained the earth he had loved and worked all his life.

The woman tried to run back into the house. The back door slammed shut. The doorknob would not turn. She screamed and hammered at the door. She felt her feet jerked out from under her. She fell heavily to the porch, knocking the wind from her. She felt herself being dragged by some force off the porch, to the ground, her head banging on the steps as she was dragged, screaming and kicking and trying to dig her fingers into the wood of the porch.

She was lifted off the ground, high into the air, screaming as she was flung about. The force smashed her to the ground, landing her on her head. The sound of her neck popping was like a gunshot. She was conscious, but could not move from the neck down. She could only move her eyes, and she wished she could not see what was happening. She lay on the ground and watched the hideous-looking creature squat down and begin eating her husband.

It did not take the Old One long.

Then it was her turn.

"I beg your pardon, Father?" Dan asked.

"I cannot undo what has taken place," the priest said. "I can only attempt to help those who want help. I cannot halt the birthing of Satan's Old Ones—his minions. You spoke of placing a dynamite charge down the hole. You could put a hundred charges of explosive down there and it would do no good. Only God can kill Satan and his minions. The Old Ones must be driven back into the earth, reburied. Once that happens, conditions here in Ruger County will return to normal. The spell over the animals will be broken. Those unfortunates who are infected . . . I'm afraid they must be killed. They can be forgiven, for what they have become is not their fault." He sighed. "I might be able to stop the Old Ones. And I stress *might*. What . . . you people, and the others in this county, are about to witness, be a part of, will be a living nightmare. But do not think your God has forsaken you. He has not. He had nothing to do with this. He is not testing you or your faith. These things . . . happen, that's all. It is not punishment, as some preachers will loudly proclaim."

"Father Denier, shall we include the other religious leaders of this community in . . . whatever it is we are going to do?" Dan questioned.

Denier smiled at that. "By all means, Sheriff. Do call the local Baptist ministers and tell them that a Catholic priest is about to perform the rite of exorcism on Ruger County. They would all get a good laugh out of that."

Vonne got tight-lipped at that remark, not reading any of the priest's humor in what was said. "That's a rather smug statement, Father."

"Oh, I didn't mean it like that, Mrs. Garrett," Denier said. "Indeed, many *priests* don't believe in exorcism. Many of the new, young priests don't even believe in *Satan*. Really. I have no quarrel with any church. Just think what a marvelous thing it would be if we could all get along. Think of what wonders we could perform if we spent our time helping instead of constantly bickering and back-biting and criticizing the other's religious choice. Do you know what I believe? I don't think it makes one whit of difference what church a person attends. Just go to *some* church. Believe in God. That's what is important. Be all that one can be. Try to practice what the Bible teaches. Turn the other cheek if possible. If it isn't possible, get in the first punch and make it count. Now do you see why I was, and am, in constant hot water with the Church hierarchy?"

When the laughter had died down, Vonne smiled and said, "You are an unusual priest, Father Denier."

"I am merely a human being who has spent his entire life in the study and worship and praise of God, Mrs. Garrett. I despise ignorance."

"*Do* we include the other religious leaders?" Dan persisted.

"We would be remiss in our duty if we did not," Denier said. "A few will probably believe us. Very few. But we have to try, for there are many who would not believe any but their own preachers. But," he held up a warning finger. "Please consider the panic it will cause, *if* we are believed. Where would the people go? And is this a county-wide concern—at this moment— or centrally located right around this town, as I believe is the case? You have ten thousand residents in this county. How many churches? Fifty? That is where the people will flock. In panic. Blind, stupid, panic. All of them. For as in combat, Sheriff, there are no atheists in the foxholes. The churches could not contain the people. They would be fighting to get in, rioting in the streets. The churches would collapse under the weight of the people."

Dan stood up. " Well . . . but . . . Goddamnit, Father!" He lost his temper.

Denier chuckled at the man's embarrassment. "It is a dilemma, is it not, Dan?"

"Well," Dan said, sitting back down. "Whatever we're going to do, we'd better be getting to it. It's full dark outside."

"What does that have to do with our situation?"

Denier asked, that slightly amused look on his face.

"Well," Dan said. "The *night* belongs to Satan, doesn't it?"

The priest shook his head. "All things belong to God, Dan. It makes no difference to Satan whether it's day or night. For in this particular situation, the Dark One is all-powerful. The Old Ones will rebirth. One is already free of the womb. The others are still struggling. But they'll make it."

"What is that one doing?" Taylor asked, curious and fearful of the priest's answer.

Denier met the man's eyes. He saw both fear and strength in the man. "Eating," he said.

The trooper leaned forward, not sure he'd heard correctly. "I beg your pardon, Father?"

"The Old Ones will be very hungry. Ravenous. They will be killing humans and eating them."

"Jesus Christ!" Dodge blurted. "Like that thing out at the hole did?"

"Yes."

Dodge shuddered.

"How many of . . . uh, the Old Ones are there?" Dan asked.

"Six, probably," Denier said. "Satan is very fond of sixes."

Chuck did some fast counting. He breathed easier when the number in the room exceeded six.

Denier had watched the chief deputy. Mountain boy, he thought. Tough as wang leather. He's spooky, but he'll stand firm.

"When you blessed the house and grounds," Dan said. "I mean . . . I'm not Catholic. I don't understand what you did."

"I blessed the house and grounds and asked God to protect those inside. Like a Jewish friend of mine is fond of saying, 'It don't hurt!' "

They all laughed at that. Dan thought: this Father Denier is a character. But I'm glad he's here.

Denier glanced at his watch. "This . . . situation, for want of a better word, will be over by this time tomorrow. One way or the other."

"Suppose it's the . . . other?" Chuck asked.

The priest said, "Then we will all be dead."

3

His Christian name was William, but everybody called him Billy. Had for as long as he could remember. He had been a deputy for two years and thought he might like to run for sheriff someday. Someday. For sure, though, he was going to be married next month and he and his wife were going to have three kids. Two boys and a girl, he liked to say with a smile.

He was thinking of his bride-to-be as he pulled into the driveway of the Service farm. He sat in the car and looked around him for a moment. He didn't know what he was walking into here. Dispatch couldn't make much sense out of the old lady's call. She was hysterical. Hollering. Hard to understand.

Billy radioed in and 10-97'd with dispatch. He got out of his car, his flashlight in his hand. His eyes swept the darkness for cats, monsters, and whatever else might be lurking in the night. It really made him mad being left out of that SST rig that overturned north of town. Bastards wouldn't even let him *see* the damned accident. Couldn't get close to it. Snooty civilians at the scene told him to go back to his regular duties and stay out of the way. Hard-eyed bunch of folks, too. Damned unfriendly. Sheriff Garrett just said to ignore them. But Billy could tell the sheriff didn't much like it, either.

Billy walked up to the front porch and knocked on the door. He waited. No sound came from within the house. He looked in through the picture window. Everything looked fine. No furniture knocked over like there usually is after a family fight. No holes in the walls, busted TV's, and torn-down drapes and curtains. This place looked just fine.

Anyway, he didn't figure this to be any sort of family disturbance. Not old Mr. and Mrs. Service. He'd known them all his life. But . . . you never knew about old folks; sometimes they could be as vicious as the young couples that fight and scrap.

"Walter?" he called. "Mrs. Service. Ya'll sing out. Where are you?"

The darkness greeted him with near silence. Only the sighing of the light night wind answered his calls.

Then an odor drifted to him.

Billy knew what that was. He'd worked enough killer wrecks to know it well. Relaxed bladders and bowels and blood. He started to walk around the house and then remembered Sheriff Garrett's words: No one lone-wolf's it if you think it might have something to do with the current situation facing Ruger County.

Sheriff had a nice way of putting it.

Billy walked back to his car, trying to ignore the tingling in the center of his back. He knew something awful had happened here. But what? He was soaking wet with sweat when he opened the door to his car and got in. He knew, *knew* there was bad trouble here. He reached for his mike.

It had taken Dan four years and a lot of arguing to do it, but Ruger County had finally come through with the money. Every call coming into the department pertaining to department business, every dispatch between officers, was taped. It helped in court, and it lessened the chances of lawsuits and other foul-ups.

It also virtually stopped all non-business calls coming out of the office.

"Base, I'm still ninety-seven at the Service house. Requesting backup."

"Is this ten-thirty-five?" That is the confidential information signal. Dan had settled on that one for anything pertaining to cats, creatures, the OSS, and whatever the hell else might be mysteriously occurring in his county.

"Ten-four."

"Stay put. Backup on the way."

"Base? I'm backing out of the drive and back onto the road. I'll wait there."

"Ten-four. Anything firm?"

"Negative. Hunch."

"Stay with it. I'm notifying Ruger One."

"Ten-four."

Billy began backing out of the drive. Halfway to the road, he jammed on the brakes as his headlights caught a glimpse of . . . He didn't know what it was. He blinked and stared. Nothing. Must have been my imagination, he thought.

No. There it was again. Something moving by the side of the house. But what was it? He mentally vacillated for a few seconds. What to do? He made up his mind and removed his shotgun from the rack, getting out of the car. He pumped a round into the chamber and began walking slowly up the gravel drive. His headlights were on high beam, casting artificial light over the front yard, creating deep pockets of darkness in the bushes and shrubs around the house.

Billy moved closer to the house, once more smelling the odor of death. And . . . something else. God, what was that smell?

There it was again. That movement by the side of the house. Billy knew it wasn't Mr. or Mrs. Service. Thing was too small for either of them. But whatever it was, it was short, stocky, and wide. Kinda like a bear.

Billy took a few more steps. "Walter? Mrs. Service? Answer me, folks!"

Deep silence, accompanied by that awful smell, greeted his words.

"You!" Billy called. "By the house. Step out into the light."

Faint chuckling drifted to the deputy.

Chuckling! "You think it's funny?" Billy shouted. "Move it—now!"

He lifted the shotgun to his shoulder. He wished his hands weren't so sweaty.

The shotgun was savagely torn from his grasp, the butt of the weapon striking him on the lower jaw as it flew from his hands.

Billy, blood leaking from his busted mouth, stood in shock for a few seconds, not understanding what had happened. He jerked out his .357 and fired, the booming shattering the nighttime quiet of the country. When his hearing returned, Billy heard the sounds of strange laughter. The . . . thing, man, bear, whatever it was, shuffled backward, into the deep darkness at the rear of the house.

Billy did a slow turnaround in the yard, looking in all directions, trying to figure out who, or what, had jerked the shotgun from his hands. He was soaked from sweat, his heart pounding as fear gripped him and adrenalin surged through his blood. Blood dripped from one corner of his mouth. He could see nothing human.

"Billy!" Walter's voice wavered through the night; a voice filled with pain. "Oh, God, Billy. I'm hurt bad. Help me, boy."

"Walter!" Billy shouted. "Where are you, Walter?"

"Behind the house, boy. Come quick. Mother's hurt real bad. Hurry, boy!"

Billy ran into the darkness, beyond the limits of the headlights. His boots slipped in something slick. He knelt down and touched the slickness with his fingertips. Blood. He was standing in blood. But whose blood? Walter's? Mrs. Service's? That thing he'd shot? If it was blood from that unknown, the thing sure had a funky sense of humor, laughing like it did.

"Oh, Lord, Billy!" Mrs. Service groaned. "Please help us, Billy."

Billy ran around the corner of the house, into almost total darkness. He ran right up to the most awful-looking thing he'd ever seen in his life. He froze, numb with shock and fear. He began screaming as huge, clawed hands dug its fingers through the cloth of his shirt and into the flesh of his belly. Blood squirted as the fingers dug deeper.

"Ruger One," dispatch radioed, "I can't get Billy to respond."

"Oh, no!" Dan muttered. "Didn't you tell him to stay put?"

"Ten-four. Said he was backing out into the road and waiting for backup to arrive."

Taylor rode with Dan in the lead car. Dodge and Father Denier sat in the back. Chuck followed behind. Langway and Hawkes made up the third and fourth vehicles. The priest was silent, sitting quietly, his bag on the seat beside him.

328

Chuck had wanted to ask him what he had in that bag, but he wasn't that sure he really wanted to know. He'd seen a lot of those movies about exorcism. Those priests who really did that sort of stuff—like Denier— had to be ballsy. Even if they didn't use them like other guys.

They all saw Billy's car parked in the drive, the headlights on high beam. The cops parked and got out. Dan and Chuck carried M-10's, set for full auto, in addition to their sidearms. The troopers carried pistols and shotguns. Dodge carried an M-16.

Father Denier carried his black bag in one hand and a large silver cross in the other.

"It's here," Denier said.

"What's here?" Dodge asked.

"Death and the Old One. They are one and the same."

"Don't you want a pistol, or something?" Chuck asked the priest.

Denier lifted the large cross. "I have one of the most powerful weapons in the world," he said.

"*One* of the most powerful?" Dan asked.

"Faith in God tops the list," Denier said.

Chuck didn't want to sound like a wise guy and get the priest down on his case, but he'd take his M-10 any day.

Denier looked at him. "You will soon see that your weapons are useless against the Old Ones."

Chuck's flesh got goose bumps when he realized that Father Denier had read his mind.

"Is Billy dead?" Dan asked.

"I don't know," Denier replied. "I only know that somebody is dead."

"Captain," Dan said, "you and Langway take the left. Dodge, you come with me to the right side. Chuck, you and Hawkes stay with Father Denier."

329

"No," the priest said. "I must lead the way."

"Father . . ."

The priest didn't hesitate. He began walking toward the rear of the house, his stride firm. The others had to move out just to keep up with him.

Denier suddenly stopped, holding up his arm for the others to halt. "Stay where you are," he ordered, his tone telling the others he would not tolerate any argument. He was running this show. He began praying, softly but firmly.

A ragged howling sprang from the darkness, the roaring filled with rage. The cops almost blasted the night with gunfire, nervous trigger fingers easing up just in time.

"Spawn of hell," Denier said quietly, no fear in his voice. "I am not afraid of you." He lifted the large silver cross, the moonlight reflecting off the polished silver.

The howling became a wild shrieking in the night, so loud and high-pitched in its anger, it momentarily deafened the men.

Odd, Dan thought. But I can clearly hear Denier's praying over the shrieking. How can that be?

The night seemed to literally shake from the insane howling and shrieking and roaring. Lightning licked across the dark sky and thunder rolled in a rhythmic flow; a sky filled with insane drummers. A limb ripped from a huge old tree in the back yard as the winds screamed in, raging with a stormy fury.

Denier stood like a solid rocky point against a surging sea. The rains came, lashing the men standing by the house. The raindrops, heavy and fat, were hot and stinking. Denier lifted his face to the sky and prayed, his arms spread wide, the cross in his right hand.

The men, as if under the control of one mind, one

body, stepped backward as the Old One approached the priest. They stared in horror and revulsion at the hideous sight. The Old One came at the priest in an awkward, running shuffle, its long arms almost dragging the ground. Its bluff failing to move the man of God, the Old One stopped a few feet from Denier. Denier looked down at the wicked hideousness.

The Old One and priest exchanged glances for a moment. Then the rain stopped. The winds ceased. The lightning no longer licked across the dark night sky. The thunder faded away.

The priest smiled.

"Stupid fool!" the words rolled from the Old One's mouth. It was Walter's voice. "So your power is strong enough to stop me. But will it stop all of us?"

"If I can sustain my faith, perhaps."

"Your God is not going to help you," the Old One said, this time speaking in Billy's voice, shocking the men who knew the young deputy. "He is not going to interfere. And your faith will not be strong enough against all of us."

"That remains to be seen, doesn't it, you walking piece of filth?" Denier replied.

The Old One laughed, a high-pitched cackle. It was Mrs. Service's voice.

"I don't believe I'm seeing this," Dodge said. "I think I'll shoot the son of a bitch!" He lifted his M-16.

"See this!" the Old One howled, looking at Dodge, its eyes glowing.

Dodge's entire body erupted in flames as all present felt the force spring from the Old One's eyes. Dodge's hair burst into flames, the skin from his head peeling away under the intense heat. Dodge's head exploded as his brains bubbled and cooked, his eyes melting, running down his face.

"Fire!" Dan yelled, lifting his M-10 and pulling the trigger, holding it back. The others joined him. The walking, living foulness was knocked around the back yard, pieces of it flying all about as the lead impacted.

Denier's shouting silenced the weapons. "Cease firing!" he yelled. "You're only making it worse."

A ball of fiercely glowing light stood where the Old One had stood. The men watched as the light began to dim. All about the yard, tiny balls of light were glowing. The huge ball of light faded away, melting into darkness. The Old One was gone. But pieces of it remained.

They looked at the charred body of Dodge. The intense heat had turned the man into a pile of ashes. His M-16 had melted.

"Where'd that . . . thing go?" Chuck asked, fighting back the sickness that threatened to boil from his stomach.

"That is not important," Denier said. "It is close, believe it. What is important is to destroy all the pieces of it. See them glowing, becoming one with the earth. Be careful to avoid them."

"You don't seem in any big hurry," Langway said.

"They are vulnerable," the priest said. "At this stage, they can be destroyed by fire. If they are not destroyed, in a few days you will have a hundred like the Old One you just saw."

Denier walked toward a whiteness glistening on the ground, a few feet from the back porch. He stopped before he stepped in something.

Dan followed the priest. "Oh, my!" he said, his eyes finding why Denier had stopped.

Billy was spread all over the back yard.

Only a few scraps of meat was left of the old couple; their bones lay white on the ground. But the head of the young deputy had been torn from the body. The head rested on the steps leading to the porch. The eyes were wide open, staring in shock and horror at that one hot second of agony before the head parted from the rest of the body. Intestines dangled with a gray slickness from the lower limbs of a tree. Various organs, still warm from life, littered the back yard.

Dan leaned against the house, refusing to be sick. He lost the fight, doubling over as nausea hit him hard.

Denier looked at the carnage. He prayed and then lifted his head. "Take pictures of it all," he said. "Including agent Dodge. We will need them in our efforts to convince the other religious leaders that Satan is alive and well in Ruger County."

"How do we destroy the little . . ." He looked around him. He pointed to the tiny glowing specks around the yard. "Those little things?"

"Burn everything," the priest said. "Pour gasoline over the grounds, the house, the outbuildings, and destroy it."

"But, Father? . . ." Chuck said. "Sir, we don't have the authority to do that. The heirs? . . ."

"Burn it!" Denier shouted.

4

The three full-time members of the Valentine Fire Department stood together in the night, on the road in front of the Service house. The three men had viewed what was left of Billy, and Mr. and Mrs. Service. They had then promptly lost their suppers. They stood quietly by the two trucks, their minds numb, drained of any emotion except shock.

All of them wondered what a priest was doing out here. They knew the Services were not Catholic. And what were those tiny glowing things?

But with that grim expression on Sheriff Garrett's face, none of the firemen were about to ask.

The firemen had worked with raw gasoline, saturating the area. Now they waited while that out-of-uniform state trooper did something.

The firemen looked up as the men walked to the road. "Burn it and stay with it until it's safe," Dan ordered.

"Yes, sir. Sheriff? How come the ground is so wet around here?"

"It rained," Taylor said.

"Just *here*?" another fireman asked.

"Just here," Taylor said flatly. "Burn it. Don't go into the yard for any reason. Just burn it. Everything. Move out."

Trucks in position, the firemen did as ordered. Dan radioed two deputies, Herman and Frank, to the burn site. He told them to stay with the firemen until the job was done. Dan then turned to Father Denier.

"The Old One, Father. Where is he?"

"It isn't a he," the priest explained. "Or a she. It is nothing and it is everything. It is evil, through and through. That is the only reason it exists."

Dan sighed. "Thank you. But that doesn't answer my question."

"Perhaps it is unanswerable for a mortal. Oh, it is watching. Waiting. I doubt it will interfere. It knows it cannot defeat me alone. It will wait until it is joined by the other Old Ones. Your bullets did nothing to harm it; indeed, that is probably what it wanted you to do. You must order your people not to use their weapons."

"I can't do that," Dan protested. "My people have a right . . ."

Denier brushed that aside. "You still don't understand. The Old Ones can turn the bullets against your people. You saw what it did to Dodge. These creatures from hell are all powerful; they are spawns of Satan. They are . . . how can I explain this? They are flesh and blood, yes; but they are more energy than anything else. They are nearly immortal. Perhaps they could be killed, but I don't know how. They can be stopped, halted for a time. But I don't know how to kill them."

Dan looked at the man, the priest's face, red-hued from the flames of the burning home and grounds.

"Well then, Father. What are we going to do?"

"I haven't the vaguest idea," Denier replied honestly.

The young couple sat up in bed. At first they thought the scratching they had heard was the wind pushing a branch against a window screen. But now the scratching seemed to be covering the entire roof and much of the outside walls of the two story home. They listened more intently. Whatever it was seemed to be not only outside but downstairs as well.

"Honey? . . ." she said.

"I don't know what it is," he said, getting out of bed and pulling jeans over his pajamas. He stuck his feet into house shoes.

"You don't suppose it's termites?" she questioned.

He looked at her to see if she was serious. She was. "Well, if it is, I sure don't to come face to face with one."

"Oh, you!" she giggled.

He reached over and cupped a young breast, the scratching almost forgotten. They had been married for only six months; still honeymooning. Still playful. She hadn't told him yet, but she thought she might be pregnant.

Then the scratching intensified.

"I'll be right back," he said.

"You be careful," she cautioned him.

"It's just the wind," he replied. He opened the bedroom door and stepped out into the hall. He looked back at his wife and winked at her, then closed the door.

She sat in the middle of the king-sized bed, naked from the waist up, hugging a pillow close to her.

She waited for what seemed to her an eternity.

About three minutes.

Once she thought she heard a muffled cry. But it was not repeated.

Then she heard the most hideous scream she had ever heard. She stiffened in bed. The scream came again. "Larry?" she shouted.

He screamed again. The sounds of running feet came to her. A thumping sound. Loud. Like a body falling. That was followed by a wild sort of screeching. It sounded like . . . like *cats* fighting.

"No!" her husband screamed. "Oh, God, no!"

"Larry! Where are you? Answer me. This isn't funny a bit, Larry."

A door slammed. Was it the hall door or a hall closet door. She couldn't be sure.

"Sylvia?" Larry called, very weakly, very faintly. "Don't come out here. Please. Lock your bedroom door. Call the police."

"Larry? What is it, Larry?"

But that screeching sound was all she could hear, and it was getting louder. Then it seemed to die out. A very faint dragging sound came to her. Her husband howled outside her door. She knew it was Larry. She also knew she had never heard any human being howl like that.

"Larry!" she screamed.

"Lock . . . door," he mumbled. His words were just understandable; a slurred sound.

Purring drifted through the closed door.

Sylvia reached up with a shaking hand and locked the door. That purring noise was louder, and something was scratching at the door. Through panicked eyes, she looked down at the rug beneath her feet. The carpet was changing colors, the beige changing to a deep dark red, slowly covering the bottoms of her feet.

She was standing in blood.

She began screaming.

Dan had pulled in all his deputies, with the exception of Herman and Frank. They were still at the burn site. He had called in his few auxiliary deputies and briefed them. He allowed them a few moments to call home and tell their families to lock the doors and stay inside. Don't leave the house for any reason. Don't let anyone in unless you're sure who it is. No one.

"All this has to do with that engineer out there on the mountain, don't it, Sheriff?" one of the reserve deputies asked.

"Yes. It has everything to do with it. All right, you people, listen up. I want this town, and the county, working three miles outside the city limits, covered by you people. Use the speakers on your cars to warn the people to stay inside. Lock their doors and pull down their windows. I . . ."

"Sheriff?" the dispatcher called. "Sylvia Quitman's on the phone. Hysterical. Something about her husband being attacked. Inside their house. That's eight-oh-eight Poplar."

"Susan, you and Woody handle it. Stay in contact at all times. All times. Take your handy-talkies. Move out."

Dan paused. He just could not order his people not to use their weapons if attacked. He just couldn't. And something else was nagging at him; something he'd read, or learned at the university. But he couldn't bring it to the fore. Father Denier had said the Old Ones were flesh and blood, but more energy than anything else. Very well, next question: what was energy? What stopped energy? What kind of energy was their make-up? Potential energy? Kinetic energy? The Old Ones for sure were not mechanical

338

energy. All right. Fine. It was coming to him now. That left electrical, heat, atomic, and chemical. And all those forms were transmutable.

"You all right, Sheriff?" Langway broke his thoughts.

Dan looked at the sergeant. "What? Oh. Yeah. Deep in thought, that's all." He looked at Chuck. "Take over here, Chuck. Captain Taylor, Father Denier, let's go into my office, please."

In his office, the door closed, the men seated, Dan looked at Denier and said, "You said the Old Ones are flesh and blood and energy. Right?"

Danier nodded.

"What kind of energy?"

"Ageless energy," the priest replied, not understanding where the sheriff was going with this line of questioning. "They have been here forever."

Dan waved his hand; a gesture of impatience. He knew time was running out, the hands of the clock moving toward disaster. "No, no, Father. You're not following me. Let me try it this way: energy, in physics, is defined as the ability to do work, right?"

"Ah!" Denier said. "Yes. All right. I'm with you, Dan. Go on."

"We can certainly assume with some degree of accuracy the Old Ones are not mechanical, so that leaves electrical, heat, atomic, and chemical, That Old One at the Service house set Dodge afire with some sort of intense force, right?"

"It was the force of Satan, Dan. We're not dealing with anything . . . any *power* really understood here on earth. Please bear that in mind."

"Yes, I know that, Father. But everything has to have a source, right?"

The priest leaned back in his chair. "Yes. Perhaps even the Old Ones. Interesting concept. I've always used a religious angle in pursuing this. Go on, Dan."

"Father Denier, Taylor, I have nothing to base my idea on except a gut feeling. I'm going to place the future of this county on a hunch it isn't atomic energy. I'm betting it's a mixture of chemical and electrical."

Captain Taylor's eyes narrowed. "Virginia Power boys, Dan?"

"Yes."

"All right, we're on the same track. But what if you're wrong?"

"We'll only have a split second to feel sorry about it," Dan replied.

Denier looked first at the trooper, then at Dan. "What are you two talking about?"

Dan sidestepped that with a question of his own. "Father, these Old Ones have a leader here on earth, right?"

"Well, yes, in a manner of speaking. The girl. Presuming she is actually here."

"Let's say she is. They—the Old Ones—would go where she goes, right?"

"I would imagine so."

"Then we've got to find her. Okay, we've got a lot of work to do tonight, boys." He caught himself. "Excuse me, Father."

Denier smiled. "Just one of the boys. That's fine with me, Sheriff."

The Quitman house was dark except for one lighted window on the second floor. Susan and Woody got out of the car, carrying shotguns. They walked slowly up the sidewalk to the small porch and knocked on the door. Nothing. Woody tried the doorknob. Locked. A slight scratching sound from the roof caused Susan to look up.

340

She paled.

"Woody," she said softly. "The roof is covered with cats." She took a deep breath, calming herself. "Look through the glass in the door and tell me what you see in there."

Woody looked. He swallowed hard. "The whole damned house is filled with cats, Susan. All of them are just sitting still on the floor, looking at the door."

"Well, Woody," Susan said, raising her voice a bit. Woody looked at her strangely. "I guess nobody is home, or else we got the wrong house. Let's drive on up the street."

She stepped off the porch, Woody right behind her. Susan said, "I'm about ready for a cup of coffee, Woody. How about you?"

"Yeah. Me, too, Susan." He followed her, wondering if his partner had lost her mind?

They made it to the car and got in, closing and locking the doors. His heart racing from the sight of hundreds of cats, all staring silently and savagely at them, Woody said, "What the hell was that all about?"

She glanced at him. "It worked, didn't it?"

Woody blinked. "You mean . . . I mean . . . you think those cats *understood* what you were saying? Come on, Susan! That's wild!"

"Yes, I do believe it." She reached for the mike and called in. "We're at the Quitman house. The roof is covered with cats and the inside of the house is filled with cats. That's probably what got Mr. Quitman. Advise calling Mrs. Quitman on the phone. Tell her to stay inside . . . whatever room she called from and to lock the door. Don't open it for any reason."

"Ten-four. Here's the sheriff."

"Susan? You and Woody stay in the car until help arrives. No heroics, now, from either of you. What?

341

Okay. Susan, dispatch has reached Sylvia Quitman. She's all right. She's in their bedroom and has the door locked. Father Denier is talking with her now, trying to keep her as calm as possible. She says there is a lot of blood oozing under the door. She guesses it's her husband's blood."

"Good guess, I'd say." Susan looked up at the lighted window. "She's looking out the window at us now, still talking on the phone."

"I'd have Father Denier tell her you're friendly; standing by until help arrives."

"Sheriff? Exactly how are we going to get her out of there?"

She could hear Sheriff Garrett sigh. "I don't know, Susan. I honest to God don't know."

"Sheriff, I . . ." She looked up at the window of the Quitman house. Lifted her eyes. The cats were gone from the roof. They had left as silently as they had come. She put the car in gear and drove slowly up the driveway, her lights on high beam.

"Susan! What's wrong?" Dan's voice cracked out of the speaker.

"Everything is fine, Sheriff," she assured him. "The cats are gone from the roof. It's completely clean." She looked in her rearview as lights flashed on the drive behind her.

"Backup's here."

"I can't tell you how to play this, Susan," Dan said. "I'm not on the scene. Play it by ear, but for Pete's sake, be careful."

"Ten-four."

The backup consisted of Deputy Ken Pollard and Virginia Highway Patrolman Lewis. Both were armed with shotguns in addition to pistols. Susan and Woody met them in the front yard. All around them, they could hear the sounds of loudspeakers, telling the residents of Valentine to stay indoors, do not come outside, lock your doors and windows, don't open them unless you know the person. It was repeated over and over.

All around them, in the houses nearby, they could see the frightened and confused faces of men, women, and children looking out of lighted windows.

The four officers clicked on their flashlights and searched the dark pockets where their high beam car lights did not reach. There was not a cat to be seen. But the odor of cat excrement was sharp in the hot night air.

"It's a hell of a lot warmer tonight than it was last night," Ken observed. "Temperature's not much different than this afternoon."

"Yeah," Woody said. "You're right. Weird things going on in this county."

"How about the front door?" Ken asked.

"Locked," Woody said. "I tried it."

"Under the circumstances," Susan said, "I don't think Mrs. Quitman would object to us kicking it in."

"Let's do it," Lewis said. He added, "*After* we check the house for cats."

While the cops checked the house from the outside, inside the house, locked behind her bedroom door, Sylvia huddled on the floor, a few inches from the thick stain of blood on the carpet. Her husband's blood. She knew that; accepted it with silent tears and shock.

Something scratched on the door.

She muffled a cry of fear.

The scratching came again, and it did not sound like cats.

Sylvia listen more intently. There it was again. Whatever it was was scratching on the door.

A low bubbling moan drifted to her. That was

343

followed by a choking cry.

It was Larry. She just knew it was. "Larry?" she whispered. "Larry? Is that you?"

More moaning drifted to her. That was followed by more scratching. And grunting.

She pressed her cheek against the door and listened. She could hear ragged breathing. She put her hand at the bottom of the door. She could feel breath coming from under the crack between door and carpet. Hot breath.

"Larry?"

Grunting and moaning whispered from the other side of the door. Downstairs, she heard the sounds of glass and wood breaking, footsteps hard on the floor.

"Mrs. Quitman!" a woman's voice called. "Stay where you are. The cats are gone. We're coming up there to get you."

"Cats are gone!" Sylvia whispered, her voice ragged. She was on the verge on shock and hysteria. "Cats! What cats?"

That dry scratching once more rasped at the door. Sylvia unlocked the door. The scratching became more urgent. Gruntings became louder. Sylvia slowly opened the door.

A hand fell through the space. Sylvia screamed in horror. The hand had been stripped of all flesh. White bony fingers dug into the shag of the carpet. Through eyes that were approaching madness, Sylvia opened the door wide. She looked at the whiteness of skull bone; a face stripped of all flesh. The eyes were gone, the lips gone. Blood leaked out from under what remained of the scalplock.

From the lipless mouth, the woman heard moaning, grunting sounds. She crawled out of the bedroom and squatted by the man. She did not look up at the approach of the cops. Larry's feet shone red/white in the dimness of the hall. Bloody white bones stuck out from under his jeans. What had once been her husband died on the carpet in the hall, his bony fingers digging into the carpet as his bones clacked and rattled in death.

Sylvia began shrieking. And rocking back and forth in the hall. She banged her head against the wall as her eyes grew wild with madness. Drool slobbered from her mouth as her mind snapped.

Then she could remember nothing. And never would.

5

Mille and Kenny had heard the sounds of shouting outside, all around the huge terminal complex, but neither knew what was going on. They both had shouted at the guard who was supposed to be just outside the door. They had received no reply. They both had listened at the door. Neither could detect any sign of life outside.

"I think he's split," Kenny said. "Boy! It's hot. What's happening around here?"

"I don't know," Mille said. "It's miserable. Get the lock, Kenny."

Using a stiff piece of wire, Kenny went to work. It did not take him long to open the cheap lock. "Piece of junk," he said.

"Here goes nothing," Mille whispered.

They opened the door a crack and looked out. Hot winds hit them in the face. The huge open sided building seemed void of life. They slipped out and closed the door. The door locked automatically behind them. They made their way cautiously and carefully through the huge, empty old building. They would occasionally catch the silver streaks of flashlights darting and bobbing in the outside night. They paused, squatting down near the open front of the building, trying to get their bearings.

"Where is Hoyt?" the shout came out of the night.

"Those things got him. He just opened the door to the trailer and was covered with those maggot-looking things. They brought him down and stripped him bare in half a minute. I never saw anything like it in my life."

"I'm gettin' outta here!"

"Goddamnit!" the harsh voice of Lou Lamotta came ripping through the turmoil and confusion. "Get yourselves together, people. You're trained agents. Get those drums of gas over there and flood the ground around the trailer with it. That'll kill those vermin. Do it!" he roared.

A woman screamed, shaking the night. "Get them off me!" The scream changed to one of agony. "They're eating me alive!" she wailed.

"Somebody shoot that lady and put her out of her misery!" Lou yelled. "Move."

A single shot blasted the hot air. The woman's screaming ceased.

Kenny and Mille squatted in the darkness of the cavernous old building, neither of them understanding what was going on around them.

"Maggots?" Kenny whispered. "Did she say maggots?"

"I think so. Listen!" Mille hissed.

The echo of the gunshot had died away. The faint sounds of munching took its place.

"Whatever it is out there is eating that woman," Mille said.

"Oh, wonderful!"

"That mummy-man is gone!" a voice shouted.

"So is the deputy," another voice was added to the confusion.

347

"Gone!" Lou screamed in anger. "What do you mean? Gone where?"

"How do I know?" the man yelled. "What am I, Lamotta, a fortune-teller?"

"Hey, Carson!" Lamotta shouted. "You watch your mouth. Don't get too cute with me."

"Too bad, man. I'm gettin' away from this place. Right now."

"You pull out now, and I'll contract your hide," Lou warned him.

The man offered no reply to that.

Gasoline swooshed into fire, adding an unreal note to the happenings.

"Contract?" Mille whispered.

"Kill him," Kenny said flatly. "I warned you about these guys."

"Kenny, what are we going to do. I'm scared." She sought his hand in the red-tinted night. "And why is it so *hot*?"

"I don't know. But I'm scared, too. We'll make it, Mille." He looked around him, spotting some old crates and boxes piled against a wall. "Over there," he said, pointing. "Outside, we might get shot. We'll hide over there until we can make a break for it."

The reporter and the investigator ran, hunched over, to the pile of crates and boxes and slipped behind them. They inched their way into a large packing crate. Where they sat, they could see the reflection of the fires in the compound, the images leaping and dancing on the wall that faced them.

"Looks like witches dancing," Kenny whispered.

"God don't say that! It looks like we traded one cell for another."

"That's one way of looking at it," Kenny returned the whisper. "We've got to be quiet, Mille. Real quiet."

348

"I'll tell you something, Kenny."

"What?"

"I'm scared. Real scared." This from a woman who had covered stories in countries ruled by harsh dictators; who had faced interrogation from secret police; and was known as one of the most fearless of the new, young breed of international reporters.

"We'll make it, Mille," he assured her. I hope, he thought.

The Old One had widened the crack in the concrete floor. Now his powerful clawed hands were jerking off chunks of concrete from the lip of the hole, widening it still further. Betty Reynolds and her kids sat on the stinking, blood-soaked floor and watched the Old One pull its horrible bulk free of the womb of the earth. It crouched on the floor, staring at those staring at it.

"Can I help you?" Betty asked.

"Now that you mention it," the Old One said, in her voice. "Yes. Yes, you can."

She leaned closer to it. "Tell me how."

The Old One laughed, a high, girlish giggle. "I'd rather show you."

"All right."

The Old One reached out and put both clawed hands on Betty's neck. It jerked, tearing the woman's head off. Blood squirted as if from a garden hose, spraying the walls. The Old One peeled the flesh from the head like the skin from a grape. Cracking her skull, the Old One began eating the still warm brains. It pausing, looking at Betty's children.

"Excuse me. I'm very hungry." Bits of gray matter clung to its lips.

The kids shrugged. The oldest boy said, "Have it all, man."

"Thank you."

At the bubbling hole not far from the chainlink fence around the old terminal, a faint cracking sound ripped from the pool as the earth around it parted. The Old One leaped from the hole to stand in the darkness and snarl and shake itself, flinging blood from the foulness that it was. Its long arms touched the ground where it stood. It looked at the flames jumping from the gasoline-soaked earth around and including the trailer. It smiled as it heard the sounds of frightened screaming and yelling voices. The Old One sensed if it stayed close, there would soon be more than enough food. It smiled again as it looked at the fence surrounding the bubbling pool. It shuffled to the fence, reached up, and tore it apart, flinging the fence into the brush. The Old One moved closer to the fence around the terminal. Choosing a spot behind some brush, it squatted down and waited. And listened to something only it could hear.

There were signals in the air. But they were conflicting and confusing.

The Old One snarled softly. The signals were missives between its Master and the Master's foe. All was not well. The Dark One was hurling oaths and curses and challenges at its lifelong enemy.

The heavens spoke with laughter, seeming to taunt the Old One's Master.

No, all was not well.

"I do thank you for waiting," the Old One said to Mickey Reynolds.

Mickey grunted.

The Old One laughed. The cat beside Mickey

seemed to laugh along with the foul hideousness.

The Old One paused, sensed something in the air that only it could sense. Messages. Angry messages. The Master was raging his dark fury.

No matter. At this time, the messages did not concern the Old One. The Old One reached out, its big, clawed hand covering the top of Mickey's skull. It squeezed. Mickey's head popped as the skull shattered. Pulling the dead, once human close, the Old One sucked out the brains, smacking its lips. It then began tearing the flesh from the carcass, stuffing the bloody strips into its wide mouth.

The cat watched and waited.

The Old One listened for a moment, not fully understanding the silent signals bouncing back and forth between heaven and earth. It shook its great ugly head and looked at that which had once been Eddie Brown.

"You have no idea why you are here, do you?" it asked, in Eddie's voice.

Eddie grunted.

"Fool!" the Old One said, then smashed a fist against the animal head of Eddie, cracking the skull with the single powerful blow. Eddie slumped to the wet floor, dead. The ugly Old One began to dine, slowly, savoring each bite. It had plenty of time—hours. But this one miserable creature would not begin to be enough to appease the Old One's ageless hunger. But it would do for the moment.

The cat waited. And watched.

The six Old Ones were free of the damnable tomb-like womb in which God had sealed them. There had been others before them to break free, but that had been centuries before. All six had heard or were listening to the signals that raged about them. None was sure of what lay before them. They were certain of only one thing: they must obey.

The cat sat and watched Anya. The girl appeared to be in a trance. But Pet knew she was receiving instructions from the Master.

It was almost time.

In the house next to where Anya and Pet were hiding, the windows were down and locked, the doors closed and locked. As the sounds of the loudspeaker faded, the man looked at his wife. "I wonder what in the world is going on?"

"I don't know." She looked out the window. "But the number of cats outside has increased. And I don't like it."

"I thought you liked cats?"

"One at a time," she corrected. "I don't like several hundred of them hanging around. It's . . . well, eerie."

"Several *hundred*?"

"Look out the window."

He rose from the couch and looked. "For pity's sake!" He clicked on the outside lights for a better look.

The yard was full of cats.

One of the cats closest to the window snarled and leaped at the window, its claws digging in, shredding the screen. It clawed and howled, almost a human-like scream of fury, unable to get at the man.

The man stepped back, startled at the violence of

the attack. "I don't like this. I don't know what is happening, but it's unnatural. Try the police again."

"I just did. The phone is still dead."

Both of them stood silent in the large den for a moment, listening as the roof of the big, two-story home seemed to come alive under the feet of hundreds of cats.

"I don't want to alarm you," the man said. "But I think we'd better reinforce these windows."

The couple began working hurriedly, moving cabinets and furniture around, barricading the windows. That done, and done well, the man went to a closet and took out an old double-barreled, side hammer shotgun. Then he forgot where he'd put the shells. He remembered and loaded the old coach gun.

She looked at the sawed off shotgun, doubt in her eyes.

"What's the matter?" he asked.

"Is that the gun you got from my brother?"

"Yes."

She arched an eyebrow dubiously.

He said, "You don't think? . . . No, he *wouldn't*!"

"Yeah, he would, too."

"Yeah," he agreed. "He would. Help me find my other shotgun."

"Good luck. I think it's in the attic."

"At least these shells will work in it."

"If they go off."

"Why shouldn't they?" he asked, sticking out his chin.

"Because you bought them at a rummage sale back in 1965."

"Turn the air conditioning up," Dan told a deputy.

"It's wide open, Sheriff," the deputy said, after

checking the thermostat. "It's got to be a hundred and twenty degrees outside."

"All planned," Denier said softly.

Everyone in the room looked at the priest. "Planned?" Taylor asked.

"People will have to open their windows after a while," the priest replied. "Soon every air conditioner in this area will be operating at full capacity. Breakers and fuses will go; the air conditioners will break down; the load will be too much on old wiring. The people will be forced to open windows in hopes of catching a breeze for relief. But there will be no breeze to catch. With the windows open, the cats can enter."

"That is the most ridiculous thing I have ever heard," a local minister said.

Dan ignored the man. He said to Denier, "You're just full of good cheer aren't you, Father?"

"Satan is playing," Denier said. "He knows what you're planning. This heat is his way of telling you he knows."

"Hogwash!" the very vocal and opinionated minister said. "Sheriff, you *can't* be taking anything this man says seriously." He looked at Denier.

Denier smiled. He was used to this type of reaction, from that type of minister.

Dan looked at the Methodist minister. "Jerry, what do you think?"

Jerry Hallock said, "You saw the thing, didn't you, Dan?"

"I certainly did. And you saw the Polaroids we took out there."

"Well," the Methodist said, "I fully believe Satan is very much alive and well. This . . ." He waved his hand toward the outside. "This is a little hard to accept. But I'll go along with it until somebody—" He looked at Louis Foster, the doubting minister. "—

354

can come up with a better explanation."

Louis snorted his contempt.

"Matt?" Dan asked the Presbyterian minister.

The other ministers in the town had flatly refused to even listen to Dan and Father Denier. One, upon sighting the priest, had slammed the door closed.

That had irritated the hell out of Dan. The priest had shrugged it off.

"I'm with Jerry," Matt Askins said. He looked around him. "But is this it? Out of all the ministers in this town, is this the sum total of all who believe in Satan? My God, if that is so, what have the others been preaching?"

"You're both losing your grip on reality," Louis said.

He was ignored.

"You call the power boys?" Taylor asked Dan. The trooper was getting a gutful of Louis Foster.

"Yes. They said they had no authority to do what I requested. Said they wouldn't do it. I asked them if they'd ever spent much time in jail. After thinking that over, they said I'd have to put my request in writing, sign it, and take full responsibility for it. I told them I would be happy to do that."

"I'll sign it, too," Taylor said. He met Dan's eyes. "The other plan still Go?"

"Yes."

The trooper nodded.

"Sheriff," a deputy interrupted, seconds after the radio squawked. "That was Jake. He says he spotted a big fire out at the old terminal."

"Now what?" Langway asked.

"They are free from the womb," Denier said.

Louis looked at Denier, open, ill-concealed hostility in his eyes. "What is free? What are you babbling about now?"

"I do not babble," Denier said, at last showing a bit of temper. "The Old Ones are free."

"Balderdash, poppycock, and pure hogwash!" Louis said.

Methodist just about told Louis to shut his mouth.

Presbyterian was on the verge of putting his sentiments a great deal more bluntly. And crudely.

"I gather then," Dan said, "that means you will not help us in any way?"

"Sheriff," Louis said, his tone that of an adult speaking to a child. A not-very-bright child. "All that has happened can be explained in a logical manner. You and your men are tired. I understand that. You've all been working under a strain lately. Fatigue tends to cloud the mind. You're all seeing things that aren't there. As for the weather, well, it's a front, that's all. You'll see. You'll all laugh at your behavior later, believe me."

Methodist now shared Presbyterian's views. He said a silent prayer asking for forgiveness for the profanity in his mind.

Dan bit back a sharp comment and said, with great patience, "Louis, it's well over a hundred degrees outside. That is far above the average for this time of year. The *daytime* average. And don't you presume to tell me what I did or did not see."

Susan Dodd had stood quietly against a wall, listening to the exchange. She now stepped in, telling the minister what had happened to Larry Quitman. The strange behavior of the cats in this area.

"My dear," Louis said smugly, not knowing just how close he stood to getting a pop across the chops from "My Dear." "It can and will all be explained. And the devil," he chuckled, "has nothing to do with it."

"All right then," she challenged him. "Go ahead."

"Go ahead—what?" Louis asked.

"Explain it!"

"Well . . . I can't."

"Well, then, until you can explain it," Susan told him. "Why not shut your mouth and sit down!"

Louis Foster's mouth closed with a snap. He sat down.

6

"That woman deputy of yours can play on my team anytime she likes," Taylor told Dan, on the way out to the terminal. "I just might try to steal her, if I can convince her to become a highway cop."

"She's a good one," Dan said. "But do you think either of us has much of a future in law enforcement after all of this?"

"Good point," the captain agreed.

"Slow down!" Denier spoke from the back seat. Dan braked. "Pull in at that driveway."

Dan cut to the right, almost missing the drive. His bright lights picked up the shadowy shapes of hundreds of cats.

"Holy smokes!" Taylor said. "There must be hundreds of cats. Half the cats in the county have to be gathered around this house."

There were cats almost anywhere the men looked. They covered the roof of the large home. The cats sprawled on the vehicles parked in the yard. They lay around the two story garage and storage area.

The men sat in the patrol car and stared.

Denier stirred on the back seat. "The girl is here," he said. "Can either of you feel that intangible?"

"Something is making my flesh crawl," Dan said.

"The hair on the back of my neck feels like it's standing up," Taylor said.

"Evil," Denier said. "In its darkest form. Pure evil, if you like."

"I wish Louis was here to see this," Dan said. "And to feel it."

"He'd probably dismiss it as cats in heat and the high humidity," Taylor replied.

"Don't be too harsh on the man," Denier said. "He was voicing his convictions and is entitled to them."

"But you don't agree with him," Dan said, looking at the priest, then back at the cats.

Denier smiled. "No," he said softly.

"A car in the drive," the woman said, looking out through a crack in the barricade over the window. "It's a police car."

"I'm gonna kill your brother," her husband said, looking at the double-barrel coach gun on the couch. "I'm gonna get him for this."

She smiled, despite their predicament. "Nobody twisted your arm to buy it, did they?"

"Don't remind me. He should have been a snake-oil salesman." He looked out the window. "Car's coming closer. Sheriff's department, I think."

Dan pulled in close to the house and used his PA speaker. "You folks all right in there?" He cracked his window a bit.

"Yes!" the man yelled. "Sheriff Garrett? Is that you?"

"That's right."

"What's going on around here?"

Dan looked at Taylor. "I was afraid he was going to ask that." He looked at his hood. Several cats were walking on it. He hit the siren. It did not bother the cats at all. "Can any cats get inside?" he asked.

359

"No," the man yelled. "I don't think so. We have plenty of food and water and have barricaded ourselves in the den. But it's very hot."

"It's very hot all over the county. Weather front, the National Weather Service says."

"You lie so convincingly," Taylor said. "You missed your calling. You should have been a politician."

"I am a politician," Dan said.

"Sheriff?" the man yelled. "What is going on?"

"We've got a very dangerous situation in this county, sir. Those cats are attacking people. We're ordering all people to stay inside and do not, repeat, do not, go outside for any reason. Keep your doors and windows locked. We'll try to have this problem solved by late tomorrow."

"Wonderful," the man said to his wife.

"Can you get rid of those cats?" the woman yelled.

"I don't know how, ma'am. But we're working on the solution. All I can tell you is to bear with us."

"He's as bad as your brother," the man said, smiling, no malice in his comment. He wiped sweat from his face. He raised his voice, "You don't sell used shotguns, do you Sheriff?"

"I beg your pardon, sir?"

"Skip it. Our phones are out, Sheriff. We have no way of communicating with the outside."

"I'm sorry, sir. The county has been closed off. Orders from the federal government. Very dangerous wreck up the road. Hang on, sir."

"Right, Sheriff. Hanging on." He looked at his wife. "Going to be a long, hot night, lady."

Dan backed away from the house, hoping his tires would squash some of the cats. They darted out of the way. "Bastards," Dan said.

Denier said, "The home seems secure and they barricaded themselves in. They seem reasonable

360

people. If they can stand the heat, they'll make it."

"Yeah," Dan said, looking at a cat sitting on his hood as he backed away. He slammed on his brakes and the cat went sliding off, yowling. "At least we know where the girl is—I guess."

"I don't care what the sheriff said," the burly, unshaved man yelled at his wife. He looked at the houses left and right of his. Not their house. His. His neighbors' homes were dark. All the windows pulled. "Stupid," the man said. "Right in the middle of town and have to stay locked up. I ain't gonna do it. I'm opening the goddamned windows. I can't take no more of this. And what's the matter with that lousy air-conditioner?"

"Vic," his wife pleaded. "Let's get in the center of the house and barricade ourselves in. Please?"

"No! I'm not movin' all that junk around for a bunch of pussycats."

"The cats are dangerous, Vic. They . . ."

"The heck with the cats, Grace. It's just a bunch of pussycats. Lemme get my gun. I'll scatter the little pests."

"Vic, I'm begging you. Don't go out there. Do this one thing for me, Vic?"

The man looked at her, disgust in his eyes. He drained his beer can and belched. He squeezed the lightweight beer can in his hand, crushing it. Marvelous feat of strength. Something the average six year old could do. But considered by some to be very macho. "Grace, just get me my shotgun and that box of shells. Don't argue with me, just do it."

The much vocally and occasionally physically abused woman stared at her husband. As she had done so often, she thought: Why did I ever marry you? Why? She slowly nodded her head. She knew why. Big hot shot in high school. Big dud later. "Okay, Vic. Whatever you say." She turned and went to their bedroom, returning in a moment with her husband's shotgun. She handed it to him, along with a box of shells. She said nothing. She didn't have to. Her eyes were saying it all.

Vic loaded up the shotgun and stuffed his pockets with extra shells.

"You can open the windows now, baby," he said with a smile. "I'll scare all the big, bad cats away."

She continued to stare in silence at him.

He wanted to slap her silent face. "You really hate me, don't you, Grace?"

"No, Vic," she said wearily. "I just don't feel anything anymore."

"Look at all them houses around us," Vic said, waving his arm. "Right in the middle of town and they are scared out of their gourd. Not me. I ain't scared of no house cat. Not Vic."

She turned away and sat down at the kitchen table, pouring a glass of iced tea.

Vic unlocked the back door and stepped out onto the porch. He heard Grace lock the door behind him. "Stupid witch," he muttered. He stepped off the porch and into the unnaturally hot night. "Here, kitty, kitty, kitty," he called. "Come to Ol' Vic. Ol' Vic's got a present for you."

The cats came. Silently, deadly, the blood lust high within them.

Dan pulled onto the road leading to the terminal. The three men could see the lights from the dying fire.

Denier looked at the dim outlines of the buildings and said, "You chose well, Sheriff. It's evil. Can you feel it?"

"Yes," both men replied. Dan saying. "But not as strong as I felt back at that house a minute ago."

"It will increase," the priest assured them. "Tell me something, if either of you can. Has any business ever succeeded here?"

Dan thought back. "Come to think of it, no. Not as far back as I can recall. I remember my dad telling me that during his lifetime, a dozen or so businesses were located, at one time or the other, in this vicinity. They all went under. Granddad said about the same, I remember. That's odd, isn't it?"

Denier was silent, staring at the terminal site. "There was a road through here at one time. And a village."

Taylor twisted in his seat, staring at the man. "Back during the Revolutionary War, yes, sir. The whole town burned and was rebuilt twice. After the second fire, the people moved to what is now Valentine."

"Yes. For a very good reason. They were trespassing," the priest said.

"Trespassing, sir?" Dan asked.

"Satan has claimed this land as his own."

Both lawmen felt their skin turn clammy.

"Be careful at the terminal, gentlemen," Denier said. "There are . . . well, *things* moving about."

"Things, Father?" Dan asked.

"Things. Little spawns of hell. Be careful."

Dan put the car in gear and moved out. The gate was closed and chained and guarded. A man carrying an M-16 walked up to the gate.

"Sheriff Garrett," Dan called. "Open the gate or I'll ram my way through."

"No need to get hostile, Sheriff," the guard said. "You can come in. Lou said you'd probably be out, all hot and bothered."

Dan muttered an obscenity under his breath. Concerning Lou.

The guard opened the heavy gate and waved Dan in and to a halt. "Be careful in there, boys," He looked at Denier. "Father. Bless me, Father?"

Denier nodded and did. "A believer among the heathens?" Denier asked with a smile.

"Yes, Father," the guard replied solemnly. "It's hell in there. I mean it, be careful. The mummy-man is loose, and so is that infected deputy of yours, Sheriff. We've got guards all along the fence line. More coming in. We hope," he added. And there is . . . well, some sort of maggot-like worms loose. Worse than piranha. That's why you see those gasoline cans stacked over there. Fire seemed to kill them. But they breed like rabbits."

"What do you mean, you hope you have more people coming in?" Taylor asked.

The guard shrugged. "Lou can't get through. He thinks something's gone sour."

"Electrify the fence," Dan said. "That should stop them. You've got the capacity to do that, I know."

"Good idea. I'll radio that into Lou." He waved them on.

"Don't bother," Dan said. "I'll tell him myself." Dan dropped the car in gear and rolled on.

"Maggots?" Taylor asked. "Yukk!"

"Little creatures of hell," Denier said. "I told you, Satan is playing. All this is nothing but a big joke to the Dark One."

"Weird sense of humor," Dan said. "What if the maggots get out of this area?" he mused aloud.

Taylor looked at him. "Easy, Dan. Let's take one problem at a time, huh?"

Dan parked by the hospital trailers. He saw a

364

shattered window in one, a broken door in the other. Bowie and the engineer, he guessed. He spotted Goodson and got out. "Getting a little out of hand, isn't it, Doctor?" he asked drily.

"If that is supposed to be funny, Sheriff, it isn't," the doctor said testily.

Dan said nothing. He noticed that Goodson would not meet Father Denier's eyes.

"When did you add it all up, Doctor Goodson?" Denier asked.

"A few days ago," the doctor said. He still would not look at the priest.

Denier stood in the night, staring at the doctor. "You should have contacted me when you first suspected."

Without replying, Goodson turned around and walked slowly into his lab.

Denier sighed and shook his head.

"Goodson!" Dan called.

The man looked around, standing in the door of the trailer.

"Where are you people keeping Ms. Smith and her friend?"

Goodson looked startled. "What?"

"Yeah, you probably don't know," Dan said.

Bennett and the other doctors joined Goodson around the open door. "What about this Smith person?" Bennett asked.

"She and a male companion were kidnapped by Lou Lamotta," Dan informed the doctors. "They're being held out here, somewhere."

"I don't believe that!" Bennett said.

"Believe it," Lou said, walking up. He carried an M-16. He looked at Dan. "You boys come out to join the festivities tonight?"

"In a manner of speaking, Lamotta. First I want

Ms. Smith and Kenny."

"Maybe I don't want you to have them."

"Maybe I don't care what you want any more, Lamotta. From now on, I'm running this show."

Lou laughed, a big, booming, arrogant laugh. "I tell you what, Sheriff. You may be dumb, but you sure don't lack for guts, buddy-boy." He wiped sweat from his face. "Now, Sheriff, just how do you think two cops and one priest are going to take over here?"

Dan smiled grimly. He glanced at his watch. "Because, Lamotta, in exactly twelve minutes, if you have not turned over control to me and Captain Taylor, eight regular deputies, a half a dozen auxiliary deputies, my chief deputy, and four Virginia Highway Patrolmen will storm this place, and they will be coming in shooting." He lifted his M-10, pointing the muzzle at Lou's belly. "And, *buddy-boy*, I'll start the dance by killing you."

All around the tight little tense knot of men, Lou's people had stopped, listening to the exchange. Some of them lifted their weapons. Bolts snicked in the night, just audible over the dying crackle of flames.

"I think you're bluffing, buddy-boy," Lamotta said.

"Try me," Dan flung the challenge at him.

The men engaged in a silent staring contest for half a minute. Finally, a slow smile crinkled Lou's lips. He shrugged his shoulders. "Okay, Sheriff. But you're dumb, buddy-boy. Just plain dumb. You know why? 'Cause all you had to have done to keep your ass clear, is just stand back. The government would have had to take all the heat for this . . ." He waved his hand. ". . . Mess! But now, buddy-boy, *you* got to take it. Okay. Fine. No sweat." He smiled, wiping his face with a handkerchief. "Figuratively speaking, that is."

Lou looked around at his people. He looked back at Dan. "You want it, buddy-boy. Okay. You got it. Me and my bunch are through here. We're pulling out. Forget about all this equipment, you can have it."

"My people are staying," Doctor Bennett said, his voice firm. "I should imagine we'll be needed before it's all over."

Lou snorted derisively. "The noble physician." He looked at the OSS doctors. Again, he shrugged. "Aw, what the hell! We'll stick around. Maybe we can help out."

At precisely that moment, a young man was stepping off a plane at Oceana Naval Air Station near Virginia Beach. The Navy pilot and co-pilot who had flown him in from Washington state were glad to be rid of their passenger. The guy had not spoken one word during the entire flight. Just sat in the back and read reports of some kind. Then stuck the folders back in his briefcase. They both had seen that kind of briefcase before, too. The kind that if someone fools around with it, it blows up. Guy wasn't very old. Maybe twenty-four, twenty-five, at the most. But hard-eyed. Odd looking, kind of slanty, icy eyes. Not really Oriental eyes; but more Eastern European, Slavic eyes. The guy had a car waiting for him. He got behind the wheel and drove off without even looking back.

Oh, well, the pilot thought. He'd flown Agency guns and spooks before. Probably would again. But this guy was military. Everything about his bearing smacked of hard discipline. The cold-eyed dude could have put on a clown's costume and any career GI could have recognized him as military.

The pilot put his passenger out of his mind. Neither he nor the co-pilot would ever mention him to anybody. Even each other. They knew better. They both knew a walking gun when they saw one.

They just wondered, silently, who was about to get

wasted? And why?

Grace sat in her hot house and sipped iced tea. It was so hot the ice melted just about as fast as she put it in the glass. She had heard Vic scream in fright. Once. Then she heard him howl in pain. Once. Then the night had swallowed any further sound, returning to its hot, silent gloom. Through the closed windows, she had heard the sounds of what she guessed to be chewing. She knew she should be horrified; should be feeling terror and revulsion and all sorts of other emotions.

She felt only one emotion.

Relief.

Emily and Alice sat in the Ramsey's den looking at their husbands, sitting across the room from them.

The phones had stopped working. Dead. The men and women had no way of knowing what was happening outside the closed, very hot house. Only that the town seemed to be filled with cats. God, where had they all come from? It was frightening. Eerie. The cats were everywhere.

A couple of miles outside of Valentine, the man and woman stared at the dark outline of the garage/storage area. That was where the bulk of cats were. And the cats were behaving very strangely. They were circling the building. The inner circle moving clockwise, the next circle counter-clockwise; that system repeated for a dozen circles.

"I've never seen anything like that," he said.

"I have," his wife said.

He looked at her. "Oh? Where?"

"In a horror movie. It's some sort of devil dance."

"In that movie, who won?"

"Satan."

The town of Valentine, and a three mile radius, circling the town, lay like an egg on hot pavement—gradually cooking. The area's population of dogs lay under porches, in sheds, by the sides of houses. They lay in packs, for protection. They had seen what had happened to dogs who shunned the safety of the pack. They had been torn to bloody bits by the cats. When this was over, if it ever was, the dogs would return to being friends or enemies—whatever. But for now, a canine truce was holding. The dogs did not understand what was happening, only that survival was the most important thing in their lives. When they rose for a drink of water, they went together, en masse, some standing guard while others drank. They maintained a very low profile.

Dozens of the thumb-sized, savage little worms escaped the fire around the trailer. They hunched and slithered away from the heat, crawling into empty buildings, holes in the earth, into vehicles, and under the fence. They slipped silently from the terminal grounds, into the country. And began to breed.

7

Mille and Kenny had crawled out of the crates at the sight and sound of Dan and his men. They stood silently, listening. They made no attempt to conceal their fear.

"Stay with us," Dan told them. "But stay out of our way."

"Yes, sir," they said.

"All right, Lou," Dan said. "I want a half circle cordon around the grounds where we believe the girl is hiding. At first light, we'll try driving them toward this area. You game for this?"

"Sure, Sheriff. But what happens when your hard-nosed buddy, Gordon, finds out about this and moves his people in to stop us?"

"I don't know," Dan admitted. "I've thought about that. It's a surprise to me that he isn't already here, right now."

"Yeah," Lou said, his voice low. "I think something's in the wind. Gordon made his appearance just about dark, then split. Said he'd be back, but I haven't seen him. Aw, what the heck, buddy? I don't see where he presents much of a problem. Dodge thought he was working for the Reds, didn't he?"

"That's what he told me."

"Well, that's easy, then. If I see him, I'll just shoot the traitor. I hate a Commie."

"Dan?" Chuck said, walking up. "The power company boys are here. And they sure are goosy about this. One of 'em stumbled upon what's left of that woman the worms ate. I 'bout had to handcuff him to get him to stay."

"He'll stay if I have to chain him to his truck," Dan said. "How about the wire?"

"We've got every roll of wire we could find in this part of the county. I busted into the hardware store and swiped a dozen rolls of five foot chainlink. And something else, too. This situation is gettin' weird."

"Good God!" Taylor said. "Now what?"

"Cruisin' patrol just called in. All of Miller's people, the civilians, have left. No SST rig, no nothin.' Just the military guards manning the road-blocks. The others just vanished. The MPs say they don't know what is going on."

"I do," Lou said. "It's all gone sour. I guessed it about an hour ago. You guys hang on for a second. I'll find out what's going down." He walked to his trailer, leaving the door open. They could hear his voice, muffled, as he talked with someone on the phone. He returned a few minutes later, a strange look on his face. "We're high and dry," he said to one of his people. "Beached like a whale. The Office of Special Studies no longer exists. Period. The FBI is rounding up agents all over the country. Dodge's last report cinched it. Federal warrants everywhere. Most of our civilian money has dried up. The bigwigs are diving for cover."

"How about us?" Lou was asked.

"We cooperate with the sheriff here, and that will be taken into consideration. In our behalf."

7

371

"Good," Chuck said with a grunt, glaring at Lou. "That means when this is all over, I can kick your butt."

Lou looked at the much smaller man and grinned. "You'd really try to do it, too, wouldn't you, you little hillbilly?"

"No, I'm not gonna try, Lou," Chuck told him. "I'm gonna do it."

Lou grinned hugely. "Maybe. But later, fireball, later. First things first. The Company's put a contract out on Miller and the bitch with him." He looked at Mille and mock-bowed. "Excuse me, my dear—the *lady* with him. Some top gun is coming in. Maybe already here. I'll know him—or her—if I see him. I probably won't see him."

"I'm going to report everything I hear and see around here," Mille said.

"Have at it, darling," Lou said. "You'll never see the touch. You won't be able to prove a thing."

"The what?" Mille asked.

"The hit. The kill. The burn," Lou told her.

"How grotesque!"

"I don't believe it," Doctor Goodson said. "That only happens in the movies."

"That's what you think, Doc," Lou said. "It don't happen everyday; but it sure as hell happens." He looked at Bennett. "It's gonna be a long night, Doc. Pass out the bennies."

Bennett nodded and went into his lab. He returned in a moment with a large bottle of white pills, handing the bottle to Lou.

Lou shook out a handful of the powerful amphetamines and began passing them out.

Captain Taylor recoiled in horror. "I most certainly will *not* take dope."

"Don't be a jerk, goody-two-shoes," Lou told him.

"We're all gonna need all the help we can get staying alert tonight and in the morning. These are government issue tabs." He looked at his watch. "These will kick your butt for about eight hours. Don't wait until you're down before taking the second one. When you feel this one wearing off, pop another."

"Good Lord!" Taylor complained. "And I've been preaching against dope for twenty years." He grimaced as Lou put two pills in his hand.

Lou grinned. "Just think of yourself as an old hippie, Captain."

"I can't think of anything more disgusting," the captain said, swallowing the pill. "I don't feel anything," he said with a smug smile. "Probably won't work on me."

Lou just laughed. "Oh, but when it does, man, you're gonna be a sight to see."

"Never," the captain said grimly.

Dan said, "Captain, get on the horn and pull as many troopers in here as possible. We're running the show now. Have your men beef up the roadblocks. Have the rest of them join us."

Taylor nodded and walked off toward a Virginia Highway Patrol car.

"Your people ready to go, Lou?" Dan asked.

"Sure." Lou slapped the sheriff on the arm. "I told you we'd be allies before all this was over, didn't I, buddy-boy?" He waved to his people. "Let's go, boys and girls. Time to round up the hants and spooks."

Dan just shook his head and stared as the man yelled for his people to get moving. He thought: Lou may be the world's biggest maniac, but he was long on courage and so were his people. They knew, to a person, the risks they were taking, walking headfirst into the unknown.

"He's a complicated man," Denier said, watching

Lou leave the area.

"That would not be my way of describing him," Dan said. "I wonder if he knows what he's getting into, or if this is just a game to him."

"He knows," the priest said quietly.

Chuck walked up to Dan's side. "We found breaks in the fence. Looks like that's where Bowie and the engineer got out."

"Pass the word to all units, county and state, to shoot them on sight and bring the bodies back here. They've got to go up with the others."

Chuck sighed. A hard choice for Dan to make; rough to put it into words. Bowie had been well-liked by everybody.

"I know," Dan said softly. "But it has to be. I just wonder where he's—*they've*—gone."

The men turned as Goodson walked up, a glass tube in one hand, flashlight in the other. "Look at this," he said.

"It looks like a great big maggot," Dan said, reluctant to even touch the glass containing the squirming, ugly worm.

"What is it?" Chuck asked.

"Bennett says his resident entomologist has never seen anything like it. It's a brand new species. But this one appears to be dying. So they have a very short life-cycle. About twenty-four hours."

"What can kill them?"

"Fire," Goodson replied. "Crushing them. Nothing else seems to faze them."

"Wonderful," Taylor said, catching the last bit. "On top of everything else."

The men noticed that Goodson kept shaking the tube. Chuck asked him why he was doing that.

"To keep it from eating through the top. They'll eat anything except glass and metal."

Taylor looked at the ugly worm and shook his head in disgust. He walked off to join his troopers.

And outside the terminal complex, someone began screaming, the faint sounds drifting over the night air.

Dan looked in the general direction of the scream. "Someone didn't follow orders and left his house."

"It's probably gonna get worse," Chuck said.

No one had looked in on Wally, lying in the hospital trailer. Wally had begun a hideous metamorphosis. What was left of his shattered leg had blackened with stinking rot. The darkness had wrinkled and spread, now covering most of his body. He jerked in agony as the mutation spread to his neck, up his head. His face contorted and altered, becoming wrinkled and dark. He rolled from the bed, tumbling to the floor. No one heard the noise.

He lay for a moment, the pain gradually subsiding. Dragging his shattered, half eaten leg, Wally found the side door of the trailer and slipped out, unnoticed. Keeping to the dark shadows, he followed the fence line, seeking escape.

"Even if we were to kill the priest," Anya mused aloud. "I do not believe that alone would be the answer. Something is very right here, and something is very wrong. I believe the Garrett person is the key to it all."

Pet sat by the girl's feet, listening, the cold eyes unblinking.

Both knew the woods around their location were filling with humans. But neither knew the why of it. They both knew the Old Ones were free of their entrapment. They both knew that at dawn they must make their move. They had twelve hours to complete what they were created to do. Dawn to dusk. They

375

had been birthed to be worshipped and to serve the Dark One. The thrust of their existence was to deliver evil, to spread it wherever they might roam, to recruit souls for Satan, to cause pain and suffering and disease.

And they had twelve hours to establish a firm foothold here. If they could dominate for twelve hours, no power in heaven or earth could dislodge them.

But they had never been able to complete that task. Not since the religious base in the desert had been destroyed.

But now? . . .

Perhaps.

And they both knew it was all a game. Nothing more. Just a game. Good on one side, Evil on the other. It was a game their Master always started, but seldom won in any great numbers of souls. But the Dark One was winning, little by little, slowly but surely, and in the strangest of ways and places and people.

This new dawning, only a few hours away, could bring the greatest coup in recent memory. And if Anya and Pet could see it through, they would have eternal life. They would be immortal.

But Anya knew something was wrong. She did not think He was interfering—not directly. But as was usually His way, He was working quietly, remaining unseen and gently manipulating lives and events. And as usually occurred, that damnable, meddling Michael was sticking his nose in affairs that did not concern him. God's warrior. God's mercenary was a better way of putting it.

Anya had been told that earlier that evening. She had also been ordered not to fail.

That was that. One simply does not disobey the

Master.

And not too far away from where Anya and Pet waited for the first rays of dawn, Bowie staggered toward the Garrett house.

8

The crew chief of the power crew stared at Sheriff Garrett in utter disbelief. Finally, he blurted, "Jumpin' Jesus Christ, Sheriff! Do you have any idea what you're asking me to do?"

"I am perfectly aware of what I am requesting," Dan said.

The man shook his head. "The devil caused this weather, huh?"

"That is correct."

"Sheriff," the crew chief said. "Let me get this straight. You want me and my boys to divert all the power from those high lines," he pointed, "and feed it into a metal grid your people are laying down?"

"That is correct."

"Sheriff, are you aware of just how many volts are running through those lines?"

"Not really. But it's ample, I'm sure."

"*Ample!*" the man yelled. "Ample! The man says ample. Oh, yeah, yeah, it's ample all right. Sheriff, when all that juice hits that wire, I don't want to be within ten miles of this place. It's gonna look like the Fourth of July. It's gonna fry that wire. It's gonna . . ."

"Calm down," Dan told him. "It isn't a question of whether you like it or not. It isn't even a question of *whether* you're going to do it. If it can be done, you are *going* to do it. The question is: *can* you do it?"

Just think, the crew chief thought—I voted for this nutso! "Oh, yeah, Sheriff. Yeah, we can do it. But what if we refuse? What if we decide to take your threat of jail instead?"

"Then I'll have it blown down," Dan told him. "I have the people to do it, and the explosives are right over there." He pointed.

"You're really serious!"

"Yes, I am."

The crew chief sighed. "For the record, you are ordering me to do this, knowing I am opposed to it?"

"That is correct. I will take full responsibility."

"Along with the state police," Captain Taylor said.

"Okay, Sheriff. Do we get hazardous duty pay for this?"

"Free sandwiches and all the coffee you can drink."

"And then you'll tell us what's going on in the county? Really going on?"

"I've already told you."

"Wonderful. I can tell my boss the devil made me do it. Come on, Sheriff!"

"You'll see. If we all live through it."

The man paled. "See *what*?"

"Let me put it this way, chief. What would happen if several million volts of electricity were to hit . . . well, atomic matter?"

"I don't know! I'm a lineman, not a scientist. Probably blow up, I guess. How much atomic matter are we talking about?"

"I don't know," Dan admitted.

"Oh, that's just great. Wonderful." The crew chief removed his hard hat and wiped the sweat away. "The

379

devil is in Ruger County? This place belongs to Satan? We got monsters crawling around the county? Little bugs that eat people? Zombies? You know what I think, Sheriff? I think you're *nuts*!"

"Think what you like. Just get to work. Before I lose patience and blow that tower down."

"Yes, sir!" The lineman saluted. "Right now, General." He yelled to his men. "Call the plant in Valentine. Tell 'em to stand by for a shut-down. Get that cherry-picker right over there. Adjust those spotlights." He looked back at the Sheriff, Captain Taylor, and Father Denier. "Sheriff, you know this is going to knock power out all over the place."

"I know. But only for a short time. When you're finished with the bypass the power can be restored until we need it, right?"

The crew chief sighed. "It's not quite that simple, Sheriff. I still think you're nuts."

He turned and walked away.

"Perhaps we are," Denier muttered.

"Why do you say that, Father?" Taylor asked.

"Mere mortals doing battle with Satan." He looked at Dan, a strange glint in his eyes. Almost as if he could see something about the man that Dan did not know.

It made Dan uncomfortable. He said, "You're a mortal, Father. And you've fought him before."

"Not on this scale."

"Are you a betting man, Father?"

"I have been known to dabble from time to time."

"How would you put the odds in this?"

Denier shrugged in the deep night. "Oh, fifty/fifty."

"That good, huh?" Taylor smiled.

When the new troopers arrived, Taylor assigned them out, putting most of them helping to lay the many rolls of wire, most of it four and five foot fencing. About an hour after Lou and his people had pulled out, Captain Taylor stood straight up and looked around him, his eyes large.

"Holy cow!" he said.

"What's the matter, Captain?" one of his men asked.

"Nothing!" Taylor said. He blinked his eyes and rubbed his hands together. "Get to work, men! Time's a-wasting. Work, work, work!" He began walking rapidly around the compound, yelling orders, unable to stand still or keep his mouth shut.

Denier watched the captain's antics for a moment, then asked, "Is the man ill?"

"Naw, Father," Kenny said, an amused look on his face. "He's just speedin' his butt off, that's all."

Bowie stood by a bedroom window of the Garrett house. He had walked through hundreds of cats on his way to the home. None had bothered him. They were all answering to the same silent call. The hot winds carrying dark voices. Bowie looked through the wire covering the screen and window. He could see that the window was unlocked. Carrie and Linda were asleep on the double bed. The faint glow of a digital clock was the only illumination. The hum of the central air conditioning would cover any slight noise he might make. He stared. The girls were dressed only in bras and panties.

Bowie licked his now thick lips, the lust in him rising, the now-wild blood surged through his veins.

He fumbled for his pocket knife and tried to open it, his animal fingers, gnarled and clawed, clumsy with the blade. He dropped the knife several times. Growling low in frustration, he used a long, thick, curved fingernail to quietly rip the chicken wire and screen. His wild eyes on the girls, drool leaked from his mouth, the thick ropy drool staining his shirt. He reached for the window. One of the girls stirred restlessly in her sleep. Bowie froze until she settled down. Carrie abruptly sat up in bed.

"S'wrong?" Linda muttered.

"Bathroom," Carrie said softly. "Go back to sleep." She padded from the room, leaving the door open.

The cats gathered around Bowie's ankles, rubbing against him, restless, sensing prey was imminent. Their low purring a menacing soft buzz in the hot night.

Bowie opened the window and leaped into the room. He hit Linda on the jaw with a hard fist, grabbed her, and tossed her out the window, to land heavily on the ground. He jumped out of the bedroom, picking up the stunned and bruised girl, and ran off, across the road.

The cats leaped into the house through the open window. They filled the room, sitting on the bed, the dresser, covering the floor. One of the cats brushed against the door, the jar closing the door. It closed with a soft click. The cats waited.

Returning from the bathroom, Carrie stopped in the hall. The door to her bedroom was closed, and she distinctly remembered leaving it open a bit.

Maybe the wind blew it shut?

No, the window was closed; Dad's orders. Besides, there was no wind.

Maybe Linda had closed the door?

Not likely. She was sound asleep before Carrie had left the room.

Then . . . what?

Carrie put her ear to the door. She could hear something, but couldn't quite identify the sound. Fear gripped her as she stood, undecided as to what to do.

She ran up the hall to her mother's room. Vonne sat up the instant the door opened.

"Something's wrong!" Carrie whispered. "Come on."

Vonne woke Carl and Mike, as they pulled on jeans, Carrie told them about the door.

"Let's go," Carl said, leading the way. At the bedroom door, he held up his hand for silence and put an ear to the door.

Purring.

He looked at his mother and motioned them all back down the hall. At the archway, he said, "The room is full of cats. I can hear them purring."

"But how did they get in?" Carrie asked, close to tears. "I was only out of the room for about a minute. And the window was closed!"

"Settle down. I don't know. But I don't understand why Linda didn't scream."

"Maybe she . . ." Carrie swallowed hard. "Maybe she didn't have time to . . . before the cats, I mean, got her!" She began crying softly.

Vonne pulled the girl close and held her.

"I don't think the cats got her," Mike said. "She would have yelled, knocked over something—anything. But we've got to find out. Maybe somebody opened the window and grabbed her. Carl, you game to cracking the door a bit?"

"Yeah. I don't see that we have a choice. How are we gonna handle it?"

"Well, I guess the cats are back outside, too. Obviously, we can't go outside. We'll . . ."

Carrie broke away from her mother and ran down the hall to her bedroom door. "Linda!" she screamed. "Answer me, Linda. Are you in there?"

Low menacing purring greeted her question.

"Linda!"

Vonne grabbed her daughter by the shoulders and literally dragged her back down the hall. She pushed her into her bedroom and looked back at the boys. "Do you best, boys. And please be careful."

"Let's put on boots," Mike said. "And get what's left of that chicken wire. It's on the back porch. Get enough for four or five layers. We'll take down a closet door and cut a hole in it, nail the wire on both sides for extra protection. When you open the bedroom door, I'll hold the other door in place while we barricade it shut, or nail it, or some goddamned thing. We'll look through the wire. How's that sound to you?"

"Let's go!"

Bowie ripped the panty and bra from the girl and held her to the ground, opening her legs. Twice he was forced to stop his crazed assault and beat the girl into submission. Unhappy with the position, Bowie twisted the girl to her hands and knees, mounting her from behind, like the animal he had become.

Finished, he pulled up his trousers and stood over the sobbing and bruised girl. He threw back his head and howled at the dark sky, the howling echoing through the hot, sticky darkness.

Bowie used his belt to tie her wrists together and secure the other end to a small tree. Then he growled and trotted off into the night.

"What do you want us to do?" the oldest of the Reynolds' kids asked the grotesqueness.

"Remain in hiding, here, until dusk of this day. If all goes well, you will know. If we fail, you will know that as well. You are all young and have reproductive abilities. That is one of the reasons you are still alive. There are others like you around this area. If by some chance we should fail, you and the others will be left to carry on. You are marked, your children will be marked. You and they are servants of the Master—forever. Do you all understand?"

They nodded their understanding.

"Then, goodbye. I hope to see you all in a matter of hours. If not? . . ." It laughed evilly and shuffled out into the darkness.

The Old Ones were moving. In the church, in the auditorium, the Old One looked at the trappings of Christian faith and laughed. Its eyes glowed with fury. The pulpit exploded in a mass of flame. Lifting its eyes, the cross on the wall behind the blazing pulpit melted under the heat. The communion table disintegrated under the force, bits of blazing wood flying about, landing on the carpet, the drapes. Fire leaped to fire. The Old One looked at the piano and laughed. The keys were depressed, a loud, discordant noise filling the burning church. The Old One chuckled and shuffled out into the hot night.

In the basement of the school, the Old One stepped over the sucked bones and climbed awkwardly up the steps leading to the main hallway. At the door, the Old One's eyes glowed. The door burst into a thousand burning pieces, the door knob shooting forward like a large bullet, white hot with heat. The door knob smashing into and through a wooden locker, setting it on fire.

The Old One laughed, filled with new strength, the laughter echoing throughout the empty school. The lockers on both sides of the long hall were blazing as the spawn of hell shuffled out into the sweltering night.

Another Old One walked the streets of Valentine, unafraid. The Old One set cars blazing, the gas tanks exploding under the force from its eyes. All the Old Ones were moving toward the location of Anya and Pet.

The cats went wild. They hurled their bodies against doors and windows, yowling and shrieking in fury, trying to gain entrance into the houses. They sought blood and human flesh. They could smell the fear of those locked inside and that scent drove them crazy. A few homes were penetrated. The screaming of those trapped inside the homes ripped through the heated air. The odor of blood hung heavy.

The cats moved, en masse, from house to house, searching, seeking, the ancient hunter's bloodlust raging within them.

"Now!" Mike yelled.

Carl pushed the bedroom door open, knocking a dozen cats spinning and sprawling and howling and hissing. Mike slammed the closet door over the opening. Several cats had their heads caught between the door and the jamb. The boys stomped the heads flat with their boots. The hall carpet oozed blood and brains. Vonne began nailing boards across the new door, securing it. She hit her thumb twice and cussed. Inside the room, the cats howled and hissed their rage at being trapped. They leaped and flung themselves at the door, at the screen covering the hole. Several managed to stick their paws through the wire. Mike and Carl hacked at the paws with butcher knives; slashed at furry heads and sharp teeth with the knives. Blood spattered the walls, leaking down the door.

"Mother!" Carl yelled. "Get Carrie. The two of

you fill every container you can find with hot water. I bet that'll get rid of them!"

"Carrie!" she called. "Get that piece of garden hose out of the pantry. The one your father was using to repair the line from the washing machine."

"All right!" Mike said. "I'll get some duct tape. I know where it is."

They fitted one end of the hose over the faucet and taped it tight. Vonne turned on the water, Carl began spraying the room. The pain-filled yowling of the cats increased as the steam from the hot water rose in gray-white waves, the hot water scalding the cats. The enraged cats jammed up the window trying to escape. Mike cleared the hole by sticking the muzzle of a shotgun through the wire and blowing the window free of wet, squirming cats.

Vonne handed Carl a flashlight and he shone the beam all around the room. Linda was not in the room, alive or dead.

"We've got to contact Dad," he said.

Then the lights went out.

9

The roaming hordes of cats, hundreds of them, stopped en masse as all the lights in town went out, plunging the area into darkness. The cats milled about, momentarily confused.

Then the lights popped back on.

"What happened?" Dan asked the crew chief.

"Relax, Sheriff. We just had to shut it down for a couple of minutes. The power that normally flows through these lines," he said, waving his hand, "has been diverted until we get this bypass hooked up. It won't take us long. Power is already restored in Valentine and the outlying areas. But let me tell you something: that bypass is not going to hold for very long. It's gonna self-destruct, like that tape recorder in that old TV show. That's the way I rigged it; that's the way it's gonna stay."

"What happens when the bypass blows, or goes, or whatever?" Taylor asked.

"Well, Captain, y'all are gonna have some mighty furious power company executives."

"Can't you fix it afterwards?" Dan asked, thinking: If there is any afterwards for any of us to worry about, that is.

"We won't have to. The current will automatically start flowing normally when the bypass burns out."

"Well, then!" Taylor said. "What's all the flap about?"

"Captain," the crew chief replied wearily, "man, we're regulated, overseen, controlled, inspected, monitored . . . you name it. Look, a lot of this juice," he said, again waving his hand, "is being sold; Florida, North Carolina, up in Pennsylvania. Disrupting the normal flow is bad enough. Let me put it this way: you boys know what a power surge is?"

"We're not idiots!" Dan snapped.

"That remains to be seen, don't it?" the crew chief popped back. "And me along with you guys for doing this," he added. "Well, just think what's gonna happen to transformers and relay stations when this much power goes off, and then kicks back on with one big jolt. You see what I mean? Sure you don't want to reconsider?"

"Get on with the bypass," Dan said.

The crew chief walked off, muttering highly uncomplimentary things under his breath.

"Dan!" Chuck called. "Trouble at your house. Carl's on the radio now. Cats got in the house. Carrie's little friend, Linda, is gone. They don't know where."

"Take over, Captain. Father Denier, come with me, would you, please."

Mille and Kenny watched Dan and the priest pull out. Mille said, "I can't figure what he's planning on doing here, can you?"

"He's gonna give somebody one heck of a hot foot, it looks like."

389

"But, he can't kill a . . . a *spirit*!"

"Sure looks like he's gonna give it the old college try, though, don't it?"

Denise walked through the woods and meadows and pastures, a pale once human form that glided more than walked. Her companion, the cat, walked with her. Once, they stopped beside a tree as the sounds of running feet came to them. They waited, watching unnoticed as Bowie ran pass them, snarling and growling as he ran.

They angled off, going in the direction Bowie had come. They soon found Linda, awake, scared, and struggling to be free of her bonds.

Her eyes widened at the sight of the naked, and dead, so she thought, Denise. She jerked in fear, then fainted at the sight of the girl.

Denise knelt beside the unconscious girl. She ran her hands over the girl's smooth body; not scarred and marked as hers. Linda stirred. Her eyelids fluttered. She opened her eyes and stared at Denise. The cat watched.

Denise removed the leather belt, freeing Linda's hands.

"You're *dead*!" Linda hissed.

Denise smiled. "Only as you think you know death. Now we are sisters."

"What! . . ."

But Denise and the cat were gone, melting into the darkness.

Then all memory of Denise and the cat left her. She could remember the rape, but no more. She sat up, pulling on the tattered remains of panty and bra. She stood up, a bit shaky. She looked around and got her bearings, then started walking toward the Garrett house. It was not that far off.

It was odd, she thought. I feel so . . . so lightheaded. Like there is something I am supposed to do, but can't remember what it is.

It would come to her. In time.

"Not a cat to be seen anywhere," Dan spoke to Vonne. They stood on the porch of their house. "And I don't know what, or who might have carried off Linda."

"I'm right here," Linda called from the side of the house. "Please toss me a robe, Mrs. Garrett. I'm practically naked."

Vonne got a robe from the house and led the girl inside. There, she told her story.

Dan glanced at Father Denier. The priest was looking at the girl, his eyes hooded, giving away nothing. "I'm going to get Doctor Ramsey," Dan said. "If I can find him."

"I'll stay here," Denier said.

The phone rang, its shrillness startling them all. "I thought the phones were out?" Dan asked.

"They were," Vonne said, rising to still the ringing. She listened for a moment. Her face drained of blood, becoming chalk white. She held the phone out to Denier. Her hands were shaking so badly she almost dropped the phone. "It's for you, Father."

"What's wrong, Vonne?" Dan asked. "Who is that on the phone?"

"He . . . he . . ." She stuttered. ". . . Said it . . . he much prefers the personal touch."

"Who, mother?" Carl asked.

"Satan," she said.

Then fainted.

Father Denier had not spoken a word since he took the receiver from Vonne's pale, cold hand, listened for a moment, and then hung up. He sat in a chair, unmoving. Dan broke all speed records getting to the Ramsey's house and piling Alice and Quinn, Emily and Bill into his car, roaring back to his house. It was only then he noticed the flames leaping into the sky from several locations around town. He tried to use his radio to contact the fire chief. It was dead. He clicked on the AM/FM car radio. Nothing. Cold. Not even static. He searched the bands. Nothing.

And he did not see a single cat.

Quinn checked Vonne. He shook his head. "Her pulse is normal. Her color has returned. Her blood pressure is normal. I . . . can't explain her unconsciousness. I know she's as healthy as anyone in the county. I gave her a physical a few weeks ago. She's just . . . *out*. And I can't explain it."

"I can," Denier finally broke his silence. "No mortal can look upon the face of Satan and live. I suppose listening to the Dark One would have somewhat lesser effects. She will awaken and be perfectly all right once her mind is ready to accept what she heard."

"But listening to . . . the devil didn't knock you out," Doctor Harrison said.

"I have spoken with . . . *him* before," the priest said. "While doing God's work in upstate New York not too long ago. I know Satan well. He hates me and I despise him."

Those words spoken, the heat intensified. Denier looked up, anger on his face. He waved his hand. "Oh, *get away!*" he shouted. "We know you're here. Stop your bragging, you bastard!"

The head abated slightly.

Denier stood up. "I must go," he said abruptly. "I'll get my bag out of your car, Sheriff."

"But . . ." Dan said.

Denier waved him silent. "This is something I must do alone. You would only be in my way. The cats won't bother me." His eyes touched Vonne, on the couch. "She will be all right. She is a fine, Christian woman. Goodbye." He turned and walked out the front door.

"I wonder what . . . Satan," she stumbled over the word, "said to him."

"I'm not sure I want to know," Dan replied.

Linda's eyes held a strange glow.

"Where is Father Denier going, Daddy," Carrie asked.

"To fight Satan."

Hate glowed fiercely from Linda's eyes.

Dan looked at Linda. He saw the strange glow, mistook it for fever.

Leaving the doctors and their wives at his house, Dan drove back to the terminal. The power crew was gone.

Captain Taylor said. "They pulled out. About five minutes ago. Said they wouldn't take any further part in this insanity. But they hooked everything up when I shoved a shotgun in the crew chief's face."

"Get them back here!" Dan said. "I want them to see this."

Taylor yelled the orders and several of his men took off after the crew.

"They show you how to operate the . . . whatever?" Dan asked.

"Yeah. Several of us. Simple. Come on, I'll show you the bypass. Or rather, the switch that will cut in the bypass."

The first hues of silver were streaking the eastern sky. Dan explained what had happened at his house. He finished with Father Denier leaving.

"And you let him go?"

"How could I stop him?"

"Good point."

The power company crew had run a line as far as they could from the metal grid that covered hundreds of feet inside the terminal complex. What looked like a huge breaker box was mounted on a pole.

"That's it?" Dan asked.

"That's it. Just pull that handle and, to quote the crew chief, 'Get ready for the ground to tingle.'"

"Get everybody clear of the grid." Dan looked at his watch. Looked toward the east. "Full light soon. Let's get a sandwich and get ready to move out."

"I'm not hungry," Taylor said.

Dan smiled. "I'm not either. But I know when you're taking speed you'd better eat something. I've taken it before."

Taylor looked at him. "Dope. When?"

Dan laughed. "Working stakeouts with the Bureau."

10

"What'd you do with June?" Gordon asked the pale-eyed young man with the silenced automatic in his right hand.

"I didn't do anything with her. She popped a capsule before I could. Dead in thirty seconds."

"You look familiar to me," Gordon said, straining his eyes to peer through the silver-streaked gloom. "Naw! He's dead."

The young man said nothing.

"I got a right to know who's gonna burn me!" Gordon said.

"You have no rights. You sold out your country. You're a traitor. And you endangered a lot of innocent lives in this county."

"Oh, goody! I get a sermon early in the morning."

"No. Just a bullet."

The young man smiled and pulled the trigger, twice. The .22 caliber slugs hit Gordon in the face, one entered his eye, the other making a tiny hole right between his eyes.

He picked up his brass and walked away.

He would be eating dinner in the mess hall at Fort Lewis that evening.

11

"It's a little girl," the woman said. "She's walking among the cats. Petting and talking to them. Where did *she* come from?"

"And who or what the hell is she?" the husband asked.

They watched as Anya looked toward the house and laughed. She pointed at the house. The cats came, leaping and snarling and hurling their bodies against the door and the windows. The windows shattered but the barricades held firm. The man picked up the double-barrel coach gun, thumbed the hammers back, and stuck the twin muzzle out through a crack in the barricade. He pulled both barrels at once, the recoil of the sawed-off knocked him backward. That window was cleared of cats. Several dozen mangled furry bodies lay in bits and pieces around the side of the house.

Anya was down in the yard, screaming in pain and fury.

"You hit the little girl," the woman said.

"I think she's part of this . . . nightmare," the husband replied.

"The shotgun worked," she said.

"Will wonders never cease." He reloaded and looked out through the crack.

The cats were leaving, hundreds of them following the girl, who was running down the road, apparently unhurt.

"I saw the girl knocked down," she said. "I saw the shot hit her. But she's running like she is not hurt at all."

The woman turned on the outside floodlights, the yard exploding in harsh light. The little girl turned and screamed obscenities at the house.

There was not a mark on the girl.

"That's impossible!" the man said. "The shot knocked her down. It hit her. But . . . what's going on here?"

Anya was shrieking at the cats. They turned, spitting and snarling at the house. The woman picked up the other shotgun.

"You can't shoot that," her husband said.

"You watch me. Here they come!"

The cats came, urged on by the screaming Anya. They jumped at the windows and were blown apart by shotgun blasts. The cats behaved as insane troops in a suicide charge. Again and again they leaped into the shotgun blasts, only to be blown to bloody furry chunks.

The girl, standing close to the house, was screaming in fury, shouting at the house.

"What language is that?" the woman asked.

"Sounds like Arabic," he said. "But my hearing is shot after all this shooting."

"Look!" She pointed.

The woods around the property were emptying of men, all carrying automatic weapons. They had formed a crude half circle, as if driving the girl and the cats.

The cats left their insane charging of the house and raced toward the men. The men, obviously well-trained, dropped to one knee and opened fire, raking the charging cats with automatic weapons fire. A few cats made it through the deadly hail of lead. They were either shot down or stomped to death.

The half circle moved closer to the girl. The man and woman in the house watched, with a mixture of fascination and horror.

The young girl pointed her finger at the moving line. One man burst into flames, his body exploding as if hit with a howitzer round.

Anya pointed her finger at another man. He slowly vaporized, his boots all that remained.

Lou lifted his M-16 and sighted the girl in.

"Why are you trying to harm me?" she called.

Lou lowered his rifle.

"Why did you point that gun at me?" Anya called.

"Because you're . . . evil!" Lou said.

"I am what I was born to be," Anya said, her young voice carrying clearly through the heat of night.

"I didn't know you spoke Arabic, Lou," the man to his right said.

"I don't."

"Well, you damn sure were!"

Lou shook his head. The guy was nuts. He looked at the young kid. "Move!" he ordered.

She laughed at him.

"Goddamn you! I said *move*!"

She turned and walked slowly down the long driveway. "Am I moving correctly?" she called over her shoulder.

"Just keep moving."

"To the lights I see in the distance?" She pointed.

"Yeah. That's right."

"Come on, Lou!" one of his people said. "Speak

English!"

"I am speaking English!" Lou said.

Lou's gone nuts! the OSS agent thought. He and that weird kid have been gibber-jabbering in Arabic.

Those cats that were left after the bloody carnage followed Anya and Pet, the agents following the cats.

In the house, the man and woman looked at each other, neither of them having the vaguest idea what was going on, or what had gone on.

"It's over for us," the woman said. "We can relax."

"How do you know that?"

"I just do."

"Honey, sometimes you're as weird as your brother."

"I don't like me and my men being treated like criminals, sheriff," the crew chief said.

"Forgive me for bruising your tender feelings," Dan said. "I want you all to see this. Now go over there and stand by those preachers. You and Louis Foster can call me names from over there. He didn't like being hauled out here either."

Crew chief and men walked away, all of them cussing under their breath.

Dan turned to Captain Taylor. "When I yell, Tay, you pull that handle, okay?"

"Where are you going to be, Dan?"

"Right out there," he replied, pointing to the wire grid.

"Are you out of your mind, man! I won't do it. No."

"You have to do it, Tay. They . ." He waved his hand at the silver darkness, ". . . whatever you want to call those unknowns we've been fighting, won't be satisfied with anyone else but me. I've been the fly in the ointment from the beginning. You know the very first person to ever lay claim to this piece of property?"

"What? No. Who *cares*?"

"My great great great—I don't know how many greats—grandfather. It all came to me about a half hour ago. The story that no one in my family would ever talk about. But I heard it in bits and pieces as a boy. By eavesdropping on the adults. That ancestor of mine fought the devil, right here. Right on this land. Fought him for years—all his life, I suppose. No, Tay. It's me they want. Tell Vonne I had to do it. Tell her why. Okay?"

"All right, Dan. Dan?" Captain Taylor held out his hand.

Dan smiled and shook it. "Listen up, now."

"See you, boy."

Standing some yards behind the two cops, Mille turned to Kenny and said, "Looks like I'm going to write a favorable story about cops after all."

"I guess it's time we both grew up," Kenny said.

Father Denier was slowly stalking the largest of the Old Ones, pushing it, driving the creature slowly toward the terminal compound.

"I should kill you now," the Old One said.

"You can't," the priest spoke low. "And you know it. Not by yourself." He held up the large cross and the Old One averted its gruesome head and rained curses down on the priest.

The sun broke through the dawn mist, the temperature soaring.

"Move, you ugly piece of filth," Denier said.

"Move, you wretched demon!" Lou shouted.

"Are you that anxious to die?" Anya called.

"We all have to see the elephant, you witch! One time is as good as the next."

"Witch? I'm a witch, Pet. The fool called me a witch. Shall we play tricks, Pet?"

The cat jumped and yowled, leaping about in glee.

Anya turned around and glared at Lou. Lou's face began melting, the flesh cooking on the bone, bubbling and popping like pork. He dropped his M-16 and screamed once, before his tongue was melted. His eyes turned to liquid and ran down his cheek bones. Lou's clothing burst into flames as the man collapsed to the ground.

"Come!" Anya called to the stalled line of agents. "Follow us. I invite you to witness the rebirthing of the Master's disciples. Come!" She turned and began walking faster.

"What in blazes," one of the OSS agents muttered. "If we cut and run, the Feds will pick us up and poke us in the slam. If we follow her, we might make it." He looked down at what remained of Lou. "You do too know Arabic, you liar."

Vonne walked out of the house to stand alone on the front porch, her eyes looking in the direction of the old truck terminal. She felt a sense of dread in her heart. She turned as Carl and Mike joined her.

"What's wrong, Mother?"

"Your father is about to do something terribly brave." She wiped her misty eyes. "But he would not want tears. He would want us to feel proud and to be strong. So that's what we shall be."

"Mother, what are you talking about?"

"Father Denier talked to me about an hour ago," she said.

"Mother, Father Denier has been gone from here for *hours*!"

"He spoke to me. He told me the story about that piece of land where your father is meeting the devil."

"What about it, Mother?"

"I'll tell you. In a little while."

"Why not now?"

"Keep your father's image in your mind, Carl. Remember him as he is. Strong, brave, decent, and honorable."

"*Mother* . . . you sound like Dad is . . . *dead!*"

"He is about to be, son."

12

When Louis Foster got his first glimpse of an Old One, he fell to his knees and began praying, the words pouring out of his mouth in a torrent.

Jerry Hallock and Matt Askins stood and stared in horror. Then they joined Louis in prayer.

One of the linemen puked up his sandwiches and coffee. The crew chief turned his face away from the horrible-looking things.

The OSS doctors stood with Doctor Goodson and stared in disbelief and revulsion.

Then all saw the little girl and the cat.

"We have an audience, Pet," Anya said. "After all our years of searching and roaming, we have come home to an audience."

The cat jumped and yowled, sensing victory was very near.

The house cats and alley cats who had followed Anya and Pet milled around for a moment, then crouched down, waiting, watching, silent.

The heat intensified. There was not a dry thread on anyone. The sun rose bubbling out of the east, out of a cloudless horizon.

Dan stood alone in the center of the metal grid. He

had made his peace with God, and he was not afraid. He watched the advance of the Old Ones. He had never seen anything so horrible-looking in all his life. Father Denier was driving one of the hideous-looking things, prodding it forward as one might drive a cow.

Anya stood well away from the grid, sensing something was wrong. She looked at Dan and smiled.

Cute kid, Dan thought. Then he shoved that from his mind, replacing it with: Child of Satan. Evil.

Anya said, "You called me to come. I came."

"End of a long journey, girl," Dan said.

"Your end. My beginning," Anya called.

"We'll see."

"Where is your God?" Anya shouted. "Why don't you call on Him to come forward and save you?"

"I'm already saved, girl. And my God is here. I don't have to see him to know that."

The Old Ones stamped their feet and laughed. They hooted at Dan, the hooting filled with derision.

"You're a fool!" Anya spat the words. "Your God has forsaken you, left you to die alone—for nothing!"

Dan stood in the center of the grid and offered no reply. He cut his eyes as a shape became more distinct near the far edge of the grid. He could recognize the tattered remnants of a uniform. Nothing else about the creature was human. Bowie staggered onto the grid, snarling and snapping like a mad dog.

Dan watched Father Denier as the priest stepped onto the wire of the grid. He held the cross in his right hand.

Denier looked at the six Old Ones. "You have made your boast that the six of you could destroy me," the priest challenged. "Very well. I am here, with my God holding my hand. Destroy me."

The air cooled abruptly as dark clouds boiled and surged overhead. The Old Ones glared at Denier. But

405

their powers were blocked.

Denier laughed at them. He walked closer to Dan.

"That's not fair!" Anya called, her voice shrill. "That's not the way the game is played. Your God is cheating! He's breaking the rules."

"How do you feel, Dan?" Denier asked softly.

"Pretty good," Sheriff Dan Garrett said. "Slight headache is all."

"Well, we'll have to see about that when we get home," Denier replied.

"What are you two whispering about?" Anya screamed from her position outside the grid.

"Why don't you join us and find out?" Dan called. "What's the matter? Are you afraid of us?"

Anya glared her hatred at the men. She stepped closer. But she was still off the grid. She pointed her finger at the men.

The dark clouds dipped closer to the earth. The girl had no powers left in her.

She looked up at the clouds and shrieked her rage. She screamed curses at the Almighty. The clouds began leaking fat drops of rain, dampening the ground.

Anya squalled her outrage as the clean drops of water touched her flesh. "Cheater, cheater, cheater!" she shouted. "You're not playing fair."

The temperature cooled even more, the rain picking up, lashing the earth.

Dan rubbed his temples. "I wish this headache would go away."

"It will," Father Denier assured him.

The smaller of the Old Ones rushed toward the men, howling in anger and frustration.

Denier held up the large cross. The Old One stopped, putting its paw-like hands in front of its eyes, shielding them from that which it hated.

"Kneel," Father Denier spoke quietly. "Kneel before the power of God, you filth."

"Don't you dare!" Anya shrieked. "You must not."

"*Kneel!*" Denier said.

The Old One dropped to the grid.

Anya spat and hissed and yelled curses at the men. She stepped onto the grid. She motioned the Old Ones to join her. Pet stepped onto the grid.

Captain Taylor watched, moving his hand closer to the switch. He prayed steadily and softly.

"You're all mouth, kid," Dan told the girl, his words just audible over the hard rain. "You're afraid of our God. You're afraid of *us*."

Anya bared her teeth in a snarl. She came closer.

Denise climbed the fence surrounding the compound and stood for a moment, outside the hard rain. Then she walked toward the small gathering, stepping onto the grid. She could not understand what was happening.

A VHP car slid to a halt, the trooper jumping out and running toward Captain Taylor. All communications were out; everything had to be done person to person.

"We got some sort of . . . I don't know what it is, Captain. Mummy-looking thing trapped inside a barn. What are we supposed to do with it?"

"Burn it," Taylor ordered. "Burn the barn to the ground and then burn the ashes. Move!"

He had never taken his eyes off Dan and the priest.

"Yes, sir." The trooper sped away.

"Come on, little girl," Dan urged. "Destroy me. I don't think you can. My God is more powerful than yours."

Anya moved closer to Dan. "Touch me and you die," she said.

Dan held out his hand. "Then here is my hand.

Come on, take it. I think you're afraid of me."

Never taking her dark furious eyes from his, Anya stepped closer and stretched out her arm.

Just before their hands touched, Dan looked at Father Denier. "I wish I had had time to tell my wife that I love her."

"She knows it," the priest replied.

Anya's hand was moving closer, the hands only inches apart.

"Going to be one hell of a bang," Dan said.

"Interesting way of describing it," Denier said with a smile.

Anya's small fingers closed around Dan's.

Dan jerked the girl to him.

"Now!" Dan shouted. "Now, now!"

13

The metal grid exploded in a shower of sparks, the wet ground actually moving as the heavy voltage fried the wire grid.

One instant the forms on the grid were there, the next instant, they were gone. The impacting current knocked every spectator to the ground. The bypass exploded under more current than it could handle. Clouds of steam rose from the fried wire and the wet, boiled earth.

The rain abruptly ceased. The dark surging clouds blew away. The sun burst forth.

The most beautiful rainbow any present could remember ever seeing arched across the sky, the colors brilliant. The rainbow lifted from the horizon and formed a colored circle.

"A halo," Captain Taylor said, kneeling on the ground. "It's a halo!"

The multi-colored halo grew smaller as it soared into the clear blue sky.

Then it vanished into the heavens.

18

The Reynolds' kids walked out of the old building and began their trek homeward. They had rehearsed their story and would not deviate from it.

They would behave normally and await instructions. They knew they would be contacted. Soon.

Captain Taylor drove back to his division HQ and tossed his badge on his desk. "That's it," he said.

"What are you going to do in retirement, Captain?" he was asked.

"I'm going to a retreat up in the mountains," Taylor said. "For a long time."

"What happened over there in Valentine, Captain?"

"God won," the captain said mysteriously. "I think."

The thumb-sized worms continued breeding in hiding, devouring the weaker, so only the strongest survived. They ate mice and rats and bugs and dogs and snakes. No cats.

And Linda was driven home by Vonne.

15

A cat was waiting for her, sitting on the girl's dresser. A black cat, with very cold, yellow eyes.

"Hi!" Linda said. "Where did you come from?"

All the cats in town had returned to normal, purring and playing and behaving as . . . well, *cats*.

The cat put its paw on Linda's left forearm. There was a slight burning sensation. The cat withdrew its paw. Linda looked down at her arm.

There was a very small mark on her arm. She looked closer. The mark was in the shape of a cat.

Linda smiled, looking at the cat on her dresser. "I think I'll call you Pet."

The cat smiled.

THE FINEST IN FICTION
FROM ZEBRA BOOKS!

HEART OF THE COUNTRY   (2299, $4.50)
by Greg Matthews

Winner of the 26th annual WESTERN HERITAGE AWARD for Outstanding Novel of 1986! Critically acclaimed from coast to coast! A grand and glorious epic saga of the American West that *NEWSWEEK* Magazine called, "a stunning mesmerizing performance," by the bestselling author of THE FURTHER ADVENTURES OF HUCKLEBERRY FINN!

"A TRIUMPHANT AND CAPTIVATING NOVEL!"
— *KANSAS CITY STAR*

CARIBBEE   (2400, $4.50)
by Thomas Hoover

From the author of THE MOGHUL! The flames of revolution erupt in 17th Century Barbados. A magnificent epic novel of bold adventure, political intrigue, and passionate romance, in the blockbuster tradition of James Clavell!

"ACTION-PACKED . . . A ROUSING READ"
— *PUBLISHERS WEEKLY*

MACAU   (1940, $4.50)
by Daniel Carney

A breathtaking thriller of epic scope and power set against a background of Oriental squalor and splendor! A sweeping saga of passion, power, and betrayal in a dark and deadly Far Eastern breeding ground of racketeers, pimps, thieves and murderers!

"A RIP-ROARER"
— *LOS ANGELES TIMES*